The Hanged Man's Wife

by

Artemis Greenleaf

Other books by Artemis Greenleaf

Earthbound

Cheval Bayard

Confessions of a Troll

Dragon by Knight
(as Coda Sterling, Belinda Tate's nom de plume)

The Magician's Children

Dragon Killer
(as Coda Sterling, Belinda Tate's nom de plume)

Exit Point

Brain's Vacation

Anthologies

Space City 6

Tides of Impossibility

PUBLISHED BY:
Black Mare Books
Houston, Texas
www.blackmarebooks.com

ISBN: 978-0-9888070-1-3

The Hanged Man's Wife

Acknowledgements

As always, thank you to my wonderful family. This endeavor would not be possible without your love and support. I also appreciate the invaluable editorial and structural help of my critique groups and beta readers. You know who you are, and I couldn't do this without you. Finally, a big shout-out to the Houston Citizen's Police Academy and officers I've had the opportunity and privilege to interact with. Thank you!

Table of Contents

The universe is full of magical things, patiently waiting for our wits to grow sharper.
Eden Phillpotts

Chapter 1
Undiscovered Country

Rural Texas, 12:06 AM

I HAD JUST TURNED out the light and settled back onto the pillow when Amos, my Rottweiler mix, growled. I stroked his back to calm him and felt the hackles standing straight up on his shoulders.

A sharp rap sounded from the wall above the headboard.

Amos shifted and I put my arms around the big dog's neck.

"Who's there?" I asked, knowing I was the only one who was supposed to be in the house. At seventeen, I was old enough to stay home alone while my mother worked the graveyard shift at the truck stop. Dad was a long haul truck driver, and he was gone a lot. Right now, he was on his way back from California, but it would be tomorrow night before he made it home. Too late to help me now.

The silence was thick enough to suffocate me. My heart thudded against my ribs so hard I was afraid it would beat its way out of my chest.

Two sharp knocks cut through the gloom, now coming from the outer wall to my left.

Amos snorted.

I sat up just far enough to peer out the window at the foot of the bed. No one was there.

Maybe it's only an animal in the wall. I didn't believe that for a minute.

Burglars didn't prowl around knocking on the walls, did they?

Four knocks, hard and fast, made me jump. This time, they came from the inner wall on my right, across from the bed.

"Is someone there?" My voice sounded thin and shivery in the dark.

There was no answer. Mom and Dad always told me the noises I heard were just the house settling. I never quite believed them – the sounds were too much like footsteps and whispering. But this knocking. This was different – I'd never heard it before.

"If there's someone there, knock twice for yes and once for no," I called out, pretending to be brave.

Two knocks sounded near the ceiling above my head.

"Are you a man?"

One knock.

"A woman?"

Two knocks.

"Do you live here?"

Two knocks.

That totally freaked me out. I didn't want to know any more about who- or whatever this was. I was done.

Amos sat up and growled. I reached over and snapped on the lamp by my bed. The small pool of light gave me just enough courage to jump out of bed and flip the overhead light switch. Amos remained crouched on the bed, head cocked and staring at the wall. Eventually, I was able to work my way around the house and get all the lights turned on. When I got to the living room, I pulled myself into a ball under the hand-crocheted afghan my grandmother had made and turned on the TV. I watched infomercials until Amos padded into the room and curled up next to me, and I just couldn't stay awake anymore.

Nine Years Later
Mundane Activity Monitoring and Intervention Center (MAMIC)

"I think that's all of them," Quinn said.

"Excellent. You take your team back out to the border and see if you can help shore it up. We'll take care of the refugees," the woman said. She turned and strode down the corridor, her long velvet dress flowing behind her.

"Hey, Aleksei!" Quinn called to a tall Lesovik, who was helping an elderly boggart find a chair. "Have you seen Siobhan recently?"

"Ni. Not since we have arrived here."

Quinn frowned at his blue-skinned friend. "Dame Rowan said to go back out to the breach. Maybe we'll pick Siobhan up on the way."

Aleksei nodded and continued toward a settee with the wispy boggart.

Eoin and Malik, two other members of Quinn's Mundane Intervention Team, stood near the entrance to the great hall. Quinn hurried toward them.

"Have either of you seen Siobhan?"

Eoin blotted some sweat off of his forehead and bare chest. His goat hooves clacked on the floor as he turned to survey the heaving room behind them. "Not since early this morning," he said.

Malik, the djinn, just shook his head as he levitated himself about four feet off the floor in a cross-legged position.

"We're supposed to get back out there, see if we can help," Quinn said. He scanned the great hall one last time. Might be better if she stays here.

As soon as Aleksei caught up, they went outside to the emergency portal. Quinn could have left a message with the guard, but decided against it. It was selfish, he knew, but if Siobhan was still here, he wanted her to stay out of harm's way. Things could get ugly in a hurry, where they were going.

They stepped through a full length looking glass in a brass frame and found themselves at the edge of a dark forest. The sky flashed rainbow lightning and dark shapes moved, as if in a fog, just beyond the trees. Fae of all types, along with a few elementals and nature spirits, scurried around like ants after their nest has been poked with a stick.

Demons had definitely been at work here. The realm of Faery overlaps and interpenetrates the Mundane world, and the borders between the two are narrow, but tough. Here, the boundary had been scraped so thin that the shadows of humans were plainly visible. The fae were busy trying to repair it before the demons returned, because the membrane was on the verge of failure. Inexplicably, the demons had left while the locals were being evacuated to the nearby MAMIC.

Demons did not belong in Faery. They didn't belong in the Mundane world, either, but a terrible magickal accident had ripped a hole through space and time and enabled them to escape their world before it tore itself apart. They'd been eradicated from Faery for millennia, but many still prowled the Mundane world, multiplying almost as fast as they were captured. Descendants of those responsible for the accident formed what eventually became MAMIC and trained special teams to hunt those remaining demons. The demons, to be sure, did not appreciate this, and fought back vigorously.

More rainbow lightning flashed. Soon, the shadowy figures disappeared, and there appeared to be a vast meadow just past the trees. The near-breach was sealed. Guards would be posted, to monitor the repair for a few days. If it remained stable, the residents would be allowed to return home. Quinn, Aleksei, Malik and Eoin returned to MAMIC. And they were back before lunch.

Siobhan was still nowhere to be found.

"Malik, do you think you can locate her for me?" Quinn asked.

"As you wish."

The djinn closed his eyes. The smile on his face slid into open-mouthed horror.

"What's wrong? Where is she?" Quinn demanded.

"She is at her cottage in the Mundane world."

"And?"

"Frost Giants have been there."

Fourteen Months Later
Houston, Texas

Ryan was over an hour late coming home.

I glanced up at the clock and then looked out the window, as I'd done for just about every minute since I got back. Ryan was often late from work, but he was usually home by now. It had been chilly and rainy for the third day in a row – not uncommon for a Houston winter – and the wet streets had snarled traffic. I was sure that was all there was to it. Still, congestion was worse than usual today, and the traffic report on the radio said there was police activity on I-10. Usually meant a fatality investigation. What a shame, especially so close to the holidays.

I went into the kitchen and looked in the oven. I'd picked up takeout from Ryan's favorite Thai restaurant on my way home from my shift at the ER, and had put it in there on low to keep it warm. I was a lot of things, but domestic wasn't one of them. I laughed to myself. Jarred pasta sauce and cooked dried spaghetti just didn't rate as special occasion fare. Our third anniversary was only two weeks away, but I couldn't wait that long. Ryan would be so surprised.

I could not stop smiling. I even smiled at the photo of us taken at the zoo that was stuck to the fridge with a tacky tourist magnet from San Francisco. Ryan had a uniquely splendid look. His mother was Vietnamese and his father was Norwegian. His eyes were dark, almost black, and his hair was dark honey blond. He had black belts in both Tae Kwon Do and Hapkido, and had the body to prove it.

A knock at the door interrupted my pouring of the sparkling grape juice.

Who could that be? I really hope it isn't those Jehovah's Witnesses again.

If only it had been Jehovah's Witnesses.

Ryan's shiftmate, Nick, and Frank Helmsly, the Watch Commander, stood on the porch, hats in their hands.

It could only mean one thing, and it was the last thing a policeman's wife ever wanted to see.

All the color drained out of the world and I couldn't seem to get enough air. My hands were shaking so hard I could barely open the door to let them in.

Nick put his arms around me and I sobbed into his chest. I could feel his silent tears on my shoulder. When I was able to get a hold of myself enough to speak, I pulled away from Nick, but didn't let go. It was only then I noticed the splashes of blood on his face. Was it Ryan's? I was afraid to ask.

I closed my eyes in a hopeless attempt to try and contain the waterfall. "Tell me what happened," I whispered.

"Supposed to be a routine traffic stop," Nick answered.

"Don't watch the news tonight, Marti. It's better if you don't," the commander said, patting my shoulder. "We think they were enforcers - they had military grade weapons and body armor. And Russian gang tattoos."

I could feel Nick starting to shake, and I hugged him tighter. "We had no idea what we were getting into," he said. "Ryan pulled them over 'cause they ran a red light. Idiots barely missed getting hit by a bus. Wish they had. Bastards." He paused and took a deep breath, struggling for control. "Their car was stolen, and I rolled up to assist. Before I knew what was happening, there was an AK-102 sticking out of the car window and Ryan was down," said Nick, his voice breaking.

"We got 'em, though, Marti. We got 'em," Helmsly broke in. "There was one holy hell of a chase. I-10 was shut down for four hours because of that and the standoff with the SWAT team. One shooter died at the scene. The other was DOA at Ben Taub. I know that's not much comfort." He shook his head and swallowed hard. "Ryan was a good man and a good officer. We're gonna miss him. The department sends its condolences."

Nick released me and stepped back. "Emily's on her way over. I'll go next door and get your mom."

Ryan and Nick hadn't been just shiftmates . They were also brothers-in-law. I had met Ryan at my sister's wedding. I was Emily's maid of honor and he was Nick's best man.

Commander Helmsly fidgeted on the front porch while Nick went to fetch my mother. I went into the bathroom and tried to vomit, but my stomach was empty. On the way out, I picked up the pregnancy test with its two blue lines and threw it in the trash.

Chapter 2
Information

———————— ஃ ————————

QUINN RAN HIS HAND through his thick black hair and sighed with frustration. This mission wasn't going well.

The rumor was that a drug dealer had managed to get his hands on some actual zombie powder. He was planning to use it to enslave dryads and make them hide his product inside trees, where he wouldn't have to worry about it being disturbed, as only the dryads could get it in or out.

Quinn didn't believe that stuff would work on fae, but his team had been sent to investigate, anyway. They'd spent a month hanging out with assorted criminals, junkies, and dealers. They hadn't had any luck, and were about to declare the whole thing a hoax when the first dryad turned up.

She wasn't dead. But she wasn't exactly alive, either. She just shuffled around in a catatonic state, staring blankly ahead of herself, moaning and bumping into objects. Quinn had sent her to Blackthorne in the fae realm to see if she could be helped. Then two more dryads in the same condition appeared, then another. They all died.

Quinn had just run down yet another dead-end lead. He was out of ideas and out of patience. Taking a short-cut, he turned down a grimy alley, and was assaulted by the rusty, salty-sweet odor of blood. Human blood, and lots of it.

A metallic click caught his attention.

A man, wearing nothing but a holey pair of boxers, was advancing down the alley. The handgun he carried was elongated by the silencer attached to the end of the barrel.

"Hey, you! Just let him die, okay?" the gunman said, his voice cracking with hysteria.

Quinn's eyes followed where the gun was pointing. He had to crane his neck to see around a dumpster. A police officer was trying to give first aid to a man who was sprawled on the asphalt in a congealing pool of blood. Quinn could tell by looking at the man's aura that he was a lost cause.

The cop looked up at the gunman. He kept pressure on the injured man's abdomen, trying to cover multiple gunshot wounds. "Easy, now. There's an ambulance on the way. He's going to the hospital. Just put the gun down and back off. Be cool, alright?" His voice was even and calm, but firm.

"I said, let him die! I shot him cuz he's a vampire. Don't help him!" The gunman's hands shook so hard he could barely point his weapon.

Quinn let his serrated teeth show and his eyes go to solid black before he stepped from behind the dumpster. The gunman took one look at him, then screamed and fled, tossing the gun into a pile of trash. Unfortunately for him, he ran smack into the arms of another officer, who was just coming around the corner.

"Vampire! Vampire!" the gunman shrieked, pointing at Quinn. "He's gonna get me!"

"Let me put you in the car, where you'll be nice and safe," the second officer said.

The quivering gunman held out his arms to be cuffed, then scrambled into the back of the police cruiser and cowered on the floor.

"Holy shit! Holy shit!" said Quinn, acting as if he'd just noticed the gunshot victim for the first time. He covered his mouth with his hand before he turned and retched behind the dumpster. No theater there – the taste of human blood made him nauseous – and with that much blood in the open air, the smell was as good as a taste. All he had to do was let his control slip a little.

The approaching ambulance wailed in the near distance like a banshee, foretelling death.

"Wish they were all that easy. Ryan, you okay?" the second officer asked, his eyes on Quinn.

"Yeah. But he's toast," the first officer replied, trying to close the dead man's eyes before he got up. But they stubbornly refused to stay shut, staring blankly at the pale November sky. He glanced at Quinn, who looked perfectly human. "That guy's higher than a kite," he said, nodding toward the police car. He stripped off the blue disposable gloves he'd been wearing and tied them up in a plastic sack. "I'll go bag the shooter's hands and call Homicide."

"So what are you doing hanging out in this alley?" the second officer, whose name tag read N. Benson, asked Quinn pleasantly. But his hand rested on the butt of his gun.

"Me?" Quinn whipped through his mental inventory of cover stories. Seconds ticked by, stinking like fried food and fresh blood. "Just moved here. Looking for a job."

"In an alley?"

Quinn looked at his shoes. "No, man. Had to take a leak."

Benson's lip curled in disgust. "Dude. No. Don't ever let me catch you doing that. You carrying? Got anything sharp in your pockets?"

"No."

"Mind if I check?" Benson asked.

Quinn raised his arms and took a wider stance, and Benson frisked him. Quinn didn't like it, but he knew it looked very suspicious, him showing up in an alley where someone had just been shot, even if someone else was holding the gun. In Benson's place, he would have done the same thing. Best to just go along while he worked out how to turn this obstacle into an opportunity.

Quinn was aware that beat cops know a lot of people in a lot of neighborhoods. They usually have a good idea of who's dealing and who's using, even if they can't prove it. Quinn needed to know what they knew, but he couldn't just come out and ask them. And it was never a good idea to stalk police officers. Maybe, though, they would be interested in some information. And if they thought they were cultivating him, he just might be able to get close enough to find out what he wanted to know and track down the dealer with the zombie powder. But they had to think they had some leverage to use against him. They wouldn't trust someone being helpful for no apparent reason.

By this time, three other patrol cars arrived, EMS had pronounced the victim, and the ambulance had been released in favor of the coroner's van. Yellow police tape blocked off the alley and the Crime Scene Unit was on its way. The first officer, the one who had been attempting first aid, approached Quinn and Benson with a clipboard.

Quinn glanced at the officer's name plate. R. Keller.

"I need to get a statement and some contact information from you, in case the DA wants to call you as a witness. If I could see your ID, please?"

"Sure," Quinn said, reaching for his back pocket. Then he reached for the other pocket. "Shit. It's gone. My wallet's gone!"

Benson rolled his eyes and shook his head.

"When was the last time you had it?" Keller asked.

"I was filling out an application at the dry cleaner a few blocks over. I had it then. Maybe I left it there."

"Maybe. You can go check after I get your statement. What's your name?"

"Marc McLeod. That's Marc with a c, last name m-c-l-e-o-d."

"Address?"

"4003 Allen Parkway. Smitherson House." He'd done a favor once for Tim Arbuckle, the manager of the well-known half-way house, who knew him as Marc McLeod. Quinn knew Arbuckle would vouch for him, if anyone ever called to check on McLeod. The real Marc McLeod was a petty criminal with a heroin habit he couldn't afford. Or he had been, until he tried to rob his dealer and ended up in a Pasadena landfill. He also was not the sort of person anyone would bother to report missing.

Quinn pretended not to notice when the officers exchanged knowing looks. Benson left. Good. He was pretty sure that meant he was going to the patrol car to check out Marc McLeod on the computer. The last time he got his driver license renewed, McLeod had a full beard and the gaunt pallor of a junkie. Quinn could pass for a healthier, clean-shaven version of McLeod, if the officers didn't study the picture too closely. Which is exactly why Quinn sometimes borrowed his identity, although he thought it was a sad commentary on the man's life that he was much more useful dead than he had ever been alive.

Keller's voice derailed Quinn's train of thought. "And a phone number?"

"Don't have one. You can leave a message with the office at Smitherson."

As the officer asked him questions, Quinn tried to locate anything or anyone that could help his cause. The area was filthy and mostly cemented over, and there didn't seem to be any fae or elementals around. Still, he kept calling out for assistance. Other fae could hear him, if they were close enough. But this sound was pitched far above the range of human hearing.

Benson returned and gave Keller the slightest of nods. "What made you decide to shave?" Benson asked casually.

"That was the old me. Trying to get myself straight. Been working out, too." Quinn flexed a bicep. He felt some of the tension drain away. They believed he was McLeod. Now, if he could just find a way to capitalize on this deception.

Keller had almost finished his questions when a ragged and sinister-looking bauchan appeared in a sagging doorway. "What do you want?" it growled at Quinn.

Information, he answered, glad the officers couldn't see or hear it. Something bad must have happed to it to make it so rough. Bauchans are related to leprechauns, and they normally looked more or less like small, cheerful humans.

"About what?" the bauchan grumped.

Who's the dead guy? Why is he here? Quinn suspected he knew the answer to the second question already.

"If I tell you, will you leave me alone?"

Yes.

"They call him Pepé. He sells little crystals and white powder, mostly to humans." The bauchan licked his lips and smirked. "He shouldn't have branched out into new products. Keeps his packages in the AC intake. Now stop bothering me." The bauchan vanished.

"Okay, if you could just sign this," Keller said, holding his clipboard and a ballpoint out to Quinn.

Quinn took it, then frowned. "Couldn't you guys just say you talked to an anonymous bystander or something?"

"You don't want us to use your name?" Benson asked. "Why's that?"

Quinn made a dramatic sigh. "Man, I'm going to catch so much shit if Arbuckle finds out I was down here. I'm serious as a heart attack, sir. I'm clean, I swear. I'll piss in a cup, if you want. But jobs are hard to get right now, 'specially if you've got complications. Rent's due next week and I haven't found nothing. Pepé," Quinn glanced at the corpse, "told me he'd slip me a couple hundred if I ran a package for him."

"What kind of package?" Benson asked.

"Didn't ask." Quinn looked down, scuffing one foot against the other. "But it might be in the AC intake. That's where he used to keep his stash, anyway."

"Nick, why don't you go grab a couple of the guys, take a look. I'll keep Mr. McLeod company," Keller said.

Benson went to talk to some of his colleagues, then they went into Pepé's "office." It didn't take long before they called the crime scene photographer inside.

Benson and Keller had asked Quinn to talk to some Vice Squad officers, but he'd refused, knowing there was a chance that some of them might have encountered the real McLeod. He did say that if he heard anything at the halfway house, he'd pass it along, provided they never used his name on any reports.

After a while, they gave him a cheap, pre-paid cell phone. Five and a half excruciating weeks of giving them information about petty thieves and pimps, and Quinn was no closer to the zombie powder dealer. There was lots of talk from all sorts of folk about the dealer with zombie powder. But no one, fae or human, not even Malik, the djinn, could find a name or point to a location that was of any use. Three more Dryads died. Aleksei and Eoin spent the entire time talking to and watching over dryads. But there was no way to protect them all.

Then, Benson and Keller told him they wanted to set up a meeting between Quinn and an investigator from the DA's office. A man by the name of Ian Chambers. Since Quinn's information on everything else had been spot on, the DA wanted to find out if Quinn knew anything about some home invasion robberies that were about to go to trial.

The day before the meeting, Keller told Quinn he wanted to meet with him privately, after his shift. The spot was off one of the hike-and-bike trails that ran along Buffalo Bayou.

Quinn got there first. The cold drizzle reminded him of home. He was focusing on the smell of rain and the feel of cool water on his face, and allowed himself to be caught off guard when Aleksei stepped from behind an ash tree, appearing human.

"Quinn! You are hard to find this evening."

"Aleksei! Don't sneak up on me like that," he chided, even though he knew it was his own fault for not paying attention. "Is anything wrong?" Aleksei's sudden appearance was not protocol.

"Ni. Nothing wrong. In fact, we have located zombie powder." Aleksei's Ukranian accent was thick and difficult to understand, but Quinn was used to it.

"That's fantastic! How…?"

"You were right. Animal cruelty investigation you said to check."

"Yes!" Quinn hissed as he fist-bumped Aleksei. Sometimes it paid to listen to the officers' radios when he met with them.

"Drug dealer was, how you say? Voodoo queen, from next state over. Used dark magick to hide herself from us, but neighbors did not like for her to be killing chickens in back yard. She is no longer problem."

"Already neutralized? That was quick." Quinn did not envy her fate, especially if the dryads got a chance at her.

"Come. There is much—" Aleksei stopped short when he heard footfalls approaching in the soggy December grass. It had been raining for two days straight, and the park was more puddle than pathway.

"I'm expecting someone. Stay human," Quinn whispered. "Over here," Quinn said to the approaching flashlight. He could easily see Keller holding it, knew he was alone.

"Who's your friend?" the officer asked.

"Him? That's Alek. He's my roomie. Gave me a ride down here."

Aleksei lowered his head slightly. "Is good to meet you. I was just going." He gave Quinn a pointed look. "I see you later at car."

He turned to leave, but the wet Texas gumbo got the better of him. His foot slipped, then stuck in the heavy clay and he lost his balance, tumbled down the bank, and splashed into the bayou.

"He can't swim!" Quinn shouted.

Quinn and Keller scrambled down the bank and found Aleksei holding on to an exposed tree root. The water level was high from all the recent rain, and it was hurrying down towards Galveston Bay as fast as it could. Quinn didn't dare jump in the bayou. Water fae could be extremely territorial, and any that had claimed this area would have known immediately that their space had been violated. Quinn couldn't risk a confrontation and have Keller caught in the middle.

Keller was already holding his baton out to Aleksei. "Grab on. I'll pull you out."

Quinn grabbed Keller's free arm to help anchor him. Aleksei was a lot heavier than he looked.

Aleksei tightened his grip on the root with his left hand and reached for the baton with his right. As soon as Keller started to pull, a floating branch smacked into Aleksei's shoulder and he lost his grip on the baton. He flailed around, but caught the root again before he could be washed downstream.

"Hold on!" yelled Quinn. "We'll try again."

Again, Aleksei reached for the baton. This time, he grabbed on with both hands, and Quinn and Keller hauled him out of the water.

"Diakuiu. I thank you," Aleksei panted, lying on the muddy bank like a beached river dolphin.

"No problem. Just doing my job," Keller replied.

"You okay?" Quinn asked.

"Da."

The three of them struggled back up the slippery bank, using small bushes and tree roots to pull themselves along.

"Do not be long. I've need of dry clothes," Aleksei said to Quinn. "Good night," he nodded to Keller.

"See you in a few," replied Quinn.

"He going to be alright?" asked Keller, eyeing Aleksei's retreating form.

"He'll be fine. You saved my friend's life. I owe you one."

Keller looked around, shining his Maglite into the bushes all around them, as if he was wary that another unexpected guest was going to pop out of the shrubbery. When he seemed to be satisfied that they were alone, he switched off the light.

"You didn't hear this from me. But don't trust Ian Chambers. There's something about that guy...I don't know. I've got to talk to some people about him," Keller said.

Then his cell rang. He'd slid his finger across its face and a thumbnail image of a pretty young woman glowed in the dark. "Hey, Bright Eyes," Keller answered. "Let me call you right back, okay?...Love you, too." Then he hung up and slipped the phone back into his pocket.

"We'll see you tomorrow. Do the street preacher thing. We'll pick you up after lunch. The usual place. I have to go. Watch your back, okay?"

"Thanks for the warning," Quinn replied. "Tomorrow."

But Quinn hadn't seen Keller the next day. Or Ian Chambers.

Benson texted him that the meeting was canceled.

With headlines blaring from every newsstand, it was impossible for Quinn not to realize why. It made him sad – as humans went, Ryan Keller had been a pretty good one. Quinn reminded himself that even the oldest humans were very short-lived, compared to fae. It didn't make him feel any better.

A few days later, Quinn attended the funeral, even admired Keller's pretty widow, whom he recognized from her image on Keller's phone. He wanted to offer his condolences, tell her that her husband had been a good man. But she already knew that, and it was better he stay in the shadows. Besides, he'd gotten what he came for, and it was time for the helpful police informant, Marc McLeod, to skip town. Quinn asked the dryads in Keller's yard to keep an eye on his wife and contact him if she got into any trouble.

Chapter 3
Dinner Theater

⸙

Nineteen months later
Memorial Day Weekend, Houston, Texas

CASSIE GIGGLED WHEN HER grandmother tickled her chin.

"She is so close to walking now, Mom," I said, shifting the baby on my hip.

"Well, she is her mother's daughter. You walked and talked before you were a year old, Marti," she replied.

"Happy Memorial Day," Nick said as he hugged me.

Emily just waved. Their third child was due a couple of weeks, and even if she weren't holding a huge pan of seven-layer dip, she couldn't get close enough to anyone for a hug. Their twins had already made a break for the ancient swing set.

Mom took the big foil-covered pan from my sister and set it on the picnic table. "Who's your friend, Em?" she asked, looking at the clean-cut, pleasant looking man, about my age, who trailed into the backyard after them.

"Adele, this is Ian Chambers. Ian, this lovely lady is my mother-in-law, Adele Schmidt."

Ian took my mother's hand in his right and clasped her elbow with his left.

"And this is my sister-in-law, Marti Keller." Nick squeezed my arm.

"Hello, Ian. Nice to meet you," I said, barely glancing at the sandy-haired man. I turned and handed Cassie over to my mother. "Nick, I could use your help with the potato salad. If you'll excuse us?"

I hustled Nick into the house. I had to nip this in the bud. Who knows? Ian Chambers might be a great guy and I might even be interested in him, but if I didn't set Nick straight here and now, he'd never stop.

As soon as the door closed I whirled to face my brother-in-law. "I don't need you to fix me up with anybody."

"Come on, Marti. Ian's a nice guy. He saved my life, back in college. He dragged me and three other people out of a burning building. He's a hero."

"I'm sure he is. But I'm not ready. I wasn't ready for the last three guys you tried to set me up with, either."

"Marti, it's been almost two years now. Ryan loved you. He wouldn't want you and Cassie to be all alone."

"We're not all alone. We live next door to my parents. You and Emily are only six doors down."

"That's not what I meant, and you know it. Look at yourself, Marti. You quit your job and hardly see your friends, like a hermit or something. Ryan wouldn't want that for you."

"I don't need you to tell me what Ryan would want. Just back off, Nick. I know you mean well, but it's my life. Got it?" Bottles rattled in the door as I jerked opened the fridge, with more force than I intended.

Nick sighed and shook his head. "Ryan died. You didn't. For Cassie's sake, don't forget that." He started for the back door.

"Where do you think you're going?" I asked him.

He turned around and grunted as I shoved a large, cold bowl of potato salad into his arms. "Don't forget this," I said, with as much smile as I could manage.

After the screen door banged behind him, I went into the bathroom to splash some cold water on my face. I had managed to hold it together while I was talking to Nick, but I was rapidly coming apart now.

"For Cassie's sake…" His words stung. Who the hell did Nick think he was?

Wasn't everything I did (or didn't do) for Cassie's sake? It was for Cassie's sake that I quit my job. She was the only link I had to Ryan, and I couldn't stand the thought of her being in day care, where she would never be as precious to them as she was to me. What if something happened to her? Why didn't I date? It wasn't only because I wasn't really over Ryan. How many times as an ER nurse had I seen children brought in because their mothers' boyfriends hurt them?

Maybe part of the problem was that I never got to say goodbye. Ryan was there…and then he wasn't. There was no closing parenthesis.

I wished for the thousandth time that I hadn't waited the extra day to tell Ryan that we were expecting. I don't suppose it would have made a difference. He'd still most likely be dead. But at least he would have died knowing about our baby. She wouldn't have just been my little secret.

The house that Cassie and I lived in had been a wedding present from Mom and Dad. My car was paid for. I didn't have a lot of expenses, but my savings and the insurance money weren't going to last forever. I needed to come up with a way to get some cash flow before it became a serious problem. I'd have to worry about it later, though. Now, I had to go show my smiling face at the barbeque.

Even after our little talk, Nick still contrived to have Ian sit next to me while we ate. He was actually kind of funny. As an investigator for the district attorney's office, and he'd probably never run out of 'stupid criminal tricks' stories. Kinda reminded me of Ryan like that. Maybe that's why I gave him my email when he asked. I told him I'd only let him have it if he didn't mention it to Nick.

It was four o'clock, and Mom's resin hummingbird garden thermometer read 96°F. Every ice cube in every cooler had melted, in spite of the shady back porch and ceiling fan.

Dad, who was holding my sleeping Cassie, waved at me from across the porch. "Little Sugar, won't you run down to the Stop-n-Go and get some more ice?"

"Sure, Dad." The corner market hadn't been a Stop-n-Go since 1989. The name changed every few years, but to Dad, all convenience stores were Stop-n-Go's.

He was doing well since the accident. In a cosmic spasm of irony, his pickup truck had gotten nailed by an 18-wheeler. He had problems adjusting to the artificial leg and he sometimes had seizures, but all and all, he was doing amazingly well.

Ian was in the bathroom, and I slipped out of the back yard before he came back. I wanted some space. Ian was certainly not hard to look at. And he was smart. And funny. But I needed to step back a little, and use the little grey cells. I stopped by my house on the way and got the little plastic wagon. I didn't want to get in the car to drive three blocks, but I didn't want to carry six bags of ice home in my arms, either.

I found myself humming as I walked along the baking sidewalk. I went out of my way to walk in the shade of the shop awnings to avoid the blistering sun. I squirmed as beads of sweat crawled down into my bra.

I was still trying to decide whether I wanted to hug Nick or slap him for bringing Ian along to the party. Ian was a pretty boy. He didn't have Ryan's body, of course, but he wasn't too shabby. Well, I didn't think he had Ryan's body, but there was only one way to be sure. Marti Renee Keller. Don't even think about going there – you don't know anything about this man. Not entirely true. I knew he worked for the DA, had a cousin who was a circus clown, and had sinfully beautiful blue eyes. Nick thought enough of him to bring him around Dad. He saved Nick's life, back when they were college roommates.

The next thing I knew, I was lying on the sidewalk.

"Oh! I am so sorry!" a plumpish woman leaned over me. "Are you okay, honey?"

"Yeah, I think I'm all right."

Another woman, scrawny with lanky, salt and pepper hair, peeked out from behind a large, battered bookcase that leaned against the brick wall of the storefront. "Did I not just say, 'Lulu, what is that noise?'? But you just kept backing up, knowing you couldn't see around that bookshelf."

"Oh hush, Belinda." The first woman extended her hand to help me up. "I'm Lulu Miranda and this is Belinda Tate. We're opening up a shop here. Trying to get all the counters and whatnot in this week. They won't fit through the back door, so we had to come around to the front. I was going backwards with this shelf and I never even saw you. Sure you're okay?"

I dusted off my butt. "I'm fine. I'm going to go now."

"We'll be open next week, so make sure you come by the shop and choose something for yourself. On me, of course. I didn't catch your name."

"Marti. I'll see you around." I walked away, suddenly aware of how loudly the little wagon rumbled along behind me.

They'd finished this new strip center over six months ago. So far, the only tenant was a nail parlor, although I think that all strip malls are required by law to have nail shops.

Loaded up with ice and headed home, I noticed an enormous sign in Lulu's window:

Coming soon! The Tenth Sphere

– Art * Books * Gifts * New Age –

Featuring original jewelry designs by Belinda's Blessed Beads.

Huh.

But back to Ian. He was good looking, had a stable job with respectable pay, had his own house (in the gentrified Heights, no less), was thirty and had never been married. Why was he still single? Was he really too good to be true, or was I just trying to talk myself out of getting to know him?

I could hear Cassie crying from half a block away. I started to jog, the wagon lurching along behind me, bumping and scraping my heels. She must have woken up from her nap and not seen me. I tried to hurry into the backyard with my payload, but it got stuck in the stepping stones at the gate.

"I've got it. You take care of the baby," Ian said, getting up from his shady camp chair.

"Thanks."

My mother was bouncing Cassie on her knees and singing, but it wasn't helping. I scooped up my little girl, but she was mad at me. Little tears fell on her cheeks and stabbed me right in the heart. I took her inside to see if nursing would calm her down.

On Wednesday, Emily called me. "Hey. Why don't you come over for dinner Friday? Dr. Fredericks scheduled my c-section for Thursday a week, and we wanted to have a last hurrah before the baby comes and we drop off the radar."

Sounded fishy to me. "Who else is going to be there?"

"Oh, Mom, Dad, a friend or two."

"Like maybe Ian Chambers?"

My sister sounded sheepish. "Maybe."

I didn't tell her that Ian had already sent me an email, asking if I'd be at the get-together. I hadn't responded yet. Wasn't like I had any prior commitments. I liked Ian. I liked to look at Ian. But I didn't like to be rushed. It was less complicated to admire him from afar, where the concept couldn't clash with the reality.

"If I come, will you make Nick promise, cross his heart and hope to die, that he will stop trying to fix me up?"

"I promise that I will tell him to promise you."

My sister, the lawyer. "Fine. I'll be there. 7:00?"

"Yep. Bring a pie."

"Got it. Bye."

I replied to Ian's mail, saying I'd be at Emily and Nick's on Friday. I felt a little thrill as I clicked "send." But then I closed the window and saw the wallpaper on my screen, a photo of Ryan and me at Niagara Falls, and I felt horribly guilty, almost like I was having an affair. I decided to take Cassie to the park, where there were no pictures to remind me.

Cassie skipped her Friday morning nap, which meant she had a two and a half hour afternoon nap. While she was sleeping, I tried on every outfit in my closet at least once. I finally decided on a floral print summer dress. It was big enough to cover the scaffolding of the nursing bra and small enough to be cute and maybe just a little flirty. I hung it up on the closet door and put my bum-around-the-house clothes back on.

I did a few quick chores before I sat down to look through a magazine I'd picked up at the bookstore. It promised tip-filled articles on work-at-home jobs for moms.

Appointment setter. No.

Virtual administrative assistant. No.

Computer programmer. No.

Medical billing coder. Maybe.

Tarot card reader. What?

"Learn to read Tarot cards! Be the master of your own destiny with a career that never goes out of style. Set up your own storefront! Entertain at parties! The future is in your hands with this people-pleasing career. For more information, request packet 008799685."

I was going to check in with the interwebs about that, but Cassie started crying. I put her in the high chair with some Cheerios and fruit puffs while I started on the pie. She didn't like to be fed anymore – wanted to do it herself. Which was good, I supposed, but it took her forever to eat. She did okay with finger foods, but she was a menace with the spoon. I put the pie in the oven and wondered if Ian liked coconut cream. It had been Ryan's favorite.

"Da da da!" shouted Cassie as she pounded her tray. I kissed her and gave her a sippy cup with some water in it.

I pointed to myself. "Ma ma. Say Mama, Cassie."

"Da da da!"

"Okay. Be that way." I sighed and forced a smile.

All of the books said that it was developmentally normal for babies to make the "d" sound before the "m" sound. My logical mind accepted this. My emotional mind was another story. Even though I knew it was totally unreasonable, I still felt slighted that she could call for the Dada she'd never meet, but not for the Mama that was there for her 24/7.

I cleaned up the kitchen and pulled the pie out of the oven. I should have made it this morning, so it had time to chill and set up properly. I stuck it in the freezer while I gave Cassie her bath.

When she was all cleaned up and ready, I went back into the kitchen and beat the egg whites. I took the pie out of the freezer. But the pie pan stuck to my damp fingers. I tried to blow hot breath on them, but ended up sticking the tip of my nose in the filling. Well, at least the meringue would hide the hole. It didn't take long to melt the frost. I spread the meringue on top of the custard and popped it in to bake. I checked on it ten minutes later and it looked exactly the same. I hadn't turned on the freaking oven. What is wrong with me?

I knew what was wrong with me, and it was called Ian Chambers. I almost called Emily to say that Cassie was sick and I wouldn't be there, after all. But Mom would be over here in two heartbeats and she'd know I was lying through my teeth. I was too old to sit through that lecture again.

I played finger puppets with Cassie while the meringue browned. Once I took the pie out of the oven, I went to change clothes. I even put on eyeliner. Then I took it back off. I hadn't worn makeup since Ryan died, and if I showed up at the party wearing it, knowing Ian Chambers would be there, Nick would never let me live it down.

Cassie and I were ten minutes late. Part of the meringue had collapsed and I tried to disguise it with toasted coconut. In the end, I gave up and decided to blame it on the pie carrier. Mom grabbed the baby as soon as I walked in, and I put the pie in Emily's fridge. Nick wolf-whistled at me as I came out of the kitchen.

"Don't make me have to smack you," I said.

He chuckled and whispered something in Ian's ear. I didn't want to know what it was.

"Marti! You look great," Ian said, blushing to almost the same color as the hibiscuses on his Hawaiian shirt.

I really didn't want to know what Nick said to him.

"Hey Auntie Marti!" Kyle and Aiden shouted at me as they ran by, squirting each other with water pistols.

"Boys! Not in the house." Nick warned.

They ran out the back door, and Dad limped in, leaving it open.

"Dad!" Emily shouted. "Close the door. You'll let the cat out."

Bojangles was already trotting towards the opening, ready to make his escape.

"TTTSSSSST! TTSSSST!" Ian shouted, waving his arms and lunging towards the cat. Bojangles' hair stood on end as he yowled and took off at top speed towards the back of the house.

On the way, he knocked Cassie over. She had been standing up, holding on to the coffee table. She looked around to make sure everyone was watching before she started to wail.

Ian, who was only a few feet away from her, scooped her up and brought her to me. My knees went a little wobbly when his hand brushed my back after he handed Cassie over. Traitors.

She wasn't hurt, but it had scared the poop out of her. Literally. I felt something wet, warm and squishy on her leg when I shifted her to my hip. There had been a catastrophic breach in the containment field.

"Um, Ian, you might want to go clean up." I was mortified, but it was all I could do to squelch a giggle as I pointed to the streak on his arm. I had a change of baby clothes, but no grown up clothes. "I'll take her back to the house to get cleaned up."

Ian's face froze and he looked at his arm as if it was coated in radioactive waste.

"I'm really sorry about that," I said as I retreated out the door.

Well. That was special. As we hurried home under the street lights, I kissed my baby's head. "So, Cassie-girl, was that an editorial opinion?"

"Da da da!"

꧁

When we rejoined the party twenty minutes later, the twins had been sent to the Kids Table, and Dad had already brought in the food he had cooked on the barbeque. My favorite was the grilled peaches. I could be happy eating those and nothing else. The smell of peach, nutmeg, cinnamon and butter made my mouth water as I picked up my dinner plate. They hadn't waited for us. After I buckled Cassie into the high chair, I sat down in the only available seat – next to Ian.

"Sorry about the accident," I said to him.

"Don't worry about it. I know how squirmy babies can be. It's easy to get the diaper on just a little wrong."

I looked at his face. He seemed cheerful enough, even though it almost sounded like a dig. I let it go. I was probably just being hyper-sensitive, given that I managed to go two whole minutes at the get-together before my child besmirched not only me, but him as well. Ryan would have laughed and said, "Poop happens!"

After coffee and a miserable looking (but tasty!) slice of pie, we went into the living room and Nick put the twins to bed. Cassie was wired after her long nap and I knew it was going to be a late night. She was back at the coffee table, holding the edge with both hands. A blue stuffed bunny, Mr. Buns, dangled by the ear from her chubby fingers as she sidled up and down the edge of the table. If it was going to tire her out, I was all for it.

Ian was sitting on the floor near me, and he reached over and scooped Cassie up when she came by. I expected her to start wailing at him for spoiling her fun.

Instead, she giggled and whacked him in the head with the rabbit. "Da da da! Da da da!"

Ian looked surprised.

"Out of the mouths of babes!" Nick said, as he came back into the room at exactly the wrong moment.

I put my head in my hands and shook it. There was no point in trying to explain that she'd been working on that sound for almost two weeks now. Da da this, da da that. When was she ever going to say 'Mama?' "I'll go help Emily in the kitchen."

Mom quickly took my place when I got up.

Pale and sweaty, Emily was trying to arrange leftovers in the fridge.

"Hey Em, anything I can do?"

"No, Marts. I'm just about done. Nick'll get the dishes later."

I sat down, then felt a little guilty. "Why don't you have a seat? You look awful."

"Gee, thanks."

Emily waddled over and pulled out the chair next to me. "So. What do you think of Ian?"

"I'm already pregnant with his child and we're going to elope to Canada."

"You don't have to be sarcastic. I just wanted to know if you liked the guy. Nick thinks you'd make a good pair."

"Sorry. I kinda feel like I'm under a microscope just now. He seems nice enough, easy on the eyes. What do you think of him? He works for the DA – you're bound to have had some lawyerly, public defender contact with him somewhere."

"I mostly know him by reputation, and he works for the other side, remember? They say he's smart, capable, very in control." Emily shrugged. "Sorry, Marts. Wish I had the energy to stay up and chat, but I'm whipped. I'm going to bed. Night." She stood up and ruffled my hair as she walked past.

I made my way back to the living room.

"...and so the guy asks for change, and when the clerk opens the drawer, bad guy pulls out a gun and yells, 'Give me everything in the register!' The clerk hands him all the money in the till and bad guy bolts out the door. There was $5 in the register. And he left the twenty on the counter," Nick said, almost doubling over laughing.

Ian glanced up at me and gave me a quick smile and a wink. I looked down to make sure I hadn't had any wardrobe malfunctions.

"So we had this guy," Ian started, "that went to rob a bank. He had a backpack full of something, and he told the teller it was a bomb. She gave him the money, but he left the backpack, saying he'd detonate it if anybody followed him. So they called out the bomb squad and they found the backpack was filled with books. And his library card."

"No shit!" Nick said.

Mom cleared her throat and he cringed.

"Wait, it gets better," Ian continued. "When the cops asked the teller if the man had any distinguishing characteristics, she said he had horns on his head - some kind of freaky implants - and a tattoo on his forehead, his forehead, that said, 'Born to loose.' He was real hard to pick out of a lineup."

I was afraid Nick was going to wet himself.

"Emily went to bed." I said, plopping down on the couch.

Dad was asleep in the recliner. It was almost like old times, except now it was Ian and Nick talking shop instead of Ryan and Nick.

Cassie had been playing with the twins' blocks, but she left them and crawled towards Ian.

"Hey, baby! Way past your bedtime, isn't it little cutie?" He looked up at me when he said this, then tickled the back of Cassie's neck. She laughed.

"She had a two and a half hour nap this afternoon. But you're right. I should get her home and at least get her jammies on."

"I'll walk you to the house. It's after ten."

I was never bothered about walking alone in this neighborhood at any time day or night. But maybe my safety wasn't what he had in mind.

I really didn't need Ian to walk me six doors down. But I didn't mind it, either.

"In this neighborhood? We'll be fine." I said, protesting more for show than anything else.

"Please allow me to be a gentleman." He flashed perfect, laser-whitened teeth at me.

"If you insist." I scooped up Cassie and the diaper bag and headed towards the door.

"Nice weather we're having," Ian said, looking up at the pale stars sprinkled on the clear charcoal sky.

"Well, at this time of day, yeah."

Ian laughed.

I hummed to Cassie and Ian didn't say anything else until we got to my front porch.

"It was great to see you again tonight. I know it's really short notice, and I understand if you already have other plans, but would you have dinner with me Saturday – tomorrow - night?"

"A dinner date?" Mom could probably watch Cassie. "Yes. I'd like that." Then, I immediately crawfished. "If I can get a babysitter. As you said, it is kind of short notice."

He didn't have to know I'd only leave Cassie with Mom or Emily. And Mom was usually available.

"I'll call you tomorrow afternoon."

"You don't have my number."

"Email it to me."

Duh.

Then he took my non-baby-filled hand and kissed it. "Good night."

Much later on, I fell asleep smiling.

Chapter 4
The Emerald Jar

━━━━━━━━━━━━ ෨ ━━━━━━━━━━━━

"BIT CHILLY IN HERE, don't you think?" the man with red hair asked.

"Maybe." Quinn shrugged.

The redhead picked up a log from the stack of wood near the cavernous fireplace and set it in the grate. He smiled at it.

It burst into flames.

"That's better," he said, dusting off his hands and making his way back to the bar.

"If you say so," Quinn said as he set a pint of dark stout in front of the redhead.

He ran his finger along the stein's handle. "I don't trust Malik."

"He's been with my team for ages. I trust him, Kai," Quinn replied.

"Yes, but you introduced him to his wife. He's in your debt, not mine."

Quinn sighed and blotted up a small puddle of beer on the bar. Closing time at the Waterhorse Inn had come and gone, and Kai was the only customer still inside the locked pub. The establishment had belonged to Quinn's family for as long as anyone in Blackthorne could remember, and that gave him a great deal of latitude with the front door key.

Kai took a deep draught of the stout and wiped his mouth with the back of his hand. "Djinn are always wildcards. Never sure what's going to offend them, and nobody carries a grudge like a djinn."

Quinn's smile was half-hearted. "I've heard all that. But Malik has always been solid. He's on my team, and you've got no say about that."

"I'm not asking you to kick him off your team. No," Kai said, crossing his arms. "That would probably be the worst possible thing to do. But this is a joint operation, and I'm just trying to assess liabilities."

"Malik is not a liability."

Kai noted that Quinn's eyes had changed from dark-eyed human to the edge-to-edge black of a kelpie. That often meant he was agitated and having trouble maintaining his current shape. But sometimes he just did it for effect - it totally freaked humans out. This was not one of those times.

Kai raised his glass. "To the unswerving loyalty of true friends." And chugged down the contents.

Quinn snorted and shook his head. His eyes were back to black on white. "Go home."

"See you tomorrow," Kai said as he stood up.

"It is tomorrow. Now get out, Kai."

"That's Mr. Underhill, to you."

Kai clapped Quinn on the shoulder, then turned and sauntered across the room to a floor-to-ceiling picture of a castle. He turned and waved before he stepped into the picture and was gone.

Quinn was tired of holding his human form. He went out to the millpond behind the inn and stripped naked under the platinum sliver of the new moon. As he dove into the water, he let its gelid fingers strip away his human shape. It felt good to be strong, a dreadnought slicing through the water. It wasn't that he felt nothing when he was in his natural kelpie form; but emotions receded into the background and sensations took center stage. The prickle of cold water rushing against his slippery skin. The pressure as he dove to the bottom of the pond. The searing of his lungs, screaming for oxygen, as he forced himself to stay under the surface until the last possible moment. He told himself that it was an exercise to expand his physical abilities. But he knew he was lying.

He wasn't really sure how long Siobhan had been gone. Sometimes it seemed like he'd been missing her for a hundred years, and sometimes it seemed that it was only yesterday that he'd carried her lifeless body, her blood soaking his skin and staining his soul, out of the wreckage of her little cottage. He would never forget that it had happened on a Tuesday, just before lunch. If he took a few moments with a Mundane calendar, he would know it had taken place two years, eight months, and six days ago. But time slipped into irrelevance as he scraped along the muddy pond bottom at top speed.

Quinn stayed out all night. As millponds go, this one was large – it had to be to accommodate generations of Waterhorse Inn kelpies – but it was still only a pond, not a deep loch. He had to be creative to find ways to push himself to exhaustion, and he managed to do so. He'd had a lot of practice. As the eastern sky lightened to grey, he shifted into human form, scooped up his clothes, and went inside.

"Morning, Robbie," Quinn said to the man arranging breakfast plates on the sideboard.

His older brother shook his head. "Put on some breeks, will ya? You'll frighten away the lodgers."

Quinn only smiled and trotted up the stairs. His hair was still damp, but the cool morning breeze had already dried his skin. He dropped his bundle of clothes on the floor and slipped under a heavy featherbed, too tired to dream.

When he woke up, it was well past lunch time. Stomach growling like a Tasmanian devil, he got up and got dressed, brushing one of last night's fish scales out from between his front teeth. Too bad it was only a small pond, with small fish.

The smell of baking bread in the kitchen made Quinn even hungrier. As he raided the pantry for something to eat, his younger brother, Kade, came in. There was one brother younger than him (Graham), and one older than Robbie (Laurence, but they called him Laurie). Neither of them kept rooms at the Waterhorse.

"So how long are you gone this time?" asked Kade.

"Not sure. A fortnight, probably less, if everything goes well." Quinn knew Kade was just asking because he wanted to make sure the work at the Inn was covered, but having his affairs probed by his younger brother still rankled him.

Kade nodded. "Keep yourself in one piece." He continued through the kitchen and out the back door.

"I always do," Quinn said softly to the closed back door.

Deer season in the Angelina National Forest had been over for months, and this was not a righteous kill. Quinn squatted by the carcass of a white-tailed doe that had been shot and left to rot. It was too late at night for bottle flies, but the scavengers had been busy. Even so, he could see the ragged gunshot holes in the tatters of her stiff hide.

That wasn't the only thing wrong in the forest. It should have smelled like pine trees and earthy leaf litter. But there was an underlying industrial smell, hints of sulfur and plastic that set Quinn's nerves on edge.

"It's gotten really bad here," a quiet voice rasped behind him.

Quinn pivoted around. "Columbia?" he asked, his voice cracking with disbelief.

The dryad should have looked like a pretty young woman. Instead, the tree spirit was gaunt and pale. Oozing sores covered most of her skin, and bald spots glared from her scalp where clumps of her hair had fallen out.

"They poison everything. The trees are dead or dying," she panted.

"Sit down. Rest," Quinn said. "That's why we're here."

Quinn breathed in deeply, trying to quash his anger. He knew if he let it flow, let it control him, he would be blinded by it. But if he could smash it into a smoldering ball of energy deep within himself, he could harness its power later, when he needed it.

Kai's team was drawing off the heavily armed defenders and arranging an encounter between them and the human state police. When Quinn got the signal, his team would sweep in, bind the guards left at the camp and leave them like Christmas presents for the park rangers, who would be on their way. They'd leave the marijuana plants and equipment for the authorities to find. Once the growers were in custody, the forest would have a chance to heal. The pesticides and harsh artificial fertilizer would stop washing into the creek, burning and killing everything they touched.

A tiny ball of light, a flower fae, suddenly glowed by his head, then was gone. It was time.

Quinn whistled like a chuck will's widow three times in quick succession. The first guard never had a chance to grab the Kalashnikov slung over his shoulder as Eoin, the urisk, kicked him in the head with his iron-hard goat hooves. He dropped with a soft grunt and the half-man, half-goat took the guard's weapon, then triple-bound his hands and feet with zip ties.

A second guard had apparently heard something and came to investigate. Quinn slipped up behind him and locked him in a sleeper hold before he could raise an alarm. Eoin again set to work with the zip ties.

"Two down, two to go," Quinn whispered.

He scanned the camp and frowned. He could see as well in the dark as he could in daylight, yet he could detect no movement, no personnel. The growers' camp was too still.

"Something's wrong, Eoin. I can feel it. Not worried about Aleksei and Malik, but Tam's so green."

They crept towards a camo-patterned tent, the kind deer hunters sometimes use. Quinn could see Aleksei standing just behind the tent, although any human who looked at him would see nothing more than a large shrub. A flicker of eye contact, and Aleksei mouthed "Trap!"

But it was too late.

The ground next to Quinn and Eoin erupted and four hulking trolls burst out of the earth. One grabbed Eoin and another snatched Quinn. In human form,

Quinn was just over six feet tall, but the troll was easily half again that height. Its hairy arms crushed the air out of his lungs as it picked him up and dragged him out in front of the tent. Eoin fought back, but even his hard hooves were no match for the living stone body of his captor. Quinn fought to breathe, then gagged on the moldy rot of the troll's breath.

"Welcome to the party," said a chunky man, who had been hidden by the tent.

The pupils of his bulging yellow eyes were vertical slits and his reptilian face was a scaly parody of a human's.

What was a demon doing here? No one had mentioned demons were involved. Although, Quinn told himself, one should never be surprised to find demons with their claws in any rotten pie they could find.

The air shimmered behind the demon and Quinn knew that Malik was stalking it.

"Catch!" shouted the demon. It tossed something that glittered green, even in the wan moonlight, in Malik's direction.

When it made contact with the djinn, it started to glow, so brightly that Quinn had to squint and turn his head. Malik seemed to crystalize out of the air, then he crumbled like a sand painting. A colorful stream, grains of Malik, was sucked into the hovering green jar. The demon snatched it out of the air and jammed a stopper into it.

Quinn and Eoin struggled to free themselves, but the trolls just squeezed them tighter, harsh laughter gurgling in their ears.

The demon pulled out a cell phone and sent a short text.

"Special bottle, you see. Carved from a single emerald. Coated in magick. Your djinn friend is mine, all mine. At least, until I sell him for a pile of cash."

The bushes near the demon rustled. No troll was holding Tam, and the young glastyn leaped from the shrubbery, his long horse ears pinned against his black hair and his sharp teeth bared. He scrabbled frantically at the green jar, but the demon coolly caught him by the throat with its free hand. Looking Quinn straight in the eye, it licked its scaly lips and sank its fangs into Tam's throat. He tried to scream, but it came out as a wet, choking gasp.

"No!" Quinn yelled, kicking uselessly at the stony legs of the troll. He heard a bone in his foot snap, but didn't feel it. He shifted into kelpie form, but the other two trolls anticipated this and grabbed his tail and neck. He wasn't any more use to Tam than he had been before. His cousin was going to die and there was nothing he could do to stop it.

Tam shriveled and collapsed in on himself as Quinn, Eoin and Aleksei watched, helpless and horrified. When the demon had finished sucking the last of Tam's life force, it threw his shriveled husk to the ground.

"I'm leaving you alive," the demon said to Quinn, "so that you can crawl back and report to your master that this is what happens to any of you stupid little fae that meddle in Balcones' business." The demon scowled and shook his head. "I can't have a big damn sea monster lying around when he gets here. Shift back to human form."

Quinn shook his head.

Balcones looked at Eoin. "Shift back, or I'm having barbequed goat for breakfast."

Defeated, Quinn shifted.

The demon nodded, and one of the trolls punched Quinn in the face. Everything went dark.

He had no idea how long he had been out, but Quinn awoke to the sound of voices. His head felt like it was in a vise and his broken ribs made breathing painful. He felt soft dirt underneath him and could hear someone nearby, breathing heavily. He hoped it was Eoin.

"And I told you, Chambers. You can have the merchandise as soon as I get a text that the funds have been transferred. Bad things will happen to you if I have to repeat myself."

Chambers. Why did that name sound familiar? There was something he should remember, but it stayed just out of reach, dancing at the dark edges of his memory.

Quinn's eye was swollen nearly shut, but he could open it enough to see the demon, disguised as a human, talking to a sandy-haired man. They were probably twenty yards away, and he doubted the human could see him in the tree-shadowed dark.

Chambers glanced at something in his hand. "My employer is not a patient man," he replied.

"Your employer's gonna have a job opening, if you don't shut up," Balcones snapped.

Chambers shut up.

Quinn let his eye close, and he wasn't aware of anything but the throbbing in his head until an electronic double beep snagged his attention. He opened his painful eye again.

"Money's cleared. Merchandise is yours. Now get back to Houston," the demon said.

He tossed Chambers the emerald bottle.

When Quinn opened his eyes again, his body was well, but his heart was sick. He could tell by the fact that everything was green that he was in a healing room. Quinn sat up and took a deep breath. It felt good to be pain free, at least physically. Then he lay back down and wondered if his mother knew that he'd gotten her cousin's youngest son killed.

"Hey! He's awake."

Quinn turned towards the door to see Kai and Eoin coming to his bedside.

"Weren't sure you were going to make it there, for a bit," Eoin said.

"Well, here I am, all in one piece."

"Kade's downstairs with your mum. He and Robbie have been taking turns sitting with you," Kai said. "She only leaves to eat."

"How long have I been here?"

"Three days," Eoin replied.

"So she knows then. About Tam."

"That was not your fault. Nobody blames you," Kai said, squeezing Quinn's shoulder.

"They should. I knew something was wrong. I should have aborted the mission and sent the team back to the rendezvous point."

"Second guessing yourself doesn't help anything, Quinn," Kai said. He cleared his throat.

"I'll go let your mum know you're awake," Eoin said, taking Kai's hint.

"It's just like before. I couldn't save Siobhan then and I couldn't save Tam now. I'm no good at this. I'll be turning in my resignation as soon as I'm out of here."

"No." Kai's voice was soft, but forceful. "That's just what Balcones wants you to do. If you quit, he wins, and Tam will have died for nothing." Kai shook his head and continued. "Siobhan knew exactly what she was doing. If she hadn't lured the demons away, it would have been a bloodbath. She saved a hundred lives, maybe more. It was her choice to make, not yours."

Quinn turned and faced the wall.

"I didn't even question it when she bought that little house in the Mundane world. She never so much as hinted that she'd volunteered for a suicide mission."

"Because she knew you would have stopped her. Or gone with her." Kai chewed his lip. "I'm sorry about Tam, really, I am. I know he was your cousin. I know you feel responsible. But it isn't your fault. When Tam saw what the situation was, he should have made a tactical retreat and called for reinforcements. That's SOP." Kai paused, his eyes softening and his voice changing from military commander to friend. "Take some time off. Get your head straight. But don't quit."

The door opened and Quinn's mother strode in, followed closely by Kade. She glared at Kai, but did not speak to him.

Kai squeezed Quinn's shoulder. "Think about what I said." Then he turned on his heel and left, avoiding eye contact with Quinn's family.

"How are you feeling?" Quinn's mother asked, laying her hand on his forehead as if he were a feverish child.

"Been better."

"I can see that." She patted his hand. "I hope you've finally come to your senses and you'll give up this ridiculous meddling in the Mundane world. If you really want to save it, you shouldn't be rescuing humans – you should be eating them, and the more the better."

Kade cringed in the background.

"They're not all bad, Mother," Quinn replied.

"Shall I convey that to my cousin Alice? I'm sure that will be very comforting as she's mourning her dead son."

"It was a demon, Mother. A demon killed Tam, not a human. We were ambushed, and Tam failed to follow protocol. He should have gone for help." Quinn struggled to keep his voice even.

"Is that what the red-haired monstrosity told you? His kind is not like us, you know." Her eyes shifted dangerously to all black.

"So, Mumsie," Kade broke in. "Have you managed to contact Graham and Laurie yet?"

"Laurence's wife said he was out teaching the children to catch sturgeon, but she'd pass along the message. I expect he'll be arriving before long."

Quinn suspected that Kade had already contacted Graham. He hoped to see his youngest brother, but knew he would not show himself as long as their mother was around. She and Graham had a bitter falling out over a hundred years ago, and hadn't spoken to each other since. She could not forgive him for getting romantically involved with a human. He could not forgive her for eating his girlfriend.

Quinn leaned dejectedly against the cinderblock wall. He'd slipped out of the Waterhorse Inn during the night, in the middle of his family drama, and come to the Mundane world to find Malik. He'd undoubtedly pay for it when he got back, but now was not the time to think about it. He had worse problems at the moment. There were only about one hundred people with the last name of Chambers in the Houston white pages. But that didn't include any unlisted numbers or cell phones. How was he going to find Malik before something really bad happened?

A police car drove by. And that's when Quinn remembered. Now he knew where he'd heard the name Chambers.

Quinn pounded his fist into the wall. "Dammit!" All this time, Chambers had been right under his nose. Quinn ran back to the pay phone and looked up 'Chambers' in the tattered white pages that hung from a cable tether underneath the phone. There was neither an 'Ian' nor an 'I' Chambers listed.

At least it wouldn't be too difficult to find out if he was still working for the District Attorney. If not, perhaps he could renew his acquaintance with Officer Benson. He might have some idea where to find Chambers.

The best place to start, he reasoned, was at the DA's office. As soon as he found a way to get downtown.

It took him over an hour to get there on the 53 Briar Forest bus, and he still had to hike eight blocks to the DA's office on Franklin Street. It was nearly 5:00 when he arrived.

"Hey there, miss," he said to the receptionist in his best good-ole-boy American accent. "I'm an old buddy of Ian Chambers' and I was in town for a conference. Thought I'd drop by and say 'hey.' Is he in this afternoon?"

"I'm sorry. Mr. Chambers is out of the office. If you'd care to leave a message?"

"No, thanks. I'll just call him at the house. You have yourself a nice day, now."

Quinn knew that Kai had a team in place for a long-term assignment, and he was certain he could get help from them. They, more than any other fae who still visited the Mundane world, would understand.

One of Kai's team, Lorelei, loaned Quinn her car and gave him a place to crash. That made his life a lot easier. She was away for a few days, but would be back the next evening. He hadn't met her, but Kai had told him where to find the house and car keys inside a faux stone in the backyard.

Quinn arrived at the parking garage around 6:30 AM, then waited until Chambers showed up at ten to eight. He wrote down Chamber's license plate and headed to the tax assessor's office, to get the registration information, which would include Chamber's address. That took two and a half hours, and he had to convince the clerk that he had been sideswiped by that vehicle in a hit and run accident before she would release the information. He stopped for sushi on the way to scope out Chamber's address, a pricey loft in the Heights. The construction was recent, and all of the trees were small. But, three short blocks down, hundred year-old live oaks in front of a gaudily restored Victorian provided excellent shade. And dryads.

Quinn rolled down his window and waited. He was certain that Malik was not at Chambers' home – he'd undoubtedly delivered the emerald jar to his employer the same night Malik was kidnapped. But it could be helpful to see if Chambers had any visitors

It didn't take long before three curious dryads approached him.

"It is strange," said the bravest of the three, "to see one of your kind inside of a human machine."

"Why have you come to this place?" asked another, as she looked at him appraisingly.

"There is a human who lives in the first loft over there. He drives a large gold machine. I need to find out where he goes. He kidnapped my friend."

The dryads twittered among themselves.

"It is the third day of the week," said the last dryad. "He does not come here until late on this night."

"Yes! Sometimes not until the rising of the sun," chimed in the second dryad.

"Thank you," Quinn said, flashing his most charming smile. "I may see you again soon." He put the car in gear and headed back downtown.

There was no way to park close to Chamber's SUV this late in the day, so he parked on the street and fed the meter all afternoon until Chambers left his office around 6:00.

He didn't go very far, taking Quinn to an especially run-down topless bar called Specials. He also noted that it was across the street from a dilapidated motel with a surprising amount of activity, given the state of it. After Chambers disappeared into a back room, Quinn had spread some cash around the bar, but nobody had much to say, other than Chambers came in at least two days a week, and sometimes met up with a couple of cops.

It was 10:30 before Chambers emerged, alone, and went to his car. Quinn followed him back to his luxury loft.

The lights inside Chamber's house went out. Quinn gave up getting any further information and went back to Lorelei's.

He was skinny-dipping in her saltwater pool, wishing it was big enough for him to shift out of human form. Probably just as well, though, in case Lorelei had any nosey night-owl neighbors. When he surfaced underneath the diving board, she was standing at the opposite end of the pool, near the floodlit waterfall.

A sound fell out of his mouth, halfway between a groan and a grunt.

In spite of her name, he had forgotten that she was an actual lorelei. No one, save perhaps those weird sisters themselves, knew what a lorelei really looked like. To any observer, they appeared as the epitome of female beauty, so everyone saw something different.

Quinn saw Siobhan.

He knew it wasn't really her. Couldn't possibly be. His mind knew, but his body reacted anyway. He wanted her. Badly. But, he also knew that, like black widows, the lorelei always devoured their lovers afterwards. Those freshwater mermaids had a little more kink than was good for a body.

Not trusting himself, he stayed as far from her as he could. "Lorelei?"

"Yes. It is I. For you, I have a message. I was told this afternoon that Graham, your brother, requires urgently your presence at your residence."

Great. Just what I need. "Thank you, Lorelei. I'd like to use your portal, if you don't mind?"

"It is no problem."

Quinn had hoped that she'd go in so that he could get out of the pool and get dressed. Looking at her had re-opened old wounds that had been mostly healed, even if the scar tissue was still sore. But she just stood there, torturing him.

"I left your keys on the end table near the front door. Thanks again for letting me borrow your car."

She nodded slightly, then turned and started back towards the house. When she was inside, Quinn pulled himself out of the pool. He hadn't brought a towel out with him, so he just put his clothes on his sopping body. He was loath to interrupt his investigation of Ian Chambers. No telling what his boss had planned for Malik. And he dreaded going home and refereeing a reunion between his mother and youngest brother. But staying here with Lorelei was even worse.

ॐ

Quinn was usually the peace-maker in the family. But he had been at the Waterhorse for days, and had come no closer to reconciling Graham and their mother. He was ready to abdicate to his older brothers. Nothing ever ruffled Robbie, and Laurie, ever Mother's favorite, had just arrived.

Precious time was slipping away, and Malik was still trapped somewhere in the Mundane world. Taking a break from his family squabbles, Quinn had gone to talk to Malik's wife. She'd cried the whole time, their two children sniffling and clinging to her. The delay was killing him. He had to take action soon.

He was lingering at the edge of the millpond, trying to steal a moment of peace and plan his departure, when he noticed a dryad approaching. She had long, straight hair, and he recognized her instantly - she was from the pine tree in Ryan Keller's yard.

"Daphne?" he asked.

"You said come to you if there was any trouble," the dryad replied.

"What's happened?" He felt his heart beat a little faster.

"Nothing yet. But this man has been coming around late at night, while the house woman is sleeping. He peers in the windows and writes himself notes. He even has asked her to dine with him this night."

"What did she say?"

"She agreed. She does not know he has put under the windows little metal boxes that allow him to listen to what she says. He is dangerous, I fear."

"All the windows?" Quinn asked.

"Just in the back of the house. And one on the side where she parks her transport machine."

Quinn nodded. "Sounds like it's time to repay a debt."

Chapter 5
Cart Before the Horse

MOM WAS ONLY TOO happy to watch Cassie while I had a date with a respectable young man. Ian had called just after lunch to confirm our date. I asked where we were going so I could meet him there. But he said that would ruin the surprise. He would swing by to pick me up at 7:00. I reminded myself that he did work for the DA, so he probably wasn't a serial killer.

"Mom, what am I going to wear?" I complained, looking in my closet. I hadn't gone anywhere I needed nice clothes for a couple of years. The only 'little black dress' I owned, I had worn to Ryan's funeral, and I couldn't bear to look at it. But I couldn't give it away, either.

I had the cash to go buy a brand new dress, but I didn't want to spend it on something so frivolous. I needed to make the money I had last as long as I could. At least until I could get a home business up and running, or Cassie was old enough to go to school and I could go back to work part-time, whichever came first.

"Why don't you ask your sister if she has something you can borrow?" Mom said. She was standing at the baby gate at the doorway to my bedroom, and Cassie was holding on to her leg.

"Because then she'll know I have a date, and I'm not ready to let Nick crow about fixing me up just yet." Especially not after the lecture I gave him at the barbeque.

"Go to the resale shop then. It'll be time for Cassie's nap soon. I'll stay with her."

I put my arms around my mother's neck. "Thanks, Mom."

§

I tried the two resale shops I usually visit, but didn't find anything I liked. There was a huge Goodwill store on Highway 6. Maybe they'd have something.

The evening wear rack had four items in my size. One was a black crepe pantsuit that was too frumpy for even my mother to wear (and she was the queen of frump). One was a gold-sequined monstrosity that was too low at the top and too high at the bottom. One was a light blue chiffon dress with a beaded bodice that had a very mother-of-the-bride look to it. The last one was a nightmare in pleated fuchsia. I was running out of time, and almost desperate enough to try on the blue chiffon, when an employee came up with a rack of clothes. She pulled out two dresses. One was tangerine, and looked like it would fit a hippopotamus. The other one was a beautiful emerald green with sheer, shimmery organza sleeves. It was perfect – elegant and flattering without being too sexy.

"Excuse me, may I try that one?" I motioned towards the green dress.

"Sure." The employee handed it over and pushed the cart to the next section.

I held my breath and looked at the tag. What were the odds it would be in my size? The tag said it was a size nine. Close enough. I hurried to the dressing room to try it on.

It wasn't a perfect fit. It was too tight across the bust, but the designer probably didn't have nursing moms in mind. It was a little too loose in the waist, but that left extra room for dinner. I paid $15 for the dress and left. There was still a little tag from the dry cleaner on the dress, so I felt okay about wearing it as-is.

I pumped when I got home. Cassie was usually only interested in nursing first thing in the morning or last thing at night. Or if she was upset. Part of me was glad that she was starting to wean herself, and part of me was sad that she was growing up. Either way, I would miss our special bonding time.

Cassie was just starting to stir. Mom went home to check on Dad. He'd gotten more forgetful lately, and she wanted to make sure he'd eaten his lunch. She'd be back around 6:30. That gave me almost three hours with my little sweetie-pie.

When Mom showed up, I was just putting on my earrings.

"You look mah-velous, dahling!"

I laughed. "Thanks. There's fresh milk in the fridge, in the bottle and ready to go. If Cassie gets too fussy or won't go to sleep, call me. I'll come straight home."

"She'll be just fine, Marti. Don't you worry about us." Mom bit her bottom lip. "You do realize you're still wearing your bunny slippers, don't you?"

I hadn't realized.

"Yes, Mom. I know."

Ryan had bought me those slippers as a joke a couple of months before he died. I started wearing them just to tease him. Now, I wore them all the time, and they were getting a bit ragged.

I touched up my eyeliner, then went to the closet and slid on my dress shoes. I never wore heels higher than two inches. At 5'9", I was already tall enough. In fact, that's one reason Emily matched me with Ryan at her wedding. He was 6'3" and the only one of the groomsmen I didn't tower over.

I had to rummage around in the closet to find my evening bag. The doorbell rang while I was still trying to stuff my wallet, cell phone and lipstick into the tiny little purse. I wedged in a fresh pair of nursing pads, just in case.

"Ian, come in," my mother said from the living room. "Marti will be out in just a moment." Eek. Just like in high school.

I gave myself a final once-over in the mirror. It wasn't too late. I could still back out. Maybe take a swig of hydrogen peroxide to make myself vomit and convince them I was sick. I shook my head, took a deep breath, and headed for the living room.

Ian sat on my couch. I would have thought he was making an internal critique of my interior decorating, the way he was scrutinizing the living room, if his right leg hadn't been twitching up and down like a sewing machine. Was he that nervous? It was kind of cute.

"Wow," he said. "You do clean up well."

Not so cute. When had he ever seen me not cleaned up?

"Thanks. You're not so bad yourself." The tan sport coat made him look like a TV detective, but it worked for him. The jacket was almost the same color as his hair, and his blue shirt was only a little darker than his eyes.

I kissed Cassie and my mother before Ian and I went out and climbed into his gold Chevy Suburban.

"So. Where are we going?"

"It's a surprise." Ian grinned at me, but I felt nervous. Why hadn't I insisted that I follow him in my own car?

We made small talk for half an hour or so as we headed east on I-10. I squirmed and shifted in my seat and leaned against the door. My logical brain told me that I wasn't in any danger. People knew I was with him. He worked in the DA's office for goodness' sake. I supposed what was bothering me was lack of control. He was probably just trying to sweep me off my feet, but I felt more trapped than romanced.

As we took the I-45 exit, I said, "You're not taking me to the Rainforest Café in Galveston so you can get me alone in the dark on the Lost River ride, are you?" I was only half joking.

"Nope. Wouldn't dream of it."

A little while later, we took the El Dorado exit and headed east.

"Kemah Boardwalk?"

"Maybe."

Ian paid extra to leave his truck in the parking garage. As soon as I got out of the car, I was caressed by a cool salty breeze. It reminded me of the last time Ryan and I camped at the beach, our standard Thanksgiving getaway. That's how I ended up with my sweet little Cassie.

It was almost 8:00, and the sky over the Kemah Boardwalk was just starting to think about going dark. The lights on the observation tower were on, but looked anemic against the grey blue of the evening sky. To our right, the Boardwalk Bullet roller coaster thundered along wooden tracks. People screamed with fear and delight as they were dropped from a free fall tower. Music from the carousel drifted our way. The kitchens on the restaurant row were in full swing, and I could smell fish, fajitas and pizza – with notes of popcorn and cotton candy. Marquee lights flashed on the Ferris wheel.

Ian took my elbow and guided me towards The Aquarium restaurant. Train tracks ran parallel to the walkway and a little red and black train hooted at us as it passed by. The Boardwalk was heaving with people, mostly families. I swallowed the small, desperate wish that I was here with Ryan and Cassie and smiled at my date.

"You know, the Aquarium downtown would have been a lot closer," I said.

"Yes, but this one has other…features. After you," he said as he opened the door.

The hostess was a youngish bottle blond whom I inexplicably disliked on sight. She addressed Ian with bored eyes and a saccharin smile. "Table for two?"

"I have a reservation. Under Chambers."

She scanned the laminated plastic sheet on the podium and made a mark with a grease pencil. "Of course. Your table will be ready in a few minutes. You can wait in the Dive Lounge, if you'd like." She handed Ian a chunky black alert buzzer.

Ian thanked her, and we made our way to the bar.

I watched the fish swim through the bubble wall while Ian ordered a martini. About the time the server arrived back at the table with the drink, our buzzer went off to let us know our table was ready.

The hostess showed us to a table with an up-front view of the overwhelming aquarium. Actually, it was an up-front view of an ever-changing pack of children with their noses pressed up against the overwhelming aquarium. I wondered if the sharks that cruised the tank had any idea that people were sitting all around them, eating their relatives.

The rail-thin server handed us our menus. Her cheekbones were sharp enough to chop wood, but her low-cut top strained to contain her oversized bosom. At least Ian was a gentleman and didn't blatantly gawk at her. I wondered how many men had bruises on their shins from being kicked under the table by wives or girlfriends when they were in her section.

"I'm Suzette," she said, in a peculiar accent that I was almost certain was fake, "and I'll be taking care of you this evening. May I get you anything to drink?"

Ian debated with Suzette about the wine list. I wasn't much of a drinker, and he could just as easily have ordered Mad Dog for all the difference it would make to me.

"Glass of water for me, please." And get yourself a sandwich while you're in the kitchen.

Suzette fetched the wine and my water.

"Would you care for any appetizers?" she chirped.

"Dozen oysters on the half shell," Ian replied. His eyebrow twitched.

I shook my head and Suzette minced back to the kitchen on her stiletto heels.

Ian poured us each a glass of white wine, then raised his glass. "To the Boardwalk."

"To the Boardwalk," I toasted.

The wine was a bit drier than I expected, and it didn't take too many sips for my cheeks to start feeling a little warm. One glass was probably more than I needed for the entire evening. I was very glad I got the glass of water.

Suzette returned with a plate of raw oysters. She set them in the middle of the table, but I could hardly look at them.

"Have you decided what you will be having for your main course tonight?"

"I'll have the mixed grill, and the lady will have the mahi mahi and shrimp."

"Excuse me," I snapped. "The lady will have the Greek salad, thank you."

"Would you like shrimp with the salad? We can do that," Suzette gushed.

"No, thank you. I'm allergic to shellfish."

"So, no shrimp then?"

"Not unless you want to see me go into anaphylactic shock and have to call EMS to the restaurant. Might upset the other diners."

I thought Suzette's eyes would pop out of her head.

"Yes ma'am. One Greek salad and one mixed grill. Excellent choices. Thank you." Suzette's heels clicked briskly on the tile as she left.

"I'm really sorry, Marti. I had no idea," Ian said.

"I believe you were trying to be an old fashioned gentleman. I appreciate that. But don't order food for me again, okay?" I don't appreciate being treated like a child.

"Certainly, if that's how you want it."

He smiled when he said it, but his clipped words were tinged with pique.

The idea drifted into my head that maybe Ian had read an old book on how to romance women, rather than actually knowing how to do it from experience. But that was just silly.

Then he started eating the oysters. I had to excuse myself to the ladies' room while he slurped. I had seen enough septic wounds in the ER that seeing anyone eat something that looked like effluvium made my stomach churn.

I texted my mom to see how Cassie was doing. She'd fallen asleep in the rocking chair with Mom while watching a Baby Einstein video, and was now sleeping like a brick in her crib. I checked my hair and makeup to see if I needed any maintenance. I looked fine. How long would it take him to eat those oysters? I gave him ten minutes before I washed my hands and went back to the table.

When I returned, Ian had not only finished the oysters, but topped off my wine glass, which I ignored. The rest of dinner went unexpectedly well, and I started to relax. He had the rest of the wine while we ate, plus another martini. I was starting to get uneasy about how much he was drinking. When I offered to pay for my meal, he wouldn't hear of it. After he'd paid the check, I enjoyed exploring the Rainforest exhibit with him and seeing the piranhas. They're actually sparkly, and kind of pretty, for vicious little killers.

It had been fun, but I was ready to go. I was tired and starting to fret about Cassie. It was 10:45 and this was the longest I'd ever been away from her. We went outside. When Ian nearly walked into a pole, I tried to decide whether I should drive us back to town or call a taxi.

The earlier crowds had dissipated, and there was hardly anyone around near the restaurant. I started towards the garage.

"What's your hurry?" Ian asked. "You don't want to leave without riding the Ferris wheel, surely?"

"They're just about to shut everything down. I've had a great time, really, Ian, but it's been a long day, and it will take us another forty-five minutes or so for me to drive us home."

"It doesn't have to."

"What? Have you got a teleportation device in your pocket?"

"Better. I've got a beach house on the Island."

Oh, boy. Why didn't I bring my own stupid car? "I'm sure it's very nice and I'd love to see it another time. I'm ready to go home. To my home. Alone. Now."

Ian took a step closer and started to stroke my shoulder. The booze smelled sour on his breath. "Come on, Marti. I-I can treat a lady right." He planted a sloppy kiss underneath my ear.

"Back off, Chambers!" I growled at him and pulled away.

He had a hold on my sleeve and when I jerked my arm backward, the sheer fabric ripped. Ian's mouth worked like a landed fish.

"Is that what you think of me? That I'm some desperate female, who'll just fall into bed with you for no good reason?"

"I...I...I am so sorry," he stammered, organza still clutched in his fingers.

"Let go!"

"Excuse me, Miss. Is there a problem here?"

I turned my head to see a man approaching us. It was hard to tell in the poor light, but he could have been anywhere between twenty and forty. Dark hair brushed his shoulders.

"Is this man troubling you?" He had a slight accent, Scottish, perhaps.

Ian stepped away from me. He looked like a scared kid. A really big scared kid.

"It's okay. Thank you," I said.

The man stayed where he was and watched Ian suspiciously.

"Marti, I don't know what came over me. I can't apologize enough." Ian pulled the car keys out of his pocket. "Let me just take you home."

"I'm not getting in the car with you." I snatched his keys away. "And you don't need to be driving anywhere." Now what was I going to do with his stinkin' keys?

"Ian, you go inside and tell them to call you a taxi."

He stumbled towards the door. I could drive myself home in Ian's car, but then I'd have to park it in front of my house, and wouldn't Nick just love that? But maybe there was a better way.

"You sure you're okay?" the dark-haired man asked.

"I'm fine, thanks. My friend has just had a little too much to drink, that's all. I appreciate your concern."

The man's eyes half-closed and he took a deep breath. "Your arm's bleeding."

I glanced down. There was a smear of blood where Ian had torn my sleeve. He must have caught me with his nails.

"Just a scratch. I'll be fine."

He looked around as if he were counting the stragglers from the earlier crowds. I probably should have been afraid, but I wasn't. When his eyes came back to me, I could see they were very dark, almost black. Like Ryan's. They pulled me in and held me. Run! Run now, before it's too late. Run. Adrenalin, not sure if it was his or mine, made my skin feel alive. If he'd made a move to touch me, I would not have stopped him. And I didn't know why.

I shook myself and looked away. I was not like that. I did not get all hot and bothered by complete strangers.

I knew Ian would be back any second, and I needed to be gone by then. "There is one thing you can do that would really help me out..." I gave him a questioning look.

"Quinn."

"Quinn," I repeated. I took Ian's car key and remote off the ring and tried to stick them in my purse, but they just wouldn't fit. I pretended like I'd planned that all along. "Would you please tell my friend that the parking attendant has his keys when he comes out?"

When Quinn smiled, just for an instant, I could have sworn his teeth were sharp, like the sharks' that we had just eaten dinner with. When I looked again, they were as normal as mine. I knew it was just the dim light, but it was still unsettling, and I felt something that wasn't quite fear.

"Your friend? Friends like that, you probably don't need."

I gave him my best glower. My friends were none of his business. "Thanks for your help," I said crisply.

He only smiled at me, so I turned on my heel and made a show of stalking towards the parking garage. I didn't have the ticket, but I was sure they'd let me out for the max price. I found the car, got inside and adjusted the seat and mirror.

The small white square by the rear view mirror was notably absent. No EZ-Tag? Why would you not have an EZ-Tag, Ian? I didn't have any change or small bills to go through the full service booths, so unless I wanted to stick Ian with a ticket, I'd have to avoid the Tollway. I did consider it, though, after what he'd just put me through.

I counted on Ian being too embarrassed by assaulting me to call the PD and report his car stolen. I would leave his Suburban in the parking lot of the 24-hour Kroger that was about a mile from my house and leave his keys in the gap under the bumper. I'd email him and let him know where it was.

And then what?

After a wrong turn sent me to Dickinson, I bumbled my way back to I-45. I knew how to get home now, so I could chew on what had happened. I liked Ian. Or at least I had, until he started pawing me outside the restaurant. Was this just a one-off, or was this his standard operating procedure? He looked contrite enough, but was that only because Quinn showed up? Ahh, Quinn. I felt an unexpected twinge of sadness that I'd never see him again.

This was all Nick's fault. If he hadn't been so bent on setting me up with somebody. I sighed. No, it was my fault. I accepted the date. I could have said 'No.' I should have. I loved Cassie more than anything in the world, but sometimes, it would be nice to have an adult to talk to besides my mother. It would be nice to feel strong male arms around me. It would be nice to make love. But Ryan was dead and no amount of wishing was going to bring him back. Regardless of what my body might want, my heart was not ready to let him go.

I let the tears roll down my cheeks as I tried to push visions of a wailing Cassie and my frazzled mother out of my head. I found the oldies station and turned up the radio, too loud, and made myself sing along with The Clash.

After I parked Ian's behemoth truck under one of the parking lot lights at the Kroger, I sent him an email from my phone about the location of his vehicle. Ordinarily, a walk in the fresh air would clear my head. But tonight it was so muggy and warm that it just made me cranky.

A Mediterranean gecko scrambled for cover as I came up onto my front porch. Fat June bugs and assorted moths buzzed around the light. I didn't hear a sound coming from the house, so I unlocked the door and crept inside. Dad was asleep in my recliner and Mom was stretched out on the couch. I checked Cassie's room. She was sighing in her sleep, smelling like baby powder and lavender. As softly as I could, I touched her hair and caressed her cheek. "Goodnight, my sweet little thing," I whispered as I left her room.

I did my usual rounds – checked all the doors to make sure they were locked, made sure Alpha and Betty, our pet rats, had food and water. Nick had rescued them from a homicide scene. The dead man had no friends or relatives to take them and the shelter was overflowing, so euthanasia was their best offer. He'd thought Kyle and Aiden would like them, but Emily wouldn't allow them in the house. He knew I never met a stray I didn't rescue, so he brought them to me. As it turned out, the twins weren't as interested as he'd imagined, but I thought the rats were very sweet.

I made one last check on Cassie, standing near her bed and listening to her breathe for a few minutes before I went to bed. How old does your baby have to be before you stop looking in on her each night?

I went to my room and lay on top of the covers. I kept the thermostat on 80 during the summer – cheaper that way – and even with the ceiling fan on high, the heat was oppressive. I tried to figure out what to do about Ian Chambers. I couldn't make up my mind whether he was a habitual jerk or just made a one-time mistake. But it seemed like the more I thought about Ian, the more Quinn's face popped into my head. I finally found a comfortable spot and slowly faded to sleep. I woke up about every two hours, remembering fragments of a dream about riding a horse, and the horse swimming through a wonderful, cool lake.

It was just after lunch on Sunday afternoon. Cassie and I were playing with the shape sorter when the phone rang. I checked Caller ID. It was Ian. Again. I let it go to voice mail. I wasn't ready to talk to him. Not yet. Maybe never.

Cassie had just finished Monday's breakfast. She was covered in oatmeal and had squished her banana chunks together to use as a hair styling product. We were headed towards the bathroom when the doorbell rang.

On the other side of the peephole, stood a young man in a light blue uniform, holding a vase of yellow roses.

"Who is it?" I asked.

"I'm Todd. I've got a delivery from Annabelle's Flowers for a Ms. Marti Keller."

I opened the door.

Todd was holding a vase of flowers, and there were five others lined up on the porch beside him. He handed me the one with the card.

"Six dozen roses? Seriously? Are you sure there's no mistake?"

"No, ma'am. They're all for you."

I signed for them and Todd helped me bring them in the house. They took up nearly all of the breakfast table. I asked Todd if he had a wife or girlfriend who might like to have a dozen yellow roses, but he shook his head.

I looked at the card.

"Dear Marti. I am so, so, so, so, so very sorry. I don't know what came over me. It's just that you are a beautiful, smart, funny lady and I want to get to know you better. I jumped the gun. I shouldn't have tried to rush you. I hope you can find it in your heart to give me another chance."

So. He thought I was beautiful, smart and funny, did he? Maybe that should count for something. Or maybe it was just empty flattery. Was this the same Ian Chambers who pulled Nick and three others out of a burning building? Just who is the real Ian Chambers??

Chapter 6
Listen

IAN CHAMBERS STAGGERED OUT of the Aquarium restaurant, and Quinn wanted to punch him in the face. He remembered Keller's last words to him, warning that Ian Chambers was not to be trusted. And now, he was courting Keller's widow.

Chambers looked around, confused.

"She's gone," Quinn said, strolling casually over. "Said she was going to leave your keys with the parking attendant."

Chambers swore softly. "And who did you say you were?"

"A friend."

"I don't think I know you." Chambers shook his head, trying to clear the fog.

"I didn't say I was your friend."

Quinn let his eyes go completely black, just for a few seconds. Long enough for Chambers to snort and back up, trip over his own feet, and land hard on his butt.

"I didn't mean anything. I would never have hurt Marti. Please…" he mewled.

"You tied to force yourself on her. You tore her dress."

"It was an accident. I – I—"

Quinn smiled and extended his hand. "Let me help you up."

Chambers' shivering hand was soft and clammy. Quinn pulled him up, then trapped his arm and pulled him in close, so his face was only inches from Chambers'.

"Stay away from Marti. I don't want to hear about you coming around and bothering her. Understand?"

Chambers nodded.

"Go get your keys. I'm sure your taxi will be here any minute," Quinn said.

Chambers wobbled off towards the parking garage, looking over his shoulder. Quinn smiled and waved. He hoped that Chambers was sober enough to remember their conversation, but he wasn't so sure.

A figure moved out of the shadow of the building. "That wasn't the smartest thing you've ever done," Kai said. "Now he knows what you look like, and he's scared of you."

"Maybe. But I got his cell phone."

Kai laughed. "Good luck with that. Doubt he'll have a contact labeled 'Evil Second Boss.' But you ought to get it back to him before he notices it's missing."

Kai did not like to drive. And it was just as well – machines tended to fail under his touch, even when he didn't want them to. As his cover identity was that of a very wealthy philanthropist, he had a driver. His name was Frey, and he'd been burned by dragon fire. He was hard to look at, but he was as loyal as they come. And, he was good with human technology, something Quinn had never really mastered.

"Frey," Quinn said as they got in the car. "That guy I've been following? I got his phone. Not sure if his contact list is going to be much use. Do you have any ideas?"

"What is it that you want to do?" Frey asked, his blind, white eye facing Quinn.

Quinn leaned back in his seat. "I'm looking for the guy he works for, the guy who has Malik. I want to know where Chambers goes and who he talks to."

"Pah. I thought it was going to be something hard. Let me see the phone," Frey answered.

He shook his head. "Not password protected." Then he opened the phone's internet browser and surfed to a website. It took almost two minutes to download an application. "Whose phone number you gonna use to check this?"

"Kai's," Quinn answered.

"That's fine," Kai replied.

Frey typed in some data and turned the phone off. "Next time he makes or receives a call, you'll be able to hear it. If he sends a text or an email, you can read it. He's disabled the GPS on the phone, but the software will turn it on. If he notices, he'll probably turn it back off, though." Frey handed Chambers' phone to Quinn.

"Will he be able to find this program?" Quinn asked.

"Not unless he's really paranoid and runs a virus sweep on his phone with the right software."

"Guess I'd better get it back to him, then."

Quinn gave Frey Chambers' address. They drove past his house, as the taxi had just arrived and Chambers was getting out. They doubled back and Frey parked in the shadows of the old live oaks down the street. They waited until the lights in Chambers windows went dark, then they waited another half hour.

Kai and Quinn got out of the car and walked up to Chamber's front door as if they belonged there. One of Kai's skills was opening locks. He couldn't do anything about barricaded doors, but locks he could pick with a touch, unless they were magickally sealed. Any curious neighbors would think the two men had a key, given how easily the door opened for them. Quinn closed it gently behind them.

Chambers had made it easy for them. He'd left his pants draped over a chair in the kitchen. His keys dangled precariously from one pocket. Quinn slipped the phone into the other front pocket, turning it so that it didn't slide out.

Quinn wrinkled his nose. The place smelled like furniture polish and carpet freshener. He looked around the room. Everything was chrome and granite. Very modern, very sterile. Even the flower arrangement in the middle of the breakfast table was silk.

Kai was already on his way out, and Quinn hurried to catch up. In his haste, he knocked over a lamp that was perched on an end table near the sofa. He lunged for it. He caught it, but made a big thump as he hit the wood floor. He and Kai both froze. Upstairs, Chambers mumbled something. Seconds passed, then minutes. The house remained still and quiet.

Quinn set the lamp back on the table and they made their way out of the house and back into Kai's car.

"That was too close," Kai said.

"Tell me about it," Quinn replied.

Quinn lost track of the number of times he heard Marti's voicemail message, as Chambers called her over and over on Sunday. He liked her voice, he decided. It was clear and firm, but softly blurred at the edges – neither sharp authoritarian nor breathy sex kitten.

Quinn kept in close contact with the dryads in Marti's yard, keeping surveillance on her that way. It felt weird to him, inadvertently spying on her, while spying on Chambers. On the other hand, it did make his life easier. He learned her routine, knew her baby always got up at six thirty and they always went for a morning walk. If he was going to protect her from Chambers, it helped to know her habits.

Chapter 7
Happy Medium

⟶━━━━━━━━━⟳━━━━━━━━━⟵

IT WAS JUST AFTER ten on a Tuesday morning, and the heat was already all but intolerable. Cassie and I were headed home from our morning walk, and she was having a lively conversation with her stuffed rabbit, Mr. Buns. "Marti? Is that you?"

I turned to see Lulu Miranda, the woman who had knocked me over with the bookshelf, carrying a cardboard box through the parking lot of the mostly vacant strip center.

"Hi. We're out for a walk." Admittedly, I was agnostic about this woman's sanity.

"Oh, come on in. Have some cold water and a look around."

A cowbell clattered as Lulu pulled the door open. I looked into the shop. Cassie seemed happy enough. The idea of talking to an adult who wasn't a relative really appealed to me just then.

"Sure, if there's room for the stroller." I always left myself an out.

"Course there is, honey." Lulu smiled as she held the door open for me.

The Tenth Sphere smelled like sandalwood incense and butterscotch. The shop felt different from outside, the same way the weekend feels different from the work week. Very breakable-looking figurines lined the wall nearest the cash register, which was boxed in by jewelry display cases. Another wall had incense sticks, charcoal tablets and reed diffusers. Sturdy wooden shelves were crammed with crystal spheres, salt lamps, pendulums, Tarot cards and loose crystals. There was a vast array of books from astral projection to zoomorphism. Two clothes racks stood against the far wall, displaying robes, cloaks and belly dancing outfits. Belly dancing outfits?

Near the back of the shop, a staircase – closed off with a purple velvet rope – led to the second floor.

"What's up there?" I asked Lulu.

Lulu grinned as she handed me a paper cup with cold water from the cooler by the front door. "Oh, we have some classrooms and private client consultation rooms."

"What do you do in private client consultation rooms?" That sounded like a euphemism for something illegal.

"Well, we do Tarot and astrological readings. Sometimes those get very emotional for the clients, and they prefer to have some privacy."

Seems like lately I could hardly sling a cat without hitting something about Tarot card reading.

"Tarot card readings. You know, I saw something the other day about doing that as a home business."

"Did you really?" Lulu said, looking at me as if she was truly surprised. "Have you ever had your cards read, honey?"

"No. My dad always said that so-called psychic readers were nothing but con artists."

As soon as the words left my mouth, I wished I could take them back. "I mean, not that you, personally, are a con artist. That's just Dad's opinion. About psychics in general, not you." Shut up before you make it any worse.

Lulu sighed. "Well, unfortunately, there are a lot of flim-flammers, and that's a real shame, because it puts a bad light on people who really do have a talent. Tell you what. I owe you one for flattening you the other day. Would you like a reading? On the house, of course. You can judge for yourself."

I looked at Cassie, enthusiastically whacking her bunny against the stroller tray and giggling with delight.

"I don't know. I'll never get the stroller up those stairs and—"

"Don't you worry about that. I'll get Belinda out of the back. She's got four grandbabies, you know." Lulu nodded and leaned towards me, as if she were about to tell me a delicious secret. "Susan Pletcher is going to be coming in on Tuesdays and Thursdays to do readings, starting next week. She is really good. Anyway. Belinda!" Lulu power-walked towards a door marked 'Employees Only.' "Belinda!"

Belinda emerged from the back room with a barcode scanner in her hand and a packing peanut in her hair.

"What is it?" she snapped.

Lulu was unfazed. "B, can you keep an eye on this little lady—," Lulu turned to me, "what's her name, honey?"

"Cassie."

"Miss Cassie while I pop upstairs to give Mama a reading?"

"Course I can. That's the best offer I've had all day." When Belinda smiled, she looked like a fairy godmother.

"I don't know. She can be fussy around people she doesn't know." She takes after her mother.

"Belinda's got a way with babies. If it makes you more comfortable, I'll even leave the curtain open so you can see Miss Cassie during your reading."

I winced as I bit the inside of my cheek a little too hard, chewing on the idea. I wasn't sure I wanted to leave Cassie with a stranger – even if she did have 'a way' with babies. On the other hand, I was extremely curious about Tarot card reading, since it had been coming up over and over. Curiosity killed the cat. Still, it wasn't exactly like I was leaving her – I'd only be half a boutique's length away from her, and I'd be able to see her the whole time. But satisfaction brought it back.

"Alright," I said.

After setting the scanner on the jewelry counter, Belinda moved Cassie's stroller so that she could see both the baby and the front door while she sat in an enormous gnarled chair carved from a cypress tree root.

Cassie grinned at her, with all four and a half teeth, and pounded poor Mr. Buns on the stroller tray. "Da da da!"

She didn't even seem to notice that I was leaving. I looked over my shoulder a couple of times as I followed Lulu upstairs. I alternated between feeling happy that my child was independent and sad that she didn't seem to miss me.

Immediately in front of us, at the top of the stairs, was a conference room with a glass door. To the left of the conference room was a doorway hung with a purple curtain, and to the right was a doorway with a green curtain.

Wooden rings scraped across the metal rod as Lulu whisked the purple curtain out of the way. We entered a room not much bigger than a walk-in closet. A well-used night stand with an artificial African violet and a box of tissues squatted in one corner. We sat down opposite each other on folding chairs at a small round table draped with several layers of fabric.

"How long will this take?" I asked, picking at the cuticle of my thumb. If I sat just a little sideways in my chair, I could look over my shoulder and see Cassie gnawing on Mr. Buns.

"Ten minutes, give or take. Depends on the cards and how many questions you have."

Lulu opened the nightstand drawer and took out a wooden box with leaves and flowers carved on the lid. The over-sized cards she pulled out of it were so worn that they could have been one of the first decks ever made.

"Shuffle the deck until it feels right to you, then cut it with your left hand."

Lulu closed her eyes and took a deep, slow breath.

She sat there like that while I shuffled, then cut the cards. I placed them in front of her. She didn't move. I started to wonder if she'd fallen asleep. Cassie giggled downstairs and I felt a twinge of jealously. Was Belinda more fun than me?

Lulu's eyes popped open, and she leaned forward, startling me enough to gasp.

"Sorry, honey. Now, let's see what we've got here."

Lulu laid out fifteen cards and frowned at them.

She tapped the first card she had turned over. It was a drawing of a man hanging upside down by his right leg in front of a grid. His left leg crossed over at the right knee, making an upside down "4." His arms were stretched wide and nailed to green circles on the grid, and there was a large snake coiled in a pit beneath his head. There was something that looked like a white and green sun at the top of the card, where his right foot was suspended.

"This first card represents you and the kind of problem you are having, or something that is influencing you. When the card's upright like this, he represents redemption, as in undoing damage or getting back something that was lost."

Getting back something that was lost. I would give anything to get Ryan back, but I didn't see how that could be possible.

With her finger still on the card, she continued. "But it may come at a cost. Also, keep in mind that this is usually on a spiritual or emotional level, more than a physical level. You see this thing that looks like a sun at the top, and this dark area with the snake? The Hanged Man represents light descending into dark, or spirit going into matter. If you are feeling lost in the dark, he's here to hand you a flashlight. But you may have to sacrifice your fear to get back home."

I could hear Lulu talking about some of the other cards, but I didn't pay close attention, at least not until the end. I kept thinking about getting back something I'd lost and wishing she was right.

"And here you have the Six of Cups, the Princess of Disks, and the Seven of Wands. A Princess usually represents a young woman. The Seven of Wands, you see here, it's called 'Valor,' represents a struggle, but nothing you can't overcome. The Six of Cups is about happiness and success – that's why it's called 'Pleasure.' What this is saying to me is that you've been having an issue with a young lady, but you'll be happy with the outcome, even though it may be a minor victory. It may come about in as little as 24 hours, but certainly less than two weeks."

Lulu put her hands on the table. "Do you have any questions, honey?"

I wanted to ask her how the Hanged Man could get my lost Ryan back. Instead, I said, "No. No questions. That was very interesting. Thanks."

"My pleasure." Lulu scooped up the cards and put them back in the box with the others. The hint of a smile on her face made me think that she knew something she wasn't telling me.

As we walked toward the stairs, Lulu said, "You know, honey, you ought to come to our mediumship circle on Thursday nights."

"Mediumship circle? What's that about?"

"Well, we do different things each week. Sometimes we reach out to those on the other side—"

"You mean you talk to dead people?"

"That's one way to put it, yes."

Ryan. If I could just talk to him again, even if it was only to say goodbye.

"Does it work? Can you talk to anybody you want?"

"Have you ever been in the bathroom when the phone rang?"

What's that got to do with the other side? "Yeah, sure."

"People on the other side have stuff to do as well, and they can't always drop everything and come running for a little chat. We can usually find someone who wants to talk to us, but it may not be who you're hoping for." Lulu patted me on the shoulder.

I suddenly noticed the absolute silence coming from downstairs.

"Cassie?" I called, peering over the railing as I hurried down the stairs.

My baby was out of her stroller, cruising around the root chair. When she saw me, she let go of the chair and flapped her arms.

"Ma ma! Ma ma!"

"Hey, baby! Did you just say…"

"Mama!"

Cassie suddenly realized she wasn't holding on to anything. She looked from one hand to the other, and squealed with delight. Then she plopped down onto her bottom. I picked her up before she could cry, even though I was almost crying myself. Mama. She'd finally said 'Mama!'

As I hugged my little girl, I realized that it was almost 11:00. If the nap window closed, it would be a wretched afternoon for both of us.

"Thanks, Lulu, for the reading. It was interesting. I appreciate you watching Cassie, Belinda. She seems to really like you. I've got to run – it's time for Cassie's nap, and if I don't get her down…"

Lulu tucked a blue flier into the stroller bag. "Been there, done that. Hope to see you Thursday, honey." She held the door for me as I wrestled the stroller over the threshold.

Cassie was so sleepy by the time we got home she didn't put up much of a fight going down for her nap. I ate my grilled cheese sandwich and looked at Lulu's flier while my baby slept.

Was it really possible to talk to dead people? What if they told you something you didn't want to know? The truth was, especially after my disastrous date with Ian Chambers, I was missing Ryan so badly that I was willing to try anything, even if I was just grasping at straws. My logical mind told me that once your heart stops beating, that's it, there's nothing left. But I didn't really believe that. And the Tarot reading nagged at me. Lulu had predicted a small victory, the attainment of something I'd really wanted, then as soon as I got downstairs, Cassie said, "Mama." I knew it was just a matter of time before she got around to it. But she hadn't seemed to be in any hurry, and Lulu predicted a 'win' within the next 24 hours.

While I was mulling this over, I cleaned Alpha and Betty's cage. When it was ready for them to go back in, I got out some bits of cereal. I decided to let Betty, the friendlier of the two rats, make the decision for me.

"Alright, Miss Betty. You tell me if you think I should go to the mediumship circle on Thursday. If you think I should stay home, take the dark Cheerio first."

Of course, asking a rat to decide whether I should go to a meeting to try and talk to dead people wasn't any less crazy than actually going to the meeting to try and talk to dead people.

I put two Cheerios in my palm. Betty stood up on her back legs and sniffed at the air. Then bounded over and snatched the pale Cheerio. She crunched it until it was small enough to tuck into her cheek, then grabbed the dark Cheerio in her delicate paws. I scooped her up and put her back into her rat habitat with her buddy.

"Serves me right for asking you."

Betty always preferred the dark Cheerios.

I picked up the phone and called my mother.

"Marti! I was just about to call you."

"What's up?"

"Do you think you'd be able to drop off the twins at robotics camp on Thursday morning? They go from 9:00 to 3:00. I'll pick them up in the afternoon, but I want to be at the hospital when Emily has her c-section."

"Is that this Thursday? I was thinking it was next week. Sure, I can do that. What time is her operation?"

"8:30. Em and Nick finally got around to picking a name. McKenzi Belle. And Marti?" mom asked. "Would you mind hanging around with your dad while I'm at the hospital?"

"What's wrong with Dad?" Worry tugged at my solar plexus.

"Oh, the doctor adjusted his medication last Friday, and he's feeling a little off. I'll have to take him back this Friday if it hasn't straightened itself out."

"Why didn't you tell me?"

"It's just a little tweak, nothing serious. I didn't want—" She stopped herself.

"You didn't want what?"

Mom hesitated. "You've seemed troubled the past couple of days. I didn't want to make it worse. Your dad's situation is under control."

I hadn't told her what happened on Saturday night, but she knew something wasn't right.

"You don't need to protect me. I'm not a child," I huffed at her. "If you must know," I sighed, "Ian wanted me to go home with him, and I said 'No,' and our date ended on a sour note. Nothing more serious than that." I knew if I told her about the kiss and the torn sleeve, she'd tell Nick, and I really didn't want to go there.

"I'm sorry, baby."

"Well, it's not the end of the world."

"So, what is it that you were calling about?"

"Oh. I had wanted to…get together with some friends on Thursday, and I was wondering if you'd watch Cassie. But that doesn't seem like a happenin' thing now."

"Nonsense. You need to get out more. Come on over for dinner and leave Cassie with us. Nick and the boys will be here. It'll be nice."

"Sounds good, Mom. See you Thursday, okay?"

"Bye."

⟲

Emily's c-section went about as well as a c-section can go. McKenzi Belle was small, red and wrinkled, with a wild shock of black hair. I took a picture with my cell phone to show Dad. I didn't get to see Emily, but I talked to Nick for a couple of minutes. He was an overly-caffeinated proud papa, and I couldn't stay long – I had to get back to the house to watch over my father.

He was delighted to see the picture of McKenzi. He seemed mostly like his usual self, just a little more tired. We sat in the kitchen, where Cassie was having her pre-nap snack.

"I heard that Ian Chambers fellow has taken quite a shine to you," Dad said, taking a sip of iced tea.

Page ·86

"Has he?" I asked. "And what else has Nick been telling you?"

Dad laughed. "Nick's a big fan of his. Chambers acts nice enough. Can't put my finger on it, but something about that boy bothers me, Little Sugar."

I smiled, wondering if Mom had told him how my date with Ian had turned out. "Well, I'm still not really ready for another guy. Ryan was a pretty tough act to follow."

"Da da da!" Cassie added.

I smiled at her and picked a melted sweet potato puff off her cheek. "She said 'Mama' yesterday."

"That girl'll be talking up a storm in no time. Won't be long before you're telling her to be quiet."

Dad got up and topped off his tea glass before hobbling into the living room. He and Cassie fell asleep watching a Matlock rerun while I tidied up the kitchen.

Nick and the twins showed up just in time for dinner. He kissed me on the cheek. "So, Marti. Ian was asking about you yesterday."

"And what was it he wanted to know?" Probably trying to figure out if I'd told Nick what had happened on Saturday.

"How you're doing. If you're going to be around this weekend, that sort of thing."

"So how's that new baby?" Dad asked.

I nodded my thanks to him and went into the kitchen to help Mom.

After supper, Cassie was so busy playing with Mom and Dad that she didn't even notice I left. And yet, I hadn't even made it to the sidewalk when Nick burst out the front door.

"Where you going?"

"Not that it's any of your business, but I'm going to meet up with some female friends for a little while."

Nick opened his mouth to say something, but I cut him off.

"And stop badgering me about Ian Chambers. See you later."

I started striding towards my house, which was in the same direction as the Tenth Sphere. I heard the screen door bang and checked over my shoulder to be sure Nick had gone inside. There was no sign of him on the porch.

ॐ

There were already six ladies at the Tenth Sphere when I got there. Another three arrived after me, and Lulu and Belinda made the group an even dozen. I put a ten dollar bill in the jar with the "Love Offering" sign, but I noticed that at least two other ladies put in twenties. I wasn't sure if that made me cheap or thrifty.

We all introduced ourselves. I, apparently, was the only newbie.

"I think that's everybody," Lulu said. Then she locked the front door and we headed up the stairs.

We all sat on the floor in a loose circle. The lights were dim, but at least there were no hokey candelabras. Belinda lit a bundle of sage and started walking around the circle.

"She's smudging the room, to cleanse it of negative energy," Lulu whispered to me.

It was all very relaxing. Until the smoke detector started screeching.

"Hello?" a stern voice boomed like an evil spirit from the intercom in the hallway. "This is PDQ Security. We've received a fire alarm. Is there an emergency here?"

I thought that Marilyn, the lady on my left, was going to jump out of her skin.

Belinda ran out of the room, "No! This is Belinda Tate. It's a false alarm. No emergency." Then she punched in a code on the alarm panel.

"Thank you, ma'am. You have a good night," the voice said, followed by a click.

In the meantime, Lulu had turned the lights up and climbed up on a chair to remove the batteries from the upstairs smoke detector.

"Well," she said. "That was exciting. Sometimes it takes some doing to figure out all the quirks of a new place."

Everyone seemed to have recovered except for Marilyn. She had gotten up and was pacing around the room.

"It's him. It's him. I just know it!" she hissed at Lulu.

"Marilyn, honey, it was nothing more than the smudge stick." She closed her eyes for a moment. "My guides tell me there's no one here that isn't supposed to be. I think I've got some chamomile tea downstairs, if you'd like a cup."

"No, thank you. I'll be alright, I guess."

Marilyn sat back down, but fidgeted with her hair. I noticed a thick scar across the width of her left wrist and felt a chill in my stomach. She must have seen me looking.

"It was a long time ago," she said, wistfully.

She might have said more, but Lulu dimmed the lights. "Let's try this again," she said.

This time when Belinda walked around with the smudge stick, nothing happened.

"Marti, I'm going to start with you, honey, because you've never done this before. First of all, what I want you to do is close your eyes and imagine yourself surrounded by white light. Now, ask your guardian angel to help and protect you. Listen to me! This is important. Never, never, never skip these two steps. There are some bad things out there you do not want to mess with. Got it?"

I nodded.

"Good. Once you've done those two things, start visualizing the person you want to see. Imagine that they're in a familiar place, where you saw them often. See them coming to meet you there. Or, if that doesn't work, think about them being in a crowded room, like at a party. You're standing in the doorway, but you can't go in. They can come over and talk to you, if you can just get them to notice you. Ask your spirit guides to help you get their attention. Keep working on that."

Lulu moved over to Marilyn. She started brushing the air around Marilyn's head and shoulders as if she were clearing away dangling cobwebs. "It's alright, honey. He isn't here."

Marilyn's shoulders dropped, and she swallowed hard. Lulu moved on.

I closed my eyes and pictured Ryan. I could see every detail of his face, every ripple of hard muscle in his body. I tried to imagine him in our living room. No joy. Then I tried a room full of strangers, but I just couldn't see him there, either.

"Girlfriend, he ain't up in there."

I opened my eyes and saw a person standing between Marilyn and myself. I couldn't make up my mind if this individual was a drag queen or just a masculine-looking woman. Either way, she looked like she ought to be singing jazz songs in a seedy nightclub. No one else appeared to notice her.

"Don't you know who I am?" she smiled.

Two rapid, sharp knocks rang out from the wall.

Chapter 8
Severance Package

―――――――――⧸❦⧹―――――――――

WHEN THE KNOCKING STARTED, Marilyn screamed and threw herself on the floor. Lulu rushed to her side and pulled her up to a sitting position.

"Shhh. Shhhh. It's okay," she said to Marilyn, as if the woman was a small child afraid of the dark. Lulu's eyes closed and a smile spread across her face. "She says her name's Delilah. She's here with Marti."

"Marti, would you tell Chicken Little there that her stepfather is not coming after her. Not unless she start drinkin' again, anyway," Delilah said.

"Uh, Marilyn, Delilah tells me that your stepfather will only come for you if you start drinking again," I echoed. And this isn't weird. Nope, not at all. Not the least bit weird.

Marilyn started making disturbing little mewing sounds. Belinda helped her to her feet and led her out of the room.

"Her stepfather…did some really bad things to her. He just died on Monday," Lulu said. "Good for you, making such strong contact with your guide on the first try." She went across the circle to talk to a woman in a virulently orange shirt with a matching silk turban and penciled-on eyebrows.

"The first try!" Delilah nearly shouted. "Girl, I been trying to wake you up for years. Thought I did it that one time. Don't you remember? You was all 'Knock twice for yes, once for no' and I was all knock, knock and you got all scared and shit. You ran away."

"That was you?" I surprised myself with how loudly the words fell out of my mouth.

"You don't have to talk out loud, you know. Now, what did I just say? If I'm lyin', I'm dyin'."

Aren't you already dead? That was much less awkward. Nobody gave me strange looks this time.

"Look who knows so much all of a sudden. Maybe I'll just leave you be…"

Don't go! I felt as if I was drowning and a lifeline was slipping through my grasp. Please. I need your help. I really, really want to talk to Ryan.

"And I told you he is not here."

Where is he?

"Girl, I can't tell you that. If he want you to know, he will get in touch."

I groaned with frustration. Why can't you help me? What difference could it possibly make? He's dead! Fear crept over me. A cruel fear that maybe Ryan didn't love me enough to want to get in touch with me. That he even knew about Cassie, but didn't care.

Delilah pursed her lips and shook her head. "Marti, girl, there are some things you just are not meant to know. I can't tell you what Ryan is up to for the same reason I can't tell you tomorrow's Lotto numbers. It's nothin' to do with you. It's just the rules."

Can you at least tell me if he's okay?

"He's happy as a pig in poop. And he's closer than you think." Delilah winked at me.

But I can't talk to him.

"Sorry." Delilah frowned.

Fine, I thought at her, irritated that I wasn't making any headway. I exhaled too loudly, not intending to make such a show of sighing. So you can't tell me any secrets. I get it. But what I don't get is why you've been hanging around all this time. The whole knocking incident was, what, twelve years ago?

Delilah shook her head. But she was smiling, kind of. "Girlfriend, I'm your spirit guide. I been with you your whole life."

Doing what?

Delilah crossed her arms. "What do you think a guide does?"

How do you guide me, if I can't even see you? I shot back.

Delilah's arms uncrossed, and she laughed loudly. At least it was loud to me. "You remember last time at the bookstore, you were all worried and such about money, and you saw that quarter on the floor? When you bent over to pick it up, you saw that magazine about home businesses on the bottom shelf. Who you think put that quarter there?"

I crossed my arms and shifted away from her. I couldn't help feeling a little creeped out, even if she was helping me. Or so she said. Why me? Why you?

With an exaggerated roll of her eyes, she said, "Everybody got spirit guides and guardian angels. Everybody. They don't always listen to 'em, but they got 'em." She gave me a meaningful look. "Angels ain't never had bodies, spirit guides have. We understand stuff about the living they just don't. If we've figured something out, we get matched with somebody that's still working on that same problem, you see?"

So you're telling me that there's like some cosmic dating service to put spirit guides with living people. Seriously?

"Lord have mercy, girl!" Delilah shook her head and looked up at the ceiling in supplication. "It ain't really like that, but if that's how you need to see it, you go ahead."

Don't you get bored, just hanging around, waiting for me to do stuff that needs guidance? I was half genuinely curious, half dismissive. Hedging my bets, I supposed.

"Naw, girl. You ain't the only one I got to attend to. They keep me hoppin'."

Oh. It made sense, in a way. After all, as an ER nurse, no one would expect me to only care for one patient per shift. But it still made me feel a little less special. Do I know any of them? What a dumb thing to say! It made it sound like I was accusing her of having an affair.

Delilah smiled at me and shook her head. "There is something I can tell you, though. You watch out for a black horse, now, you hear?"

And with that cryptic warning, Delilah was gone. I spent the rest of the session trying to get either her or Ryan to come through, with no luck. Lulu turned the lights up, and we filed out of the room and down the stairs for light refreshments.

"I want to talk to you before you go, honey," Lulu said quietly to me as I passed her.

Belinda met us downstairs with an industrial-sized pot of hot tea and a tray of gluten-free cookies, which were surprisingly good. While the rest of the group was jawing about what successes they did or didn't have during the circle, Lulu pulled me through the Employees Only door.

"I know you're itching to get back to Miss Cassie," Lulu said. "But I needed to talk to you. Are you still interested in learning to read Tarot cards for fun and profit?" She raised her perfectly plucked eyebrows and cocked her head to one side.

"Well, I hadn't really thought any more about it."

"You have a gift. The way you just opened up and made contact with Delilah was amazing."

But it didn't get me in touch with Ryan. "Maybe."

"No maybe about it, honey. If you think you might want to develop your gift, why don't you work a party with me on Saturday? That'll give you a chance to see what reading cards," Lulu made air quotes, "'for entertainment purposes only!' looks like. Sometimes just paying attention to someone can make all the difference to that person and you do more good than you realize."

"I don't know. It's kind of short notice, and I have to get a baby sitter…"

"There's a hundred bucks in it for you."

"My mom will probably be available. What time?"

"Be at the shop at seven."

"I'll let you know if there's a problem."

Lulu smiled and handed me a pack of cards. "Have a look at these before Saturday."

෯

I felt guilty asking my mother to babysit yet again. It seemed like lately I was constantly pawning Cassie off on my parents. I felt like a horrible mother and a horrible daughter. But I needed to make some money. This gig didn't pay nearly as well as the ER, but it didn't cost me forty plus hours a week away from my baby. And if the parties or events were a few hours here and a few hours there, mostly at night while Cassie was sleeping, it almost didn't count as being away from her.

Nick had started his paternity leave, and while we visited Emily in the hospital, he took the boys out for breakfast, then to day camp. My sister was doing well. McKenzi was in the room with her when we came in. She looked a whole lot better, hardly wrinkled at all and a nice, healthy pink. What a difference a day makes. They'd be coming home either Monday afternoon or Tuesday morning, depending on when the insurance company booted them out of the hospital.

We stopped for Indian take out on the way home. I had to be really careful what I ordered – Cassie hated it when I ate spicy food. Guess it made my milk taste funny. Dad, on the other hand, was jonesing for a chicken vindaloo.

After lunch, Cassie and I headed back to our house. My phone rang just as we opened the door. Caller ID told me it was Ian Chambers. Again. He'd called me at least twice a day, every day this week. I'd already texted him to stop calling, and blocked his email. I shook my head. I had decided that he was too big a risk to have around my baby. If I never saw him again, it would be too soon.

Once Cassie went down for her nap, I opened up the cards Lulu had given me last night. They were different from the ones she had used to tell my fortune – those had a more or less Art Deco style. These looked medieval. The pictures could have come straight off stained glass windows from a European cathedral. I sat at the table with the instruction booklet, looked at the pictures and wrote down the meaning of each card. Then I tried doing my own reading. I did manage to freak myself out when the first card I turned over was

The Hanged Man, just like in Lulu's reading. Otherwise, I was utterly hopeless. Hopefully, Lulu just wanted me to carry stuff for her, and not do any actual fortune telling.

I looked at the instructions again for the meaning of The Hanged Man. Betrayal. Sacrifice. Accusation. What were the other things Lulu had said? Wisdom and seeing things from another perspective. Well, if this card represented Ian Chambers, it was right on the money with the betrayal part. I supposed the six dozen roses he sent were a kind of sacrifice, but I wasn't willing to be bought so easily. But then again, what was he supposed to do to apologize (not that it mattered at this point)? I didn't have an answer for that, so I got up and folded that pesky basket of laundry that had been sitting around since yesterday morning.

❧

I arrived at the Tenth Sphere at 6:55. The door was locked, so I tapped on the glass. I could see Lulu arranging things in the jewelry case that faced away from the door. Something struck me as odd, but it didn't register until she turned around.

Lulu was dressed up like a gypsy fortune teller – corset, chemise, tiered skirt, lacy shawl and coin belt. What have I gotten myself into?

She grinned at me as she jingled towards the door.

"Glad you could make it, honey."

"Nice, um, outfit."

Lulu grinned. "How many other jobs are there where you get to play dress up?"

I shrugged.

"Come on," Lulu said. "Belinda usually works the events with me, but her granddaughter has a dance recital tonight. She said you could borrow her costume. You're both tall and skinny, and the sizing on these things is pretty flexible."

I followed Lulu to the back of the store, where the clothes racks were. There was a pair of saloon doors with a "Fitting Room" sign above them. A garment bag hung on one of the doors. She nodded towards it. "We need to leave in about ten minutes. Everything's already in the car."

"Is a costume really necessary? At least for me? I've never been all that into dress up."

"We are paid entertainers tonight. Chop, chop. Time's a-wastin'."

I sighed. "The $100 is in cash, right?"

Resigned to my fate, I took the garment bag and went into the dressing room. The electric blue of the bodice was not a color I would have chosen for myself. But the Battenberg lace inserts on the sleeves of the chemise were very pretty. Not sure if it was by good luck or good design, but the corset laced in front. I looked in the mirror and shook my head. Halloween came early this year.

The coin belt jangled with every step and jangled my nerves.

"Excellent!" Lulu said before she put a gaudy, bejeweled barrette in my hair.

She looked at me again and chewed her bottom lip. "The tennies don't quite work, though, honey. There should be some shoes in the outer pocket of the garment bag."

I did like Belinda's lace up boots. But we had to stop at the corner market on the way and get some knee-high hose, because they were too tight with socks. Good thing I could tie them loosely.

We headed east, to a ritzy Memorial Area neighborhood. The guard at the gate found Lulu's name on the guest list, but he looked like he was having second thoughts about letting us in. He shook his head as he wrote down Lulu's driver's license number and opened the gate. We wound our way through a maze of McMansions – over-sized houses on under-sized lots – and Lulu finally pulled up in front of a three-story Mediterranean-style house.

It had to have been at least as big as my house, my parents' house, and Emily and Nick's house put together. Twilight was only just starting to settle onto the city, and landscape lighting was beginning to come on. Green floodlights cast eerie palm tree shadows against the beige stucco walls. Taking up most of the postage stamp-sized front yard, a dazzlingly lit, eight foot tall Talavera fountain cascaded into a Talavera-tiled koi pond, dotted with fuchsia water lilies. Ordinarily, I quite like the bright, colorful Mexican tiles, but this was way too much of a good thing.

As I helped Lulu get her gear out of the car, I looked at the surrounding yards: tiny, closely-trimmed patches of St. Augustine grass punctuated with Dr. Seuss-style juniper topiaries near walkways or front doors. No flowers. No unusual shrubs. The yards were all one homogenized strip of what my mother referred to as "blandscaping." I smiled to myself. Bet the neighbors hate that fountain.

The woman who answered the door looked exactly as I would have expected someone who owned an eight foot Talavera fountain to look. She had the "Texas

Blonde" thing going – dark roots and nearly platinum hair – teased into a towering beehive. I wouldn't have thought that a lime green cocktail dress with black polka dots would have been good on anybody, but it worked for her. Green rhinestones sparkled on her zebra-striped manicure as she grabbed Lulu and hugged her.

"I'd like you to meet my associate, Marti Keller," Lulu said when the woman released her. "And Marti, this is our hostess, Mrs. Stella Thorpe."

"Pleased to meet you." I offered her my hand.

Stella pulled me into a rib-cracking hug. I tried not to gasp too loudly for air when she let go.

"Ain't you two just the cutest little things?" She asked in a thick East Texas drawl. "Ya'll come on in now." Stella turned and cupped her hands around her mouth like a megaphone. "Pudge! Come and help the fortune tellers set up, you hear?"

Pudge, followed by the world's ugliest dog, trotted down the stairs. Pudge was small and wiry (except for a pot belly), with greasy, shoulder-length salt-and-pepper hair. Dandruff littered the shoulders of his polyester leisure suit that hadn't been in style since the early seventies. And he had the sniffles.

Except for tufts of long white hair on its head and the end of its tail, the dog was bald with speckled skin and crooked teeth.

Stella kissed Pudge's unshaven cheek and scooped up the dog. "Pudgie, you know Lulu, and this gal here is Marti." Stella batted her false eyelashes at me. "This here's my husband, Geoffrey, but we all call him Pudge." She patted his belly affectionately.

Pudge gave us a glassy-eyed nod. He didn't say a word, but he was very twitchy, and it made me nervous.

He wiped his nose on his sleeve, leaving a snail track of bloody snot.

"This little one here," Stella patted the dog in her arms, "is Moo Shu, our Chinese Crested. She's s'posed to look like this, you know."

She must say that a lot.

"This way," Pudge grunted as he picked up the canvas case with Lulu's folding card table and dragged it across the terra cotta tile.

"Bless his heart, I think Pudge has started on his birthday celebration a little early," Stella said, almost apologetically.

❦

We had almost finished setting up when both the caterers and the circus performers arrived. The performers would be out in the backyard (in the heat) putting on their show as best they could in the minute garden. The guests could hang around in the air conditioning, eating canapés, and watch them eating fire and juggling chainsaws and so on.

Once the first few guests trickled in, the floodgates opened, and the house teemed with people. I walked around the crowd periodically, handing out business cards and letting people know where we were. Most of the time, I managed the line – Lulu was doing a brisk trade – and I listened in on the readings as much as I could. I almost felt like I was at Cinderella's ball every time the grandfather clock on the second floor landing tolled out the hour. Customers had thinned to practically none, and Lulu had taken a restroom break. My feet were killing me, and I sat on a folding stool that she had brought. The clock had just finished striking eleven. Even though the party was still going strong, I was ready to turn into a pumpkin.

The front door opened. I'm not sure what made me look up, because people had been coming and going all night.

Two men stepped into the foyer. I couldn't tell if they'd come in together, or just happened to arrive at the same time. The strawberry blond one took Stella's hand and air-kissed her cheek. His dove grey suit looked expensive and Italian. I would not have described him as ugly, but there was something about him that was not quite right.

"Why Tucker Fellowes, you devil!" I heard Stella say. "Your secretary said you weren't coming."

"And miss your party, Stella? I canceled my other plans."

The second man was sharply dressed, but his clothes just didn't look right on him. The brown sport coat he wore was well-made, but didn't fit his muscle-bound frame the way it should have. I wondered if he had borrowed it.

"Mmmm, mmm, mmm. That is one crazy mo-fo, girlfriend. Don't even talk to that man if you don't have to."

I jumped.

Delilah was standing to my left, arms crossed and staring at the latest arrival.

"Jeez, woman! Don't sneak up on me like that," I hissed at her.

The lady in the overstuffed chair near me gave me a strange look before she got up and left.

"You know," Delilah said, "when you talk out loud to folks other people can't see, they kind of think you're crazy."

Better? I thought at her.

"What do you think?" Delilah cocked her head at me. "Lord have mercy! What do we have here?"

I followed her gaze.

A man in a white suit with a black shirt and red tie was in front of the muscle guy who had just come in the door. White Suit was waving his arms, his head cocked oddly to one side, in front of the man's face.

"Look what you've done to me! Look what you've done!" he screamed.

Muscles ignored him. So did all the other guests.

It was only then I noticed that White Suit's hands were missing, and the ends of his pristine, white sleeves were soaked in blood.

Chapter 9
Scavenger Hunt

☘

THE MUSCLE MAN CONTINUED to ignore the man in the white suit. Muscles took a step forward and walked right through him.

"Listen to me!" White Suit's head tilted in a crazy bend as he screamed at Muscles' back.

Muscles kept walking.

Why was everyone ignoring the screaming man in the white suit? This wasn't right, and even the hair on my arms prickled and stood up. Then I realized that they were ignoring him because they couldn't see him.

"This can not be good," I said to Delilah.

"What's that, sugar?" Stella asked me, flute of pink champagne in one hand and a plate of hors d'oeuvres in the other.

I'd been so intent on the guy in the white suit, that I hadn't noticed our hostess passing by. "Oh...I mean, well," I searched the room and my eyes fell on the performers in the backyard. "The flaming chainsaws they're juggling out there. If one goes over the fence and lands in the neighbor's yard, that can not be good."

Stella waved her champagne at me. "Oh, don't be silly. It'd just fall in the Jacuzzi." She walked away, shaking her head.

"I warned you 'bout talking out loud, girlfriend." Delilah said.

Fine. I get it.

White Suit stopped shouting and looked in our direction. Had he heard us? His eyes locked on mine, and he ran over to where we stood, passing through party guests on the way. That was creepy and weird and I started looking for the back door.

"Can you see me?" he shouted.

Yes. And I can hear you too. You don't have to yell.

"Look what he did to me!" White Suit screamed. His head fell backwards at a disturbing angle, and he had to use both arm stumps to drag it back into place.

"Boy, what did girlfriend here just say?" Delilah demanded.

"But he broke my neck, then he cut off my hands so I'd be hard to ID. I didn't even do nuthin', chica."

His head wobbled crazily, and I thought he was going to cry.

"Lots of interesting guests at the party tonight, honey." Lulu had come back from her restroom break and was looking at White Suit with equal amounts of surprise and pity.

White Suit turned to look at her, but his head collapsed onto his chest.

"Come on, Marti. Let me help you fix your make up." Lulu waved at White Suit to follow us.

"Step into my office," Lulu said as she held the door to the biggest bathroom I'd ever seen in somebody's house. It was bigger than my living room. Black polished granite countertops glittered around the double sinks. The toilet was enclosed in its own tiny room and there was a small, red velvet couch against one wall. An enormous vase of birds of paradise, orchids, and protea stood in one corner, and a potted fern stood in another.

"Now what?" White Suit said pitifully.

Lulu ignored him. She squeezed my upper arm. "Marti, you okay with this? I know it can be unsettling at first, when they know you can see them, and they start coming out of the woodwork."

"What are you trying to say?" White Suit glared at her.

Lulu gave him a talk-to-the-hand gesture. Her eyes were soft and kind when she looked at me.

"You are never required to help anybody. But it seems a shame to squander a special gift."

"I'm not sure seeing dead people is a gift. More like a curse." Unless one of those dead people was Ryan.

Lulu smiled. "It can seem that way, sometimes. But you had a career helping living people. Dead people can need help, too – they're just in different circumstances."

Well, that made sense. Nurses helped people in trouble, and ER nurses helped people in bad trouble. Wait a minute...

"Lulu?" I asked, taking a step away from her. "How do you know I used to having a career helping people?"

"When I touch you, honey, I can see an image of you in green scrubs in a very bright room, carrying a tray of medical instruments. You're a nurse, aren't you?"

"Ahem!" The man in the white suit glared at us. "That's all nice and sweet and everything, but what about me? I'm the one in need here."

Lulu looked at him, then back to me. "He came to you, Marti. Must be a reason. I think you should handle it," Lulu said.

"Me?!"

Delilah stood in the corner with the flowers, arms crossed and smirking. I wanted to stomp over and ask her what she thought was so funny. Instead, I turned to Lulu.

"How, exactly, do I handle it? I don't really want to get involved in a murder. It's nothing to do with me."

"How would you like it if somebody killed you and stuffed you in a culvert and nobody would help you?" White Suit asked, his head lying on his shoulder. "I don't want my little boy to grow up not knowing what happened to his papa."

I sighed. I looked for Delilah, but she was gone. Lulu was smiling at me. "Fine," I said. "Where is the culvert? What's your name? Maybe I could tell somebody down at the station."

"What are you going to tell them?" Lulu asked.

"Where he is and who he is, I guess."

"And what are you going to say when they ask how you know this?"

I hadn't thought about that. If I told Nick that a ghost at a party told me where to find this man's body, I'd be in a straightjacket within the hour. Then what would happen to Cassie? What would people think of me if they knew I talked to dead people? The phrase 'Salem Witch Trials' flitted across my brain, and I shuddered.

"I can't get involved," I said.

"People call the cops from pay phones with anonymous tips every day. Don't tell me you ain't heard of Crime Stoppers." White Suit's voice sounded desperate, but I couldn't tell if he was looking down to avoid eye contact, or if he just couldn't help it. I did wonder if his broken neck might have had something to do with an anonymous tip.

"Do they even have pay phones anymore?" I asked, still trying to find an out.

"If you know where to look." White Suit answered.

I didn't have any paper, so I unrolled a few squares of toilet paper. Lulu handed me a pen.

"Where are you located?" I asked White Suit.

"I am right here. My body is in a culvert out in the country somewhere. The main road is 529, but I don't know the street they turned off on. It was gravel, no sign."

"Wow. 529 and BFE. That narrows it down. What's your name?"

White Suit glared at me. "Nelson Ortega. But everybody calls me 'Spam.'"

"Spam?" I wrote down the name and tucked my toilet paper memo into my bra.

"Long story." He frowned and his head lolled forward. "Could I ask you one more favor? Could you get my wallet out of the trash and leave it with my body? I can show you where they threw it."

"You're already pushing your luck, and now you want me to go dumpster diving for you?"

"There's something in it I want my boy to have - a St. Christopher medal I got from my own father. They tossed the wallet on the way here. I've only been dead a couple of hours."

"We can look for it on the way home," Lulu said.

I'd almost forgotten she was standing there. "It'll be dark." I complained.

"I always keep a flashlight in my car. Never know when you're going to need one."

I crossed my arms and stared daggers at Spam. "Okay, but I'm not looking for your body until daylight."

"You know," Lulu said, "the shop doesn't open until noon on Sundays. I could come with you, if want me to."

That would give me a live person to talk to, anyway. "Alright. You want to meet me at your shop around nine?"

"Nine it is," Lulu said.

"And you," I turned to Spam. "I'll help you out, but you need to do something for me."

"Got somebody you want me to go haunt or something?"

He looked awfully eager.

"No. My husband, Ryan, died almost two years ago. I want you to find him and tell him that I really need to see him."

"I'll see what I can do. I got lots of contacts on the other side."

I'm sure you do.

"I heard that."

I looked at Lulu, then back to Spam. "So after we get your wallet, you're not planning to follow me home and watch me get undressed or anything like that are you? Because if I see you hanging around my house, the deal is off. Got it?"

The doorknob rattled.

"Just a minute!" called Lulu. She flushed the toilet and ran the tap for a minute.

We got a strange look from an elderly lady as we came out and she went in. But that wasn't the worst of it.

Not twenty feet away, standing beside the ten-gallon punch bowl was Ian Chambers.

I ducked behind a potted palm tree.

"Lulu!" I whispered.

She looked at me like I'd lost my mind.

"See that guy over there by the punch bowl? In the light pink shirt?"

"What about him?"

"I can't let him see me. I know him. We had a horrid date, and he's been calling me all week. I really, really don't want to talk to him."

"That doesn't seem like enough reason to hide from him," Lulu chided me.

"I stole his car."

"I see."

There was no way to get back to our Tarot table without passing right in front of Ian. Shielded by Lulu, I made my way to the nearest door past the bathroom. I spent the next half-hour in the kitchen, peeking out the door to see if Ian Chambers was gone and trying to stay out of the way of the caterers (although I did end up filling a tray of champagne flutes for them).

"Is he gone?" I asked Lulu when she finally showed back up.

"Went upstairs. It's nearly twelve. We should start packing up."

I followed her, continually glancing over my shoulder at the red marble staircase as we went. The coast remained clear.

"You know that guy?" Spam whispered in my ear. It almost sounded like an accusation.

Had a date with him. Didn't go well.

"No shit," he snorted at me, like I should have known better. If Spam was the career criminal I suspected he was, he wouldn't think much of an investigator from the DA's office.

It didn't take long to fold up all of the table draperies and pack everything away.

"Why don't you start taking stuff out to the car? I'll go find Stella." Lulu handed me her car keys.

After I wrestled the table and tote bags into the trunk of Lulu's car, I caught a blur of motion, just out of the corner of my eye. Something had run around the side of the house.

Holy. Crap. Where were my ghostly friends now, when I needed someone to go investigate something dangerous for me? I checked the glove box for Lulu's flashlight and found it sitting right on top of the Key Map.

A pink Hello Kitty flashlight, Lulu? Maybe if I found a burglar, he'd laugh himself to death. I snapped on the light and the anemic beam barely lit the ground five feet in front of me. I crept around the corner.

"Woof! Woof!"

An unusually large black Labrador retriever sat in front of the six foot brick wall that separated back yard from front. His eyes shone green in the flashlight and his tail thumped on the grass. Something akin to déjà vu washed over me. I shook it off.

The dog barked again. Although he didn't have a collar, he looked well-fed and his coat was shiny. Must belong to somebody. Probably just dug under the fence.

"Nice doggie," I said. I let out the breath I hadn't realized I'd been holding.

I backed away from him slowly, intending to go into the house and let Stella know about the neighbor's dog. That went well until I bumped into something solid.

"Who are you? What are you doing here?" Ian Chambers demanded.

The night was getting more crap-tacular by the second.

I turned around, keeping the flashlight down so he couldn't see my face, and I tried to deepen my voice. "No hablo Ingles."

"¿Quién eres, senorita? ¿Qué haces acqui?"

I only know enough Spanish to get myself into trouble, and this wouldn't be the first time. But I was saved from having to bumble through an answer by a low growl.

The black Lab was standing next to me, teeth bared and hackles raised.

"Good dog," Chambers said. I could see his right hand easing towards his left armpit. "I've got something for you right here."

Of course he'd be carrying. As much as I didn't want to talk to him, I couldn't just stand by and let him shoot the poor dog.

"Excuse me? Is there some reason you're harassing my staff?" Lulu was standing in the light of the Talavera fountain, hands on her hips.

Stella stood next to her, swaying a little on her platform shoes.

"Mrs. Thorpe. Sorry, I thought I'd found some criminal activity. I hadn't realized..."

"Apologize to that girl, then shut your trap and get back in the house. Salinger was looking for you," Stella demanded.

"Lo siento, se pierda," Ian said.

"Gracias." That one was easy, anyway.

Stella and Lulu exchanged perplexed looks as Ian scurried into the house.

"Why was he speaking to you in Spanish?" Lulu asked.

"Case of mistaken identity. Anyway," I said, shining the light on my protector, "your neighbor's dog got loose."

"He don't belong to nobody I know. I see the same people walking the same dogs every day, and I ain't never seen that one," said Stella. "Why don't you keep it? If anybody comes looking for it, I'll let you know."

I needed a dog like I needed a hole in my head.

"I don't know, Stella. I've got a baby at home, and I don't know anything about this dog. Besides, he really looks like he belongs to somebody."

Lulu had narrowed her eyes as she looked at the Lab. "He could be dangerous. It's hard to tell with a dog like that."

"Well, I'll wait until morning to call Animal Control. I'm sure it doesn't live around here." Stella hugged Lulu. "The guests got a real kick out of your fortune telling. Good night, ya'll. Drive safe, now."

After the front door closed, I looked at the dog, then at Lulu. "Do you really think she'll have him sent to the pound?" I didn't like his chances, if that happened.

"She's had a lot to drink. She'll probably forget," Lulu looked hard at the dog, "if he isn't where she can see him. Out of sight, out of mind."

"He did come to my rescue with Ian Chambers. Maybe I should put up some posters and feed him for a day or two until someone claims him." I'd already half-talked myself into taking the dog home. The slope was getting more slippery by the second.

"I don't believe anyone's going to claim that dog," Lulu said, moving towards the car.

The Lab headed towards the car with us. Going once!

"Why do you say that?"

The dog barked and wagged his tail when I touched the car door handle. Going twice!

"Because I don't think he belongs to anybody. He looks like a free agent."

The "free agent" scrambled into the car as soon as I opened the door and plopped himself down on the back seat. I guessed he weighed eighty pounds or more, and it wouldn't be easy to get him out of the car if he didn't want to go. Sold! To the lady in blue.

I had to laugh. "That is exactly the sort of thing my dad's old dog, Jingle, would do. It might be good for Dad to have him around, even if it's only for a few days."

I couldn't tell in the dark whether Lulu's face was sad or angry. "Maybe. But there's something not right about that dog. If he turns out to be dangerous, don't say I didn't warn you. And if he gets carsick, you're cleaning it up."

We got buckled in and Lulu started the car.

"Hey!" Spam's voice came from the back seat. "Why do I have to sit back here with the dog dude?"

The Lab yawned, ignoring the ghost.

"Dog breath. Nice. Glad I can't smell no more," Spam added.

"You don't have to sit anywhere. You could just go away," I reminded him.

"You promised," he retorted, sounding wounded.

"Your wallet. Where is it?" Lulu asked.

Spam directed us to a dumpster behind a grocery store on the northwest side of town.

"Don't look at me, he's your case," Lulu said as she pulled up in front of it.

I took a deep breath, trying to load my lungs with fresh air before I got out and faced the garbage. Hoping to be quick, I left the car door open. Spam appeared at my side.

A pile of moldy cabbage drooped over the edge. I wasn't sure if it was a good thing or a bad thing that the dumpster was mostly full. "Hey, Spam! Why don't you look around and make sure it's still there?"

He disappeared into the trash.

"It's here!" he shouted. "Between the furry cheese and the moldy peaches!"

I stacked some milk crates up so I'd have a better reach. I would have held my nose, if I hadn't had to hold the flashlight. The dumpster smelled like something dead with sour milk and rotten bananas on top of it. I couldn't stop myself from gagging.

I saw the wallet and reached for it.

"Wait!" shouted Spam.

"What?" I asked.

"You need something to pick it up with. Otherwise, you'll get fingerprints all over it."

"You've done this kind of thing before, haven't you?"

Spam shrugged.

I went back to Lulu's car and found some paper napkins in my purse. I wrapped two of them around the wallet and pulled it out of the ooze of rotten fruit.

"I don't want that disgusting thing in my car," Lulu said when I sat down. She popped the trunk. "There's some plastic bags in back. Wrap it up in one of those."

"Don't forget. You promised you'd help me." Spam waved a stump at me, probably forgetting he no longer had fingers. It might have been more effective, if his head hadn't flopped forward onto his chest. He faded into the darkness.

"Good night, Spam," I said with a half-hearted wave before I went back to rummaging around in the trunk.

A small, flat stone rolled out from under some boxes that I moved. I recognized the scratchy markings as a rune, but I didn't know any more about it than that. I found a plastic bag and dropped the wallet inside.

I handed the stone to Lulu as I buckled my seatbelt. "Found this in the trunk."

"Oh! I've been looking for those rune stones. Funny you should find that particular one, honey. It's called Eoh. Means 'horse' and it usually represents a trip or a journey."

"Huh. Delilah said something about a horse Thursday night. I don't see myself going on a trip any time soon. And I certainly can't afford a horse." I picked at my fingernails. "I suppose I should think up something to call him," I said.

"Call who?" asked Lulu.

"The dog."

I looked into the backseat. I could only see his front half, but his tail thunked against the card table.

"How about Pluto," Lulu suggested.

"As in Mickey Mouse's dog?"

"No. As in the God of the Underworld. Hades would probably work just as well."

"You really don't like him, do you Lulu?"

"I don't think bringing that dog home with you was the best decision, no. Don't you think that's awfully convenient that he just happened to show up when Ian Chambers did?"

"What? You think Ian and the dog are playing good cop/bad cop with me? For what purpose?" Even though I'd been talking to a dead guy for the past couple of hours, I still had a tough time believing in ghosts. A psychic dog on top of that was just too much.

"I don't know," Lulu sighed.

We didn't talk the rest of the way home. I actually fell asleep for a few minutes. When we got back to the Tenth Sphere, I left the Lab in the car while I changed clothes.

When I came out of the dressing room, Lulu hung a small pewter medallion around my neck. "If you're going to keep that dog, I want you to have this."

"What is it? Luck with pet care?"

"More like protection."

"Fine." I thought she was being a bit over-protective. He was just a dog, for crying out loud.

Then she handed me a white envelope. Inside were ten crisp twenties. "I thought you said $100."

Lulu shrugged. "Stella's a generous tipper. She used to wait tables in some small town diner, then she and Pudge hit the Lotto. $119 million. She never forgot what it's like to be broke, though."

⚘

Cassie was delighted to find a dog in the house when she woke up. She squealed and giggled and threw her Cheerios on the floor. The dog gobbled them up.

I felt a little guilty. "When was the last time you ate, huh fella?"

I cleaned Cassie up and we made a quick trip to the grocery store for a bag of dog chow. I bought some canned food for good measure. Scanning the bin of old movies near the checkout gave me an idea for a name.

I set out a big stainless mixing bowl and filled it to the top with kibble. "Bruce! Come and eat your breakfast!"

Toenails clattered on the wood floor, and the dog appeared in the kitchen doorway. He sat down in front of the bowl of food and sniffed it. Then he cocked his head to one side and whined at me.

"It's dog food. You're a dog. Eat it."

Bruce lay down and rested his head on his paws. His eyebrows wrinkled, and he was the saddest looking dog ever. I'd let him out in the backyard to go to the bathroom when I first got up, so I didn't think that was the problem.

"I don't have time for this, Bruce. I have to meet Lulu in ten minutes."

I opened one of the dog food cans and dumped it on top of the dry food. "Yummy, yummy, Bruce! Nom, nom, nom."

He turned his head and looked even sadder. And he sighed. I couldn't believe it. I picked up the bowl and set it on the table, thinking I should get a fork and mix up the wet and dry foods.

Cassie squealed, and I had to snatch the bowl up before she got her hands in the congealed red paté. I picked up a Cheerio off the high chair and put it under Bruce's nose. He ate it.

"Wretched dog," I mumbled under my breath as I poured a bowl of Cheerios for Bruce. He stood up and started wolfing them down.

"I'll deal with you later, Doggy McStrange."

I had my hands full, and I very nearly forgot Spam's wallet.

༄

Cassie and I pulled up to the Tenth Sphere with about thirty seconds to spare. Lulu was waiting in the air conditioning and came out as soon as we stopped.

Before she even made it to the car, Spam appeared in the front seat. "Shotgun!"

I would have insisted he get in the back, but I really didn't want him sitting next to Cassie. I didn't know if she could see him, but I preferred not to take any chances on him scaring her. I hadn't really wanted to bring her, but I had no choice. Mom was helping Emily with the baby and I couldn't exactly tell Nick that I needed him to babysit so I could go plant evidence at a crime scene. Cassie would be sitting in the car with Lulu in the air conditioning, so she wouldn't be exposed to anything dangerous. I doubted that any bad guys would be hanging out, watching Spam's body – they left him on the far side of nowhere so they could forget about him.

"So. Where's the dog?" Lulu asked as she climbed into the back seat.

She smiled at Cassie, and Cassie cooed at her.

"I left him at home. I didn't know how he'd react to being in the car with a baby." I glanced to my right. "Okay, Spam. How far out on 529 are we talking?"

"Past Katy. I know that much."

I started at Highway 6 and took a left on FM 529. Once we passed FM 362, we were surrounded by rice paddies and cattle.

"Are you sure it's this far out?" I grumbled.

"Yeah. I remember there was a big tree by the turn off. Maybe like an oak or something. A bunch of red and white cows were lying down under it. I remember 'cuz I asked the bossman why we was coming all the way out here." After a few seconds pause, Spam asked, "What do you think FM stands for? Far Mother—"

"No," I cut him off. "Farm to Market. Jecz. And watch your language around Cassie."

Spam sulked.

We drove for another ten minutes before I hit the brakes.

"Did they look like that?" I asked, pointing to a group of polled Herefords on the north side of the road.

"Yeah! That could be them."

"I think it's a little farther on," Lulu said from the back.

"What makes you say that?"

She pointed to the northwest. "Them."

A couple of dozen black vultures circled a point about a mile ahead of us, spiraling down to the ground like a tornado in extreme slow motion.

Chapter 10
Space Invaders

———————————❧———————————

"PLEASE DON'T LET THEM buzzards eat me!" begged Spam, head thrown all the way back over his shoulders.

"I'm sorry, but there's not much we can do about that. I'm going out on a limb leaving your wallet here. I don't want to disturb the crime scene any more than what I'm already doing, and I don't want to get involved."

We turned north onto the gravel road that led to the vulture feast. It wasn't long before we came to a bridge over a dry creek. Red-headed turkey buzzards had joined the party of black vultures and hunched along the guard rail on the bridge. Blow flies buzzed fitfully around the culvert.

"You probably don't want to see this," I said to Spam.

He still followed me to the big pipe. The indignant scavengers moved out of my way and glowered at me from a safe distance. I threw the bag containing Spam's wallet near where the stump of an arm stuck out of the culvert. I could hear flapping and hissing coming from inside the pipe. I really didn't want to look in there.

"Yo! Mujer! You can't leave the bag and napkins. Your fingerprints are all over them."

I groaned.

Spam's corpse hadn't taken long to ripen in the June heat. I held my nose against the sickly-sweet stench and closed my eye that was closest to his body. Even so, I caught a glimpse of it. Scavengers had been at work for a while, and the left arm was gone. There wasn't much left of his face, either. It was all I could do not to toss my cookies.

I shook the wallet out of the plastic bag and picked up the napkins I had used to retrieve it from the dumpster.

The rattling bag alarmed the birds in the culvert, and they rushed out, big wings flapping. One of them paused long enough to vomit on my shoes.

"Ugh! Gross!" I yelled at the turkey buzzard, as little chunks of Spam slid off my feet and onto the ground.

It didn't take too many steps before the vulture vomit started to seep through the tongue of my tennies. I took off my shoes and socks and put them in the plastic bag that had held Spam's wallet. I had to pick my way through the grass burrs back to the car, where Lulu was sitting in the air conditioning with Cassie. Spam marched along by my side, muttering about how somebody was going to pay for this.

I opened the back of my car and dropped the plastic bag-o-nastiness in. When I slid behind the wheel, Lulu asked why I was barefoot and slamming doors.

She laughed at me when I told her what had happened.

"It's not funny. I'm going to have to buy new shoes."

"I'm sorry, honey. It's just that you're the only person I've ever known who's had a buzzard puke on them." Lulu clamped her lips together, trying not to smile.

"I bet Spam doesn't think it's amusing."

I looked around for him, but he was nowhere to be seen.

※

Before I dropped Lulu off at her shop, I stopped by a truck stop, lobbed my ruined footwear into the dumpster and used their pay phone to call Crime Stoppers to report finding Spam's body.

When we got back to the house, I struggled to pull a wiggly Cassie out of her carseat. She kept grabbing the medallion that Lulu had given me, choking me, and out of frustration, I pulled it off and tossed it into the glove box. At least the temperature of the concrete underneath the carport was bearable. The caliche in the driveway, not so much.

"I guess no good deed goes unpunished," I complained to Cassie as I hopped across the sizzling gravel towards the side door.

A horse whinnied nearby.

"I mean, this has nothing to do with us. Seems like Spam's not even grateful for the help."

Cassie squealed with delight and lurched away from me. I had to clutch her shirt to keep her from falling.

The horse whinnied a second time.

There in my backyard, as if it was the most normal thing in the world, was a shiny black horse. I stared stupidly through the chain-link fence.

"What the—"

A loud crash came from inside the house. Burglars?!

Horse or no horse, I ran to Mom and Dad's house and called the police. I also called Emily's number to see if Nick was at home. He wasn't.

I left Cassie in the house with Mom when two patrol cars arrived a few minutes later. Dad came out with me to talk to the police. I recognized one of the officers from parties of Christmases past – his name was Robert. The other was a lady I hadn't seen before.

"Marti, what happened?" Robert asked me.

"I came back from running an errand and—" I glanced into the backyard. There was no sign of the horse. I wondered if I had imagined it, but Cassie had seen it too. "And I heard some noises coming from inside."

"Good thing you called us. Can't be too careful with something like that," he said.

The side door was locked, so I handed him my keys. The other officer went around to the front door.

Gun drawn, Robert knocked on the side door. "Hello? Anybody in there?"

The only reply was a muffled bark.

Bruce.

I'd forgotten about him. I hoped he wasn't hurt.

"Is that dog loose in the house?" Robert asked.

"He was when I left."

Robert entered the house. I wasn't sure if his partner had gone in the front, or was waiting by the door to catch whomever Robert flushed out. Either way, she wouldn't give her position away by using her radio. Minutes crawled by. Dad squeezed my shoulder and hobbled over to my car and sat down in the driver's seat.

"It's going to be okay, Little Sugar." He cocked his head and frowned. "Where are your shoes?"

"My shoes. Yes. Long story short, I stepped in some…fresh asphalt while I was out and ruined them. I threw them out so I wouldn't get it all over the floors in the house. Because that would be a real mess to clean up." I should probably stop over-explaining now.

Finally, Robert came out the side door.

"There's nobody here. We found your dog shut in the baby's room. He doesn't look hurt."

"Dog? You don't have a dog," Dad said.

"I found him last night."

Dad and I followed Robert into the house. The female officer was taking notes. I opened Cassie's bedroom door. Bruce trotted over to me and put his head under the palm of my hand.

"You okay?" I asked him, scratching his ears.

He answered with a big slurp of his tongue on my wrist.

Robert walked me around the house, asking if anything was disturbed or missing. Even though the front door was now standing wide open, none of my valuables (such as they were), including my laptop and the TV, were missing. The living room, on the other hand, was a disaster.

Couch cushions were strewn across the floor. The drawers from my small filing cabinet had been dumped out. My breath caught in my throat when I saw our wedding photo on the tile, glass broken and picture partially pulled out. All the pictures that had been on the wall were face-down on the floor, some of the frames were broken and the canvases torn. My signed copy of The Mists of Avalon lay open and face-down, the front cover partially torn from the binding.

"You have any idea what the burglar might have been looking for?" the officer I didn't know asked me. Her brass name tag read 'A. Perkins.'

"No. I don't have anything. I don't keep cash in the house, and the few pieces of real jewelry I have are still in the box on my dresser."

I was as puzzled as they were.

A. Perkins looked at Bruce. Robert asked, "You sure the dog didn't do any of this? Sometimes they get real upset being left alone."

"You think the dog was so upset he went through my files and took all of my pictures off the walls? Then he opened the front door and shut himself in Cassie's room?"

Robert shrugged. "Things aren't always what they seem."

☙

They asked me to stay out of the house until they finished collecting evidence. They let me take a few things for Cassie, and the Cheerios for Bruce, and said they'd call me when I could come back.

When Dad, Bruce and I arrived next door, Mom hugged me. Dad got out the phonebook (which I didn't realize they still made) and called one of the big alarm companies to set up an appointment for Monday afternoon.

"I'm so glad you and Cassie weren't hurt," Mom said, stroking my arm. "Good thing you heard that noise."

"Yeah." I thought of Delilah's warning – Watch out for the black horse. I'd have to see just what she knew about that. What had happened to it? How was it connected to the burglary? Did she know who was in my house? And then there was the horse rune in Lulu's trunk. Maybe after my parents and Cassie were asleep, I could try to contact her.

"So tell me about the dog, Little Sugar. He kinda looks like old Jingle."

"Found him wandering around last night. He doesn't look like a stray. I thought I'd take him to the vet and see if he had a microchip, and maybe put up some posters for him, see if anybody claims him. If not, I guess I'll keep him."

"It's good to have a dog around," Mom said.

"If he stays with us, I'll have to have him neutered. I'm not crazy about having a male dog running around, peeing on everything."

Bruce grunted and curled up.

"Tends to keep them from getting out and wandering, too," Mom said.

"He's kind of weird, though. Only thing I've found that he eats is Cheerios."

Bruce leapt to his feet and barked.

The front door rattled.

Both of my parents gasped and my heart pounded against my ribs.

Nick burst through the front door, with Kyle and Aiden close behind.

"Marti! What happened? Are you okay? I saw the patrol cars in front of your house…"

"It's alright, Bruce. Nick is a friend." I gave the dog a pat. "You scared the living crap out of us, Nick."

Then I told him what had happened, starting with pulling into the carport, and editing out the part about the horse.

He nodded and chewed on his lower lip. "I'll keep on top of it." He tilted his head. "Where'd the dog come from?"

"Found him."

"Well, you ought to keep him. You need an alarm system, too."

"Dad's already on it."

"I'll just go next door and see how it's going," Nick said.

Aiden and Kyle coaxed Bruce out into the backyard to play with them. He seemed to be very good with kids: running around in circles like a fool and leaping to catch tennis balls that they threw. No telling where they got them. I hoped, for Bruce's sake, that they weren't moldy.

$$\circledS$$

The police finished with their evidence gathering and cleared us to come home before supper. I opted to spend the night at Mom and Dad's. Even with Bruce around, I wasn't comfortable staying in my own house. That made me angry. It wasn't about the things that the burglar didn't even bother taking. It was about the invasion of my space. Whoever broke into my house had no right to do that. It was my house, dammit. And what if that horse hadn't whinnied and I had walked in with Cassie while he was in the middle of trashing my living room? What would have happened then? If I could get my hands on that jerk, I'd like to remove a few of his favorite body parts and see how he felt about that, see if he felt violated the way I did right now.

Cassie was totally unruffled, but I picked at my food. I was still too upset to eat much of anything. Nick and the boys joined us for dinner.

"Have they started running mounted patrols in this area, Nick?" Mom asked.

"You mean on horses? Don't think so. Not unless HCSO is doing something. Why?"

"The sheriff's department? Maybe. I was sure I heard horses whinnying this afternoon. Didn't see any, though."

"Yeah. Thought I heard one, too. Aren't there some ranchettes a mile or so south of here, where people are allowed to have horses? Maybe they were just trail riding," I said, hoping she'd drop it. The less said about the vanishing equine, the better.

"I thought it was just before you got back, Marti. Maybe it was on TV or something."

I shrugged.

Or something. I had almost convinced myself that I'd imagined the horse in my backyard. But Cassie had seen it, too. Were we both hallucinating? If not, where did it go?

I watched as Kyle surreptitiously fed his carrot soufflé to Bruce, who gobbled it up. If Nick noticed, he didn't let on. Bruce, you are the weirdest dog, ever.

Bruce looked up and pricked his floppy Lab ears as high as they would go. That look only lasted a couple of seconds, until Kyle slipped him some more soufflé.

Nick had left with the boys hours ago. Mom, Dad and Cassie were all asleep. It was 1:30 AM and the pull-out sofa bed was not getting any more comfortable. It wasn't the springs that poked me at every turn that were making me cry. Every time I closed my eyes, I imagined the burglar holed up somewhere, laughing at me. I had given up on trying to sleep long ago and sat cross-legged on a cushion on the lumpy sofa bed in Mom and Dad's living room, flipping through the channels. It didn't seem like there was anything on except old movies and infomercials. And really weird cartoons. Cartoons not intended for children.

I blew my nose yet again. I couldn't stop the tears of frustration, of anger, of sadness that slid down my cheeks and splattered on my shirt.

"Girlfriend, you got to get a hold of yourself." Delilah had materialized next to me on the couch.

"Easy for you to say. You haven't just had your house broken into and your things destroyed."

"Could be worse. You could be Spam."

"Is this meant to be a pep talk, Delilah? Because you're actually making it worse."

"You're talking out loud again."

Do you know anything about the black horse that was in my backyard this morning? You did say something about a black horse earlier.

"Yes. Yes, I do know something about it. You know that amulet that Lulu gave you? You might want to put it back on."

And then she was gone.

I punched the throw pillows. Why did she have to be so freakin' obscure about everything? Who did she think she was, Nostradamus?

Bruce hopped up on the couch and put his head in my lap, tail wagging lazily. I was finally able to go to sleep with both the lamp and the TV on, and Bruce snuggled up against me.

I woke up to the sound of Cassie babbling and shaking the side of the crib. I pushed my way out from under Bruce (who had managed to spread out and take up most of the fold-out) and went to my baby. She was standing up, holding onto the railing, and I swear she was trying to sing.

"You know what, baby? We're going back to our house. I'm not letting some big meanie run our lives. It's our house, and we're taking it back."

I wrote a quick note for Mom, and then Cassie, Bruce and I headed next door. The dog took care of his morning business on the way and he ended up eating more of Cassie's breakfast than she did. She was used to the Pick Up Game – she'd throw stuff on the floor and I'd pick it up. Bruce, however, just ate it. At first, I think she was a little mad, but she soon decided it was funnier that way.

I called the vet that Dad used to take Jingle to. They could see Bruce on Tuesday afternoon. I had gotten most of the living room put back in order by the time the alarm guy showed up at 2:30. Dad was watching for him, and he was at my house before the estimator even got out of his truck. Nick came over as well, although he was really antsy, so I guessed he was anxious about leaving Emily at home with the new baby and the boys.

"Mom is there. They'll be fine," I said.

"The kids make a lot of noise. It'll be obvious that people are home. In case—" Nick stopped himself.

"In case what? The burglar comes back to hit more houses in the neighborhood?" I asked.

Nick looked at the ground. "Yeah."

"Not helping, Nick. Not helping."

"Sorry."

Dad took the estimate from the alarm guy back to the house with him. Nick followed.

When Cassie woke up from her afternoon nap, we went to go see Emily and McKenzi. My sister was still sore and was having trouble getting up and down, but she seemed chipper enough.

"Who is Bruce?" she asked me. "The boys keep talking about playing with him."

"I found a dog. I'd bet money he belongs to somebody. I'm having the vet scan for a chip tomorrow, and I'll get some signs up."

"I hope nobody claims him. Kyle and Aiden would love to have a dog, but I just can't manage one right now. They'd have a blast borrowing yours."

I felt like I almost had to keep Bruce, now. And I was okay with that.

Cassie was easy to get to sleep that night. Bruce curled up on my bed, and I talked to him while I was getting undressed for a much-needed shower. I was tired from my late night, and fell asleep easily, in spite of Bruce's snoring.

The next thing I heard was the shower running. I opened one eye. It was just getting light. The alarm clock read 6:12. Ryan's getting up a little late for work this morning. I rolled over to go back to sleep.

Hang on. It couldn't possibly be Ryan in the shower.

But who was it? Bruce was nowhere to be seen.

The water shut off. Whoever was in my bathroom was whistling. The tune seemed vaguely familiar, but I couldn't think of the name of it.

"Bruce!" I whispered. No response.

I was looking for a heavy, blunt object when the bathroom door opened. Wearing nothing but a towel around his hips, water glistening over his well-formed muscles, stood Quinn, the guy who'd saved me from Ian Chambers in Kemah.

Chapter 11
Creature Feature

⎯⎯⎯⎯⎯⎯⎯⎯⎯ ᔐ ⎯⎯⎯⎯⎯⎯⎯⎯⎯

"QUINN?" I ASKED, TRYING to pick my jaw up off the floor.

He winked at me and disappeared back into the bathroom.

When he'd intervened in the drama with a drunken Ian Chambers at the Kemah Boardwalk, it hadn't really occurred to me to wonder what he looked like naked. Now that I knew, I was mad at myself for strongly approving.

Why was he in my bathroom? And with no clothes on?

I slipped out of bed, fully conscious that I was only wearing one of Ryan's threadbare tee-shirts and purple polka-dot panties.

I pushed open the bathroom door.

"Hello?"

Bruce's tail thumped against the shower curtain. He used his nose to push the shower faucet lever up, and lapped the water from the faucet. The water squealed and groaned in the pipes from the low flow.

I closed my eyes and rubbed them. I shook my head. When I opened my eyes again, wet Bruce was still in the shower, getting himself a drink.

The only rational explanation was that I was losing my mind.

I put Bruce outside to do his doggy business while I got dressed. As I filled the carafe for the coffee maker, I wondered how much a psychiatrist would cost. I knew some worked on a sliding scale. I wasn't sure I trusted myself around my baby now. If I was hallucinating naked men, no telling what else my crazy brain might come up with. What if it made me hallucinate something that caused me to hurt Cassie? Like that lady who heard voices telling her she should drown her five kids in the bathtub. And she believed them.

I did think about trying to contact Delilah and ask her for help. But somehow, asking an invisible dead person about my hallucination seemed weird and wrong.

But what if there wasn't anything wrong with me? Seems like these visions of ghosts started when I met Lulu. What if she was slipping psychoactive drugs to her unsuspecting clients? That might explain a lot of things, although it wouldn't explain the whole Spam adventure. I fully intended to get a sample of the water in the cooler, for a start. My friend Amanda still worked in the hospital lab, and she'd probably be willing to do me a favor and run some tests.

Cassie and I went for our morning walk, as usual. Except this time, we had Bruce with us. Cassie ignored Mr. Buns and laughed at Bruce as he trotted along, tongue flapping and speckling the sidewalk with little drops of drool.

We arrived at the Tenth Sphere a few minutes before opening time. Bruce plopped down in the shade of the awning.

"Oh, come on," I said to him. "I don't want it to look like we're standing around, waiting for them to open. Don't you have some territory to mark?"

Bruce just lay there, panting.

Cassie banged on her stroller tray. "Da ma da ma!"

Metal clacked against metal as Belinda pushed back the security shutters and unlocked the front door.

"Good morning!" she called to us.

"Morning, Belinda. How are you?" I couldn't help feeling a little wary. I hoped it didn't show. She seemed too nice to spike the water cooler, but in the ER, I'd seen way too many awful things that "really nice" people had done.

"Fine, fine. If you're looking for Lulu, she'll be in after lunch."

I shouldn't have made it so obvious that I was peering over her shoulder and into the shop. "No, that's alright. I wanted to thank you for letting me borrow your outfit for the party on Saturday."

Belinda opened the door a little wider. "You're welcome. You ladies can come inside and tell me about it, if you'd like."

"I'm in a bit of a rush, but I would like a drink of water, if you don't mind. Did Lulu tell you about our trip to the country Sunday?" I wrestled the stroller over the threshold. Bruce sat up and whined, but wouldn't come inside. I tugged on the leash, and he fought back. Finally, I gave up and tied the leash to the bar handle of the door.

"She did. I bet it was pretty grisly. Did you see it on the news? They said they found a wallet, but the body was too badly…damaged to make a positive ID." Belinda shuddered.

"Yes," I said, filling a paper cup from the cooler. "It was pretty gross. Lots of buzzards and flies and stuff." I saluted her with the cup. "Thanks for the water – I've got to run."

We were almost back to my house when a passing car startled a group of iridescent black grackles drinking from a sprinkler puddle in the gutter. One bird bounced off the car's windshield and lay flapping in the street. I set the brake on the stroller, double checked for traffic, then ran out into the road and scooped up the bird. His mouth opened and closed pitifully, and his nictitating membrane closed halfway over his eye.

"Cassie, we may have a trip to the wildlife rehabbers," I said as I pulled the stroller brake up with my toe.

It was hard to steer the stroller with one hand and cradle the injured bird against my body with the other.

In the end, it didn't matter. The bird stopped struggling and his head lolled limp between my fingers. I couldn't feel a heartbeat. After Cassie went to sleep, I buried him under the knockout rose near my patio. Bruce lay nearby, head on his paws, and watched.

I called Amanda, and she agreed to meet me at the California Pizza Kitchen in the mall at 12:30. The lunchtime rush had not thinned out quite enough to be what I would consider 'baby friendly.' The frazzled hostess put us in a booth at the far end of the restaurant, near the restrooms. Cassie sat at the end of the table in a high chair and threw crayons at us while we talked. I wrangled them and herded them into the space between Cassie's cup and the container of finger foods I had brought.

"You dropped off the face of the Earth after you had her," Amanda said. She gave Cassie a vaguely resentful look. I tried not to go into Mama Bear mode.

I put some Cheerios on a napkin for Cassie. One by one, she dropped them on the floor. I wondered if she was missing Bruce.

"Things would have been a lot different if Ryan hadn't died." I often felt like I had to defend my decisions around my former work friends. I supposed that's why I tended to avoid them.

"Molly just finished maternity leave," Amanda said. "She found a really nice daycare lady. She could probably put you in touch if you were interested in coming back to work. ER is way under-staffed right now – I'm sure they'd take you back in a heartbeat."

"Thanks. I'll keep that in mind. So, how's Lance?"

Amanda blushed. "Guess you haven't heard the news."

Uh-oh. Had they broken up?

She held out her left hand. A big honkin' rock glittered on her ring finger.

"Congratulations! Have you set a date?"

"Thanksgiving. Everybody's going to be travelling down anyway, so it seemed like a good time."

"Good for you." I envied her then.

I flashed back to when Ryan had proposed to me. It was 6:00 on a Saturday morning, and the ER was slow, often the case in that timeslot. A cop and one of the doctors came rushing down the hall from one of the ambulance bays with a patient on a stretcher. I was in the zone and didn't even notice the officer was Nick. Not until afterwards, anyway, when he took off his fake moustache. Dr. Vo shouted for the crash cart, so I ran to get it. When I got back, my first clue that something was out of the ordinary was a line drawing of a heart taped to the EKG monitor. Shaking his head and trying hard (but not quite succeeding) to look grave, Dr. Vo told me that the man's heart was missing. I stepped in for a closer look. The "patient" sat up, and I was surprised to see it was Ryan – they'd kept his face hidden from me when they brought him in. He said that since I'd stolen his heart, I may as well take the rest of him, too. Then he gave me his grandmother's ring and asked me to marry him. I couldn't have said 'no' if I had wanted to.

Cassie's squeal snapped me back to the present. "Sorry, I've got something in my eye," I said, dabbing at the moisture that suddenly pooled at the corners of my eyelids.

I had hardly regained my composure when Spam appeared on the seat next to Amanda.

I jumped half out of my seat and knocked over my tea.

Luckily, the tea glass was mostly empty and I had enough napkins to mop up the spill. "Sorry about that. My phone is on vibrate, and it went off in my pocket."

Amanda nodded. Everybody's done that at least once. I pulled out my phone and pretended to read a message.

What are you doing here?! I gave Spam a sharp, quick look.

"There's something you need to see. Go to Specials tonight around six."

I don't know what 'Specials' is.

"It's a club, called Specials, downtown, near West Gray."

And what is it I'm supposed to see there?

"You wouldn't believe me if I told you."

And just like that he was gone. Ghosts had the most annoying habit of disappearing so you couldn't argue with them.

I finished my pretend message and put my phone away. Cassie was gumming the crayons that I had thought were out of reach. "Babies, huh?" I said to Amanda as I traded the green Crayola for some sweet potato puffs.

"So what's the story on this water you want tested?" Amanda asked.

"A friend of mine started having some hallucinations after she started at a new job. She's afraid she's going nuts, but I wanted to find out if there was something simple, like contaminated water, before she blew a wad of cash on a shrink," I said.

"I'll run some strips on it," Amanda said. She looked bewildered as she watched Cassie recapture the green crayon and start trying to shove it up her nose.

Nick had told me I could leave Cassie at their house while I took Bruce to the vet and ran an errand. I couldn't bring myself to ask my mom again. I dropped off a mac and cheese casserole at Emily's when I dropped off Cassie. I was pretty sure that if dinner was up to Nick, Kyle and Aiden would have chips and gummy bears.

"Alright, Bruce. It's just you and me," I said when I got back in the car.

"Easy, there, Bruce" said the vet tech as the hydraulic exam table rose. "Eighty six pounds – he's a big guy." He flashed a thermometer into Bruce's ear. "Ninety-eight. Temps a little low, but that may be because of the AC."

Dr. Anderson reached to shake my hand as she entered the exam room. "Ms. Keller, I'm so sorry about your long wait. We tried calling to reschedule, but you'd already left. Did the front desk tell you I had an emergency surgery? It took a while – I ended up having to amputate the poor dog's leg. When it's car vs. dog, the dog never wins." Dr. Anderson shook her head. "So, who do we have here?"

"Well, I found this dog on Saturday night. I thought I'd have him checked to see if he's got a chip and maybe I'd put out some signs to see if anybody's lost him. If nobody claims him, I guess I'll keep him. I've been calling him Bruce."

"Anthony, would you go get the scanner, please?" Dr. Anderson asked.

The tech disappeared into the back of the clinic. The doctor looked in Bruce's ears and at his feet, then pulled his lips back and checked his teeth. She checked again.

"That's odd. He's got some extra teeth. I would expect to find forty-two. He's got fifty. He's got plenty of room for them, don't see any crowding."

Anthony returned with something that looked like a giant magnifying glass with a digital read-out in the handle. The vet took it from him and waved it over Bruce's neck and back.

"No chip."

Spam appeared in the corner, tapping his wrist.

I ignored him.

Dr. Anderson didn't find out anything else odd or unusual about Bruce, and I decided to hold off on the vaccinations and neutering until I found out whether anybody was looking for him. I did buy a tube of topical flea and heartworm medication, though. The receptionist handed me a crunchy doggie bagel from the jar while I was waiting for my receipt. Bruce made short work of it. Guess those extra teeth came in handy.

"You don't have time to take him home," Spam said as we walked out of the clinic. "It's almost 5:30 now."

I knew he was right, but I didn't like it. I stopped on the way and bought a liter bottle of water and a package of disposable bowls.

I had to drive around a little to find a parking spot in the shade. "Sorry, Bruce. This is the best I can do for now. Stay in the car – I'll be out as soon as I can."

After I rolled down all four of the windows and poured Bruce two bowls of water, I followed Spam to the club entrance.

The bouncer gave me a funny look as I went through the door. Once I got inside and had a look around, I understood why.

I was in a titty bar. And an especially seedy one, at that. Spam directed me to a corner table, and I cringed as I sat on a sticky wooden chair. What would Ryan say if he knew I was in a place like this? He'd laugh at me, then hand me a couple of dollar bills, that's what he'd do.

You might have mentioned what kind of place this was, Spam.

"Maybe, chica. But you might not have come."

I snorted. You think? Now that we're here, what am I looking for? I don't want to be in this place a second longer than I have to be.

"You see that door back on the other side of the stage that says 'Employees Only?' Keep your eyes on who goes in and out."

The odors of alcohol, stale sweat and long gone cigarettes assaulted me. I perched on the edge of the chair and crossed my hands in my lap, trying to minimize contact with anything in this place. Whomever I was supposed to see had better make an appearance soon, because I was on the verge of breaking out the disinfectant wipes that I always kept in my purse. That would probably not be inconspicuous.

A woman in a g-string and high heels slapped a napkin down on my table. "Drink?"

Are you kidding?! "No thanks, not right now. I'm…waiting on somebody."

She shrugged and left.

I wanted to tell her that it wasn't what she thought, that I wasn't the sort of person who frequented places like this, but I managed to keep my mouth shut, for a change. I hope Bruce is okay – whatever Spam wants me to see had better happen soon, because I'm not leaving that dog in the car for long.

I couldn't watch the door without also seeing the stage, and I'd bet money that Spam planned it that way. He seemed to be enjoying the show, but I thought most of the girls looked like they would rather have been anywhere but Specials. Their eyes were glazed and they seemed to be half-heartedly following a choreography that they'd gotten bored of long ago.

Except for one dancer. She looked Marilyn Monroe-esque, with platinum blonde hair, bright red lipstick and a beauty mark on her chin. She'd started out with a white halter dress and full length gloves, and was quickly working her way down to much less. I found her routine with the pole disturbing, both for her relentless enthusiasm and sheer vulgarity. Spam wore a wistful smile. I checked the time on my phone. I'd been there five minutes. If nothing had happened in another five, I was leaving.

"Be sure to avoid that one," a male voice whispered in my ear.

I whipped my head around to find Quinn sitting in the shabby chair to my right. I poked him in the arm.

"What was that for?"

"To see if you're a hallucination."

"Well?"

"You feel solid enough. What are you doing here? Are you following me?" Why were you naked in my bathroom, and where did you go, if you were even really there?

"We seem to be looking for the same person." Quinn smiled. "Seriously, though." He cocked his head towards the stage, "Avoid her like the plague."

Like I was interested in doing anything anywhere near her.

"Why you dissing, GiGi, man? She's smokin' hot – look at those chichis grandes!" Spam said. He didn't act the least bit concerned about the new arrival.

"She's a succubus," Quinn said, maddeningly nonchalant.

"She'll suck your what?" Spam asked, with such a salacious smile I wanted to smack him.

"Your soul," Quinn said. "She's a soul eater. Don't you know anything about demons? With a set-up like this, she doesn't have to go looking for victims. They come to her."

I suddenly snapped that Quinn and Spam were having a conversation. "Wait! You can see him?" I said. I was surprised at the relief I felt that lots of people saw ghosts. "I thought Lulu and I were the only ones that could see him." Maybe I'm not losing my mind, after all.

I glanced back up at GiGi and winced. Her performance made me feel like I was being assaulted. "You mean she's working like a demon. Not that she's an actual demon, right?"

"Says the lady who talks to dead people." Quinn smiled as he said it.

Spam glared at him.

"See what she sees," Quinn answered him, commanding.

He brushed his fingertips over my eyes, almost touching me. I pulled away from him, but when I looked back at the stage, I almost cried out. Instead of a modern-day Marilyn Monroe, something scaly and reptilian with bulging yellow eyes gyrated on stage in a white sequined thong. It felt like someone had poured a glass of ice water over my head and down my back. I glanced at Spam. I expected that he would have gone pale, if there had been any blood to drain from his face. I spent a moment or two being amused by his lusting after The Creature from the Black Lagoon.

"Who are you, really? How did you do that? Why are you here?" I pelted Quinn with questions.

"She wears a disguise, I know how to see through it, that's all," Quinn said. "And I told you, my name is Quinn. And it appears we are looking for the same person, you and I."

I clenched my fists in frustration. He had answered my questions, but told me nothing.

"Look! Look! Look!" shouted Spam.

The 'Employees Only' door opened and a muscle-bound man in a polo shirt and acid-washed jeans, whose appearance screamed 'bouncer,' poked his head out and scanned the room.

"That's Jericho," Spam whispered. "If he's here, Salinger's around somewhere too. He is one sneaky bastard."

Jericho waved to someone behind him. Moments later, Ian Chambers slipped cautiously out the door.

And headed straight for our table.

Chapter 12
Secret Chambers

I LOOKED DESPERATELY FROM Spam to Quinn. I didn't think Ian had spotted me yet, but it was only a matter of seconds until he did.

"I can't let him see me here!" I said through gritted teeth.

I was trapped in the corner, and the only way out led directly into Ian's path. My heart pounded so hard I wondered if he could hear it.

A warm, strong arm slid around my shoulders and my rickety chair tipped back just a little. Quinn's hot mouth covered my own. My lips, no longer under my control, parted for him. I couldn't remember how to breathe, and my skin felt electrified. It made me think of diving into a deep, icy pool on a sweltering day, shocking and overloading my senses, short-circuiting my brain. He smelled of water on parched earth and pine forests. It seemed to me that I could drown in his embrace, and it wouldn't be a bad thing.

I had never thought the word 'swoon' would be applied to me. But that's just about what I did when Quinn pulled away from me and gently lowered the front legs of my chair back to the floor. Good thing the table was there – it kept me from slithering out of the chair and lying like a limpid pool on the floor. I was dizzy and shaking, almost gasping for air. And that was just from a kiss.

"He didn't see you," said Quinn, licking his lips. He brushed my cheek with the backs of his fingers and I shivered.

It took a moment for his words to register and make sense as my mind drifted back down from the stratosphere. A fleeting aftertaste of bagels forced my mind to focus on reality. I shifted in my chair, planning to get up and follow Ian.

"Wait," said Spam. "He's still here, getting a drink at the bar."

I made sure my back stayed to the bar.

"Why are you looking for Ian Chambers?" I asked Quinn.

"You're welcome," he said.

I glanced into his eyes, then down at the table. It was hard to keep control of myself when I looked at his face. My body was desperate for another kiss like that, but my mind wanted to run as far away, as fast as possible. "Thanks. Again. That's twice, now that you've stepped in between me and Chambers."

"At least."

Before I could ask what he meant by that, one of the dancers came to our table. Her eyes looked blankly at Quinn, and I was as invisible to her as Spam was.

"Dance, mister?"

Even in the poor light, I could tell she was not young, but she probably wasn't nearly as old as she looked, either. Her smile was tired and artificial, and crow's feet cracked through thick layers of foundation and powder.

Quinn shook his head. The woman shifted the chain mail bib necklace that hugged her throat and dangled between her pendulous breasts. As she turned to go, something fluttered to the table, falling from the crease of her breast. I covered my mouth to stop myself from saying anything when I realized that it was a small, dried cockroach. Spam snickered, but I felt incredibly sad for her. How does somebody get to a place in her life where this is normal?

Shut up, Spam. It's not funny.

Quinn tilted his head like a dog does when it hears something its human can't.

"Wait, Miss."

She turned back to him, her face an odd mix of hope and disappointment. He scanned the room before pressing something into her hand.

"Have a good one." His tone was solemn.

Whatever it was, she quickly tucked it into her shoe.

"Ay caramba, dude!" Spam said. "A hundred bucks for nothing?"

"You gave her a hundred dollars? That's quite a gift," I added. Why didn't strangers just walk around and hand me hundred-dollar bills, no strings attached?

"Is it? If they don't find it and take it away from her, I'd be surprised if she doesn't buy enough drugs to overdose."

"Then why did you give it to her?" Surprise made my voice break. "If you knew it might be dangerous? Why?"

"Death isn't necessarily the worst thing that can happen to you. Besides," he shrugged, "she might do something else with it. Everything is a choice, isn't it?"

"Hey, chica, you might want to see this. Don't turn around. Look in the mirror."

What mirror, Spam? What am I looking at?

"On the ceiling. Check out Chambers' new friend."

I looked up to see that sections of the low ceiling were mirrored. If I scooted towards Quinn just a little and tilted my head at the right angle, I could see Ian Chambers.

He was talking to Nick.

I had to struggle not to stomp over and ask him what he was doing in a place like this. If Emily knew, she'd be so disappointed. But then, Nick might wonder what I was doing in a place like this. What was I doing here? Spying on Ian Chambers and making out with a total stranger in a scummy titty bar while my sister took care of her newborn, her twins and my child, that's what. What is wrong with me?

The only thing that I was sure of was that I had to get out of this place, and the sooner the better. Preferably without either Nick or Ian seeing me.

Hey, Spam. Where is the back door in this little shop of horrors?

"Kitchen."

The kitchen, of course, was at the end of the bar. Where Nick was chatting with Ian-Stop-Calling-Me Chambers.

What about the bathrooms?

They were just to the other side of the 'Employees Only' door.

"No door. Might be a window in the senoras bano, but I never been in there."

Could you go look?

Spam tried to cock his head at me, but it only sagged onto his shoulder.

Don't look at me like that. You owe me big time, Spam.

Muttering to himself in Spanish, he vanished.

I was very careful not to look into Quinn's eyes. That seemed to be where I got caught, just fell right in, like a mammoth in the La Brea Tar Pits. That, or when he touched me.

I stared at his hands. There was a slight webbing between his fingers. Not like duck feet – just at the base of his fingers, and extending maybe half an inch up. It was barely noticeable, unless I looked carefully.

"So. Quinn, you said we were looking for the same person. Why are you looking for Ian Chambers?"

"You first."

I risked glancing up at his face. He looked amused. I clenched my teeth and forced myself to take a deep breath before I spoke. Okay, Mr. Slippery. I'll bite, if that's what it takes to get you talking.

I twisted a few strands of hair around my finger. "I haven't been looking for him. We had a blind date – that night I saw you in Kemah – and now it seems like everywhere I go, he turns up." And so do you.

"Hmm. It seems you have some very—" he paused, choosing his next word carefully, "interesting friends."

"I'm baaack! Did you miss me, chica?" Spam reappeared across from Quinn.

Jeez! Stop doing that already. What did you find out?

"There's a tiny window just below the ceiling in the ladies' room, but if you go through the 'Employees Only' door, you can go behind the stage and out through the kitchen door." Spam said.

"Sounds like a terrific plan, Spam. I'm sure the bouncer won't mind at all if I go wandering around backstage." I spoke out loud, so Quinn could hear.

"Maybe if we're lucky, he'll put you to work." Spam grinned.

"Spam, I did what you asked me to. I put your wallet with your body and called in a tip to Crime Stoppers. Why are you still hanging around being a jerk? Aren't you supposed to go into the light or something now?"

Spam's grin faded considerably. "Unfinished business, chica. Unfinished business."

"That has nothing to do with me. Honestly, I don't know why I'm wasting any more of my time with you. You showed me that Ian Chambers hangs out in a cesspool. Big. Fat. Hairy. Deal," I grouched at him.

"You said you would help me. You gave your word," Spam said, each syllable an accusation. Infuriatingly, he vanished.

Quinn cleared his throat. "The bouncer won't mind you being backstage if he doesn't see you."

"And I suppose you're going to loan me your invisibility cloak?"

"No. It wouldn't work on you."

I couldn't tell if his half smile was serious or sarcastic.

"But," he continued, "What I am going to do is create a disturbance. Go to the ladies' room, and when you hear the bouncer run out of the 'Employees Only' door, go through it."

I've heard of worse plans.

"Do you want me to swing by the front and pick you up in the car?" I asked.

"I'll be fine. Don't worry about me."

A quick look into the ceiling mirror showed me that Nick was smiling and talking with his hands. Ian was pale and had dark circles under his eyes. He just nodded along as Nick spoke.

"Thanks." I made the mistake of making eye contact with Quinn. I could feel his kiss all over again and goose bumps popped up on my skin.

He closed his eyes – a long blink - and I glanced back towards Nick and Ian. "Well, those two seem busy enough. There's no time like the present." I got up, cringing as the fabric of my long shirt briefly stuck to the chair. I made my way to the bathroom as casually as I could.

The faded cherry veneer on the door was cracked and buckled, and the hinges squeaked like a startled mouse when I pushed the broken handle. I almost gagged. Specials needed a special plumber for their sewer gas problem. I left the door open just a crack, so I could get some fresh air and see when the bouncer, the one Spam had called Jericho, ran by. Within seconds, I heard glass breaking and a man shout. Did he really say, 'Hey, he stole my clothes!'?

The 'Employees Only' door opened and slammed shut. Heavy footsteps thudded on the worn carpeting towards the bar. Through the crack in the door, I could see the back of a large man moving quickly away from me. Keeping my back towards the fracas, I slipped through the other door.

The corridor was dim, and aged yellow linoleum crackled softly under my feet. A door on my left had 'Office' in peeling black letters on the frosted glass window. Another door to my right had an engraved plastic sign that read 'Stage.' I turned the handle and slowly pushed the door open.

The Marilyn Monroe dancer stood just off stage with her arms crossed, watching a woman in pleather writhing around the pole on stage. Maybe it had something to do with being away from Quinn, but she was back to looking human. She gave me a head-to-toe scan that made my skin crawl. It was more predatory than appreciative.

"You the new girl?" she asked.

"Kitchen. I'm helping in the kitchen." I said, backing away from her.

"Come back after your shift, sweet thing. I could make a meal out of you." She blew me a kiss.

Not today, lizard breath. I was not too proud to scurry like a rat behind the dusty curtains into the murky hallway that separated backstage from the kitchen. I could hear a dishwasher running, and something that sounded like deep-fat frying, but I didn't see anyone. I tip-toed to the exit and made a break for my car.

Behind Specials, there were a few employee parking spaces and a dumpster. An eight foot wooden fence blocked me from leaving in the direction of my car. I had to make my way down the driveway and take the long way back to where I was parked.

Bruce sat behind the steering wheel and whuffed when he saw me.

"Move over, you big lug. You can't drive." I was happy to see that sitting in the car for almost fifteen minutes hadn't harmed him.

Bruce squeezed into the back.

I tossed my purse into the passenger seat, then popped the trunk and raided the emergency baby change kit for a beach towel, which I used to cover the driver's seat. Then I emptied the water bowls onto a thirsty patch of grass. Bruce didn't seem to have drunk any of it, so I wondered why his head was wet. If it was drool, I didn't want to think about how it got between his ears.

I reached between the seats and patted the dog's chest. "You know, Bruce, it's pretty bad when a wet dog smells better than the place you've just been in."

I drove around the front of Specials, just in case, but there was no sign of either Quinn or an altercation. I still felt uneasy as I drove away.

"What do you think, Bruce? Think Quinn's all right? I know he said not to worry about him, but I hate leaving without knowing he's okay."

The crazy dog pushed his head between the two front seats and slobbered all over my neck, trying to lick my face.

"Okay, okay. We're going home."

Specials had a stench that went far deeper than surface grime, and I didn't want it in my house. I stripped naked and threw my clothes and the beach towel in the washer before I left the garage. I didn't like washing such a tiny load, but sometimes the bullet must be bitten. Bruce sat by the door and supervised.

I took a quick shower before he and I went to pick up Cassie. Emily asked me to stay for coffee, and Bruce exercised the boys in the back yard until dark. If Nick had noticed me at Specials earlier, he didn't say anything.

I was wiped out by the time we got home. It was too late, and I was too tired to put my mini-load on the clothesline, so I guiltily plopped it in the dryer. I fell asleep in the rocking chair, nursing Cassie. It wasn't anywhere near the first time I'd done that - I always put her in a sling during bedtime nummies for that very reason. It was close to midnight when I tucked her into her crib. I topped off Alpha and Betty's food and filled their water bottle on the way to my room.

"Come on Bruce." I yawned and patted the bed.

I felt the mattress sag as he jumped on it, but I was out before he finished getting comfortable.

I felt myself drifting up out of sleep. I was hot, sweating from the warm body snuggled up against me. I was lying on my right side and an arm, a male arm, draped across my waist and curled around me. Hot breath on the back of my neck made me quiver.

Relief washed over me like a warm shower. I'd been having this horrible dream where Ryan was dead. And now I was waking up and there he was, right where he belonged. I wanted to dance and shout. I snuggled up tighter against him.

Maybe I should wake him up.

I twisted a little so I could run my hand down his thigh. But something felt off. Some indefinable thing wasn't right. The joy (and lust) I had been feeling only a moment before started to congeal into cold little blobs of anxiety.

The warm body next to me stirred. The arm across my waist shifted, and the hand cupped around my shoulder.

I reached up and ran my fingers over that hand on my shoulder. There was no wedding band. My stomach lurched.

Then a word. A single word from dreaming male lips: "Siobhan"

Siobhan? Who the hell is Siobhan?

I shoved the arm off of me, sat up and snapped on the bedside lamp.

The silver lining was that Ryan wasn't having an affair with some chick named Siobhan.

The towering, five mile high, black-as-sin thunder cloud remained, however. What the freaking bloody hell was Quinn doing in my bed, laying there like a Playgirl centerfold?

Shock and disappointment were a one-two punch that took my breath away. I almost tripped myself up as I scrambled out of bed, taking the sheet with me to cover up my verging-on-transparent threadbare tee shirt.

Quinn squeezed his eyelids together, then rubbed them.

I hit him. On the shoulder, as hard as I could.

"What was that for?" he asked, opening one eye.

"What are you doing in my bed? Naked?"

"Lots of people sleep naked."

"Not in my bed." I shook my head.

Quinn sat up. A languid smile turned up the corners of his lips. "You invited me."

"I most certainly did not."

Quinn breathed in deeply, then he shimmered and flickered. In an instant, Bruce lounged in his place. He thumped his tail on the quilt and gave a low bark. Bruce shimmered and Quinn was back.

"Okay. I know I'm dreaming now. That did not just happen. It's a trick. You only see stuff like that in the movies. People don't just turn into dogs and back again."

"You're right. Humans don't. But I'm not human."

His dark, dark eyes fixed on mine. I felt like a deer in the headlights. I couldn't move, didn't want to move.

"W-What are you, then?" I stammered. Maybe I'm not awake, after all.

I felt his hold on me relax. When he smiled, there was a flash of sharp teeth, just like the very first time I saw him at the Kemah Aquarium. "I'm a kelpie."

I stared at him. Meant nothing to me.

"A water horse?" he tried again.

I shrugged.

"Surely you've heard of the Loch Ness Monster?"

"You're telling me that you are the Loch Ness Monster?" I arched an eyebrow and tilted my head away from him.

"Only once, when I was visiting my cousin, Vanessa. There are a lot of us, actually. Most large bodies of fresh water have lake monsters. Haven't you ever heard of Champ, the Lake Champlain monster? Or Tessie, in Lake Tahoe?"

Quinn stretched and put his hands behind his head. The move highlighted the well-defined muscles in his chest. I swallowed and looked away, remembering his kiss at Specials.

"Why don't you put some clothes on?" I asked. Less distracting that way.

"Why? Is this form not pleasing to you?" His eyes were bright, teasing me.

"I'm not in the habit of entertaining naked sea monsters in my bedroom." I tried on my best schoolmarm voice, but I could feel heat in my cheeks.

"Kelpies live in fresh water, not the ocean. Besides, I don't have any."

Funny, it looks to me like you've got some to spare. "Any what?" I was staring again. I tore my eyes away from his body.

"Clothes."

I sighed. I had never gotten around to donating Ryan's things to the homeless shelter. It didn't seem right, somehow, offering them to a stranger now. A stranger who had turned up in my bed in the altogether. But it seemed even less right to sit and talk to said naked stranger lying in my bed.

I went over to the dresser. I could feel Quinn's eyes on my back. It made my skin tingle, but how much of that was dread and how much was delight was hard to say. I didn't know what to think about Quinn. The whole turning into a dog thing had to be a trick, somehow. My mind flatly refused to accept that it was possible for a man to turn into a dog and back again, even if I did just see it happen.

"Here. Put these on," I said, handing a pair of cargo shorts and a t-shirt to Quinn. He was a little shorter and a little slimmer than Ryan, but the fit would probably be close enough.

"As you like."

I turned my back while he got dressed. Silly, I know. I'd already seen every blessed inch of him. I suppose what I didn't want to see was the way his muscles moved under his skin. Or the way he looked at me with those big, dark eyes that were so much like Ryan's.

"So. Tell me about kelpies," I said to him, my back still turned. I heard fabric slide on his skin and the zip and snap of shorts being fastened.

"We can take several forms. Normal, human, dog, horse."

"Horse! Was that you in my backyard on Sunday afternoon?"

"Yes. I needed to keep you from going inside. You can turn around now."

Seeing Quinn sitting on my bed, wearing Ryan's clothes, was almost as much of a shock as seeing him there naked. My hands flew to my mouth and I staggered back a step. I couldn't help the tears that spilled out of my eyes. The aching disappointment I had felt when I realized that I hadn't dreamed Ryan's death was sharper now.

Quinn came to me then, put his hands on my shoulders and kissed the top of my head, as if I were a child. "What makes you so sad, now?"

I pulled away from him. This was wrong, very wrong. I hardly knew the man. Or monster, if he was what he said he was. And yet, I could think of nothing I wanted more at that moment than to feel his arms around me.

That was when the dam burst and a river of tears flooded down my face, cascading onto my throat and soaking Quinn's shirt. I didn't care that he was hardly more than a stranger, and a very strange one, at that. I sobbed against his chest until I was dry.

"I'm sorry," I finally said. It felt good to be held by a man, and I wasn't quite ready to push him away.

"About what?" Quinn's voice was pure black velvet.

"When I woke up, and you were there, I thought…I thought you were Ryan, my husband, and that I'd only been dreaming that he was dead." I sniffled. "It's nothing against you," even if you are a sea monster, "I just thought I'd woken up from a nightmare and then found I hadn't. And what were you doing in my bed, anyway?"

I pulled away from him then, and he let me go. Part of me wished he hadn't.

"I told you – you invited me."

"No," I said, putting my hands on my hips, "I invited Bruce, the dog."

Quinn laughed. "Can't have one without the other, I'm afraid." Then his face became more serious. "I'm not offended. It is hard to lose a mate."

I suppose he meant that to be comforting, but it felt like he was mashing a bruise. I closed my eyes for a long moment.

A peek at the clock told me it was 4:27 AM. Cassie would be asleep for another couple of hours. Maybe I could get some answers from Quinn this time.

"Who is Siobhan?"

"She was...a colleague." Quinn closed his eyes and bit his bottom lip. "It's hard to explain to you. She was killed."

I wondered if he had ever kissed her the way he'd kissed me, and I was startled by this twinge of jealousy.

"I'm sorry," I said.

"She was—" he stopped himself. "It happens. She knew the risks when she accepted the job." Pain flickered across his eyes, but was quickly gone.

It was enough to stop me from asking any more questions about her, though, even if I was very curious what risks she knew about and how she ended up dead. I'd best change the subject.

"So. How do you know Ian Chambers?" I asked.

"I don't. It's his boss I'm looking for."

I folded my arms across my chest. "The District Attorney?" That wouldn't take much looking.

"His other boss. The one who pays for his beach house and his designer suits."

"Other boss? What are you saying? Are you telling me that you think Ian Chambers is dirty?" Cold fear gripped my innards. Why hadn't it occurred to me to wonder how Chambers had enough money to afford a beach house and a house in The Heights on an investigator's salary?

"I'm saying he plays both sides. He was the one who ransacked your house, by the way."

"What? Why would he do that?"

"I think that your husband might have had something of his, something that made him wonder what Chambers was up to. Once your husband died, Chambers probably thought people were done asking questions about him. But when I showed up, with more questions, he panicked and started trying to find whatever it is. He also bugged your house."

"Bugged my house? How do you know this?"

"Someone saw him. Under the back windows and the side one by the carport. They got blasted by the sprinklers though. Don't work anymore."

"I haven't been running the sprinklers."

Quinn smiled.

"Oh." I found I was gnawing on my thumbnail. "What could he be looking for? And why would Ryan have it? I don't think he even knew the guy."

But then I thought back to last night at Specials. Nick knew Ian Chambers well enough. And Ryan and Nick sometimes had a drink after work. Had Ryan known Chambers? I felt a little betrayed that Nick wouldn't mention this to me, even though there was no real reason why he should. And there was an unpleasant little shock when it occurred to me that Ryan might have gone to Specials with them.

I had to sit down, so I dropped myself on the cedar chest at the end of the bed with a thud.

"This second boss. Tell me about him."

"I'll tell you about him, chica. Calls himself Diablo. He was the one who had me killed!" Spam shouted, almost in my ear.

Startled, I fell off the chest, sprawling on the floor. "You've got to stop doing that!" I snarled at him as I picked myself up.

"What?"

"Just popping up out of nowhere and shouting at me. It's extremely annoying."

I suddenly became very conscious of being wrapped in a thin sheet over a verging-on- transparent threadbare shirt with two strange men in my room. Even though one of them was dead and one only looked like a man. Still felt uncomfortable.

"Spam, what did I tell you about hanging around my house? I'll deal with you later. Just go."

He glowered at me, but disappeared in a puff of wispy vapor.

I checked Cassie's room to make sure the noise hadn't woken her up. She was still blissfully a-snooze. I went back to my bedroom. And Quinn.

"Okay," I said to him as I sat on the bed. "Without waking the baby, tell me why you are looking for Ian Chambers' alleged second boss. Please."

"He took something from me. I need it back," Quinn said.

"What was that?"

"You wouldn't believe me if I told you."

"Try me. I've seen a lot of unbelievable things lately."

"What he stole is a small green bottle." Quinn took a deep breath and closed his eyes. "It's carved from a single chunk of emerald."

He avoided looking at me. There was something he wasn't telling me.

"What's in the bottle?"

"A djinn."

Chapter 13
Gate Crasher

—————————————⚬⚬⚬—————————————

"A DJINN? HE STOLE a djinn from you?" I asked. I immediately thought of one of Cassie's favorite picture books, *How the Camel Got His Hump*. "You mean like a swirling cloud of dust, a genie in a bottle, three wishes and all that?"

"Well, unbound djinn aren't obligated to give anyone any wishes. Some of them do it for their own entertainment, though."

I closed my eyes. I tapped my heels together three times. "There's no place like home. There's no place like home. There's no place like home."

When I opened my eyes, Quinn, in Ryan's clothes, was still sitting next to me on the bed, looking puzzled.

"What are you doing?" he asked.

"I seem to have fallen into the Twilight Zone, where a bunch of made up stuff, like sea monsters, ghosts and genies are real. I was just hoping to get home. It worked for Dorothy, anyway."

I smiled to cover up how scared I was. I had very clear ideas about what was fact and what was fiction, and now someone was changing the rules on me.

Quinn crossed his arms and glared at me before he got up and strode to the other side of the room. When he spoke, his voice was deeper, rougher. "Made-up stuff? I find that very offensive. My kind have been around long before you hairless apes showed up. I'm the one who pointed out Jupiter's moons to Galileo, and I'm not even middle-aged yet. Just because you are ignorant, that's no excuse to go around insulting people, especially people who have been trying to help you."

His eyes flickered, and the near-black iris suddenly bled across his entire eye, swallowing up any traces of white. I was afraid of him then. At that moment, I absolutely believed he could shift into something monstrous. I was scared, and yet…I didn't want him to go. Every logical brain cell in my head screamed at me to tell him to leave and never come back, call 911 if I had to, anything just to get him gone.

Instead, I apologized.

"I'm sorry. I was brought up being told that there was no such thing as ghosts. That sea monsters were just misidentified animals or flotsam. That fairy tales are nothing more than cautionary stories for children. It's really, really hard to accept that you are what you say you are, even if I did actually see you change into a dog. You don't understand how hard this is for me to believe. I didn't mean to offend you." What was I thinking?

Quinn's eyes softened, but his arms stayed crossed. "We get that a lot. That's why most of us don't even bother interacting with humans."

"Okay, let's just rewind and start over. Why don't you tell me more about kelpies? What do they eat? How do they spend their time?"

"Okay, a do-over works for me. Kelpies are solitary fae, and we have to live near water. What we eat depends on what form we've taken. If I'm a horse, I eat grass."

"When you're a dog, you don't eat dog food."

"Have you ever tasted dog food?"

"Point taken. What about when you're in normal kelpie form, whatever that may be?"

Quinn put his hands on top of his thighs, and then found a loose thread on the comforter to pick at. "Whatever that may be?" he quoted me. "Come on. Everyone's seen the infamous Surgeon's Photo of the Loch Ness Monster."

"Wasn't that a hoax?"

"No, not at all. But it was important for people to think it was. Chris Spurling was good enough to confess to making the model and naming the other so-called hoaxers, who had conveniently died. As to what we eat, you know. The normal stuff. Fish. Humans. Livestock."

"Wait! Did you just say 'humans?'"

"Well, not me, really. Humans give me terrible indigestion, so I go out of my way to avoid them. It's been years since the last time. Seriously."

"So what you're saying is that you could turn into a monster at any moment and gobble up my daughter and I?"

"Technically." Quinn's jaw worked from side to side. "But you know how some people can't have dairy products? Same for me with humans."

"Really? The only reason you haven't eaten us is because you're lactose intolerant? I'm not sure how to respond to that."

"No. That's not the only reason. Besides, how many times have I protected you from Ian Chambers already? If I was planning to hurt you, I would have done it ages ago. We could help each other. We're both trying to find the same guy."

"No. You're trying to find him. I'm going to talk to Nick, let him handle it through official channels. I don't need to get involved in taking down Ian Chambers and his alleged second boss."

Quinn laughed quietly. "Do you really think Nick will believe anything bad about Chambers? Your husband was suspicious of him; he must have known something. Otherwise Chambers wouldn't have turned your house over. Aren't you the least bit curious?"

"Not if it puts my daughter at risk." I crossed my arms, now.

"Hate to break it to you, but she's already at risk, and so are you. If Chambers gets desperate enough, he'll use any leverage he can find."

"So you're saying that I have no choice but to trust you?" I resented being pushed into a corner by anybody. "I don't think so. Nick may not want to believe anything bad about Chambers, but he's not unreasonable. And if he doesn't want to listen to me, I'll take it to Captain Helmsley. Somebody, somewhere will listen to me."

"Maybe. If you had proof. But what are you going to tell them? A sea monster told you that Chambers was a bad guy?" The corners of Quinn's mouth curled up into a mocking smirk.

"You said it yourself: Ryan hid something in the house. If I could find it..."

Quinn sat back down on the bed. "But you don't even know what it is."

"Well, maybe Chambers got it. He won't have any reason to come after me, then."

"Are you willing to bet your life on that? Cassie's life?"

"Then tell me what you think Ryan had. Tell me what you know about Chambers' other boss."

"That's the problem. I don't know. Ryan must have had something small – but that could be anything – a piece of jewelry, a photo, a thumb drive." Quinn threw up his hands. "And his master? That's even trickier. I know he's somewhere in the Greater Houston Area, which narrows it down to about five million people. Lots of visitors come and go from Chambers' place. One of them might be the boss man. Or not. I can't just walk up and ask them, now can I? I do know this – Mr. X has his fingers in a lot of pies, but drugs and prostitutes are his main source of income, and he has some very dangerous friends."

"And you know this how?"

"I've seen Boris Cherngelanov going into his house. He's the top dog in the local Russian brotherhood."

"Brotherhood?"

"Mafia."

I got up and stalked to the sliding glass door. I looked for the pot of red zinnias on the bistro table that took up most of the small patio. I could see nothing but reflections of the room and myself in the dark glass, and I watched Quinn watching me. I saw him get up and come stand behind me, too close. He didn't touch me, just looked out the window over my shoulder. My body was aware of him, though. My skin tingled and the little hairs along my arms stood up, alerted by danger and desire. Damned gonads. I dug my fingernails hard into the palm of my hand, trying to draw blood, trying to distract myself. Punishment for wanting him.

"What do you see?" His voice was not much more than a whisper.

"Dark."

Quinn reached past me to the light switch and flicked it off. As he brought his hand back to his body, he brushed his fingertips close to my forehead, just like he did at Specials. "Look again," he said.

Now there were small lights, like fireflies, except they didn't flicker on and off, floating around the zinnias on the table. Two young ladies in gossamer dresses were sitting in the bistro chairs, chatting away. When the light went off, they looked up briefly and smiled, most likely at Quinn, since they probably had no idea I could see them. As I looked beyond the patio, I could see dozens, maybe even hundreds of little lights dancing around the plants all the way to the back of the garden. I felt like I had fallen into a Disneyland version of my own backyard.

"What is this? Why are there people sitting on my patio, and who are they?" I tried to turn towards him, but his cool, strong hands on my shoulders stopped me.

"They're dryads. The one on the left is from the pine tree, the other is from the oak. They like your patio."

"What about the little glowing things buzzing around the flowers?"

"Flower fae. They're a little bit like guardian angels for plants."

"Is this like at Specials, with the succubus? You did something to make me see them?"

"Yes. There's a whole universe of things, Marti, that most humans have no awareness of. I've seen how you treated Bruce, how you treat Alpha and Betty. I watched you try to help the bird that got hit by a car. Your yard is a giant butterfly garden. I thought maybe you were one of those rare few who would be willing to help."

"Help? Help with what?"

"Shifting the balance. There are those - some human, some not – who prefer darkness to light. Right now, they seem to be winning."

I looked at Quinn's reflection in the glass. His face looked serious, earnest, somber. "I think you need a super hero, not a single mom. Sounds too lofty for someone like me."

"It isn't that lofty, not if everybody that can does a little bit." There was a note of something that might have been longing in his voice.

I frowned at the darkness and picked at my thumbnail.

Quinn continued. "The guy that Chambers is working for is very bad, even by human standards. The thought of him with a djinn is unbelievably horrifying."

He took a step back from me.

I immediately felt the empty space where he had been, and I sighed. "You really want your djinn back, don't you?"

"He isn't mine. His name is Malik. He has a family, and he doesn't deserve to be a prisoner. He also doesn't deserve what will happen to him if Chambers' boss finds a sahir willing to work for him."

"A sahir? What is a sahir, and what would one of those do to him?" I kept watching the dancing lights around the flowers. Were those really there all the time?

"A sahir is a sorcerer that specializes in djinn. He knows how to bind one to an object, enslaving the djinn. Can you imagine what would happen if a bad guy, a really bad guy, had unlimited power?"

"I thought you said they didn't have to grant wishes if they didn't want to."

"I said unbound djinn are not obligated to. Bound djinn are a different story. What if the first wish is to be emperor of the world?"

"People wouldn't stand for it. They'd fight back."

"What if they forgot they had ever lived any other way?"

I whirled to face him, fantasy panorama forgotten. "That's impossible! He couldn't do that."

Quinn shimmered and changed into Bruce, who looked utterly ridiculous in Ryan's shorts and tee shirt. He came to me and licked my hand. Suddenly Quinn stood in his place, so close I could feel the heat from his body. "Don't try to tell me about impossible. You don't know the half of it." His voice had a hard edge to it, and what had been so funny a moment before was now deadly serious.

My jaw clenched. There was no need for him to talk down to me. "If this is so apocalypse/Armageddon/end-of-the-world important, why are you trying to do this on your own?"

"I'm not. But we could use all the help we can get. Besides, we have a fallback position. You don't."

Even in the pre-dawn gloom, I could see his face was drawn, as if he knew more than he was saying, shielding me from the worst of it. I wanted to reach out to him, but I didn't dare.

"I need to think," I said.

Quinn nodded and slipped away from me through the darkness. He closed the bedroom door behind him. A little part of me was mad that he had left so easily, didn't want to stay with me. In my bedroom. That little part was going to get me into trouble, no doubt about it.

I sat on the bed and watched the dancing lights in the backyard. I thought it was rude to stare at the two young ladies sitting at my bistro table, but I let my eyes pass over them from time to time. I wondered if they would talk to me, or just run away if I went outside. Surely, this was just a dream. None of it could possibly be real. And yet...the heat of Quinn's body against my skin hadn't felt at all like imagination. If this was a dream, there was no harm in exploring. If it was real, well, that was a little tougher.

I tried to get my head around Quinn's nightmare scenario. Bad guy with unlimited power. Evil world dictator. And genie power. But it was just too fantastical, too unreal. I couldn't make that leap. In a book or a movie, sure. In the real world? I couldn't believe it. My eyelids started to get heavy, and I was afraid that if I went to sleep, I wouldn't be able to see the dryads and fairies anymore when I woke up. I decided to step outside and see what would happen.

My hand was on the lever lock of the door when the dryads stopped talking and looked sharply at the back of the yard. Something large was moving in the dark. It trotted towards the door. As it moved past flowerbeds, the little dancing lights were extinguished. The dryads fled. The shape seemed doglike, and for a second, I wondered if it was Quinn. As it got closer, it broke into a lope, covering the short distance with long strides. It stopped at the glass and peered up at me.

The thing was huge, and at first I might have thought it was a timber wolf. But there was something about its proportions that was not right – body too long, chest too heavy. The distorted canid rose onto its hind legs and stood like a man. Its huge paws slid on the door like hands, searching for a handle. Heavy claws screeched on the slick surface. Less than six inches away from my face, fierce teeth glinted in the dying moonlight as slavering lips pulled back into a snarl. Hot breath fogged the glass, but I could still see its eyes, glowing like campfire embers.

Run! Get away, now! Flight response had kicked in. Except that my feet weren't listening.

I could have sworn the beast smiled before it took a few steps backward, then threw itself at the door. The frame creaked, and the house shuddered. It backed up and tried again. This time, the first layer of the double glazing cracked. I was too terrified to breathe, let alone move.

I had the distinct impression that this monster wanted to get at me for no reason other than the sheer delight it would feel in watching me die in a horror-fest of blood and gore. And there seemed to be nothing I could do about it. Would it be satisfied with me, and leave Cassie alone? I thought of my baby, asleep in her crib, and rage flowed through me. If I was going down, I was going to take this thing with me. It was not going near Cassie, not while I was still breathing.

I started a mental inventory of possible defensive weapons. Both Ryan's Sig Sauer pistol and his grandfather's silver-inlaid kiem sword were packed safely away in the attic. Didn't matter – I had no time to get to them, and I didn't have any bullets for the gun, anyway.

The weird wolf backed up again, getting ready to make another run at the cracked glass.

The bedroom door opened, and the creature paused. It seemed to be looking over my shoulder.

"Whatever you do, do not turn around," Quinn said, not far behind me.

You can count on that. The air around me suddenly went cold and damp. It felt like I was standing in heavy fog, only everything looked the same. Fear crawled across my skin like a nest of spiders. I didn't have to look at Quinn to know he'd turned into his kelpie form. There wasn't enough money on the planet for me to turn around and see that. But instinct got the better of me, and I turned to look at the grey blur of motion in the mirror. I whipped my head back around, even putting my hand to the side of my face to block my peripheral vision. But not before I caught a glimpse of a long neck and a crocodile-like snout.

The monster outside twisted its head from side to side, then cowered and slunk away.

I swallowed hard, and noticed my breath was coming in fast, shallow bursts. I felt Quinn's hand on my shoulder. At least, I hoped it was a hand.

"Are you okay?"

I turned and melted against him, gasping in deep ragged breaths of air to stop the hyperventilation. He caught me when my knees buckled, and carried me to the bed.

"What was that?" I hated the way my voice quivered and broke.

"Seriously? I thought everybody'd heard of werewolves."

"There's no such thing as werewolves."

"Go outside and tell him that."

I looked at the cracked glass and started shaking. I tried to stand up, but my legs were pure gelatin, and I fell back on the bed.

"Where are you going?" Quinn asked.

"I need to check on Cassie."

"She's fine."

"I need to see her."

Quinn sighed. "Stay here."

He got up, silent as a shadow, and came back a moment later with a sleeping Cassie in his arms. He put her gently on the bed next to me. She groaned and rolled over. Tears of relief rained onto the quilt. I didn't want to cry, but the tears were cleansing, washing away the fear and evil that had shrouded me only a few minutes ago.

I knew if I touched her too much, it would chase the sleep away, but I kissed the top of her head and caressed her cheek anyway. Her nose twitched.

Quinn handed me a tissue. "You don't want to wake her up with Chinese water torture, now do you?"

I snorted, and Cassie opened her eyes. She started to cry, but I scooped her up and took her to the rocking chair. It didn't take long to get her to sleep. I decided there wasn't much point in going back to bed, so I put my baby in her crib and headed toward the kitchen, with Quinn close behind me.

"Coffee?" I asked as I filled the carafe.

"No, thanks."

"How do you like your eggs?" I normally avoided cooking as much as possible, except when I was nervous. It gave me something to do, and everybody has to eat.

"Scrambled," Quinn answered.

I heated olive oil in the skillet while I beat the daylights out of four innocent little eggs and a tablespoon of water.

"Could you find the garlic press for me?" I pointed to one of the drawers under the countertop closest to him.

I peeled two cloves of garlic while Quinn rummaged around in the drawer. He finally chose something and held it out to me.

"That would be a citrus reamer. A garlic press is a squeezy thing with handles and a basket."

"This?"

"Yep."

I deliberately brushed my hand over his when I took the gadget. I studied his face, checking for any reaction. One eyebrow twitched. That was something, anyway.

I added salt, pepper and garlic to the eggs and poured them into the hot pan. My stomach growled as the warm smell of cooking eggs filled the kitchen. I popped a couple of slices of bread in the toaster.

I looked at Quinn. "Why do you suppose that a werewolf was using himself as a battering ram at my side door? Do you think Chambers' boss is into them, too?"

"Don't know. It may not have anything to do with Chambers. Could be someone trying to set me up."

"How so?"

"Kill you and Cassie, make it look like I did it."

"Why?"

"That's a whole 'nother story. Let's just say 'revenge' and leave it at that. There are some individuals who are not above framing me for something I didn't do." Quinn frowned, "I don't think Chambers knows about me, not yet, anyway." Then he shook his head. "Werewolves are demonic, so there could be a demon behind the attack. And demons would definitely do something like that."

Demons. Oh, good. Because I need more problems in my life just now.

I dished out the eggs and got a jar of orange marmalade from the fridge.

"Your friend at the metaphysical shop. Is she any good at warding?" Quinn asked.

"I don't even know what that is."

I spread marmalade on my toast, pretending we weren't having a conversation about werewolves attacking my house.

"Protection spells."

"Spells. Right. I can ask her." Well, we've already got fairies, werewolves and lake monsters. Why not witches, too?

"I know you're getting a burglar alarm installed. That'll help against bad humans, but it isn't much use against demons, though. As soon as it gets light, I need to go out. Not sure when I'll be back, but definitely before dark."

"Is that a good idea? I mean, if this werewolf is looking for you, maybe you shouldn't be here." I shuddered, remembering the fangs on that thing.

Quinn frowned. "It knows I'm here. But it won't take me on without its pack, if it has one. Besides, what if Ian Chambers comes back to finish what he started on Sunday? Do you want to be here by yourself, you and your baby?"

I liked the idea of Quinn/Bruce being around, but I couldn't help but wonder why he did it. There must have been a dozen other ways for him to follow Ian Chambers without involving me.

"What if he found whatever he was looking for?"

"What if he didn't? Besides, I could be wrong. The werewolf may have come for you. Maybe Chambers knows more than I think he does. Wouldn't surprise me if Chambers' boss is the kind who'd make an alliance with demons."

"A pact with the devil?"

"The devil? I don't know what that is, but long story short, demons existed in an ancient, unstable universe that ripped itself apart. Demons are all about chaos and destruction. They shouldn't be here, except some managed to crawl through a hole in time – something I believe you'd call a wormhole."

Sci-fi, too. It just keeps getting better. I picked up a scrambled egg curd and popped it into my mouth. I swallowed it, and wished I wasn't out of orange juice.

"So I'm between a rock and a hard place then. It's dangerous if you stay, dangerous if you don't." If Ryan's parents were still alive, I'd go stay with them for a while in Vermont. I just wished I could take Cassie and get the hell out of Dodge right now.

"Looks that way," Quinn said around a mouthful of toast.

I stabbed viciously at a clot of egg. "I never had these problems until I started dabbling in this stupid card-reading psychic stuff."

"Ian Chambers has been a problem for a while. You just didn't know it."

"Maybe. But I didn't fish a wallet out of a nasty dumpster for him." Or tamper with a crime scene. I really hope you appreciate that, Spam.

Quinn shook his head, a hint of a smile on his mouth.

I stared out the bay window, and noticed that the black silk night had started to fade to grey. Pink and gold smudges peeked through the neighbor's trees, letting me know that the werewolf-banishing sun was on its way. At least that's how I hoped it worked, anyway.

"I guess you'll be going soon," I said.

"Yeah. You could say I have to see a man about a dog."

I groaned.

"Ma da da maaaaa!" Cassie shouted from her crib.

"I'll be right back," I said.

When I returned with Cassie on my hip, she took one look at Quinn and squealed. "Booce!"

Chapter 14
One Small Step

⚶

"HOW DID—?" I SHOOK my head. "That's not possible."

"Babies remember a lot, but they can't talk about it. By the time they can talk about it, they've mostly forgotten," Quinn said. He smiled and waved at Cassie.

"What could babies possibly remember?"

"Where they came from before they came here."

"You mean Heaven?"

"If that's what you want to call it." He got up and surveyed the backyard. "I think it's light enough that you'll be safe, now. I'll be back before dark."

He didn't wait for me to answer before he pushed open the door and was gone. Part of me was glad he was gone, and part of me wanted to run after him. I'd wanted to ask him more questions, but they'd have to wait. Besides, I had a hungry baby to feed. A beautiful baby who meant the world to me.

"Girlfriend, what did I say about putting on that amulet?" Delilah stood in front of me, hands on hips.

"I wondered where you'd gotten to. We've been having some excitement around here."

I was a little cross with her for poofing in with some cryptic message, then poofing out again before I could get any answers.

I purposely walked right through Delilah, heading towards my rocking chair. Felt like stepping in to a walk-in freezer. Cassie's shiver pricked me with guilt.

"That's what I'm talking about, girl," Delilah said, drifting along behind me. "You need to be a little less excited 'bout that shifter."

I sat down, got myself ready, and Cassie latched on hungrily. It felt like she was going to suck my spine out, as well.

"What are you talking about, Delilah?"

Her hands went from her hips to across her chest. "Your new boyfriend, that shapeshifter. Can't nobody trust a shifter. That's why Lulu gave you that amulet, girl. It keeps a shifter from shifting, but you have to wear it. It don't do nobody no good sitting in your glove box."

"I don't need the attitude, thanks. If you and Lulu want me to know something, why don't you just come out and tell me, instead of making me guess at your crazy riddles? And then you act like I'm stupid if I don't know what you're talking about."

Cassie squirmed and complained, but didn't let go. Could she taste my irritation?

I patted her back and took a few deep breaths. The baby settled in and started feeding in earnest. That child must be having another growth spurt.

Then I had an idea. "What about werewolves? Does that charm work against them?"

Delilah's outline shivered. "Werewolves. Girlfriend, they are some bad juju. They ain't natural. But you know, silver the only thing can hurt them."

"A werewolf tried to knock down my door this morning."

"I know that."

"Then you also know that Quinn scared it away."

"Girl, how do you know those two ain't friends?"

"If Quinn wanted to hurt me, he's had lots of opportunities." I surprised myself at how quickly I came to his defense.

Delilah glowered at me while I switched Cassie to the other side. I decided the subject needed changing. "So. Do you know if Lulu is any good at warding?" I asked.

"Pretty good. She kept your boyfriend out of her shop." Smirking was not attractive on Delilah.

"I wish you'd stop referring to him as my boyfriend. It isn't like that. His name is Quinn."

"You mean it isn't like that...yet." One thinly plucked eyebrow arched smugly.

"And what's it to you, anyway? I'm a grown woman. I can do whatever, whomever, I want," I snapped back at her.

Cassie started to cry, but whether it was because I was dry or angry, I couldn't tell. I stormed past Delilah into the kitchen to get yogurt and cereal for my little girl.

Thankfully, the ghost didn't follow me, and I was able to cool down a little. I got Cassie ready to go for our walk. Wouldn't hurt to ask Lulu about the warding. I knew that Amanda wouldn't find anything in the water I had asked her to test, so there wasn't any reason to avoid The Tenth Sphere. Truth was, I kind of missed the shop. Maybe I'd even do the mediumship circle tomorrow night, if Mom was available to stay with Cassie.

The Tenth Sphere was still closed when we walked past it. It seemed weird, not having Bruce, or rather, Quinn, with us. He was, as they say, conspicuous by his absence. I hadn't counted on that.

The humidity made the air tangible and the morning sun bright and thick, crouching on my shoulders like the Old Man of the Sea. By the time we had finished our loop and made it back to the shop, I had made a valiant effort to convince myself that I'd imagined the whole werewolf adventure. The cowbell jangled more loudly than I remembered when I opened the door and pushed the stroller inside.

Lulu popped up from behind the counter. "Marti! Where've you been, honey?" She looked behind me, out the door. Her eyes narrowed a little. "Where's that dog? Did he run away?" She almost looked hopeful.

"Cassie and I have just been hanging, doing lunch. That sort of thing." I thought about the anti-shifter amulet, and wondered if I was taking the right approach. "No, Bruce hasn't run away. So. Tell me what makes you think he's a shapeshifter." I smiled, kept my voice even, non-accusatory.

Lulu smiled back. "He just has that look about him. Guess you could call it his aura. Are you okay? He hasn't tried anything, has he?"

"What do you mean?" I figured playing dumb would get more information than starting out with details.

"I mean fae are dangerous. Humans are easily enthralled by them. They can make anything seem like a really good idea – jumping off a bridge, playing in traffic, having sex with them."

Enthralled…was that what I felt when Quinn looked at me? "I see. And just for argument's sake, what would be so dangerous about having sex with them?"

"No. Please tell me you haven't…"

"Lulu. He's a dog. Not my type."

She frowned slightly. "It isn't uncommon for people to die."

"Die! Seriously? Why?" Reflexively, I glanced at Cassie. She was too busy gnawing on Mr. Buns' ear to get up to anything else. Please, teeth. Hurry up.

"When the faery consort leaves, and they always do, the abandoned human often pines away and dies. They lose all interest in the Mundane world and human lovers."

I couldn't resist. "Once you've had fae, there's no other way?"

"It's not a joke, Marti. That's why I gave you the amulet. If he is what I think he is, and shifts into human form, do not, under any circumstances, let him touch you."

Too late for that. "He saved me from a werewolf last night."

Her eyes narrowed. "Did he tell you it was a werewolf, or did you actually see it?" Lulu wasn't cutting Quinn any slack.

"It was hurling itself against my patio door. It was clearly a werewolf."

Lulu scowled, and it was a minute or so before she answered. "Werewolves and fae are usually chalk and cheese. But stranger alliances have been made."

Because it's perfectly normal to have werewolves in the back yard and lake monsters in the kitchen. "Well, Delilah's not too crazy about him, either."

"Good for her."

The bell on the door clanged, and the UPS man pushed a dolly with two boxes up to the counter. He left them near the cash register.

"Have a good one, Ms. Miranda," the deliveryman nodded at Lulu as he left.

"B! Your shipment is here!"

Belinda fairly burst out of the 'Employees Only' door. She struggled to lift one of the boxes onto the counter, then sliced it open with a pair of scissors. "Oh, they're beautiful!" she cried as she pulled out a paperback book.

Lulu handed one to me. The title, Dragon by Knight, and the author's name, Coda Sterling, graced the cover in light green. A very hot guy, wearing only jeans and holding a large sword, stood in front of a seaside castle. Over his shoulder, a dragon flew underneath the full moon.

The bell jangled again, and a group of women came in. I recognized the one with the turban from the mediumship circle last week. Today, the hat was turquoise. In the daylight, I realized that her eyebrows were drawn on with pencil, not because they were plucked, but because she didn't have any. No eyelashes, either. Chemo. I wondered what kind of cancer she had.

"I saw the UPS truck. Are they here yet?" she asked.

Lulu hugged her. "Ellen! Great to see you, honey. How are you feeling?"

"Today's a good day. I'm so glad I could make it out and get a copy of Belinda's latest, hot off the presses."

Belinda's latest?

"This one's kind of steamy – you may need a cold shower," Belinda joked.

She took a pen from the cup by the cash register and signed the book in her hand – "To Ellen. Fight the good fight! Love, Coda Sterling" She signed books for the other four women, who lined up to pay. Lulu refused to take any money from Ellen.

"I have to run, sweetie. I'm due at Anderson in twenty-five," she said.

Belinda squeezed her hand. "You let us know what the doctor says, you hear?"

Ellen smiled and nodded. With that, the ladies trooped out the door. I hoped if I was older and sick that I'd have friends that took me to the hospital and sat with me. Well, I certainly wouldn't if I kept pushing them away, I scolded myself. I sighed and looked down at Cassie, who was bashing the now soggy Mr. Buns on the stroller tray.

I was curious about Ellen, but I thought it would be too tacky to ask. I guess Lulu could tell, because she said, "Ellen's had a setback. Her breast cancer had been in remission for four years, but then she developed leukemia from the chemo. She just got out of the hospital for chemo on that, and now they may have to remove her spleen."

"AML – Acute Myeloid Leukemia?" I nodded knowingly, although it was something I'd only heard of, not seen – most of the time, they went straight to M.D. Anderson, since it's the cancer research hospital. But I knew the prognosis wasn't usually very good.

The cozy atmosphere in the store had turned grim. I wanted to shake it off as best I could, so I turned to Belinda. "I didn't know you were an author."

She blushed. "Well, it's just something I do on the side, really."

I turned the book I still held in my hand over and scanned the back. It looked like it was a bodice ripper set in medieval times, with knights and dragons and all the trappings. But maybe not.

After a chance encounter with a devastatingly handsome knight, Lisabeth Stuart finds herself at the Dragon's Lair Pleasure Faire resort in Galveston. She's supposed to be reporting back to her investor cousin, but she's hoping to enjoy the merriment and feasting, and especially time with the mysterious and delectable Sir Tristan. Just when Lisabeth starts to think she's found exactly what she wants, old enemies and even older secrets threaten to take everything from her. Will finding true love save her…or kill her?

"I'll buy your book. Looks interesting." I am normally not into romance novels, but I thought it was cool to have a signed copy of a book written by someone I knew.

Belinda signed it – "To Marti – Look for the dragons in the world. Love, Coda Sterling"

While Lulu was ringing me up, she said, "Belinda and I were talking. With all the classes we've got going on, we're up to our eyeballs with paperwork. We were thinking it might be good to get someone in part time, like half a day, two or three days a week. That gives me some space to do all the back-room stuff during the day instead of staying up late to do it. I was wondering if you might be interested? Of course, you can bring your little princess." She smiled at Cassie, who shouted "Ma da da da ma ning!" Ning? That's new.

"Oh," I said. Her offer surprised me a little. "What would I be doing?"

"Mostly running the till. Maybe a little re-stocking, answering the phone. That sort of thing."

"Can I sleep on it?"

"Of course you can. Oh, listen. There's a new product we're trying. Totali-TEA. You want to have a sample and tell us what you think?"

"Sure, why not?" Cassie was back to chewing on Mr. Buns and didn't seem at all bothered about hanging with Lulu and Belinda. Having tea would give me a chance to ask Lulu about warding. I sat down in the cypress root chair while Lulu disappeared into the back.

The bell jangled, and an older couple came in. Belinda showed them some salt lamps.

The Tenth Sphere was busier than I thought it would be on a Wednesday morning. That was good. I was 99% sure I would accept Lulu's job offer, and having worked retail in college, I knew busy was better.

"Here you go, honey." Lulu handed me a cup of hot tea.

"Thanks." The tea smelled wonderful and floral. I guessed it had lavender and jasmine flowers in it. I filled the spoon and blew on it, trying to cool the tea down enough that it wouldn't scald my palate. "So, Lulu. About the werewolf that showed up last night. Would you happen to know anyone who might know how to do some warding to keep it out of my yard?"

"Oh, I could do that for you, no problem. How about this evening, when the shop closes?"

"That would be great. The tea is excellent, by the way." It ought to be for $16.99 a box.

It was almost 3:30 and there was no sign of Quinn. Cassie was having her afternoon nap, and I lazed on the couch with Belinda's book. I could see what she meant about the cold shower. I would never look at Belinda the same way again. The book wasn't actually set in medieval times, but at an adults-only Renaissance-themed resort. With an actual dragon.

I heard scratching at the door. Quinn, in the form of Bruce, sat panting on the back porch. I opened the door for him.

"You could just open the door and come on in."

The dog shimmered and Quinn stood next to me. "What would the neighbors think?" He smiled at me, and I smiled back at him. Enthralled?

"Did you talk to your friend about the warding?" he asked.

"Good afternoon to you, too."

Quinn was unfazed. "I hope that's a yes."

"Lulu's coming this evening after the shop closes."

"Good. We managed to track the werewolf. And you wouldn't believe where he went."

Before I could ask where, Cassie began to wail. After a dry diaper and a snack, she was a much happier camper. We sat in the living room while Cassie cruised around the furniture and cooed at Quinn. Apparently, he wasn't comfortable talking about werewolves in front of a soon-to-be eleven-month old baby.

BamBamBamBamBam! Sombody or something was banging on the back door.

I froze, and I was sure my heart stopped.

"Aunt Marti! Aunt Marti! Can we play with Bruce?"

I think that was the most grateful I've ever been to hear Kyle and Aiden shouting at the tops of their lungs.

Quinn shifted into dog form and beat me to the back door. At four in the afternoon on a summer day in Houston, it wouldn't take long for the heat to suck the life right out of them. Cassie tried to keep up, but she couldn't crawl nearly as fast as they could run.

So she got up and walked.

Not very well or very far, but she had taken her first unassisted steps. This called for a celebration.

"Hey, guys! Do you want popsicles or ice cream sandwiches?" I shouted to the boys.

"Popsicles!"

I got one for each child and an ice cream sandwich for myself. Had to take a picture of Cassie, who got more of the popsicle on her than in her. I felt genuinely happy. Except for Lulu's warning about Quinn, which kept buzzing at the edges of my consciousness like a mosquito at three AM. Every time I get any warm fuzzies towards Quinn, I questioned whether it was real or I was just enthralled by him. True, he had been protecting me, but was it only because he thought he needed me to help find his emerald jar?

According to the old clock/thermometer/hygrometer on the wall, Lulu'd be here in half an hour, give or take.

I picked up a tennis ball that lay near my feet. "Bruce! Here, boy."

He came bounding up to me, and I threw the ball. He caught it on the second bounce and brought it back to me. I scratched his ears and lowered my voice to a whisper. "Lulu's coming soon. I'm going to do something you may not like, but you have to trust me. I'll explain it to you when she's gone. We need to talk, anyway."

I threw the ball again, but he didn't fetch it. Hackles raised, he barked and snarled at the back gate. Nick had started to open it, but reconsidered.

"Easy, there, boy," he said.

That just made Bruce/Quinn snarl louder.

"Bruce! Come!"

He grudgingly came and plopped himself down at my feet with a grunt. His eyes stayed on Nick.

"That's just the kind of dog you need, Marti." Nick did not come into the yard. "Boys! Come wash up for supper!"

"Bye, Aunt Marti! Thanks, Bruce!"

Nick was gone before I even had a chance to tell him Cassie had taken her first steps. I was bursting to tell someone. Maybe I'd get a chance to call Mom before Lulu showed up. I got my car keys and got the anti-shifting amulet from my car. I felt bad putting it on, but I didn't want to risk Quinn taking human form and talking to her while she was here. And I wanted Lulu to feel like her advice had been taken.

Bruce/Quinn's dejected eyes said it all as the three of us went back into the relative cool of the house. I didn't want to hurt him, and I very nearly took the amulet off, even had my hand on it, when Lulu knocked at the door.

"This is what I was talking about earlier. Please trust me." I tried to pat him on the head, but he avoided my touch. What have I done?

Lulu had a fabric shopping bag slung over her shoulder. "Wow. You've really done some updates on this house. It looks so modern on the inside."

The house may be twice my age, but it's paid for. "Well, Ryan did most of the work. He said that it was like a moving meditation, very zen and all that. He was Buddhist."

"Honey, I don't want to be rude, but I've had something come up and I need to do this quickly. Can we start in back?"

"I hope it's nothing too serious." I shifted Cassie to the other hip and led the way to the back yard.

Lulu rolled her eyes and shook her head. "There's a turf war going on between my Home Owners Association incumbent president and the challenger. Lot of BS, if you ask me, but since I'm the secretary, I have to show up at the meetings, even if they only give me three hours' notice."

Bruce/Quinn slunk along behind us. He was going to be mad at me for a while. I hoped he'd get over it.

Lulu went to the northeast corner of the backyard. She pulled out a small yellow cotton bag. Quartz crystals and some dried leaves peeked out of the top of it. She lit some dried sage and placed it in a censer. She muttered something about 'spirits of air,' then pulled out a trowel. She lifted off the layer of sod like a pro, and when she was done burying the bag, I couldn't even tell there had been a hole.

Next we visited the southeast corner, in the front yard, where she buried a red bag; the southwest corner where she buried a blue bag; and the northwest corner, where she buried a green bag. The sage smoke reminded me of stuffing, and I wondered for a second what I was going to do about supper.

"Okay, honey," Lulu said. "That should fix you up. Never can tell about werewolves, though. Some of them are strong enough to punch through the best wardings."

I scooped up Cassie, led Lulu through the gate and out to the sidewalk. Bruce/Quinn stayed panting under the oak tree in the far corner.

"Thank you so much, Lulu. I'll see you tomorrow. Have fun at your meeting."

She snorted. "You take care," she said, tossing her bag into the back seat of her car. I waved as she drove away.

A slamming screen door to my left caught my attention.

Nick ran down the sidewalk towards me.

"Marti!" he bellowed.

I waited the few seconds it took for him to sprint to me. His face was flushed and his chest heaved. I knew it wasn't from running the short distance from his house. Anger flowed off of him in hot, palpable waves. "Nick, what is wrong?"

"I'm being investigated." His voice was hoarse.

"For what?!" Arrows were crooked, compared to Nick.

"Internal Affairs was contacted by the DA's office. They said they had a tip from some gang punk trying to cop a plea that certain officers were looking the other way on some drug dealers for a cut of the profits. I was on the list."

"That's just crazy."

"But listen. They may show up at your house with a search warrant."

"My house?" A tip from the DA's office? Was Ian Chambers now trying to have my house officially searched because he didn't find what he wanted on his own? "Have you talked to Ian? Can he tell you anything?"

"Can't find him. But there's something you need to know. That little POS claimed that Ryan was the original ringleader."

Chapter 15
Stalking Horse

❧

I ALMOST DROPPED CASSIE. The extra-sticky coating of popsicle juice may have been what saved her. "What did you just say?"

"I said, they think Ryan took the money and organized other cops to leave the pushers alone. This kid couldn't have been more than twelve when Ryan died. Doesn't make any sense. I have no idea where this is coming from." Nick's fists clenched by his sides.

I think I know exactly where this is coming from. "It'll be okay, Nick. You didn't do anything wrong, and neither did Ryan. They won't find any evidence, because there is nothing to find." I used the calmest ER nurse voice I could summon. I had to convince myself as well as him.

"I hope you're right. I have a meeting with the union rep first thing in the morning. I can't just stand around. I have to try and clear my head – just need to move. Later." Nick sprinted off down the sidewalk.

I watched him go, and felt my own anger welling up inside me. Some friend you are, Ian Chambers. Nick's been on the waiting list for the SWAT team for almost three years and this false accusation better not torpedo his chances. But attacking Ryan, who isn't even around to defend himself? That is lower than low, and there is no way in hell I'm going to let you get away with that.

I ran up the steps and slammed the side door behind me. The noise made Cassie cry. I ran the bath and sang absently to her while I tried to figure out what to do. It did give me a chance to cool down a little. I took off the anti-shape-shifting amulet and left it on the dining table. Bruce/Quinn remained outside. Whatever. I could only deal with one crisis at a time.

I almost didn't need my own shower by the time Cassie was done with her bath. After dinner, she was too tired to put up much of a fight, and she went to sleep quickly. I crept out of her room, and found Quinn sitting at the kitchen table, his face grim.

"I'm sorry," I said.

"So am I."

"What is that supposed to mean?" I had a bad feeling about this.

"I never should have involved you. You clearly don't trust me. I thought that you could help, that you wanted to help." His voice was like frozen blades of grass - cold, sharp and brittle.

"Don't blame me for not fully trusting you, when you used some kind of hocus-pocus magic power to make me want you." Had I just said too much?

"I am what I am. I told you up front that I wasn't human, so don't be so surprised if I don't think like one."

I crossed my arms and glared at him. Hard to argue with his logic, but I didn't have to like it.

Quinn got up and walked into the dining room.

Was that it? He was just going to get up and leave? I sat there, stunned.

He returned a few seconds later, carrying the anti-shifting amulet as if it were a piece of rotting garbage. Quietly, he placed it in front of me, then sat back down.

"Do you know what this is?" he asked.

"An anti-shape shifting amulet." Duh.

"But how is it made? Any idea?"

I had a feeling I wouldn't like the answer. "No."

"Shapeshifters, generally, are pretty strong. If you want to control them, you have to get the strongest shapeshifter of them all – a dragon – and bind it to this amulet. It no longer has any free will. Every time the amulet is used to stop a shift, a little more of the dragon's power, a little more of its life, is torn away. It suffers horribly until it dies. And dragons live practically forever."

I felt pretty much the same way that I felt when I heard about LD-50 tests – where testers force-feed beauty products to a group of animals until half of them die – and the bottom dropped out of my anger. "I didn't know." Does Lulu?

"I thought not."

"Can the dragon be released?"

"If you unmake the amulet."

"What, do I have to throw it in a live volcano or something?"

"It's not that bad. Ryan said —"

"You knew Ryan?" Who else was going to turn up that Ryan had known but I had no idea existed?

"Yes. He was a good man, and he helped us out, although I don't think he realized it. He had some questions about Ian Chambers and, unfortunately I didn't have any answers."

Quinn's expression was drawn and wistful, and I waited for the thunk of the other shoe hitting the floor.

"Did he know what you really are?"

Quinn shook his head. "No."

Well, at least I was in on one little secret. Yay, me.

"So, basically, you were investigating Ian Chambers and I stumbled into your way." My rational mind told me that I should have felt relieved that I was only on the periphery of the weirdness, rather than at its center. Even so, I was oddly disappointed that I only had a walk-on role in this drama.

"That isn't true. Ryan was crazy about you. I felt I owed it to him to keep an eye on after he died."

"You owed him?"

"One of my colleagues fell into Buffalo Bayou. Ryan pulled him out. Saved his life, so I owed Ryan a favor."

So, instead of a guardian angel, I had a guardian lake monster. That's unique. Still, I wasn't entirely sure how to take that. Kind of sweet or kind of creepy – could go either way. But I did see an opportunity.

"If you feel you owe Ryan anything, you can help me now. Somebody in the DA's office, and I think we both know who that is, has made some allegations that Ryan and Nick are dirty, that they took money from drug dealers. I know that isn't true, but I don't know how to prove it. Help me find a way to clear them."

"You know what that means," Quinn said.

"What?"

"That Chambers didn't find what he was looking for. The only way to clear Ryan is to get Chambers and his boss."

"I was afraid you were going to say that. So what do we do?"

"You never asked where the werewolf went," Quinn said.

I rearranged the salt and pepper shakers on the kitchen table. "I'd forgotten about him. Where did he go?" I don't see what that has to do with clearing Ryan and Nick.

"We tracked him to Specials."

"They already have a pet succubus. Why not a werewolf?" I shrugged.

Quinn's lips made a pale imitation of a smile. "I don't think it was a coincidence that you went to Specials in the afternoon and their so-called pet werewolf showed up at your door later that night."

"You know that's right."

I looked up to see Delilah standing by the refrigerator.

"Girlfriend, I have a message for you from Spam, since you don't want him popping up in your house. He told me to tell you that Salinger saw you at Specials. He knows who you are."

"Salinger? Now is he that muscle-bound dude from Stella's party that broke Spam's neck?"

"That's the one," Delilah answered.

I chewed my thumbnail. I only did that when I was scared and pretending I wasn't. "So what's the problem with that? He doesn't know that I know he killed Spam."

"And yet a werewolf came to kill you," Quinn said.

"I don't have time to deal with Spam's stuff right now. I've got to help Nick and clear Ryan's name. That's more important."

Quinn propped both elbows on the table and rested his chin in his hands. "Come Tuesday morning, neither of those things may matter."

"What you talking about, shifter?" Delilah asked, planting her hands on her hips.

"I got word this afternoon that one of the sahirs we've been keeping an eye on is on the move, and in the general direction of Houston. The good news is, he can't take a plane – he's on a terrorist watch list. The bad news is, he doesn't need to. He's working his way around all the wardings and shields between here and there, so the person summoning him must not have a portal. It's taking him some extra time, but he'll be here for the full moon on Monday. That's when they'll do the binding."

"Binding?" Delilah's arms relaxed and slid to her sides.

"They're going to bind a djinn to some kind of object, probably a talisman or a ring, to give the possessor almost unlimited power. And by 'they,' I mean some really bad guys," Quinn answered.

"Oh, that is not good," Delilah answered.

I still couldn't get my head around the evil-world-dictator-for-life scenario. But I really didn't have to. What I could understand was that Chambers and company needed to be stopped, and stopped soon, or else Nick's career and Ryan's reputation were in the toilet. I'd just go with that.

"It's Thursday night," I said. "That gives us Friday, Saturday, Sunday and Monday."

"Until moonrise on Monday," Quinn corrected.

"Fine. Moonrise. What's the plan?"

Quinn looked at Delilah, then back at me. "Marti, I don't think you realize how dangerous these people are. This is not a TV show. They will kill you. Or worse."

Or worse? "I can't sit around at home and hope you get the bad guys. Ryan and Nick deserve better from me." How could I look at my little girl, knowing I didn't do everything I could to clear her daddy's name?

"I'm not asking you to sit around. I also don't think you want Cassie to lose both of her parents. You can do some digging. Find out who owns Specials. Do they own any other businesses? Whose name is on the liquor license? That sort of thing will help, if you want to clear Ryan. Investigators love paper trails."

I was only mad because I didn't want to admit that he was right about Cassie. "I don't really see how Spam's stuff is going to help," I pouted, not willing to concede entirely.

"Ian Chambers didn't just go there for a drink. He came out of the back office, remember? He's connected to Specials. You need to find out how. I'm sure that's why Spam took you there."

"Fine." I still felt like I was being given busy work to keep me out of the way.

Quinn looked at Delilah. "How strong is the warding?"

"Good as it gets, shifter."

"Glad to hear it." He looked back at me. "I have to go. If you haven't heard from me by noon on Sunday, assume the worst and do whatever you have to do to keep yourself alive."

I had to swallow hard before I could speak, the coppery taste of fear flavoring my words. "You have to win." I inwardly cringed. My words came out sounding too much like a plea, like begging.

"I know." He stood up and pushed his chair in, lifting it slightly so the legs didn't scrape on the floor and wake Cassie.

I stood up and walked him to the door, under Delilah's watchful eye. He said nothing else, but he turned and brushed my cheek with the back of his fingers in a way that made my knees weak. I didn't know if that was a promise or a final goodbye. "Keep yourself in one piece," he said.

Then he stepped out of the door and melted into the twilight.

A twisting tidal wave of emotions washed over me. Fear, anger, loss, hope, desire, regret, frustration, hate, pain. I didn't know whether to scream or curl up in a fetal position under the covers. Or both. I covered my face with my hands, took a deep breath, held it as long as I could, then let it out. Dropping my hands back to my sides, I turned to Delilah. "The last thing I can afford to do right now is fall apart like a cheap plastic toy. I'm going to go take a shower. A hot shower makes everything better."

Delilah nodded and faded away.

I stood under the hot water until it started to go cold. My emotions were still vacillating wildly between terror and fury, but at least I'd narrowed the range down to two. I was drying my arms when I noticed the mirror.

It was fogged up from the hot shower. But someone had written two words on it: "Ryans File."

I really hoped that Delilah was the one creeping around in my bathroom while I was in the shower, but I tried not to think about it too much. Maybe this was something I could use. I quickly combed out my hair and put on a nightshirt, all the while thinking about which of Ryan's files this clue could mean. I looked through every file in the two-drawer cabinet. Nothing but mundane stuff – insurance papers, bank statements, tax returns and such. All very familiar, as I'd just reorganized them after Ian Chambers broke into my house and tossed them all over the floor.

It was just after ten when I picked up the phone and called my sister's house. Nick answered after three rings.

"Marti? What's wrong?" Nick's voice was deep and raspy, the way it got when he'd been drinking.

"Nothing's wrong. Nick, how hard would it be for you to get a hold of Ryan's file. The investigation of his death?"

"I can maybe talk to somebody Monday –"

"I can't wait until Monday. I need it tomorrow."

"Why?"

Good question. How can I answer that without sounding like a nutcase? "I just need to see it. Maybe there's something in there that can help get you off the hook."

"Doubt it, but I'll see what I can do after my union guy meeting."

"Thanks. And Nick? Hydrate and go to bed. You don't want to be hung over in the morning. Goodnight." I hung up before he could argue with me.

I hoped that Lulu's warding would work. I didn't need werewolves coming in my backyard at will. What had Delilah said? Only silver can hurt a werewolf. I hoped that there didn't have to be a critical mass, and any amount of silver would work. I pulled down the stairs to the attic and climbed up. The small, naked bulb didn't do much to alleviate the creepy shadows in the corners. I grabbed the box with Ryan's grandfather's sword and scooted back down the rickety steps. I would keep it with me, just in case.

I was able to use the Texas Alcoholic Beverage Commission public inquiry webpage to find out about Specials' liquor license. The listed owner, irony notwithstanding, was Friar Enterprises, LLC. I found an address for them, an executive suite at Greenway Plaza, as it turned out. According to their website, Friar Enterprises owned a wide range of strip clubs, from the dingy to the deluxe. I supposed that wasn't so unusual, but it seemed odd, for a company with that many holdings, to only have one tiny executive suite, rather than actual office space somewhere.

It was a quarter of one, and I'd decided I had done all I could do for the night. I looked in on Cassie, who was sleeping like a rock. It felt odd, walking around my house with a sword, but extraordinary times called for extraordinary measures, or something like that.

Tired as I was, I had a hard time settling down and going to sleep, my brain assaulting me with too many problems and issues: dragons and djinn, liars and louts. I worried about Nick, and Ryan's reputation, and wondered if Quinn would be okay. I had gotten used to Bruce/Quinn sleeping on the bed, and now that I was alone, it was hard to tell if I felt smaller or the bed felt bigger. And who wrote those words on the bathroom mirror? Exhaustion finally won out, and I slept.

Who needs an alarm clock when you have a baby? I could set my watch by Cassie – up at 6:30. Every. Single. Morning.

After the usual preparations, we went to the kitchen for some solid food. Cassie threw her Cheerios off her tray and looked hopefully at the door. Bruce did not come. She sulked.

"Don't worry, sweetie. He'll be back." *I hope.*

I was restless and didn't really want to be alone. Well, Cassie counted as company, but not company that I could have a rational conversation with. We stopped by the Tenth Sphere on the way back from our morning walk. Besides, I had an ulterior motive. What Quinn had told me about the suffering dragon was jabbing my conscience, and I needed to see how much Lulu knew about it.

Cassie was being especially fussy and insisted on being carried. I walked her around the shop while she gnawed on her fingers as if she hadn't eaten in weeks. Talking to Lulu between customers and a cranky baby wasn't easy, but I managed to snatch an opportunity.

"So, Lulu. That amulet you gave me. Did you make that?"

She set down the packs of Tarot cards she'd been rearranging and looked at me like I was crazy. "Are you kidding, honey? I don't have the time or patience to do those. And I don't know anything about metalwork. No. I get them from a company in Oregon. They're expensive, but they're handmade and they really work."

"So you don't know how they're made?"

"Not really. All I know is it takes three days to make one. Are you thinking of starting an amulet business?"

Maybe the dragon rescuing business.

I shifted Cassie to my other hip. "No. I was just wondering. It's beautiful, and nobody would ever think it was anything other than just a piece of jewelry. Curious about their secret, that's all."

She offered to send me the owner's email address later, and I said that would be fine. I felt relieved that she didn't know about the dragon. I would tell her next week, if the world didn't end, and see if I could get her to help me release the creature.

In the end, Cassie's incoming new teeth were giving her a lot of grief, and she was just too grouchy to continue inflicting her on innocent bystanders.

When we got home, I gave Cassie some baby ibuprofen. Betty and Alpha climbed to the top of their cage, hoping for a treat. I gave them each a yogurt drop and felt a little guilty for ignoring them for the past few days. Even with the ibuprofen, Cassie's gums were bothering her too much to allow her to sleep. I thought distraction might help, so I slipped the rats' tiny harnesses and leashes on, and the four of us girls sat in the shade under the live oak tree in the back yard. The pain reliever finally kicked in, and Cassie tried walking some more. She was getting better at it, but still had a long way to go. The little rats seemed to be enjoying sniffing around in the grass and eating the occasional pill bug. It didn't take very long for the sun's ferocity to drive us back indoors.

We had just started lunch when Nick walked in the back door, without knocking, and plopped a large brown envelope on the kitchen table. Peppery stubble littered his face, and his usual spikey hair lay flat and limp on his head.

"Jeez, Nick. You look like something the cat dragged in."

"Whatever. Here's the file you asked for. Gotta have it back first thing Monday morning."

"Thanks. How did your meeting go?"

Nick flipped one of the breakfast chairs around, and sat straddling it, resting his chin on the back. "I am so screwed. IAD is focused on nailing dirty cops, not clearing innocent ones. Even if they don't come up with a shred of evidence, I'm still tainted."

It hurt me to see Nick in this state. I was sure he'd bounce back, once he had a little time to get over the initial shock. "I'm so sorry this happened to you. But they also went after Ryan, and I'm not going to let either one of you get railroaded."

Nick smiled. "Emily says the same thing."

"Well, there you go. The Schmidt Sisters are on the case. How can you lose?" I paused long enough to give him a reassuring look. "You know, it might do you some good to take the boys to the Museum of Natural Science. Maybe you could catch the IMAX and get your mind off of this for a little bit. And you know Kyle and Aiden never get tired of seeing the enormous hall of dinosaurs."

"Maybe."

Nick looked around the room. "Hey. Where's your dog?"

"Bruce? He's…at the vet, getting a flea bath." I hated lying to Nick, even if it was a teeny white one. But I couldn't exactly tell him the truth, either.

"You need to make sure your back door's locked, especially if you're by yourself." Nick stood up to go.

Once Cassie was down for her afternoon nap, I hopped back on the internet and started researching Friar Enterprises, LLC. It was privately held, and there wasn't much to find, although I did discover that the executive director was named Cynthia Ashland.

I suppose I had put off looking at Ryan's file for as long as I could. My hands shook as I picked up the unmarked mailing envelope and slid the file out. There were some loose crime scene photographs in the folder that I couldn't bear to look at, so I held them against the front cover to keep them face down when I opened it. The file was not very thick – the case was cut and dried. Traffic stop goes bad. High speed chase and stand-off. SWAT called. Bad guys dead. The end. As much as I thought that the idea of time-travelling Russian literary stars with machine guns would make a great Quentin Tarantino movie, I didn't believe for a second that Anton Chekhov and Fydor Dostoyevsky were the shooters' real names.

I read every piece of paper, save anything that might be trapped between the photos, at least three times. The time of 12:55, when the 'Officer Down' call hit dispatch, stuck in my head. Still, I couldn't find a single thing that would do Ryan or Nick any good. Some tip this turned out to be. I picked up the loose papers and tried to get them back in some semblance of order before I clipped them back in.

A grimy, dog-eared Post-It note fluttered to the floor. I picked it up. In smeared pencil, it read: "EMT: suspect said, 'Hey, fellows!' and then expired."

Well. Interesting bit of trivia, but completely useless. Dying people often say bizarre things.

The question now was whether I'd missed something, or my mirror-writing source was wrong. Just to see if there was some report or scrap of paper I'd missed, I picked up the photos one by one, careful to keep them face-down. I'd seen some very grisly things in the ER, but none of them had involved Ryan. I needed for the pictures of him I kept in my head to stay uncontaminated. It had been necessary for the funeral service to be closed-casket.

I tucked all of the papers and photos back into the folder and slipped it into the large envelope. I texted Nick that I was done with the file, but didn't get a reply.

I had managed to get through the file without blubbering. That was something, anyway. But now, I felt dull and depressed. I made a pitcher of iced-tea and stood in the kitchen, looking out the back door. I hoped the sunlight would burn off the gloom, but it was merely hot, rather than purifying. I knew Cassie would be up any minute, and I hoped I could force myself into a better mood before then. Wondering what Quinn was doing wasn't helpful, and Delilah didn't seem to be around, either.

I went in the living room and turned on the TV.

The phone rang. I could tell by caller ID that it was Amanda. She had called to tell me there was nothing wrong with the water sample I'd given her. And to remind me that the ER was hiring.

I hung up the phone and flipped mindlessly through the channels until I heard Cassie squawking in her crib. After I brought her into the living room, she didn't want to do anything but have me hold her hands so she could walk around the house. We did that until my back cramped up and I could barely stand upright.

I called Emily to see if she needed anything, and Cassie and I ended up going over there. Nick had taken the boys out, and I was able to have a good visit with my sister – just girl talk - even though we avoided the 600 pound gorilla that was the manufactured charges against Nick and Ryan. We stayed for dinner, but I made a point of getting home before dark. I hadn't brought the sword with me – thought I'd avoid the awkward questions and explanations.

At 3:42 AM, I was awakened by someone tapping, actually, it was more like banging, on the sliding glass door in my bedroom. The same glass door that the charging werewolf had cracked. It took a moment for my brain to wake up and my hands to grab the sword. Raising it above my head, I went to the door and turned on the outside light. There was a group of four people standing on the patio. No, make that five. Someone was draped over the shoulder of one of the men. The person's backside was towards me and I could tell it was a man, but I couldn't tell if he was alive or dead.

"Let us in!" demanded a red-haired man.

I waved the sword, just to make sure they saw it. "Who are you?"

The redhead said something to the man who was carrying the body. He turned around and I gasped. Even with the hair matted to it with blood, I recognized the face.

Quinn.

Chapter 16
Bitter Grapes

— ෨ —

QUINN HATED LEAVING MARTI and Cassie. But he also knew that it was the only way to protect them. And at this point, it went far beyond saving a pretty woman and her baby. For ten thousand years, maybe longer, there were humans who had thought they could control djinn. Even bound djinn were not as helpless as they might seem, and binding them seemed to make the djinn go a bit mad. Between Malik's tricks and Chambers' employer's wishes, there was no telling what would happen. And none of it was likely to be good. Quinn was certain that the boss had paid a lot of money for Malik – the demon who kidnapped him said as much - and he probably wouldn't do that unless he had something really big and really bad planned. Why else would he need the power of a djinn? How did he even know about djinn, anyway? Were demons involved in that, too? If that was true, it added a whole other level of ugly – it could change the situation from potentially catastrophic to potentially apocalyptic. His head throbbed, from the crown all the way down into his shoulders.

Kai's car was waiting around the corner.

"Frey," Quinn said as he climbed in.

"Evening," Frey replied, then drove in silence to Kai's house.

As usual, when Frey drove, all the traffic lights were green. The journey took less than twenty minutes.

When they arrived, Quinn hurried up the stairs to the large bedroom that served as the war room for Kai's team. The walls were brightly painted, but whether it was dark yellow or light orange was hard for Quinn to say. He wasn't sure he liked the color, but he did always feel energized in that room. An oval mahogany table with a highly polished grey and orange granite top stood in the center of the room, surrounded by six matching chairs. Kai's laptop perched on one end of the table, its back to a large flatscreen, which took up most of the wall on one of the room's shorter sides. The longer sides of the room were old school, lined with whiteboards and corkboards.

He forced a grim smile when he saw those already gathered.

Eoin and Aleksei sat at the table opposite each other, eating sandwiches. Kai was on his feet, fidgeting around near the computer. And of course, there was Breena, who'd just met him at the door. Well, there were five of them, and teams were always made up of five. It should be enough. He hoped. They were going to rescue a captured team member. That's all they had to do to make the bad guys' plan fall apart. Just a day's work for a Mundane Intervention Team.

"Food is on the table," Breena said, tucking dark hair behind her ear. She gestured towards a side table spread with fresh fruit, sandwiches, and a selection of fruit juices before she moved to the table and sat down.

Quinn wasn't really hungry, but thought he ought to at least have something for politeness' sake. As he reached for the pitcher of orange juice, he caught Marti's scent on his hand. When this was over, when

Malik was recovered, when the bad guys were dealt with, when Marti was safe, then what was he going to do? The obvious answer was to go back to the Waterhorse Inn and serve up pints and sandwiches until another mission called. It would certainly keep Marti safe from his mother. It would be better for Marti and Cassie both, for a lot of reasons, if he just left her alone. But he wasn't sure he could.

"We may as well get started," Kai said. He pushed a button on his smartphone and the flatscreen flared to life. A map of the Port of Houston appeared on it in high definition. As he talked, the map zoomed in on one terminal. "Now, the source who's been tracking the sahir tells me that he's on a Liberian-flagged container ship, the MV Albatross. Best guess is that he's pretending to be one of the crew. When the ship docks at Barbours Cut Terminal, we assume he's going to slip off the boat as its being unloaded. What we don't know is how he's getting to the place they're keeping Malik. And since we don't know where that is, either, we'll have to follow him. Once we have a location, we can start planning. The ship should arrive sometime tomorrow."

Quinn knew they were necessary, but he hated planning sessions. He just wanted to get started, get things done. He shifted in his chair and tried to force himself to pay attention.

Kai clicked the button again. "This is what he looks like." An image of an elderly, leather-faced man appeared on the wall. His eyes were a nearly colorless grey, and they matched his thick, grizzled beard. "He's only human. He can't shift or use glamour. But he is likely to be disguised. And he's also probably the only one that will be sneaking out of the terminal."

"Is he travelling alone?" Eoin asked.

"Excellent question. I don't know," Kai said.

"If he is user of dark magick, is easy to tell," Aleksei added.

"Maybe. If he isn't expecting anyone to be looking for him and he hasn't bothered shielding himself. But one doesn't get to be as old as he is without being paranoid. Not sure we can count on seeing the anti-glow," Kai said.

Quinn knew that all living things have an aura, a field of glowing colors that surround them. Most humans have trained themselves not to notice it, but they can see it, with a little practice. People who do good things glow brightly, while those who do bad are dimmer. He saw it all the time, and had taken it for granted. Still, he hadn't thought about magick. Add magick, and the effects are amplified. Magick itself isn't good or bad, but when it is used for bad things, the aura of the person using it glows dimmer and dimmer, until he finally has a negative aura, as if light is being sucked away – an anti-glow.

"There is one thing to look for – he always wears a ring on the middle finger of his right hand. Has a large peridot stone in the middle and some ancient script on the sides. It's the source of his power – he won't take it off." The picture zoomed in to a cocktail ring-sized green stone on the sahir's hand. "Now what I was thinking," Kai continued, "is that one of us could be inside the terminal, watching the boat, and the rest of us could be keeping an eye on the exit."

"Security's going to be really tight there, could be a problem," Quinn said.

"Maybe not, if that individual was in the water."

Quinn's smile was more grimace than grin. "Because you know how much I love swimming in nasty seaport water."

"I'm sure Malik would do it for you," Kai shot back.

"Of course he would." He was the only one, apparently, who recognized Kai's dig at Malik.

More pictures were displayed and all the organizational details were worked out. Quinn didn't relish simply hiding in the port water, keeping only his eyes and nostrils above the surface, so he'd simply look like flotsam, if anyone spotted him. He hated waiting – he preferred doing.

"Alright," Kai said. "I think we should try and get some rest. It's going to be a long day tomorrow."

There were enough bedrooms in the house for each of the guests to have their own, but Aleksei and Eoin preferred to sleep outside in the back yard. The marble tiles inside were too slippery for Eoin's hooves, and Aleksei needed to get his toes in the soil to recharge.

Upstairs, Quinn lay on a soft bed, staring at the pale blue ceiling. He was too tired to sleep. Or perhaps it wasn't that at all. His arm stretched across the empty expanse of the bed. He'd quickly gotten used to not sleeping alone, even if he had been in dog form. He forced his mind in another direction, focusing on tomorrow's plan. He visualized the mission going smoothly, recovering Malik, introducing Chambers and his boss to the human authorities. His debt to Ryan Keller would be repaid. And then what? He couldn't think about that, not now. He started over with the visualization.

෯

Quinn and company left early in the morning, while it was still dark, and drove about an hour to Seabrook. No one there would pay much attention to a wade fisherman in the surf. Quinn eased himself further into the water, deeper and deeper, until he could slip under the swells and shift. He swam out into Galveston Bay and followed the line of ships until he found the one he was looking for. The Albatross had not been difficult to locate. It was queued up to enter the mouth of the San Jacinto River and move into the Ship Channel. Once he spotted it, it would be nearly impossible to miss. All of the other ships were stacked high with generic yellow, white and grey containers. But the Albatross also had one small, sea-green refrigerated container with grapes painted on it.

He kept himself submerged as much as possible – but he could only hold his breath about two hours, if he was mostly still. He got as close to the ship as he dared, but he made sure he stayed well away from the depth finder, and especially far from the boat's thirty foot propellers.

Watching an anchored ship was excruciatingly boring. The crew was below decks in the shade, rather than soaking up the punishing Texas summer sun. Quinn amused himself by catching redfish for his breakfast. Finally, the tugboat and the channel pilot came out to the Albatross, and the ship began to move towards the terminal. It wasn't moving quickly, but it was moving.

Quinn's relief was short-lived.

He had just gotten a breath when he saw it. It was medium grey, hints of vertical stripes, with a blunt nose and low, wide dorsal fin. Tiger shark.

At fifteen feet, it wasn't much smaller than he was. The shark was probably attracted by the scraps of Quinn's fish, but it wouldn't be opposed to having a meal of kelpie with a redfish garnish. He knew it would approach slowly, trying not to spook him, then when it got close enough, it would attack, its powerful tail giving it a burst of speed that he couldn't match. So the trick was not letting it get close enough.

Quinn dove, swimming away from the shark faster than it was moving, but not at his top speed. He wasn't as fast as the shark, but he was more maneuverable. The shark picked up its pace, easily shadowing him. Quinn skimmed along the bottom, twisting and turning to avoid debris and other hazards. He was making for one of the many abandoned oil platforms, or a shell reef, whichever came first, across the river in Trinity Bay. With any luck, the tiger shark would decide that the schools of fish that swarmed the submerged structures were easier pickings than Quinn.

He ducked behind a pipe stand that looked like over-sized, barnacle-encrusted monkey bars. He stuck his head over the top of it and looked for the shark. It was nowhere to be seen. Perhaps it had given up. Swimming far and quickly had depleted Quinn's air reserves, and he needed to get to the surface. He checked again. No sign of the shark. He started to rise, slowly, carefully. The water wasn't deep, scarcely more than the millpond at the Waterhorse. Quinn tilted his head upward, so he could just break the surface with his nostrils.

The shark hit him from behind, crashing into his side and grabbing one of his flippers in its mouth. The teeth were so sharp he didn't feel them cutting into his skin, and he was momentarily amazed by the dark cloud of his own blood floating around him. The shark shook its head, tearing at the flipper. Quinn's lungs were burning. He had to have air, and soon. Even sooner, he had to get twelve hundred pounds of shark off of him.

Sharks aren't the only ones with mouths full of razor sharp weapons. Quinn sank his own teeth into the flesh just before the fish's stumpy dorsal fin. The shark wasn't used to its prey biting back. Startled, it stopped the attack and reversed course, thrashing and snapping its bristling jaws. Quinn let it go. His straining lungs would force him to gulp in seawater instead of air if he didn't get to the surface soon.

His head shot out of the water, and he gasped for oxygen. A startled fisherman nearly fell out of his bass boat. Quinn gave him a toothy grin. Cursing and fumbling, the man started his outboard motor and sped away.

Quinn had to get out of the water. Between his bleeding flipper and the injured shark nearby, other sharks would be coming to investigate. And this would quickly become a very unhealthy place to be. He swam towards the opposite bank the fisherman had headed to, and he let himself take on human form as he left the water.

The shark had bitten his arm all the way to the bone, and it was bleeding badly. Muscle and skin hung in strips. He sat on the beach and put the ragged flesh back in place as best he could, then he had to apply pressure so the tissue could knit itself together properly. He covered most of the wound with his hand and other arm, and after a minute or two, the bleeding slowed considerably. Kelpies heal very quickly. In two hours' time, there would hardly be a scar. Nevertheless, he was light-headed from blood loss.

But now the mission was compromised. He'd lost track of the Albatross. And he couldn't risk getting back into the water until the shark bite healed, or at the very least, stopped bleeding. And if those problems weren't enough, his clothes were somewhere on the opposite side of the bay, so he couldn't go walking around to get back into the water further away from the shark.

Quinn looked around, trying to get his bearings. He was surrounded by brackish estuary, low, scrubby bushes, and thick marsh grass. He sat partially in the water so it wasn't obvious that he was nude. The last thing he needed was somebody wandering by and calling the police.

A shadow seeped across Quinn's face.

"You're out of your element, kelpie," a hoarse voice croaked.

Quinn turned his head to see an especially ugly ichthyuxoris standing over him. She was mostly human-shaped, with large external gills that started behind where her ear would be if she were human and ended at the base of her throat. They dangled and swayed like fat, spiky earthworms in the breeze. Her face was more frog than human, with bulging tawny eyes and an unpleasantly wide mouth filled with jagged bony plates, like some prehistoric fish. Sunlight glinted off of her green-black scales.

There are virtually no reports of these creatures, partly because they are very rare, and partly because humans who saw them almost never lived to tell anyone about it. In fact, the favorite hobby of ichthyuxori is tipping over small boats and drowning the occupants. Still, Quinn knew the reason the ancient Romans had called them Fish Wives.

Quinn raised his injured arm. "I'll be on my way in a bit, as soon as this heals enough."

"This is my territory. Get out," the ichthyuxoris snarled, pointing a dangerously clawed, webbed hand toward the land.

"I understand that. I'm not planning on staying here, and I'm not hunting. I just need to rest for a little while."

The ichthyuxoris hissed and took another step towards him. "Leave!"

In human form, Quinn didn't stand a chance against her, especially not in his weakened state. In his kelpie form, he was clumsy on land, but still quite dangerous, and he would have the advantage. He couldn't leave via land, and she would fight him if he got in the water. He didn't wish to hurt her, but he had to get back to the other side of the bay, and see if he could still find the Albatross and salvage the mission. Without being torn apart by frenzied sharks.

Blood still oozed from his arm, but it was a lot better than it had been a few minutes ago. He eased himself slightly deeper into the water, as if the swells were carrying him out into the bay.

"Not that way!" the ichthyuxoris growled. "My territory."

Quinn stood up, as if he were going to come on shore. Then he hurled himself backwards into the water, changing into kelpie form as he did so. The water was a little shallow, and he scraped his belly on the rocky bottom, but he shot away from the ichthyuxoris. With a screech, she dove under the waves and followed him. He'd counted on that.

Quinn built up speed, stretching out like a long-necked torpedo. He headed straight towards where he'd left the injured shark.

So far, it was holding its own against some small sharks that had come, hoping for an easy meal. The big tiger's teeth added some of their blood to its own. Larger sharks would not be far away.

As soon as the ichthyuxoris saw the wounded tiger shark, she broke off her pursuit, swam to it, and lovingly stroked its nose. Surveying the small sharks harassing the injured tiger, she opened her mouth wide and emitted an infrasonic growl that nearly knocked Quinn over. Its frequency was too low for humans to hear, but the attacking sharks couldn't get away from her fast enough. Quinn twisted his long neck around as he shook his head to clear the ringing in his ears. The ichthyuxoris was guiding the shark by its dorsal fin, most likely to her lair to treat its injuries. Fish Wife, indeed. Quinn wished there were more of her kind.

The line of ships waiting to enter the channel was easy to find. The Albatross was not. It must already be in the terminal. The channel was relatively narrow and shallow, with lots of traffic. He'd have to maneuver his large body perfectly, if he wanted to avoid being converted into chum by the huge propellers. The problem was, his eyesight was blurry and his head seemed like it was no longer attached to his neck.

Quinn's flipper felt like it was on fire. The strain of frantic swimming had been too much for the healing wound. It hadn't held, and now he was pouring blood into the bay again. He wasn't going to do Malik any good if he bled to death, so he reluctantly made his way back to the shore.

He converted to human form as soon as the water got shallow enough. He heaved himself onto the crushed concrete, and lay partially submerged in the shade of a rotting pier. He held pressure on his arm. It took a lot longer for the bleeding to stop this time. The water in the Gulf of Mexico during summer is like bathwater, and the warm gentle waves caressed and relaxed his exhausted body. His mind drifted with the whitecaps, not really awake, but not quite asleep. Something brushed against his thigh.

"Marti?" he mumbled.

But it was only a clump of seaweed.

๏

When Quinn opened his eyes, Breena was pouring something cool down his throat. It tasted green and sweet – like mint and basil and thyme and honey, all mixed together.

He swallowed and coughed.

"Welcome back," she said.

Quinn was lying on the second row of seats in Kai's SUV. His clothes were on, although his shirt was backwards. His arm was bandaged.

"When you didn't check in, we got worried. Frey found you." Breena helped him sit up. "You may still feel dizzy. It'll pass soon. You're going to be fine, although it will probably be tomorrow before you're a hundred percent."

Quinn nodded his thanks to Frey, who was playing a game on his cell phone.

"Then it's a good thing we're just doing recon today," Quinn replied.

Kai, who was sitting in the front passenger seat, put down his binoculars and turned to Quinn. "What happened?"

Quinn told them.

"You saw an ichthyuxoris?" Kai asked. "That's amazing. There are only about three of them in the entire Gulf of Mexico. I think one's near Padre and the other is in the Florida Keys."

"Okay. Good to know. I'd rather have seen the sahir."

"Yeah, well, you have to take whatever wins you can get, sometimes," Kai replied.

The remark irritated Quinn. It wasn't his fault he got attacked by a shark, was it? It might be possible later for him to slip into the water from the other side of Barbours Cut Boulevard and swim into the terminal to watch the water side of the Albatross, but right now, he was too weak and clumsy from the shark attack to be able to pull it off. If the sahir had brought diving gear, and if he waited until well after dark, he just might be able to slip over the side of the ship and make his way out of the terminal underwater, away from the watchful eyes of the Coast Guard and the Port Police. He'd escape while Quinn and his team all sat in the car, wondering what to do. If Quinn had just taken the time to eat breakfast and left the stupid redfish alone, the shark wouldn't have showed up, and he'd be in place, ready to intercept the wretched sahir. He wanted to hit something, but didn't dare, not in the vehicle's close quarters with the others nearby. With any luck, he'd be strong enough to get back in the water in a few hours, and could still redeem himself. If the sahir was not stopped, Malik would be enslaved. And it would be all Quinn's fault.

Quinn sighed and looked out the window. "Is it my imagination, or are we really parked in front of a cemetery in the middle of a cargo terminal?"

Breena snorted softly.

"Morgan's Point Cemetery. It was here long before the terminal. Quite handy for Aleksei to get up in those trees in the corner. He and Eoin can watch the ship, we can watch the exit." Kai handed Quinn a pair of binoculars before he put his own pair back up to his eyes. Quinn glanced to the back row, slightly ashamed he hadn't even noticed that Aleksei and Eoin were missing. He lifted the glasses and focused on the gate.

It was 4:30. The gates would close at 5:00. If anyone was planning on leaving tonight, they'd have to do it soon. Quinn watched the exiting vehicles. Silver pickup. Green pickup. White semi. White semi. Orange semi. Red semi.

"Now that's interesting," Quinn said.

"What's that?" asked Kai.

"That pickup truck with the flatbed trailer. He's taking one half-sized, refrigerated container. I'm sure it was on the Albatross. I haven't seen any other green containers with grapes painted on them."

"Are you thinking what I'm thinking?"

"That the sahir isn't in the crew — he's in the container."

"Bingo."

Frey flashed the SUV's headlights. Eoin and Aleksei were at the doors within a minute.

"Think we've found him," Kai said.

Frey pulled slowly out of the parking lot and turned onto Barbours Cut Boulevard. The pickup was just ahead of them. Aleksei and Eoin ducked below the windows and Quinn lay back down on the seat, bending his knees so Breena would have space to sit. If the pickup driver noticed the SUV, two men and a lady probably wouldn't look suspicious. Five men and a lady might.

They followed the driver until he pulled into a warehouse near the train depot in downtown Houston. Frey passed the driveway and parked around the corner a few blocks over. They could see if anyone entered or left the premises, but they couldn't see anything that was going on in the yard.

Frey scowled at the steering wheel.

"What's wrong?" asked Kai.

"Perhaps it's nothing. It just seems that he went well out of his way to get here. He should have just stayed on 225. There was no reason at all for him to go all the way down to the Beltway and back up on 288."

"Maybe he just took a wrong turn?" Breena asked.

"If so, he's a bloody bad driver," Frey responded.

"The great thing about walking a dog is that you can wander around all kinds of places, and no one thinks twice about it," Kai said.

Eoin chuckled.

"You be gentle with him. His arm's still healing," Breena said sternly. "Maybe I should do it."

"No. They'll notice you. They won't pay any attention to a male. I think Aleksei should go with him," Kai replied.

Quinn shifted into dog form, and Aleksei forced his blue skin into a more human shade. They strolled down the sidewalk, pausing for a sniff here and a dig there. He only limped a little bit – the arm bandage was far too big for a dog leg and had to be removed. The skin had healed, but the muscles were still weak. Aleksei and Quinn verified that there were no back exits to the warehouse yard. They could even see the nose of the truck sticking out from behind the warehouse. Eight vertical feet of chain link fence, topped with razor wire, encircled the yard. A faded, rust-flecked sign on the front gate read "Beware of Dog." That was all there was to report when they returned to the SUV.

By the time it was dark, the warehouse district was asleep. A few security guards occasionally appeared and disappeared around corners. No one had left the warehouse. The truck was still parked behind the building.

"I don't like this," Breena whispered loudly.

"Did you notice any place that a dog might be able to get into the yard?" Kai asked.

"Where the gates join in the middle is not quite flush. If somebody pushed on the bottom half of one, I could probably squeeze in."

Breena frowned after he and Aleksei as they left the SUV and headed towards the warehouse, knowing Quinn wasn't fully healed.

Aleksei looked around. There was no one is sight. The chain rattled as he pushed against the lower half of the gate. His feet were strong, like the roots of a tree, and the metal was no match for him. The gate started to bend, and Quinn slipped through, wagging his tail.

He snuffled around and trotted towards the truck. The trailer was still attached to it, but the container was gone. Must be inside.

Light poured out of the windows and left square puddles on the ground. Quinn found some five gallon buckets stacked along one wall, and a couple of them were under windows. He cringed as each click of his toenails was amplified by the empty containers. He stood on his hind legs to peer in, but the three men inside didn't seem to notice. One was tall and beefy, probably a body guard. He stood with his arms crossed and feet apart. Next to him was a man with reddish blond hair, who was doing a lot of talking. The other man had a grizzled beard and leathery skin. The sahir. He was holding the emerald jar. A jewelry box, a stick of chalk, a box of charcoal tabs, cone incense and a censer lay haphazardly on the table next to him.

Quinn climbed down from the buckets as quietly as he could, then bounded toward the gate. Aleksei pushed the bottom open for Quinn and he slipped out. He galloped toward Kai's SUV as fast as his three good legs could go. He heard Aleksei pounding along behind. Eoin opened the back door and Quinn leaped in, then shifted to human form.

"They aren't waiting," he panted. "Looks like they're getting ready for the ritual right now."

"Damn," Kai said.

Aleksei clambered into the middle row. "What is plan?" he asked.

"How many?" asked Kai.

"Three," answered Quinn. "That I saw, anyway."

"We are five," Aleksei said.

"We should probably count the sahir as two," Kai said.

"And the body guard," Quinn added.

"They probably aren't expecting any visitors," Eoin said. "We could just barge in. Surprise will be on our side."

"He's right. I doubt we'll be able to sneak in and get the bottle," Breena said. "Not if they're just about to perform the binding ritual."

"Right. Not much of a plan, but we're out of time. Let's go in there and see what happens," Kai said.

They started getting out of the SUV. Breena closed the door on Quinn. "You might want your clothes on first."

When they got to the warehouse gate, the padlock came off in Kai's hand as if it had never been locked. He opened the gate quietly. The other four slipped in, and he pulled the gate shut behind him. The heavy smell of incense leaked from the windows and hung stagnant in the moist air.

The warehouse had a drive-through passage, with garage doors on either end. On the end nearest the gate, a metal door opened into a small office, which opened into the warehouse. The opposite end of the warehouse had another metal door next to the garage door. Quinn and Eoin went to the far door, while Kai, Breena and Aleksei crept in through the office. They burst into the warehouse more or less simultaneously. The strawberry blond sat on a table, his legs dangling.

The sahir sat in the middle of a twelve foot chalk circle. The emerald jar was in his lap.

"You're a little too late," said the man on the table. If he was surprised by their appearance, it didn't show.

The sahir chanted, getting gradually louder. Quinn could see the cone of energy, a swirling blue flame, surrounding the chalk circle. They would not be able to get inside it. The only way they could save Malik was to get the sahir to come out and break the circle.

"I thought you said there were three of them," Eoin said softly.

Quinn glanced around. "There were."

A wooden crate near the sahir burst into flames. Then another. Then the wooden table. It was good to have a firestarter on your team.

"Get out! This whole place is going to go up!" shouted the strawberry blond. "We'll do this later!" He got halfway towards the far door, and looked over his shoulder. The sahir had stood up and was pacing the circumference of the circle, chanting, oblivious to the intruders. The man shook his head. "You idiot! Come on," he shouted at the sahir.

Then he stopped, looked at Quinn and smiled. A bad kind of smile.

Quinn started to turn his head and glimpsed a blur of brown fur as the werewolf barreled through the door and sank its teeth into his shoulder. It had been aiming for his jugular, but he'd had a split second to move out of the way. He cried out as his collar bone splintered.

Without even thinking, he shifted into kelpie form. His long neck snaked around the werewolf and grabbed its leg. It yowled and let go of him, scratching and clawing at Quinn's body as he pulled it away from himself. He shook the werewolf like a rag doll and flung it into the flaming blue cone. The impact was enough to knock the sahir out of the circle. As soon as he crossed the chalk line, the blue flames vanished. Aleksei strode forward, snatched the emerald jar from him and pinned his arms. Breena took his ring and handed it to Kai. He set it on the concrete floor and stared at it. The ring started to melt.

"No! Stop! You cannot do this!" screamed the sahir. His face was white with terror.

An amorphous, boiling cloud began to form over the molten gold and the loose gemstone. Lightning flashed around it, and fountains of sparks erupted as the bolts of energy struck the metal framework of the warehouse.

"That would be one really pissed-off djinn. We need to go. Now," said Kai.

The far door banged shut. The strawberry blond man was gone.

Aleksei ran to help Eoin with Quinn, who had reverted to human shape.

"No!" Eoin shouted. "Get back. Did you not see that werewolf?" He hoisted Quinn onto his shoulders, and the five of them fled out the back door.

Frey was waiting for them at the gate. Aleksei opened the SUV's back door and Eoin pushed Quinn inside, then got in with him. Tires squealed as Frey took off, not waiting for Kai's door to close.

"I don't know how, but they knew we were coming," Kai blurted out. "They were expecting us."

"I see. Where to?" Frey asked.

"Can't take him to our place. Too much MAMIC traffic, and this mission was beyond unauthorized. Take him to his girlfriend's house," Kai said.

"She's not my girlfriend," Quinn replied weakly from the back.

Eoin pulled some paper towels off of the big roll in the cargo area and used them to help staunch the bleeding as he held Quinn's shoulder tightly. "What about Malik? Can you free him? We could do with his help."

Kai shook his head. "No. I don't know how far they got with the ritual. He might be compromised. If we let him out, he might kill us all."

Chapter 17
If Wishes Were Horses

I THREW DOWN THE sword and fumbled with the lock, flipping the lever and jerking the door back along its track.

"No! Don't touch him! He's covered in blood," a dark-haired woman shouted at me as I lunged towards Quinn.

I felt that familiar helpless dread, like my soul was being sucked down a bathtub drain with the dirty water. Not again.

"What happened? Is he…?"

"Dead?" asked the woman. "No. Not yet, and not if I can help it."

She went out to the patio and started talking, apparently, to the zinnias in the pot on the bistro table. The man who had been carrying Quinn laid him down on my bed. That's when I noticed that only the top half of him was a man. The goat-legged bottom half was very disturbing.

I turned on the overhead light. Quinn looked bad. His eyes had rolled back in his head, so mostly white was showing. A huge bite mark marred his left shoulder and part of his neck. Many, less serious, cuts and bruises dotted his body. As I watched, he started to twitch and shiver.

"Hurry!" the redhead called to the woman.

"He's seizing!" I yelled.

The red haired man held onto my arm and prevented me from going to Quinn. "Don't touch him! Are you deaf, woman?"

I could have sworn that I saw a disembodied hand suddenly appear in front of the woman on the patio and pass her a two-handled cup. However she got it, she came in and drizzled some of the cobalt-colored liquid on Quinn's gaping shoulder wound. It hissed and smoked when it touched the bloody areas.

"I need a spoon for the smaller areas – more precision," she said, not looking at me.

Obediently, I trotted into the kitchen and retrieved both a regular spoon and a serving spoon. That wound on his shoulder was big.

When I got back, the redhead, the half-goat and the third man were holding Quinn down on the bed as he thrashed and moaned. His shredded clothes were lying in a pile by the door. The woman was trying to dress his wounds with the blue stuff, but he was doing his best not to let her. I'd seen scary grand mal seizures before, but this was worse. He snarled like a trapped animal and groaned as if he were in unbearable pain. I shut the door behind me, hoping to muffle the noise enough not to wake Cassie. I didn't need to contend with her as well.

"Here!" I said handing the woman the spoons.

"Good. You take the small spoon and put the medicine on any place you can find where the skin is broken. He won't like it. Don't let the liquid get on your skin. And whatever you do, don't touch his blood. Eoin's immune. You're not."

I would ask her what Eoin was immune to later. Now, I had work to do. I took the spoon from her and dipped it into the cup. My ER training made dabbing smelly stuff on a struggling body seem like second nature. While I was searching out punctures, I could feel Goatboy's eyes on me. It seemed that he wasn't just looking at me, but into me; peeling away the layers of myself, until he could see my bare soul. I didn't have time to worry about being uncomfortable.

The third man grumbled. "I don't understand why you wanted to bring him here. We should have just taken him to—"

The red-haired man shushed him and nodded towards me. "Aleksei. You know he can't go there if he's infected."

Infected? There it was again. Infected with what?

I looked at the third man, who was holding one of Quinn's legs. I knew he was there, but he seemed to fade into the background and I had to concentrate to notice him. His face was greyish-blue and elongated, and something about it made me think of gnarled, ancient trees.

The woman had finished with the big wound. To my surprise, it was already starting to close. She helped me medicate the last few scratches on his front and sides.

"Roll him on his side," she ordered the men holding Quinn.

Fortunately, there weren't many wounds on his back – we were almost out of the blue serum.

"Gotta get him out of this blood," the woman said. "It may be live."

Live?

The men lifted Quinn while she stripped off the sheets. There was one small spot where Quinn's blood had soaked through the pad and into the mattress.

"That mattress is going to have to go. Sorry," the redhead said.

They laid Quinn back down, as far away from the spot as possible. He had stopped struggling, and appeared to be asleep. I shook my head in disbelief. The enormous wound on his neck and shoulder was completely closed, covered by new, pink flesh. There was no sign of the other cuts and scratches.

The woman gasped. "Blood!" she shouted to the red-haired man.

A deep red streak stood out in shocking relief against his pale wrist. She grabbed the spoon from me and smeared the residue of the cobalt liquid on the blood. Then she did the same with the other spoon. The blood sizzled and smoked as it evaporated.

"That was close. Please tell me no one else is contaminated."

The four of them checked each other for blood spots, then the woman gave me a careful once-over. Everyone was clean.

I opened the cedar chest at the end of the bed and pulled out a cotton blanket. Careful not to touch him, I draped it over the unconscious Quinn.

The red-haired man took out his mobile phone and started sending a text.

"Okay," I said. "Can someone please tell me what is going on? What happened to Quinn?"

"Werewolf," said the woman. "Big nasty one, too."

I really hoped that it was the same one that had come to my door. I didn't want to think that there was a whole pack of them prowling around. "Did he kill it?" I asked, hopeful.

"Not sure," said the red-haired man. "There was a lot going on when we left."

I looked at Quinn. "Will he be all right?"

The red-haired man looked at the woman, and there seemed to be some unspoken communication between them, but it was nothing I could decipher.

"Maybe," she replied, glancing at me. "Werewolves are kind of like Komodo dragons. Except instead of lethal bacteria, their saliva contains parasites, which can infect the victim and turn him or her into a werewolf, too, if there is a sufficient load. That's why you can't touch his blood – it may be full of them. Eoin's an urisk – think Scottish satyr – and the parasites can't live in his blood. The rest of us are all susceptible, and humans are particularly vulnerable." She shook her head slightly and looked at Quinn. "We killed off as many as we could, but it's up to him, now. If his body can fight off the invaders, he'll be fine."

"And if it doesn't?" I was fairly sure I already knew the answer.

"He'll either die slowly and painfully, or the parasites will take him over and we'll have to kill him," Aleksei said quietly.

That seemed incredibly unfair. "Isn't there some kind of antibiotic or anthelmintic you can give him?"

"A dewormer? I wish there was," said the woman, with a sigh. "Sunlight helps some."

"Got no shortage of that," I replied. "Well, at least we won't in another couple of hours. How did Quinn get attacked by a werewolf?" Guilt was already gnawing at me. Had he taken on that monster to protect me? My eyes lingered on his face, so peaceful now. Please, please, please be okay.

"We were retrieving some stolen property," the redhead said, "and it ambushed us."

Stolen property? Could it be the bottle containing Malik, the djinn? Might be just what the doctor ordered.

"Were you able to get your stuff back?" I asked.

Another long look between him and the woman. "Yes," he said, with no elaboration.

"That's nice," I said. These folks don't give anything away, do they? I continued. "We haven't been introduced. I'm —"

"Marti Keller. We know. I am Mr. Underhill," he replied. One corner of his mouth quivered, as if an automatic smile was suddenly quashed.

Quinn moaned softly and his fingers twitched as if he were dreaming. I watched him carefully.

"You can go to him now, if you want," the woman said. "He's cleaned up, should be safe enough. For now, anyway."

I tried not to be too dismayed as I went and sat on the edge of the bed. I stroked his forearm and the back of his left hand. "Just because I said there was no such thing as werewolves, you didn't have to go and try to prove it. I believe you. You're going to be just fine. All you need is some rest."

I leaned over and kissed his forehead. "I'll see you soon."

I hadn't noticed Eoin and Aleksei leaving, but when I turned around, they were nowhere to be seen.

I got up and made my way to the dark-haired woman. "How long does it take? To know if he's going to become a werewolf?" I whispered.

"If he hasn't turned by Tuesday morning, he isn't going to," she replied.

"Tuesday? Today is Saturday. Where are you going to take him to recover? Can I come visit him?"

"Take him? He's too unstable to be moved."

The last thing in the world I needed was a werewolf incubating in my bedroom. But I couldn't just throw Quinn out and risk his recovery, either. Do I choose Scylla or Charybdis?

"Won't the werewolf come back to finish Quinn off? It knows where I live, and it knows Quinn has been staying here."

"Unlikely," Mr. Underhill answered. "For one thing, it was badly injured – I think Quinn broke one of its legs. For another, if our treatment doesn't work, either Quinn will die or he'll turn. If he turns, he'll seek out the alpha, the one who infected him. No real reason for the werewolf to come back. Besides, you've got a pretty good warding set up."

"Worst-case scenario: what happens? I have to know what to do to protect my child."

"In the worst-case scenario, there's really nothing you can do, other than to not be here. If he starts to turn and takes us out before we can neutralize him, he becomes a full-blown werewolf. If the parasites are able to harness his full kelpie strength, well, I don't fancy anyone's chances against him."

Fantastic. "On a slightly different subject, there was an event, with a sahir, on Monday night that Quinn was concerned about. Is that—"

"That situation is under control," Mr. Underhill said, cutting me off.

I seemed to mostly have traded one crisis for another, except that now I was back to square one on taking down Ian Chambers and his boss. The world might be safe from an evil dictator, but Nick and Quinn (and Ryan's reputation) were still in jeopardy. The more

I thought about it, the more I knew what I had to do. I just hoped I hadn't missed my chance.

"I need to go to the restroom. If you'll excuse me?" I went into the bathroom and locked the door behind me, turned on the exhaust fan, then flipped down the lid and sat on the toilet.

"Delilah!" I thought as hard as I could.

"Girlfriend, what have you gotten yourself into now?" She stood directly in front of me, shaking her head.

I need your help. Can you find out which one of them has the bottle with the djinn?

"They can see and hear me, remember? Nothing I can do about that."

Damn.

"Since you wouldn't take my advice about the shifter, I know you ain't gonna take my advice about messin' around with djinn. But I'm gonna tell you anyway. Do not even go there. You think that shifter's friends are slippery. They ain't nothin' compared to a djinn. I know what you're thinking and you need to just forget about it."

But don't you see? It would fix all of the problems in one easy step.

"Baby girl, I got two words for you: unintended consequences. You think you're the first person to fool around with stuff like that? Ain't nobody, in the history of time, ever got what they thought they would."

What do you want me to do? Quinn may turn into a werewolf and be killed by his friends. Nick's career may be finished, and Ryan's reputation could be tarnished forever if I don't do something.

Delilah's eyes softened. "Marti, why do you think this is all on you? Nick's union lawyer will take care of him. When he's cleared, Ryan's cleared. There's not a thing you can do for that shifter. He'll either be okay or he won't. But it's not about you."

I never said it was. I can't just sit around and hope things will work out. I have to do something. It's the way I'm made.

Delilah shook her head. "Girl, I knew you were going to say that. Please let that djinn alone. And when you ride the black horse, don't trust its driver."

And poof! Delilah was gone.

Aaaarrrgh! Ghosts could be so annoying.

I flushed the toilet and washed my hands, just in case they were listening outside in the bedroom. If they had a djinn in a bottle, who was Quinn's friend, why didn't they just ask the djinn to heal him? There was probably some elaborate protocol, red tape and paperwork, I reasoned. At least that's what I hoped it was. But me, I had plausible deniability. I could just plead ignorance.

I brushed my teeth and splashed some water on my face. Man, I look rough. Still another hour before Cassie got up. I may as well have breakfast.

I did a very poor job of stifling a yawn as I went back into the bedroom. Quinn hadn't moved, but the woman was sitting on the cedar chest, and "Mr. Underhill" had his cell phone held up to one ear with his finger stuffed in the opposite one.

"I'm starved," I announced. "You guys want some breakfast?"

The woman hesitated. "Do you have any fresh fruit?"

"Always."

She followed me into the kitchen and rooted through the fruit bowl while I put the coffee on. I had hoped to get a chance to talk to her. But she washed the peach she had chosen, ate it over the sink and was gone before I could think up anything more or less intelligent to say. I am so not a morning person.

What am I going to do? I can't abandon my house to these strangers. I think they're trying to help Quinn, but I can't be certain. Quinn did say that someone might be trying to get revenge against him, so I suppose it's possible that this whole thing is a crazy conspiracy. But if they wanted revenge, it seemed weird they would have bothered patching him up. Besides, Delilah never said anything against them. And Quinn had said 'we' several times. I didn't think he meant the royal we, as in 'We are not amused.' What if Cassie and I left the house and Kyle and Aiden came to play with Bruce, but found a were-kelpie-wolf in his place? How would I explain that to Emily and Nick? 'I'm so sorry that your kids were eaten by a werewolf...' I had to keep Cassie safe. Not like I could leave her at Mom's for three days. I wanted to help Quinn, if I could, but I wasn't sure that any of my nursing skills translated into de-wolfing someone. And what about Nick and Ryan? How was I supposed to work on nailing Ian Chambers with a possibly mortally wounded Quinn lying on my bed and being watched over by people who just might have to kill him? And me, for that matter. All this made my head hurt. Maybe coffee would help.

I had propped my elbows on the table and cradled my chin in my hands, just to rest my eyes for a moment. I didn't realize I had fallen asleep until Cassie's wakeup alarm sounded. The coffee had thickened and scorched while I had been sleeping, filling the kitchen with a bitter reek. I unplugged the machine and went to get my little sweetie.

I stopped by my bedroom on the way, to check on Quinn. I suppose no news was good news.

Once Cassie was dressed and ready to come into the kitchen, I set her in the high chair. She dropped Cheerios on the floor and looked around expectantly. When Bruce didn't come, she cried.

"It's okay, baby," I said, stroking her short, wispy hair. I picked her up and carried her around the house. "Let's go for our walk, okay my dumpling?"

I knew it wasn't required, but I checked in with the dark-haired woman, whom I decided to start calling Morgaine (just not to her face).

"Ba ba ning!" Cassie exclaimed, flapping her hands.

The woman smiled, and Cassie grinned back at her.

"How's he doing?" I asked.

"No change," she replied, shaking her head gently.

"We're going out for our morning walk. Need anything from the corner market?"

Morgaine opened her mouth as if she were going to say something, then shut it again. "No, nothing, thanks. Have fun."

I was hoping the fresh air, make that dense, muggy air, would help me find a new perspective, to look at these multiple problems from a different angle. That, and the Tenth Sphere was on the way. Maybe Lulu would have some insight into demonic parasites.

I could hear the rumble of a big truck outside. Odd. It wasn't garbage day. I looked out the front window and saw a furniture delivery truck parked in front of my house. Two men were lowering the ramp.

"New mattress," Mr. Underhill said. "You didn't really want to keep the blood-soaked, parasite-infected one, did you?"

"Not when you put it that way."

"They'll also take all of the contaminated clothes, sheets and so on and dispose of them properly."

I nodded. I never expected to have a bio-hazard containment team in my house. Even if it had to be done, I didn't want to watch them take away the mattress from the bed I'd shared with Ryan. I grabbed Cassie and we hurried to the Tenth Sphere.

"So, honey," Lulu asked as soon as I walked in the door. "Have you thought any more about coming to work here at the shop?" She was dusting the Tibetan singing bowls.

"Yes. Yes, I'd love to do it. When do you want me to start?"

"How about Monday?" Lulu wiped down the counters with glass cleaner.

"How about Tuesday?" Morgaine said we would know one way or the other by then.

"Deal."

I sighed. The walk hadn't done diddly-squat for my perspective. If anybody could help, it would be Lulu. And I needed every ounce of help I could get. After all, she had accompanied me to tamper with a crime scene. If I couldn't trust her, I couldn't trust anybody. "So. How much do you know about werewolves? Delilah said the only thing that can hurt a werewolf is silver. Is that true? If so, will wearing a silver bracelet help?" I was trying my best to come up with ways to protect

Cassie that wouldn't make me look like a tinfoil-hatter to the casual observer.

"They do seem to be allergic to it – blisters them on contact and it'll kill them if it gets in their bloodstream. Not sure how well a bracelet would work, but it couldn't hurt, I suppose. Is that werewolf still giving you trouble?" she asked. "Didn't the warding help?"

"It's not that. I wish that was it. It's Quinn. Well, you know him as Bruce, the dog. He's been attacked by a werewolf."

"Goddess help us!" Lulu exclaimed. "Well, honey, I did tell you not to take that dog home," Lulu said. "But anybody that is fighting werewolves can't be all bad." Then her eyes narrowed. "How do you know that's what happened? And I'm not even going to ask how you know his name is Quinn."

"They told me when they brought him to my house at 3:30 this morning."

"They who?" she shot back.

"A man that calls himself Mr. Underhill, a dark-haired woman, a goat man, and a guy that made me think of trees, if that makes sense."

Lulu dropped the duster. "Does this Mr. Underhill have red hair by any chance?"

I felt my jaw go limp. "How did you know that?"

I shifted Cassie to my other hip. She'd been gnawing on her fingers and drooling like a faucet. My left shoulder was soaking.

"If this Mr. Underhill is who and what I think he is, any anti-werewolf measures he's got are miles better than the best I could come up with. Excuse me, honey."

She left to help a customer choose a Tarot deck and some incense.

"Patchouli," she said when she came back.

I snorted. "Hmph. He going home to fire up a joint?" I snarked.

Lulu gave me such a look that I felt like I should run out to the parking lot to apologize to the man for something he didn't even hear me say.

"Patchouli is good for divination – it boosts clairvoyance. Fertility, too, if you must know."

"That's very nice," I snapped. I was pacing back and forth behind the cypress root chair and bouncing Cassie a little harder than I probably should have. "But I have to know: how could you possibly know Mr. Underhill?"

I puffed out my cheeks and exhaled my frustrations. Didn't help any. I shifted Cassie to my other hip. The air conditioning blowing right on my head and slimy shirt didn't make me feel any more cheerful.

"I don't know him," Lulu replied. "I know of him."

"And?"

Lulu shrugged. "He's fae. He and his group are about as much on our side as their kind are ever likely to be."

"What's that supposed to mean?"

The door jingled and a woman wearing a gauzy, flowing skirt in a floral print strolled in.

"Oh, dear," Lulu muttered just loud enough for me to hear. "Hold that thought, Marti." She cleared her throat and smiled rigidly as she went to greet the customer. "Virginia! What brings you to this side of town?"

"Lu! Love the shop. This is a great location for you."

She ran her fingers over the glass counter as she went by the cash register, passing Lulu and making her way deeper into the shop.

"Yes," Lulu said. "We're liking it a lot. Well, thanks for stopping by."

"Oh, my, my, my. I'm in no rush." She cast her eye around to the shelves nearest her. "I thought I'd have a look at your loose crystals."

Lulu never let the strained smile slip. "Of course you did." She turned to me and mouthed something. It looked like 'Go get Belinda,' so that's what I did.

I found her in the store room, organizing inventory.

"Hey, Belinda? Lulu asked me to come find you. Some woman named Virginia is up front."

Belinda' eyebrows arched into fearsome points and her nostrils flared. I was concerned for her blood pressure, the way her face darkened.

"Yeah, well, I think Cassie and I will be on our way now." I backed away from her. Whatever was going on with this Virginia person looked like way more than I was willing to get involved with right now.

I wished I could have hung around the shop and helped a little bit, but between Virginia (whoever she was) and trying to keep Cassie from making the acquaintance of any number of breakables, I was stretched too thin. It was time for Cassie's nap, anyway. We went back to the house. Wasn't sure how that was going to work when I reported for duty on Tuesday, but I supposed I would find out. If it was just half a day, two or three days a week, my mother might even be able to swing watching her. But how on Earth did Lulu know about Mr. Underhill? Stupid Virginia. She couldn't have waited five minutes to waltz through the door and mess everything up?

I hadn't intended to, but I surprised the alleged Mr. Underhill sitting at the kitchen table with the green bottle-o-djinn in his hands. He quickly stuffed it back into his left pocket. Now at least, I knew where it was. No idea how to get it, but I'd worry about that later.

Cassie struggled against sleep, but lost the battle. She would be giving up her morning nap soon, I guessed. Soon, but not yet.

I got a drink of water and went to my bedroom.

"How's the patient?" I asked Morgaine.

"He's stirring a little. Why don't you try and talk to him?"

She hovered in the doorway when I went to see Quinn. I couldn't tell who she was watching more closely, me or him.

I laid my hand on top if his. "Quinn? How are you feeling?"

His smile was weak and half-hearted. When he opened his eyes, I pulled back and gasped. I hadn't meant to.

Instead of near-black, his eyes were orange, and burned with fever.

"Is that supposed to happen?" I asked, glancing over my shoulder to the woman in the doorway.

"It's not a good sign," she answered. "But he isn't lost yet."

"Marti?" Quinn's voice was quiet, but it was a hoarse growl that turned my insides to ice.

"I'm here." I squeezed his hand harder.

"Sorry. Didn't. Get. Him." He rasped.

"It's okay," I said. "We'll get him later. You need to rest, and get yourself well."

His lips parted, as if he was going to say something else, but I put my finger against them. "You can tell me all about it later." The fact was, his rough new voice frightened me, and I refused to think about what it meant. He was losing the battle and I knew it. I'd seen the signs all too often in the ER.

I had to act now, before it was too late. If I didn't do something, and right now, Quinn was going to die. Or become a werewolf. Not sure which was worse.

"Be back in a minute," I told Morgaine on my way out.

Fortune smiled upon me. Mr. Underhill was headed down the hall towards me. I adjusted my pace so that I would pass him just at the open door of the half-bath.

I pretended to trip on the throw rug and fell into him. Instinctively, he reached up to catch me. I plunged my hand into his left pocket and felt the emerald jar, cold and sharp-edged. He must have felt me pulling it out. He tried to grab me, but I twisted away and ducked into the powder room, slamming the door behind me and slapping the bolt latch closed. The door was an old-fashioned solid wood one, not the flimsy hollow core ones that most people have inside their houses. Still, I knew the latch wouldn't keep him out for long. But hopefully, it would be long enough. I wedged the laundry hamper under the doorknob for good measure.

I hadn't really thought through what I was going to do when I got my hands on the emerald bottle, so I was going to have to wing it.

"I claim this bottle," I said. "And the djinn within," I added for emphasis.

"Open the door, Marti!" Mr. Underhill shouted. "You don't know what you're doing."

"No! I know exactly how to fix everything. Go away!"

My hands were shaking from adrenalin and my heart pounded. I almost dropped the bottle on the tile when I tapped it with my fingernail. I wasn't sure how to get Malik's attention, and that seemed like a good idea.

Out of the corner of my eye, I saw the door's bolt latch sliding open. I grabbed the little knob on top and slammed it closed. I leaned on the hamper and door and didn't dare let go of the latch. Whatever Mr. Underhill was using on the other side to pull the latch back was strong and I struggled to hold it in place. I wasn't sure if the laundry hamper was hurting or helping at this point.

I addressed the bottle. "I have a deal for you. One wish for your freedom."

I twisted the cork top out of the mouth of the jar. I expected smoke to pour out and turn into someone who looked more or less like Mr. Clean.

Nothing seemed to happen. I had to drop the bottle onto the rug and hold the latch with both hands now.

"Don't let him out!" shouted Mr. Underhill. "Open the door!"

"Well? Aren't you going to answer him?" asked a deep voice.

I looked over my shoulder to see a man in a wool sport coat standing between the toilet and the sink. His pale lavender silk tie was impeccably knotted and held in place by a diamond tie-tack. A carefully shaped and closely trimmed beard hugged his chin and jaws. The only thing that prevented him from looking like he'd just stepped out of a Fortune 500 shareholders' meeting was his weirdly green eyes. They were absolutely the wrong shade for eyes – pale and metallic – and it seemed to me that there was a cold fire raging behind them.

Mr. Underhill pounded on the door. "Marti? What have you done?"

My fingers ached from holding the tiny knob on the latch. I knew it was only moments before my grip failed. I leaned against it even harder.

"A trade," I said to the djinn. "One wish for your freedom."

"A single wish? Nothing more than that?" he replied.

"Marti! Stop!" pleaded Mr. Underhill from behind the door.

"I wish I was back to the day before Ryan died."

The room began to spin. I threw out my arms for balance. I felt the powder room door opening and pushing against my body as I faded away.

I heard Mr. Underhill shout, from what sounded like a very great distance away, "Malik! She doesn't know what she's doing. Give her an out!"

"Oh, very well," the djinn grumbled. "You have chosen to change history and create an alternate timeline. I cannot prevent you from forgetting this version of reality, but I can slow it. You have thirty-six hours before your memories of this timeline are completely erased. You can change your mind until then."

And I was utterly alone in the dark.

Chapter 18
Horses for Courses

―――――――――― ❦ ――――――――――

I OPENED AND CLOSED my eyes. Made no difference. The blackness was absolute. Then I started to fall. I flailed my arms and kicked my legs, searching for a non-existent solid something to grab onto. I tried to scream, but nothing would come out of my mouth.

I landed hard on my back and gasped for air. I was cold and felt mildly claustrophobic, almost like I was trapped in goo in a small space.

I smelled something spicy and familiar. My eyes flew open.

I was lying in my own bed. The bathroom door was ajar, and Ryan was just finishing up shaving, wearing nothing but his boxer-briefs, as usual. And what a delicious sight that was. He hummed to himself as he stretched his lips and chin for the razor. I almost laughed out loud. I knew he'd think I was having some kind of episode if I ran in there and hugged him, so I stayed under the covers, basking in my secret good fortune.

It was still dark, and he didn't have to be at work until eight. He usually went to the gym first, unless I could persuade him to skip it. But that wasn't going to happen today. I felt queasy and I was over a week late. I would wait until after Ryan left to take the test, just in case I was wrong. But I knew I wasn't. Still, I'd need something to show Ryan – he'd want proof. I thought of Cassie and smiled.

Everything was put back to where it should have been. Ryan was alive, and I'd tell him about the baby before he left for work. Not sure how I'd stop him from pulling over that car tomorrow, but I'd come up with something – I had to. It was now almost two years before Quinn would encounter the werewolf, and if Ryan didn't die, and Ian Chambers had no reason to come to my house, perhaps Quinn and the werewolf would never even meet, and he'd be safe. Maybe I'd even changed things enough that Malik would never be imprisoned in the emerald jar. I could hope, anyway. I could expose Ian Chambers before he had the opportunity to frame Ryan and Nick, and they'd be safe. But most important, I had Ryan back and Cassie would have a chance to grow up knowing her daddy. It was an all-around win.

Ryan stepped out of the bathroom and pulled a t-shirt and sweats out of the dresser. He was half dressed before he noticed me watching him.

"Hey, Bright Eyes."

"Hey, yourself." That was it. I couldn't lie there and not touch him. I peeled back the warm covers and swung my legs out of bed. And lay back down. There wasn't anything in my stomach, but damned if it wasn't trying to come up anyway.

"You okay?" Ryan asked, concerned.

"Yeah. Just got up too fast, that's all," I fibbed.

Ryan scowled. "I hope you're not getting that flu that's been going around."

"I'm sure it's not the flu. I'm fine. Actually, I think it's something else. Something very, very different." I stood up and took the few steps I needed to join him by the dresser.

He wrapped his arms around me, and started to kiss me. But I wouldn't let him. I hadn't brushed my teeth yet. I nestled my head against his shoulder, savoring the feel of his body, the smell of his aftershave, the beating of his heart. If I got any happier I would explode. Now was my big chance to tell him.

The first heave wasn't too strong, and was easy to stifle. But I knew the next one wouldn't be. I pulled away from Ryan, more slowly than I needed to, but faster than I wanted to.

"Bathroom," I said, smiling at him.

He nodded and went back to getting dressed.

Behind the closed bathroom door, I tried drinking some water. But the sound of the running faucet made me really have to pee. I tore open the pregnancy test I'd stashed under the towels in the étagère above the toilet. I held up the tiny plastic cup. Seriously? But I had to go – it was that or nothing.

Drinking the water had been a bad idea. Now there was something to heave up. I knew I had fifteen weeks of vomiting to look forward to. Or was it twelve? Details were starting to get a little fuzzy already. I supposed that was a good thing.

I completed the test and set it on the floor beside the toilet to let it develop while I brushed my teeth so I could give Ryan a proper send off.

"Ryan?"

No answer. He can't have left already. I haven't told him!

I ran into the kitchen and looked out the back door window. His car was just pulling onto the street. No! I'd never stop him now. I had no choice but to wait until tonight. I could call him, I supposed, but this was the kind of news that ought to be told in person. I sighed and told myself that regardless of what happened tomorrow, he'd still know about the baby.

I went back to the bathroom. The second line had appeared, as I knew it would. I left it on the vanity where Ryan could see it when he came home. Today, I was working the two-to-ten shift, and he'd be home first. The last time, I'd kept it hidden. But now that I had another shot at it, I wasn't going to blow it. I missed holding Cassie, but I knew she was in the safest place she could possibly be. In another eight months or so, both Ryan and I would have the chance to hold her.

I walked around my house, touching the curtains, straightening the picture frames, like I had just moved in. I reveled in my second chance – I was the cat who got the cream. Before I knew it, it was time for lunch.

Lunch…Officer down at 12:55. That was it! I'd get Ryan to have lunch with me tomorrow. That's what would stop him from pulling over that car – he would be safe and sound in a restaurant. I didn't know what Mr. Underhill had been so upset about. This was a piece of cake.

My shift in the ER was busy, as usual. The only thing that stood out was just before I was scheduled to go off duty, a couple brought in a six year-old boy. He was a beautiful child, with enormous hazel-brown eyes and milk chocolate brown hair. And a broken arm. The mother was frantic. I recognized the father. I knew him from somewhere, but I just couldn't place him. 'Spam,' the mother had called him. I couldn't think of a reason why I would know Spam, but I was sure that I did.

Something bad had happened to him. He didn't seem to know me, though, and he even got edgy with me at one point. Could Ryan have arrested him? Maybe, but how would I know about it?

"Take a picture chica; it'll last longer," he snapped at me.

"I'm sorry. I was sure I knew you from somewhere. Must be mistaken."

Maybe he was from the other reality, the bad reality that was fading away. It couldn't fade fast enough for me.

Ryan met me at the door when I got home.

"Is that what I think it is in the bathroom?"

I grinned at him.

And then we celebrated. Right there in the middle of the living room floor.

After we migrated into the bed, I snuggled against Ryan, and he draped a territorial leg over mine. He fell asleep almost immediately. It was early December, and the Christmas lights across the street bled in around the edges of the mini-blinds, blinking and flashing. I blamed them for keeping me awake, but, if I were really honest with myself, I'd have to admit that I was afraid if I went to sleep, I'd wake up and Ryan would be dead again.

So, I tried to organize my life. Had I done any shopping? I'd check my closet in the morning. That's where I hid everything. Maybe stepping into my life exactly where I'd left off almost two years ago wasn't quite as easy as I thought, but it sure beat the alternative.

The sound of Ryan's slow, deep breathing was starting to lull me to sleep. My eyelids were now so heavy I couldn't keep them open.

A sharp rap pierced the cozy quiet of the room.

My eyes flew open like cartoon window shades. The noise had come from the wall above the headboard, on Ryan's side.

At first, I couldn't see anything, but as I stared into the darkness, a pale mist seemed to be floating next to the bed. Or it could have been my imagination. Then, I remembered.

"Darla!" I whispered as loudly as I thought I could without waking Ryan.

"Darla? Girlfriend, that is messed up. Delilah. My name is Delilah. And you're talking out loud, again."

"Oh. Right. Why are you here?" I asked. I hadn't learned to see her until after Ryan died.

"I'm always around, Marti-girl. Even if you don't see me. I'm trying to help you. You need to undo this wish."

You are out of your mind. No way in hell I would change this. I've got Ryan back, and there are some other things I'm sure I fixed. I will not un-wish.

I could only see a faint mist, but I imagined that Delilah shook her head, and I could hear the sigh in her words. "Remember that I warned you."

The mist faded away, and I slipped into an uneasy sleep.

Nick and Ryan met me at 12:39 at the IHOP. It was too soon to tell Nick our good news, but he could tell we were hiding something. I have no doubt he guessed at what it was, especially given my sudden and obvious aversion to food. I was equally sure that Nick would wheedle it out of Ryan. That was okay. I'd already told Emily, but sworn her to secrecy.

I didn't pay very much attention to the conversation – my attention was on the green plastic clock on the far wall. 12:50. I squirmed in my seat.

"Do you need to get out so you can go to the ladies room?" Ryan asked.

"No, I'm fine."

12:55 came and went with no fanfare. I knew it was an important milestone. And that it had something to do with Ryan, but I couldn't quite remember what. Only that it was good that it had passed.

Outside of the IHOP, a man stood on the sidewalk in the parking lot. He wore a sandwich board made from two ragged pieces of cardboard. The message scrawled on the front with a ball point pen read, "The end is near! Repent, sinners!" and on the back, it read "World ends December 18! Believe it!" He flapped a handful of photocopied, handwritten fliers at anyone who didn't walk across the parking lot to avoid him.

"Are you saved?" the man shouted at Ryan.

"Sorry, sir. You're going to have to move along. You're trespassing," he replied.

The man handed Ryan a flyer, which he folded and put in his pocket. I guessed he did that just to be polite. That, and there was no trash can around.

"Fine, fine. The truth is too much for these wretched sinners to handle, anyway," the man grumbled as he started to shamble away.

He paused to look at me when he passed by. His eyes were dark, almost black, and they were clear and bright. Not the vacant eyes of the addict or the intense eyes of the psychopath. The dirt on his face looked cosmetic, not the ingrained grime of the long-term homeless. In fact, he smelled more like evergreens and rain than unwashed masses. I was horrified that his scent made my heart skip a beat. I glanced at Ryan and Nick, but their expressions gave nothing away.

The preacher took off his sandwich board and tossed it to the sidewalk.

"Hey! Pick that up. You're littering," Nick called after him.

The man waved one arm, as if he were swatting at Nick, and kept walking.

"That's it. We're going to have to run you in," Ryan said.

"Do what you've got to do," he replied.

Ryan cuffed the preacher and put him in the car while Nick put his makeshift sign and flyers in the trash.

Idiot. It was almost like he wanted to get arrested.

Thoughts of the incongruous street preacher niggled at me as I drove to work. And Delilah's warning from last night didn't help, either. I hadn't even clocked in when Ryan called on my mobile.

"Hey! What's up?" I asked.

"Marti," his voice was soft, and I was suddenly afraid. "Your mom was out shopping with Emily and the boys. Some guys ran a red light and hit her car.

Adele and Kyle are okay, just bumps and bruises. Aiden's been Life-Flighted to Hermann hospital."

"Oh, God." How could this happen to a four-year old boy? It wasn't fair. It took me a second to count heads. "Emily. You didn't say anything about her."

"I am so sorry."

"No. My sister is not dead. She wouldn't leave her boys right before Christmas. You're wrong." It couldn't be true if I refused to believe it, right?

Ryan didn't argue with me. "I just dropped Nick off at the hospital. I'm on my way to pick you up. Be there in about twenty. I love you."

My hands shook so hard that it took three tries to get my phone back into my handbag and I could barely see through tear-blurred eyes.

Mom and Dad had taken Kyle out to feed the ducks and get something to eat. Ryan and I sat with Nick, who looked more like a wax figure of Nick than the actual person. I had to look closely to see if he was breathing. I was still waiting for Emily to come around the corner and say, "Ha ha! Fooled you!"

It was almost 5:00 when Aiden came out of surgery. Both his legs were broken, he had a ruptured spleen, and a fractured skull. Even though he had taken off his surgical scrubs, the doctor's scent was a sour cocktail of latex, iodine and sweat, and he looked exhausted.

"Aiden had a subarachnoid hemorrhage. We had to perform a craniotomy, that's cutting a hole in his skull, to relieve the pressure and stop the bleeding. If he makes it through the night, there's a reasonable chance he might pull through. We've put him in a drug-induced coma to help the swelling go down and give the brain a better chance to recover. You need to know that both cognitive and physical disabilities are common with this kind of injury."

As soon as he had said 'subarachnoid hemorrhage,' I knew it was bad. Really bad.

Smart-ass, swaggering Nick stared blankly at the doctor. I'd never seen him like that, and it broke my heart.

"Can we see him?" Ryan asked.

"In about half an hour, you can go to the ICU."

I couldn't look at Nick, and I felt too guilty to cling to Ryan while Nick was sitting there all alone, so I stood up and looked out the small window in the waiting area. Winter dark was already descending, and the city was on the night side of twilight.

Somehow, this was my fault. I wasn't sure how it could be, but I knew it was. Not the first time I'd wished for a CTRL-ALT-DEL in real life. My stomach was a little crampy, but I figured that was because I'd eaten six saltines and half of a pancake all day. I left the waiting area to find a drink of water, but it didn't help much.

Ryan had followed me out into the hall.

"So," I said. "Did they at least get the person who did this?"

"Yes and no. Adele was westbound on Memorial and there was a Metro bus headed east. The southbound SUV hit your mom's car, pushing it across three lanes of traffic. The bus T-boned them immediately after."

"Them?"

"Two men, we think. Car was registered to Friar Enterprises. But it's going to take some time to identify the occupants."

I cringed. Enough details. Back in the waiting area, a woman in scrubs was talking to Nick. I wasn't sure if she was a nurse or a doctor, but she had come to take us to Aiden.

We stumbled like zombies to the ICU. I got a Snickers bar from the vending machine on the way. My hands were starting to shake, and the cramps were getting worse. Even so, I couldn't bring myself to eat the candy bar.

Aiden was dwarfed by the machinery that surrounded him. Tubes stuck out of his head and his throat and his arms. Drain tubes, trach tube, IVs. He was so pale. EKG and EEG readouts scrolled along above his head. The respirator clicked and hissed. I was too numb to cry. This couldn't be happening.

But my day wasn't bad enough.

The cramps I'd been having suddenly got worse. A whole lot worse. It felt like my entire midsection was being crushed in a vise. I hadn't meant to cry out as I doubled over and hit the floor. I must have peed myself, because something hot and wet was running down my leg.

I stayed curled in a fetal position on the floor. I could hear Ryan swearing (he never did that) and rubber-soled shoes scurrying around the room. Then the clatter of a gurney, and hands lifting me up.

I heard someone moaning and groaning as they wheeled me down the corridor. I wondered if it was me. I found the smell of hospital disinfectant oddly comforting.

"Was she pregnant?" a female voice asked.

Was? What do you mean was? Is. Was is past tense. I am pregnant.

"Yes." Ryan's voice was hoarse.

Another wave of mega-cramps hit me. I was sure I heard the word 'miscarriage' floating in the air above my head.

NO. No. No. No. No. I am not losing my baby, too.

Too much. Too much tragedy for one day. I didn't think I could survive it. I tried to say something, but the only thing that came out was a whimper.

"Is there supposed to be that much blood?" Ryan asked. His voice was edged with panic.

I didn't hear what the woman said because someone was whispering in my ear. "Marti? You're almost out of time, girlfriend. If you're gonna un-wish this, you better do it quick."

Un-wish? I could almost remember something about making a wish, but it skirted the edges of my memory.

"You can go back to where you were before you made the wish. Ryan is dead, but your baby, her name is Cassie, is alive, and Emily and Aiden are fine. Or you can stay here."

Cassie? The baby's a girl? I'd always wanted a little girl, but I'm not sure I would have named her Cassie.

If Ryan was alive, I could probably have another baby. Wouldn't be this baby, but lots of women had miscarriages and went on to have healthy babies. Happened every day. The ER docs always said most early miscarriages were due to chromosomal abnormalities.

If my choice was to sacrifice Ryan for an unviable baby, there was no contest.

But it wouldn't bring back Emily. I'd lose my sister, Mom and Dad would lose their daughter, Nick would lose his wife, and Kyle would lose his mommy.

I thought of Aiden, lying in the ICU, so small and so very fragile. A medically-induced coma was a Hail Mary, a last resort. Something they did when there was nothing left to lose. He was only four.

And I did this to them. I knew it in my bones, even if I couldn't figure out how.

Why do I have to choose? Ryan or my baby, my sister, and my nephew. That's so unfair.

"Sorry, girlfriend. I don't make the rules."

My baby, though. Carrie?

"Cassie."

She's healthy? Nothing wrong with her? And Emily and Aiden are fine?

"Yes. She's beautiful. You have to choose now."

Dammit. Dammit. Dammit. I knew, if I were able to ask Ryan to choose, what his choice would be. Why? Why did this life have to be so damned hard?

I opened my eyes and looked up at Ryan. I needed to see his face. I squeezed his hand. My throat was so tight with misery and pain that I could barely get the words out. "I love you," I wheezed.

And then, I un-wished.

I fell up, spinning away into the night sky. The stars glittered coldly, so bright and so close. I felt nothing, no fear, no pain, no joy. I was just...aware. Galaxies spun. Stars died and were born. I watched it all and I didn't know if I was there for a millisecond or a millennium before I started to fall back down.

Faster and faster I went, feeling as if the breath was being pushed out of me, and there was too much pressure to let my lungs expand and take in more. Fear gripped my innards with icy fingers and sharp claws. Just when I thought I must surely implode, everything stopped. I gasped for air and opened my eyes.

Chapter 19
Down to the Sea in Ships

—————————— ❧ ——————————

I SPRAWLED IN THE middle of the powder room floor, the fallen laundry hamper on one of my legs. Mr. Underhill bent over me and snatched the emerald bottle and its stopper out of my hands.

"What did you do?" he asked.

"I didn't do anything. There was nothing in the bottle," I snapped at him. Still, I wondered why my cheeks were wet with tears and my abdomen felt like the Jolly Green Giant had squeezed me nearly in half.

He frowned. "What did you think would be in it?"

I took a deep breath and let it out. No reason to keep it a secret anymore. "Quinn told me that his friend, Malik the djinn, was trapped in a bottle made from an emerald. When you said that you had gotten what you were looking for, I assumed it was Malik. I thought I could save everybody if I wished myself back to the day before Ryan died. He wouldn't get killed, Quinn wouldn't have to fight the werewolf, and Ian Chambers would have no reason to frame Ryan and Nick. But the bottle was empty. Nothing happened." I didn't know whether to be angrier with myself, for believing in some stupid fairy tale genie, or Mr. Underhill, for treating me like a naughty child. Or the fact the whole crazy plan didn't work.

"What is the last thing you remember?"

Oh, for Pete's sake. "You pounding on the door and yelling at me."

What could have possibly happened in the nanosecond between me opening the bottle and him crashing through the door?

I picked myself up off the fuzzy rug and pushed my way past Mr. Underhill, shoulders back and chin up, trying to salvage the remaining shreds of my dignity. All the noise had woken Cassie up, and I had to go to her.

I sat her in her high chair with a sippy cup and veggie puffs while I cut up grapes for her. She didn't throw anything on the floor for Bruce to eat, and that made me a little sad.

Something shiny caught my eye. The anti-shifter amulet was still on the table where Quinn had left it. Once Cassie was done eating and wiped down, I took the amulet into my bedroom and gave it to the dark-haired woman.

"I don't know if this will help. It's an anti-shifting amulet. Quinn says there's a dragon bound to it."

She shrugged. "Maybe. Werewolves are unnatural shifters, so the type of magic in the amulet doesn't sync with theirs. But then again, dragons are powerful healers. Can't hurt to try."

I could tell by her expression that she didn't think it would do much good, but she hung it around Quinn's neck, anyway.

He immediately started groaning and writhing. The strange characters on the amulet glowed pale blue. His eyes darkened from bright orange to amber.

"That's good, right?" I asked.

"Not sure," she replied.

The noises Quinn was making frightened Cassie, so I had to take her out of the room. In fact, the walls were closing in on me and I really needed to get out of the house.

Mr. Underhill sat in the living room, messing with his phone.

Fae, huh? And all this time, I thought fairies were tiny little women in skimpy dresses with sparkly butterfly wings. And just what is it, Mr. Underhill, that you do that makes you so locally well known that even Lulu has heard of you?

"I'm low on diapers, so I'm going to get a few things from the store. Need anything?" I asked him.

He didn't look up. "No, thanks."

☙

The HEB grocery store was about three miles from my house. Kroger was closer, but I had HEB diaper coupons. We were a little over halfway there when the giant primer grey and red Suburban on my left decided to change lanes. Unfortunately, he didn't bother checking to see if the lane was occupied.

There wasn't a lot I could do to avoid him. I laid on the horn and ran up on the curb. He still sideswiped my fender before he took off, tires squealing. His windows were tinted too dark for me to get a look at the driver and I couldn't see his license plate – there was an over-sized spare tire bolted to the back. Cassie and I were shaken up, but unhurt.

As I was getting her out of the car, a metallic blue convertible Ferrari pulled up in front of us and the driver got out, "Hey Miss! You okay? I saw what happened."

"Thanks for stopping," I said. Where did I know this guy from?

"No problem." He handed me a business card. 'Tucker Fellowes, Attorney at Law Board Certified Estate Planning and Probate.' An address and phone numbers followed. "If you need a witness, just give me a call."

"I appreciate that. I was just calling my insurance."

The fender could have been worse, but the front tire on the passenger side was flat, and I was afraid the axle was bent. Great. Just what I needed.

I thought it was a little odd that Tucker Fellowes waited around while I talked to my agent. She was sending a tow truck. I used my phone to take photos of the damage and email them to her, as well as Tucker Fellowes' contact information. Then it suddenly occurred to me where I had seen him.

"You know Stella and Pudge? I'm sure I saw you at their party last Saturday."

A broad grin spread across his face. I wouldn't say he was handsome, but his features were well chiseled, and if anything, he was over-groomed. Clear nail polish on men really didn't work for me, though. "Yes, I was there. Sorry that we didn't meet at the party."

He said this while staring at my chest, and I found that I wasn't particularly sorry we hadn't been introduced.

"Excuse me for a minute, okay?" I said.

I tried to call Nick to see if he could come and get Cassie and me, but I couldn't get a signal. Of all the times for my cell to crap out. It had been working fine a few minutes ago.

Flashing yellow lights at the next traffic signal made me feel better. The wrecker driver would be here in a minute.

"You Marti Keller?" the driver asked when he got out of the tow truck. The name Earl was embroidered on his blue uniform shirt.

"Yes, I am,"

Earl handed me a card from the towing company. "Let's get 'em hooked up here." He spat tobacco juice on the sidewalk and then walked around my car.

Tucker Fellowes even helped Earl get the car lined up to pull it onto the flatbed truck. Once it was secured, I thought Cassie and I would ride to the dealership with him. If my phone didn't work there, at least they'd have a landline I could use.

But there was a problem.

There was enough room in the cab for Cassie or me, but not both.

"Can I just hold the baby in my lap?" I asked the driver.

"No ma'am. Can't do that. Insurance won't let me."

"Can I give you a lift somewhere?" Fellowes asked.

I weighed my options. Walk about two miles with a twenty-three pound baby in a carrier - a squirmy twenty-three pound baby who did not want to be in the carrier – or get into a sports car that cost about three times more than my house with a board certified probate attorney who freely gave his name and contact info to my insurance agent. Fellowes might be a creep, but I didn't think he was dangerous.

"Will the baby carrier fit in the back of your car?" I asked. There was that out again.

"Are you kidding? A baby is about all that will fit in that back seat," Fellowes said with a chuckle.

Even with the top down, it took a lot of contortion and awkwardness, but I got the baby bucket strapped into one of the miniscule back seats. I wasn't convinced that the two seats in the back were intended for anything other than decoration. Or maybe for chauffeuring Pomeranians around.

The front seat, on the other hand, reeked of luxury. Leather seats, satellite navigation, back-up camera. All very high tech and very expensive. If I won the Lotto, I don't think I'd buy a car like this, but I didn't object to going for a ride in it.

My plan was to have Fellowes drop me off at the Tenth Sphere. Close enough to easily walk home, and he wouldn't know exactly where my house was. I gave him directions.

We were on surface streets, but the top was down and the engine was loud. Sometimes it was hard to understand him, and I had to shout to make myself heard.

"What are you doing, chica?"

I could see him hunched in the back seat, next to Cassie. Getting a ride home, Spam. What did you expect me to do, hitchhike? With a baby? Where have you been, anyway?

"How do you know Stella and Pudge?" Fellowes asked.

"Stuff to do, people to see," Spam replied.

Having two completely separate conversations with two different people is a lot harder than it looks. I turned to Fellowes. "I don't exactly know them. I was there working with Lulu, the Tarot card reader."

Glancing up into the rearview mirror, I thought at Spam. What are you doing here?

"I remember there were entertainers there. How long have you been in the business?" Fellowes asked.

"'Bout a week," I answered, trying to look calm, cool and collected.

"Why'd you get in the car with this pendejo? What were you thinking?"

What am I supposed to think, Spam? I was getting more irritated with him by the second. If he wanted to tell me something, why couldn't he just come out and say it?

Fellowes continued through the light.

"Um, you missed the turn. You should have made a left there."

"Oh, did I? Sorry." But he kept driving.

"Told you," Spam chirped.

If you aren't going to help, go get someone who will, like maybe Delilah?

"Okay. This has gone far enough. Just pull over and let us out." I tried to sound calm, but my voice was scratchy and cracked from all the shouting.

"Can't do that, Marti. You decided to stick your nose in my business, so now you're going to get to experience it first-hand," Fellowes said, with a rancid smile.

I did not like the sound of that. "I thought you were a probate attorney. What are you going to do? Force me to read wills?" If I sounded flippant, maybe he wouldn't realize how scared I was.

"You're a funny lady, Marti. My estate planning practice is just the entrée, gets my foot in the door. Helps me find clients for my real business," Fellowes replied.

"And what would that be?" It had only just occurred to me the Ferrari logo was a black horse on a yellow background. "When you ride the black horse, don't trust its driver," Delilah had said. Crap.

"Haven't you guessed by now?" Fellowes asked, his tone implying I was stupid.

No, I haven't guessed what the business is, but I bet I know one of the employees. "Would Ian Chambers know?"

More laughter. "We'll be seeing him later. Why don't you ask him then? But out of the goodness of my heart, I'll give you a hint: Cynthia Ashland, since I know you've been doing some research. You have been to my website, after all."

Cynthia Ashland? The name seemed familiar, but I struggled to recall where I'd seen it. I mentally back tracked through the websites I'd been researching. Which one was Tucker Fellowes'?

"He owns Specials," Spam said.

You could have mentioned that earlier, Spam.

"No, I couldn't have. You have to be here. Sorry."

I looked at the back seat in the rear view mirror. Spam was fading away, and Cassie was getting glassy-eyed. There was no way I could jump out of the car without leaving my little girl behind.

At the next red light, a couple of homeless men were going from car to car with a paper cup.

"Help me!" I shouted at them. "Call the cops!"

Tucker Fellowes laughed. "You do realize you're asking junkies to call the police?"

I casually put my hand in my shorts pocket, where my cell phone was. Surely I'd get a signal by now. That dead spot had to have been a fluke. I ran my fingers over keys, trying to remember where the numbers started and the special characters ended. I hoped I was dialing 911.

Tucker Fellowes just smiled.

Nothing happened, so I tried again. Still nothing. Damn.

Then I suddenly remembered where I'd heard of Cynthia Ashland. She was the executive director of Friar Enterprises, LLC. Which owned Specials and a range of titty bars. Must be a front for Fellowes. That explained why Friar Enterprises only needed an executive suite – it was just a puppet theater. It also wasn't too hard to guess what types of services Friar Enterprises might be providing. So Tucker Fellowes wanted me to experience his business first-hand, and he was a pimp. I shuddered.

When we got to the Beltway, we headed south. I had tried calling 911 twelve times now.

I looked back at Cassie. She was falling asleep. Car rides did that to her. "Where are we going?" I asked.

"Boat ride." Fellowes answered. "And just an FYI – I turned on the cell phone jammer, so you can give up trying to call anyone. Might save yourself a lot of effort and frustration. I let you call the insurance agent and tow truck to get your car off the road so it wouldn't be attracting any unwanted attention. Your mother has already gotten a text saying that you and the baby are visiting a friend in Austin over the weekend. By the time anyone misses you, you'll be long gone."

I swallowed against the metallic taste of adrenalin and tried to force myself to breathe deeply. If I did that, my heart might stop thumping against my ribs like a caged animal. "Gone where?" I tried to sound casual. But my voice split the difference between 'terrified' and 'casual' and came out 'concerned.'

"Probably Asia, but we'll have to bleach your hair – they prefer blondes. Don't look so worried. You're way too old to go to Bangkok. I expect you'll go to a private collection. In fact, I've already contacted several likely interested parties. One of them likes to make snuff films, but I don't think he will be able to afford what I'm asking for you."

Knowing Fellowes was trying to intimidate me, I closed my eyes. I'd only caught a glimpse of Quinn in kelpie form on the night of the werewolf attack, so I substituted a mosasaur. I pictured it snapping up Tucker Fellowes in its huge jaws and swallowing him, screaming for his mama, in one gulp. There. You're not so tough.

Then I had another thought. I was afraid of the answer, but I had to ask. "What about Cassie?"

"The baby? She's not old enough to sell on to Bangkok." He smiled a greasy smile at me, knowing that wasn't at all what I meant. "If you cooperate, I won't hurt her. I could have her left at a hospital or fire station, with her name pinned on her shirt and everything. Your mother would get her back eventually. But only if you do exactly what I tell you."

That didn't make me feel a whole lot better.

I knew it was grasping at straws, but I had nothing else to grasp at. I may not be able to transmit anything from my phone, but I could record. It was a long shot, but I couldn't think of anything else. I fumbled with the buttons.

"So. Just out of curiosity. Why did you have Spam killed, Fellowes?"

"Spam? You run in interesting social circles, Ms. Keller. Yes, I was disappointed that they were able to find and identify him so quickly. But then you wouldn't know anything about that, would you?" He paused for me to answer, but continued when I said nothing.

"Spam was a long time employee. He was good at doing odd jobs and procurement. It's a real shame he started to develop a conscience and began questioning some of my business practices. It was only a matter of time before he started running his mouth to the wrong people."

Spam did like to run his mouth. "What kind of procurement?"

"Well, well. Aren't you full of questions?" Fellowes downshifted and took the I-45 exit off the Beltway. "Do you have any idea how expensive law school is? Neither did I, until I enrolled. I cooked meth to pay my way. Spam smurfed for me. Yep. If there was something you needed, Spam could get it."

"I'm sure he could." I shifted in my seat, feeling more sickened by Fellowes by the second.

"Estate planning and probate didn't pay nearly as much as I thought it would, so I had to branch out, add goods and services to my line of offerings."

"You disgust me."

"You'll have plenty of practice being disgusted once I've received payment and shipped you to the buyer."

If I didn't think it would make him crash the car and possibly hurt Cassie, I would have slapped his smarmy face. I pushed the button on the phone again, ending the recording. I didn't want to talk to Fellowes any more. Right now, I was too angry to be scared. But I knew that would change.

When we got to the private marina where Fellowes had his yacht docked, he raised the top and locked me in the car while he took Cassie out of the back seat.

Then he opened the door for me. I had no choice but to follow as he carried my sleeping baby along the pier.

"Did you really name your yacht 'Mary Celeste'?"

Fellowes grinned. "I couldn't resist. We'll be here for a few minutes, until the others can join us."

Anybody who would name a boat after an infamous ghost ship really liked to push his luck, was all I could say.

Fellowes found a shady spot under an overhang and set down the carrier. He pulled up a deck chair and sat next to Cassie, blocking my access. I paced back and forth in the glaring sun, looking for a way out. There wasn't a soul on this side of the marina. And what was I going to do if there was? Fellowes had Cassie. No telling what he'd say if the cops showed up – nasty custody battle that I'd lost? I was a stalker? I'd be the one getting arrested, and by the time they figured everything out, he'd be long gone with my baby.

Still, the sun shone and the waves sparkled. White boats bobbed on the swells. In the distance, a rainbow triangle skated over the water, pulling a sailboat along underneath it. The luxuriant frivolity pissed me off.

The ugly primer and red Suburban that had run me into the curb pulled up in the parking lot. Ian Chambers and Salinger-Spam-Killer got out of the truck. They pulled a large duffle bag from the back and Salinger slung it over his shoulder, more or less fireman style. The two men came down the pier and climbed aboard the boat.

I didn't know what had happened to Salinger, but I'd hate to see the other guy. Both of his eyes were blackened, although the bruises were a little blotchy, like they were a day or two old. Two deep, scabby cuts barely missed his left eye and skidded down the side of his neck to his collar bone. He limped badly under the weight of the duffle.

"Ian, can you get her cell phone? It's in her right pocket," Fellowes said.

Chambers complied, refusing to look me in the eye, and handed the phone to Fellowes, who sealed it in a cardboard envelope. "I picked a random storefront in Austin to FedEx this to. You can run it up to the drop box before we leave."

Ian Chambers paused before following Salinger below decks. "I'm sorry it had to come to this, Marti."

"I'll bet you are."

"Let's all go below, shall we?" Fellowes said with a gesture. "After you, mademoiselle."

He had Cassie's baby bucket, so there wasn't much I could do but curse him silently and shuffle down the steep stairs.

Chambers fixed himself a drink at the minibar. Salinger plopped the duffle on the floor, where it toppled over. I was sure I heard a groan. He opened a drawer and worked a fresh roll of duct tape out of a large multi-pack. He pulled some off and came over to me. He taped my hands together behind my back.

"Sit down," he said, nodding toward the built-in bench sofa behind me.

I sat, and he taped my ankles together.

"Really?" I asked. "Where is it you think I'm going to go?"

Salinger responded by slapping a piece of tape across my mouth. Asshole.

Tucker Fellowes had taken Cassie into another cabin.

"Hey, Fellowes," Salinger called.

I suddenly thought of the dog-eared sticky note in Ryan's file. Hey, Fellowes. Hey, fellows! Isn't that what the guy who shot Ryan, Fydor Dostoyevsky, said in the ambulance just before he died? Holy shit. What is going on here?

"What?" Fellowes came back in without Cassie.

Salinger prodded the duffle bag with his foot. "Leave him in or tape him?"

Fellowes looked at me with a wolfish grin. "By all means, tape him. I don't want my property damaged."

Chambers set down his drink and helped Salinger open the duffle bag and shake its contents onto the white Berber carpeting.

Mouth freshly bloodied, and still wearing the anti-shifter amulet, lay Quinn, looking much the worse for wear.

Chapter 20
Pretty Maids All in a Row

━━━━━━━━━━━━━━ ᪥ ━━━━━━━━━━━━━━

"WHAT HAVE YOU DONE to him?" I tried, without much luck, to shout at Salinger. He only smirked at me.

I hopped over to Quinn and flopped down awkwardly beside him. Laying my head on his chest, I could hear his heartbeat, slow but steady, and I felt his breath on my cheek. I wanted to peel back an eyelid and see what color his eyes were, but it was impossible with my hands taped behind me. Had they darkened or turned even more fiery? And what had happened to Mr. Underhill and the dark-haired woman?

I sat up and glared at Salinger. I tried scowling at Salinger, but the duct tape on my mouth was too stiff. Then I looked back at Quinn.

Salinger didn't try to roll Quinn over, just taped his hands in front of him, then his ankles. He didn't bother taping Quinn's mouth – maybe he didn't think it would stick with all the blood.

When he was done, he tossed the duct tape back in the drawer, looked at Chambers and nodded toward the stairs. Chambers picked up his drink, which was sweating almost as profusely as he was, and started for the steps. He paused to give me a sad, lingering look. I imagined hundreds of little knives flying out of my eyes and ripping him to shreds. He sighed and left. Salinger closed the door on his way out and locked it.

ᪧ

I don't know how long our boat ride lasted. It felt like several years, but I was sure that it really wasn't more than a couple of hours. It was long enough for me to make myself sick with worry, at any rate. Was Cassie okay? Where was she? Would I be able to get us out of this mess before I ended up in a brothel? Was Quinn still Quinn? Where the hell was Fellowes taking us, anyway?

If there is a way to get comfortable while bound and gagged with duct tape, I couldn't find it. Eventually, I sat next to Quinn and used his prone body to prop myself up.

Someone cut the engine and the boat stopped moving forward, but it still rocked enough to make me feel a little ill. I could hear men shouting and Cassie crying. I cried along with her. It'll be okay, sweetie. It'll be okay. Mama loves you. I struggled against the duct tape, but nothing I did seemed to help much. My shoulders ached from my arms being pulled behind my back and the stink from the tape on my mouth was giving me a headache.

I wished yet again that Lulu's anti-shifting amulet wasn't hanging around Quinn's neck. It was probably the one time ever that I needed him to turn into a big, nasty monster, and he couldn't do it. But then again, I couldn't be sure what kind of big, nasty monster he would turn into now, so maybe it was just as well.

I didn't know what Fellowes' plan for him was, but I was sure it wouldn't be good. I was reviewing my options (currently, none), when heavy footfalls thudded down the stairs. Then the snick of metal on metal as the lock turned, followed by a squeal of the door being opened. Salinger loomed in the doorway.

"We're here." He went to the mini-bar and opened the cabinet high above it. When he turned to face us, he had a box cutter.

He used it to cut the duct tape from our ankles. He wasn't very careful and he nicked my shin. He wiped the blood off of my leg with his finger, and then licked it. I gagged. He grinned.

Salinger got a chilled bottle of water from the mini-bar and splashed it on Quinn's face. His lids fluttered (but not enough for me to see what was going on with his eyes) and he groaned. "Wake up, you little sneak," Salinger snarled at him, before dragging him roughly to his feet. Semi-conscious, Quinn staggered and stumbled up the metal stairs ahead of me. He went to his knees twice on the way up, and I winced for him both times. That's going to leave a mark.

Out on the deck, I filled my lungs with the fresh, salty air. I quite liked the smell of the sea. Although, the smell of the sea, mingled with duct tape stench, was not so nice. It was late in the afternoon, and the yacht was moored to the barnacle-encrusted leg of an oil platform. A shabby nylon rope ladder dangled down the side, its tattered ends drifting it the water next to the boat. Were they expecting us to climb up that? A diesel engine growled to life somewhere above us. I looked up to see that a crane high above was lowering what looked like a giant metal basket towards us. Quinn collapsed to his knees on the deck, leaning his head against the side railing.

"I'll deal with you later," Salinger growled at him.

Then he stood behind me, hands on my shoulders.

Something bad was about to happen.

Tucker Fellowes picked up Cassie's baby carrier. She started to cry, I was sure she was wet and hungry, and I ached to hold her. Salinger's nails dug into me.

"You know how I said that I could leave her at a hospital or a fire station for your mother? I could...but I won't."

And then he dropped her over the side of the boat.

I jumped after her, but Salinger was expecting that, and grabbed me around the waist. I screamed as well as I could with duct tape over my mouth. I kicked that muscle-bound idiot for all I was worth. I thrashed around and head-butted him. Still, he didn't let go. I am not small, but he was a mountain of meanness and muscle. I didn't think I could save Cassie with my hands taped together, but I'd rather drown with her than stay on the wretched boat. Out of the corner of my eye, I saw Quinn lunge for the gunwale and topple over the railing. His hands were taped together and he was wearing the anti-shifter amulet. What was he thinking? Now, I'd lost both of them.

Salinger jerked up on my wrists until I heard a wet crunch and felt one of my shoulders pop out of joint. The pain was nothing compared to watching Fellowes drop Cassie overboard like she was a piece of trash.

It was too late to do anything now. Despair and hopelessness closed in on me, and I stopped fighting. Salinger dumped me into the middle of the basket and sat down with his feet on me so I couldn't get up. The metal floor was unpleasantly hot and stank of ammonia.

Fellowes looked over the side of the boat where Quinn had thrown himself in. "Well. That saves me a lot of trouble."

He and Chambers stepped onto the basket, and I felt us being lifted up. I couldn't bear to open my eyes and look at the horrible murky water that had swallowed up Cassie and Quinn. If I didn't see it, it wasn't real. Inside, I was dead. Why wouldn't my heart stop beating? How could it work when it had been shattered into a million tiny fragments? I curled more tightly into a fetal position and focused on the throbbing of my dislocated shoulder. Maybe it would distract me from the unbearable pain in my heart.

On the platform, Fellowes and Chambers scrambled out of the personnel basket, which hovered just above the deck. Salinger picked me up and handed me to Chambers. I went completely limp, forcing him to carry me.

"Put her in with the others, for now," Fellowes said.

I was carried and dragged down a couple of flights of metal stairs. A door was unlocked and it scraped across the cement floor when it was opened. Chambers set me down carefully on the floor of a dimly lit room. He peeled off the tape from my mouth, then my hands. It hurt like hell when he moved my dislocated arm, and I let out an involuntary cry.

"I'm so sorry, Marti," he whispered before he left, and the door slammed shut and locked.

In one corner of the room, a girl sat with her knees clasped to her chest, rocking herself. It was hard to tell in the poor lighting, but she looked about fifteen. Her face was bruised and her pants were crusted with something dark. Dried blood? Another girl, more or less the same age, I guessed, cowered against the wall near her. Long brown hair covered her face. Two other girls watched me from the shadows.

There was one other girl. I knew she was dead – a ghost – because I could see through the gaping hole in her chest. Her pale face was spattered with blood, and she used both hands to cup something small against her belly. She said nothing, only glared. I didn't have either the strength or the will to try and contact her.

"Welcome to Hell," said a voice behind me.

No shit. I sat up gingerly and turned to face her, grimacing as my dislocated arm dragged along my thigh. This girl looked closer to twenty than the others, but I didn't think she was there yet. "I need out," I answered. "I'm going to disembowel Tucker Fellowes and hang him with his own intestines." I felt like I was watching a movie of myself. Cue the action hero to swoop in for a daring rescue.

The girl snorted. "You and what army? I'm Rayne, by the way." She indicated the two girls in the shadows. "That's Mercedes and Daniella. The other two are Veronica and Crystal. Don't think we haven't tried to get out of this shithole."

"He threw my baby overboard," I said. Though my logical mind told me there was only one possible outcome, I refused to accept it. It wasn't real, true, or possible. It just couldn't be.

The ghost girl raised her head and took a step closer.

"I'm very sorry about that," Rayne said, glancing at the other girls. "But we're on an abandoned oil platform on the far side of nowhere. Nobody is coming to help us. Nobody is going to make him pay."

Dolphins. Dolphins often help shipwreck survivors and drowning people. Maybe there were dolphins that could save Cassie and Quinn. Please, let there be dolphins.

I said nothing, absently watching the ghost girl. I was sure she knew I could see her, but she made no move to speak to me. She kept looking at whatever it was in her hands.

"Boats," Rayne said, apparently feeling the need to explain. "Easy pick up and drop off. There was even a chopper here two days ago. They took Charlotte." She looked down at the filthy floor.

The rusty door skreeked across the cement floor again. A scrawny man with bad teeth and a stained ribbed tank top appeared in the doorway. He had an electric cattle prod in one hand and a large plastic dog bowl filled with an unidentifiable mass in the other.

"Here, bitches! Supper." He laughed as he roughly dropped the bowl on the floor, and a fair amount of the contents slopped out.

He brandished the cattle prod, causing Veronica and Crystal to shrink against the wall and cry.

"Get out," I snarled. After all, I had nothing left to lose, and there was nothing he could do to me that would be anywhere near as bad as what had already happened.

He took a big step towards me.

I did not back down. All of the impotent rage that I thought had burned itself out on the deck of Fellowes' yacht suddenly crystalized into a cold-blooded need to make somebody pay. And he was available.

He must have read the intention on my face, because he backed away and scuttered out the door like the vermin that he was.

The door slammed and locked.

"You go, girl," said Rayne.

Behind her, the other four girls were using their hands to scoop the mush out of the dog bowl and eat it. Under other circumstances, I probably would have been appalled. But I found it hard to care much at the moment.

"There has to be a way out of here," I said.

"Yeah, sure. Just ask Billy nicely and I'm sure he'll let you out." Rayne's voice dripped sarcasm. "And if you get out, what do you think you're going to do? This platform is sixty miles offshore. At least that's what they told me, anyway."

The door scraped open again. This time, Salinger hulked in the opening. "Keller, Mr. Fellowes wants you to join him for dinner."

"Not hungry."

"Then you can watch him eat."

He grabbed my dislocated arm and dragged me through the door. It brought tears to my eyes, but I refused to cry. Not in front of him.

I tried to visualize dolphins, lifting Cassie and Quinn out of the water on their wide backs, taking them to the safety of a passing boat.

We tramped up two flights of metal stairs and ended up in a cafeteria-style dining area. There were several plastic tables, but only one had a crisp, white tablecloth. And a putrid scumball called Tucker Fellowes.

Salinger pushed me down into a plastic chair. I winced as he patted my shoulder.

"Not again!" Fellowes' voice bristled with irritation. "What have I told you? It costs me money when they're damaged. I have to give a discount. It's coming out of your pay, that's all I can say."

Salinger grunted and lumbered off.

Ignoring the plate of lobster scampi in front of me, I leaned back in my fancy plastic lawn chair as far as I dared. I tried to cross my arms, but quickly decided against it as hot pain stabbed my dislocated shoulder.

"I have great news. I found a buyer for you. He'll be here for a test drive in the morning, and if he likes, he'll take you with him."

I considered eating the lobster tail. If I went into anaphylactic shock and died, it would serve Fellowes right. I'd be with Cassie and Ryan, away from this horrible, horrible place. I smiled a wicked little smile at this idea.

"You'll get your own room, here on the upper deck," Fellowes continued. "After all, my client will expect a play area. You'll get your hair done in a little while - this one likes redheads. And you get a shower. Oh, and I get a fat wad of cash. What's not to like?"

I examined his face, wondering if I could jam the plastic knife by my plate far enough into his eye socket to reach his brain before it broke.

"Oh, come on. The poor are the nation's greatest untapped natural resource. Crystal's mother sold her to me for five rocks of crack. I can get her conditioned, clean her up for almost nothing, then turn around and sell her for maybe ten grand. It's all in the presentation. I get a fantastic return on investment, and she gets a job. How is that bad?"

"Are there many dolphins out here?" I asked.

"Dolphins?" Fellowes looked both puzzled by my question and genuinely surprised that I didn't congratulate him on his jobs creation program.

Death by shellfish was looking more attractive by the second. I closed my eyes. I could just about see

Ryan standing there, Cassie in one arm, the other open to welcome me. The joke's on you, Fellowes. I couldn't help laughing.

I opened my eyes when I heard Fellowes sigh. He was shaking his head.

"Well, eat up. I don't want you looking drawn and waxy when my client comes to shop. In fact, I think I'll give you a little something to keep you going later. The client is…quite vigorous."

I smiled at Fellowes as I thought of Cassie and speared an especially large hunk of lobster with my fork. It kept sliding off the plastic, so I grabbed the big chunk in one hand and a smaller piece in the other hand. This was going to be so easy. Two bites of lobster, then I'd be free, and there would be nothing Fellowes could do about it.

With the worst timing in the world, Ian Chambers came into the dining room. "Here's the number you wanted. Hey, Marti, I thought you were deathly allergic to shellfish."

Fellowes dived across the table, knocking my chair over and trying to pin my wrists to the floor.

"No! Let go of me!" I screamed at Fellowes, kicking and snapping at him with my teeth. I got close enough to the piece of lobster in my right hand to taste the garlic butter sauce, but Fellowes smashed my wrist against the concrete floor until my hand went numb and he scraped the shellfish out of my cupped palm. I had no strength in my injured arm, and he had both hands free to pry the little bite of lobster, my salvation, out of my other hand. But not before I bit his forearm hard enough to draw blood. He rewarded me with a hard slap across the face.

"Nice try. But I'm not going to let you cheat me out of my hard-earned money. Chambers, take her to the Honeymoon Suite." Fellowes got to his feet and wrapped a paper napkin around his bloody arm, cursing softly.

If I couldn't join Cassie in death, then she must somehow be alive. The dolphins must have come to save her. I was sure of it. Now, I just had to find a way to get to her.

Ian Chambers held my arm and guided me through a labyrinth of low, narrow corridors. He stopped and opened a door painted a cheerless, gaudy red. "After you," he said, gesturing inside.

There was a king-sized bed with a faux fur leopard blanket over zebra print sheets. The ceiling was mirrored and sex toys spilled out of a compartment in the lighted headboard. A fake bearskin rug stretched across the floor at the end of the bed, lying on top of white shag carpeting.

Ian Chambers looked both ways down the hall before he stepped into the room and closed the door behind him.

"I'm going to get the key tonight," he said, slumping down onto the bed.

"Key to what?" I asked. I stayed as near the door as possible. If I could just get out to the water, the dolphins would take me to Cassie. Maybe they'd saved Quinn, too.

"The key that unlocks the cockpit of Fellowes' yacht. Then I'm going to get you, and the girls downstairs, and we're going to leave this hellhole."

"Fellowes will kill you," I said. And if he doesn't, I might.

"Nick'll kill me, when he finds out what I've been doing. Either way, I'm a dead man walking." Ian's lips smiled, but his eyes glistened with pain.

I didn't care. I just wanted out.

"Don't know how I got here, Marti. It was never meant to be like this. I was supposed to be one of the good guys, you know? And have the house with white picket fence and a dog." His voice was soft, and thick with tears I knew he would not cry.

"How did you get mixed up with Fellowes, anyway?" Dumb thing to say. I did not want to be his confessor. I didn't have the strength to forgive him for his sins. I just wanted to find the dolphins, and if I kept him talking, maybe he'd let his guard down, and I could escape.

They call him Flipper, Flipper...

Ian looked at the floor. "You know Fellowes runs crank and hookers between Houston and Tulsa, right? Well, not all of them are female."

I swayed to the music in my head. Faster than lightning...

"You're a male prostitute?!" I asked.

No one you see is smarter than he...

Ian almost laughed as he shook his head. "Not me, but I...receive their services."

That took a minute to sink in, and it interrupted my little song. It was the only dolphin song I knew.

He'd gotten my attention, at least for a minute. "So. Catching a DA investigator doing something illegal was too good to pass up?"

"That, and he covered some gambling debts for me in Vegas."

It was my turn to shake my head. "How did Nick not know about this? About you not liking girls, I mean." And I had thought he was just being a gentleman at the restaurant, when he didn't ogle the waitress with the too-low top.

"Well, you know Nick. He's 110% Alpha male. It would never occur to him that another man wouldn't want the same things he does. And I did everything I could to hide it. If Nick wanted to go jump out of airplanes, I was the first to say, 'Hell, yeah!' He was always fixing me up with girls. I think most of them knew, on some level, anyway, that nothing was ever going to happen between us."

"Okay, so now I have to know. If you don't even like girls, why did you ask me on a date and try to rip my clothes off?" I started humming the theme to Flipper again.

"Yeah. Sorry about that. I had to get drunk to come on to you, and I overdid it. It was never about getting in your pants. It was about getting in your house. I had to figure out where Ryan had hidden it."

Hidden it? I swallowed hard. "What did he have on you?"

Ian closed his eyes and shook his head. "A credit card receipt. Sounds stupid, I know. But Nick and Ryan had picked up one of Fellowes' mules, Richard Murphy, for DWI and possession. He only used Fellowes' street name – he calls himself Diablo - but Murphy did way too much talking for his continued good health. Three hours after he made bail, he was found in a dumpster with his neck broken. I was supposed to be deposing him at the time he was killed. Instead, I was having a beer with Nick and Ryan."

"The guy didn't show. You did something else. That's not a crime." I said, still not understanding why a credit card receipt mattered so much.

"It is when you falsify court documents."

"You just made up his deposition?" I said, too loudly.

"No. Fellowes had it messengered over. And I filed it. With a huge red timestamp on it that declared I had deposed Murphy at the same time I was sitting on a stool at Specials. It was in my valise, which got kicked over, and Ryan helped me pick up the papers that fell out. I knew he saw it. In spite of Nick's cheerleading, he never liked me, never trusted me. It was only a matter of time until he put two and two together, if he hadn't already."

I did not like where this was going, and I felt cold, in spite of the heat. "What did you do?" I couldn't control the quiver in my voice. It reminded me of a dolphin chattering.

"I didn't know at the time that they'd already iced Murphy. I swear, Marti. If I had—" Ian's voice broke and he gasped for air. "I would never have told Fellowes about Ryan. I knew he was a heartless bastard, but I didn't realize he was a cold-blooded killer. That's not exactly true. He keeps his hands clean. He's always got someone else to do his dirty work. That traffic stop, it didn't just go bad. It was an execution. And it's my fault."

I felt like Ian had just thrown me over a cliff. The oxygen-depleted world spun until I could finally stop it. Now I understood why the dying shooter was talking about Fellowes.

In three strides, I was pounding on his chest with my fists, although my injured arm was too weak to do any harm. "You. Worthless. Piece. Of. Shit," I snarled at him.

Chambers managed to grab my wrists and held on to them until I stopped trying to hit him. I wanted to scream with rage. But I pushed it down, holding it in reserve. I knew I'd need it later. I turned my back on Chambers and stalked to the door. Then I leaned my back against it, pressing myself as far away from him as I could get.

"I never intended for Ryan to get killed. I don't know what I thought. Maybe that Fellowes would change his operation, or lay low for a while. This has been eating me alive for almost two years now." His cheeks glistened and he snuffled, a deep, wet, miserable sound that shook his entire body. "I knew when Spam turned up dead that I was probably next. Regardless of what happens out here, I sent a FedEx to the DA. First thing Monday morning, an envelope will arrive containing my resignation and a full confession. I detailed how I set Ryan and Nick up. I named every name I could think of, and I even included my journal in case I left someone out." Ian sighed deeply. "I know it doesn't bring your husband or your baby back. I wish…"

His misery washed over me and broke on the rock that used to be my heart. Inside, I had become a frozen wasteland – harsh, implacable ice. I didn't object to getting the girls out of this place, but I also knew if we left Tucker Fellowes alive on this platform, he'd either escape and go somewhere with no extradition treaty, or some way, somehow, he'd manage to bend the law in his favor and get a slap on the wrist, if that. I could almost see the dolphins swimming away, breaching and chattering in the setting sun. Without Cassie.

A weight, a cold oppressiveness, settled on me like a granite cloak, squeezing out any glints of hope. "There aren't any dolphins around here, are there?"

Chambers frowned. "I have no idea."

I was going to make sure Tucker Fellowes, that despicable excuse for a human being who took my family away from me, was going down, or I would die trying. And I was okay with that.

Chapter 21
Tangled Web

"WE CAN'T JUST SNEAK out and leave Fellowes here. He'll find some way to escape," I said.

"I can radio the Coast Guard from the boat. He won't get away."

The problem was, I knew Ian Chambers was a double agent. I had no way of knowing if this was some Machiavellian plot to get me to trust him and manipulate me into doing what Fellowes wanted me to, or if he'd really had a change of heart. If he was acting, he was damned good, and really should try out for the Alley Theatre Company. That is, if he survived.

But ultimately, I didn't really have a choice. I could sit here, passively waiting to be raped and living the life of the walking dead, or I could try to save those girls and get them on the boat. And then get Fellowes myself. Trustworthy or not, Chambers was the only chance they had. Besides, I had no chance of taking down Fellowes if I was locked up in this tragic and cheesy porno hell room.

"What's your plan?" I asked.

"Fellowes has to go to sleep at some point. I'll slip in and get the keys to the yacht, then I'll get you and the girls and we'll climb down the rope ladder onto the boat. "

"And what could possibly go wrong?"

"If you have a better idea, let's hear it," he snapped.

I started to cross my arms again, but my shoulder screamed at me. "What about Salinger? And there's at least one other goon. I saw him when I was locked in with the girls." And I'm not leaving Fellowes behind, alive and well on this stinkin' platform.

Chambers scowled. "There are two of them, Billy and Trey. And he's got a cook, Charles."

"I saw what they're feeding those girls. I don't know why you call him a cook."

"He isn't that kind of cook. He's a chemist. Fellowes built a state-of-the-art meth lab on the top deck. He puts out primo stuff."

"Can we torch the lab?" That might be a great diversion.

"Not likely. It's designed to be fire proof."

Chambers looked at his watch. "I've been here too long already. I have to get back before Fellowes misses me."

"Doesn't he trust you?" I toned down the sarcasm, but it still came out too harshly.

"He doesn't trust anybody. That's why he's still alive."

Chambers locked me in the room. I tried pacing, but each step jolted my shoulder. I lay down on the bed, hoping to give it some support. It helped a little, but not much. I needed a sling, or at least a pillowcase and a pair of scissors. I had a pillowcase, anyway.

The bedspread smelled like new carpet that had been sprayed with fabric deodorizer. Sleep wasn't an option, and I knew I should try to come up with a plan. I didn't know very much about the layout of this place and the whole thing was a game of chess. But I was the world's crappiest chess player. I couldn't even beat Kyle, and he was only six.

"Chica?"

I turned my head to see Spam standing near the end of the bed. I didn't want to admit I was glad to see him. "Long time, no see."

"I tried warning you about this pendejo. You should have listened better."

"You said Salinger killed you. How was I supposed to know he worked for Fellowes?"

Spam shrugged. "Guess it doesn't matter. He was going to grab you anyway. You just made it easier for him."

"Did you just pop in to criticize me, or are you planning to do something useful?"

"Don't count on Chambers, chica."

"I knew it! I knew it was some kind of miserable plot." I slapped the bed with my good hand.

"No. Fellowes brought him out here to get rid of him. Chambers is becoming a liability. Just like I was. Fellowes is going to shoot him up with smack and leave him on the beach by his house. It'll look like just another dead dumbass, messin' with stuff he couldn't handle."

"Or suicide, when the DA gets his confession. Does Fellowes know what Chambers sent to the DA?"

Spam's smile was grim. "No. But the DA ain't gonna catch Fellowes. He's got too many escape holes. Something bad's only gonna happen to Fellowes if the Russians find out he's been shorting them. You got no idea what he's capable of."

I looked around the room. "I think I do."

"No, chica. You don't. Fellowes paid some Russian hackers to break into the EZ Tag system. He can track anybody that gets on any tollroad in Texas. That's why Chambers wouldn't put a tag in his car. If it has an EZ tag, Fellowes knows if it's coming his way. He can listen to any cop's cell, not just the scanners. He's also jacked into TranStar and the traffic camera net."

"I thought that was strange that Chambers didn't have an EZ tag. But haven't they turned off the red light cameras?"

"Just because the city ain't using them, doesn't mean Fellowes isn't.

I nodded.

"I gotta tell you something," Spam said. "I was there."

I sat up. "You were where?"

"I was there when they killed your husband."

If Spam had still been alive, I would have strangled him, dislocated shoulder notwithstanding. "You were there? And you've been hanging around, acting like you're here to help and asking me to do stuff for you? You're a bigger tool than Chambers," I spat, out loud for God and everybody to hear.

"It wasn't like that, chica. They didn't know I was there, but I was tailin' them the whole time. They were a present from the Russians, and Fellowes wanted to get rid of them – they were too sloppy, and probably spies. He also wanted to get rid of your husband. He thought he could do both at the same time. After they pulled the trigger, they ran, because that's what Fellowes told them to do. But he double-crossed 'em. He was supposed to have a second vehicle waiting for them in a parking garage, so they could switch cars, but it wasn't there. They couldn't even get in the garage – that's why they headed for the freeway, instead of just hiding inside. Once the cops stopped them, it was my job to make sure they left in body bags. Those pendejos were going to get out of the car and give up. If that happened, Fellowes was gonna kill me. You see how it was? Me or them. I knew he'd look at the message, thinking it was instructions from Fellowes, so I sent the driver a 'shopped picture of his girlfriend bangin' a cop. That's why he started shooting."

"Spam?"

"What?"

"I'm glad you're dead."

"That's cold, chica."

"So are you, you heartless son of a bitch."

Spam faded away. I suppose it was good information, about Chambers. He might want to know that Fellowes was planning to kill him, if it wasn't already too late. There was no clock, here in the Museum of Tacky. It seemed like such a long time between Spam leaving and Chambers showing up, that I had convinced myself that he wasn't coming. I couldn't allow myself to think about Cassie, or I wouldn't be able to function. But it was especially hard not to think about her. It must be way past her bedtime, because my breasts were engorged and sore. It was just one more layer of hurt piled on to this already unbearable day.

I stared at what looked like a small bloodstain on the wall as I scrambled to think of something else. Anything else. My thoughts wandered to Quinn. Was he trying to help my poor, sweet baby? I guess I'd never know. I had gotten used to having him around, and his absence was more painful than I would have expected. I had to force myself to stop thinking about him, too. That left Mr. Underhill and the woman. I don't think they liked me, especially, but they were Quinn's friends. I hoped they were okay. I called for Delilah, but she didn't answer.

I jumped when the lock turned and the door started to open.

"Are you ready to go?" Chambers half-entered the room and whispered.

"Past ready." I said as I slipped out of the Porn Palace. I noticed something shiny on the threshold. It was a key. Chambers must have dropped it, so I picked it up and stuck it in my pocket.

Chambers was already a dozen yards down the dimly lit corridor, so I pushed the door shut and turned the bolt to lock it, then hurried to catch up.

We crept down the hallway, our footsteps echoing on the metal floor. I stayed as close to Chambers as I could. I had no idea where we were or where we were going.

"Did you know Fellowes is planning to kill you?" I whispered to Chambers.

"Not surprising. Did he tell you that?"

"Not directly."

"You overheard it?"

"Something like that." Now, I wished I hadn't said anything.

Footsteps clanged on the metal floor, coming towards us.

Shit. I'd forgotten about my hair appointment.

"They're supposed to dye my hair tonight," I whispered in Chambers' ear.

"Then we'd better get a move on."

"Hey!" a voice shouted. Salinger. He'd seen us and he started running our way, his footsteps thundering on the metal flooring.

"Go that way!" Chambers pointed to a darkened hallway up ahead.

I sprinted for the connecting passage, but Chambers ran back the way we had come. Guess Salinger couldn't follow both of us. I ran a short distance and came to a T-intersection. I hung a right and plastered myself against a wall to listen for a second. The only sounds were my heavy breathing and pounding heart. I'm going to have to start doing more cardio, if I get out of this alive.

This part of the platform didn't appear to be used much – there were no lights and it smelled rusty and dank. Once I had turned the corner, it was almost like being in a cave. I felt my way along the wall and tested the floor with each step. It was slow going, but the only appointment I had was with Fellowes, and it was flexible.

I could hear water dripping, somewhere off to my left, and something scuttled around in the dark. I really hoped it was roaches. They were big and disgusting, especially when they flew straight at your face, but they wouldn't stop me from getting Fellowes.

The wall suddenly disappeared, and I fell through the stairwell opening and tumbled down a few stairs.

I was sitting on the top step, trying to shake it off, when the dead girl I had seen earlier appeared in front of me, two stair steps below.

"This way," she beckoned. Her eyes flashed a metallic green that made my skin crawl.

I need to get to Rayne and the others, I thought at her, not sure where she intended to lead me, and not sure I wanted to go.

"I know."

What did you say your name was?

"Kamli."

She glided down the stairs so fast it was hard for me to keep up with her. She waited for me at the bottom. Kamli was still holding something in her left hand, petting it with two fingers from her right. Only this time, she was clutching it up to her chest, where her heart would have been if there hadn't been a yawning hole there.

"Not his to take," the ghost said, frowning.

What wasn't?

A smile flickered across her face and she hugged whatever she held in her hands closer. "Josh promised he would marry me. Promised. But then he said he didn't want no stupid tramp to be the mama to his babies. Josh sold me to Tucker Fellowes."

She chose a corridor and started floating down it. I followed her.

And Fellowes did this to you?

"Nah. It was that big ole guy that works for him. Too bad he cain't see me, or I woulda got him, just like I got Josh."

Oh?

"I stood at the end of his bed every night. Just stood there and stared at 'im. Didn't take long before he was sittin' in the corner, talkin' to the walls. His mama had to haul him off to the crazy house."

I see.

"Guilt'll do that to a person, eat ya up like a cancer."

That's true. Are we nearly there? It didn't seem to me that we were going the right way. It was too dark.

"Almost."

Kamli led me deeper into the musty labyrinth. I was just about tell her I thought she'd made a wrong turn when she stopped.

"Here. Open this door."

Are you sure? This doesn't look like the same door.

"Open it."

I frowned at the door, but pushed down the handle and went into the room. I couldn't see my hand in front of my face. But I could hear the ocean and feel a little breeze. It seemed to be coming from the floor. I froze, afraid to take another step. I could hear the wush-wush of my pulse pounding in my ears.

Kamli? What's going on?

She giggled behind me. I turned to look at her. She held up the thing she'd been cradling, and it seemed to stretch, nearly doubling in size. I dropped to my knees.

Mr. Buns, Cassie's lovie, dangled from Kamli's fingers. He glowed, the same way she did. Her giggles turned to guffaws.

"How did you get that?" I shrieked at her, struggling for air.

"This old thing?" Kamli asked.

Then she tossed Mr. Buns over my head, towards the corner of the room. I snatched at him as he sailed past, but I missed badly – one arm was useless and the other was exhausted. Instead of landing on the floor, the stuffed rabbit disappeared through it.

"Why did you do that?" I couldn't stop the sobs that powered their way out of my chest, so I sat back on my heels and let them come.

"Revenge," Kamli said sweetly.

Then she started to shimmer and twist in the air. A man stood where the girl had been a moment before. He had a carefully shaped, closely cropped beard. He looked very business-like in his expensive sport coat, a diamond tie-tack holding down his silk tie. Except for his weird, metallic green eyes.

"What happened to –"

"Kamli. Malik. Same difference."

"Malik? I-I tried to release you. You weren't in the bottle," I stammered.

"Of course I was. You just don't remember."

The djinn waved his hand at me, and a flash flood of memories washed over me, nearly drowning me in misery. The pregnancy test. Making love with Ryan. The car accident. Losing my baby. Losing Ryan. Again.

"Stop!" I screamed at him. "Stop this!"

Malik only smiled. "You begged me for a wish. Do you remember?"

"Yes," I whispered.

"And then you spurned my generous gift to you! You unwished it." Malik's eyes blazed.

"I had to. I had Ryan back, but I lost my baby, my sister and my nephew. It just made things worse for everybody." My voice was squeaky and pathetic.

"You can't shift one part of a timeline without affecting the rest of it," Malik said, as if he were scolding a naughty child.

"I didn't know! How was I supposed to know that?"

Malik raised one eyebrow and shrugged.

"I thought I was helping you by letting you out of that bottle. I would have been better off just letting Mr. Underhill keep it," I snapped at him.

Malik's face darkened, and his eyes burned bonfire bright.

My body reacted, leaning away from him. I lost my balance and toppled over to my side. "I am sorry. I am so sorry I offended you. Please. I beg your forgiveness." I had to get out of here, and telling him what he wanted to hear seemed the quickest way to do it.

Malik crossed his arms and the fire in his eyes dimmed a little. "It is only because you freed me that I am giving you a chance."

The djinn raised both his arms, his hands circling as they rose. A dim light appeared on the ceiling. I could see that there was a hole about the size of a large pizza box in the floor behind me, where Mr. Buns had vanished. On the wall in front of me were three doors, frames glowing neon green.

"One door leads to certain death. One door is the exit. The other door…is a surprise. Choose wisely."

"What if I don't choose?" I asked, knowing that wasn't really an option.

Malik cocked an eyebrow. I heard a splash behind me. I spun around to see that another pizza box-sized chunk of floor was gone.

"One will fall every minute that you don't choose."

With a grin, he was gone.

Chapter 22
Eenie Meanie

⚶

I LOOKED AT THE double pizza box-sized hole in the floor. I guestimated that the room was ten pizza boxes wide by twelve pizza boxes long. That gave me about two hours.

I stared at the three glowing doors. Malik was wrong. I didn't have to choose. I could just wait until the floor dropped out from under me, and I joined Cassie in the water. It was tempting.

But that wouldn't get Fellowes. And it wouldn't save the girls. If I ever needed guidance, it was now.

"Delilah! Where are you? I really need your help!" I said to the middle door.

Behind me, another tile dropped.

To my great relief, Delilah appeared next to me, hands on her hips.

"Girlfriend –"

A blue light surrounded her and she froze.

"Delilah?!"

She didn't move.

Then I heard Malik's disembodied voice. "Unh-uh-uh. That's cheating."

His laughter faded, but Delilah remained a statue.

Dammit. I looked at the doors again.

Another tile splashed into the sea. There didn't seem to be an entire minute between each splash, but perhaps my perception was distorted.

The doors were identical. There were no visible clues as to what might be behind them. I scrambled to the first one and put my ear against it. I held my breath, listening. Silence. Same with the other two. There was no keyhole to peer through. I even tried sniffing at the border where door met frame. Nothing.

Another tile dropped. The first row was about halfway gone.

I growled with frustration. For lack of a better idea, I started "Eenie, meanie, miney, mo. Catch a tiger by his toe. If he hollers let him go. My mother told me to pick this one." I was pointing to the door on the right.

I took a deep breath. As I pulled the door open with my left hand, I gripped the frame tightly with my right, hoping I could pull myself back if it looked like I was facing certain death.

Instead, I found myself in my own kitchen. I had just come in from the outside door. I smelled tobacco. Not the bitter smell of cigarettes, nor the dusty smell of cigars, but tobacco from a pouch, earthy and sweet.

"Oh, there you are, darling," said Quinn. He sat at the table, hair oiled back, wearing slacks, a button down shirt (with an undershirt), reading a newspaper. And smoking a pipe.

"I just wanted to bring in yesterday's mail," I said, looking at the envelopes in my hands. It was then I noticed that I was wearing a cotton A-line dress and a ruffled apron. I knew the ring on my finger was my wedding ring, but it seemed alien, wrong somehow.

I felt like I had just woken from a dream, but strands of it lingered, dusty, obscure cobwebs in my head that fluttered away every time I tried to grab at them.

"Don't forget to take the cinnamon rolls out of the oven, Dear," Quinn said.

"Oh! I had forgotten about them."

I got an oven mitt and pulled a pan out of the oven. The rolls weren't burned, but they were on the far side of the done spectrum. There was a bowl of frosting sitting on the countertop, and I started spreading the contents on the bread.

Quinn came over and eyed the rolls. "Tsk, tsk. You're completely useless in the kitchen." He smiled as he said this. Then he patted my butt. "It's a good thing I love you for your other, much more accomplished skills."

As he walked away, I wanted to smack him across the face and tell him just where he could shove that steaming hot pan of cinnamon rolls.

Instead, I said. "Yes, Dear, I know. I'm so lucky to have married you."

I didn't have a lot of control over what I did, and even less over what I said. I seemed to be trapped inside the body of a 1950s sitcom wife. This had to be the dream, the nightmare, and the other thing I couldn't quite remember had to be reality. Now, if I could just figure out how to wake up.

Four children, two boys and twin girls bounded into the kitchen. The boys book-ended the girls, and the youngest looked six-ish while the oldest looked twelve-ish. I would guess the girls were eight or nine.

The oldest child looked disapprovingly at the pan, rolls half-smeared with icing.

"Father said you had a snack for us, before he took Harry and me out to ride bikes," he said.

What about the girls? Don't they get to go ride?

"Yes, David. But you know how I am in the kitchen. Why don't you children just wait at the table. I'm sure I'll get this done in a minute."

Where is the stapler, so I can just staple my lips together and not spew this tripe all over the place? I am going to make myself ill. The side door. If I can just get to the side door.

I put a cinnamon roll on each of four plates, along with a knife and fork. I served the boys first, and when the four of them were finished, the girls picked up all of the plates and put them in the sink.

The boys left with their father. By the time they came back an hour later, the girls and I had washed the dishes, dusted the knick-knacks and swept the floors. I did manage to wrest a fragment of control from the automaton who was hosting me.

"Didn't you girls want to go and ride bikes as well?" I finally managed to ask.

The looked at each other, then back at me. "Mother!" said Peony. "We're not boys!"

Then she and Petunia trotted up the stairs to play with their dolls. I sighed and started mopping the floor. Peony and Petunia? Harry and David? Who named these children? I had hoped I could work my way to the side door and escape, but I just wasn't able to force my hands to turn the door knob.

Quinn came downstairs, hair oil-free and still damp from his shower. I didn't think this was the actual Quinn, but a creation that looked like him.

"You know what would be good, Darling?" he asked.

"I'm sure I don't," I said, wanting to gag on those words.

"If we had some fresh-cut flowers for the table when my boss and his wife come over for dinner tonight."

So, I have to cook a fancy dinner for the boss and his wife, after Quinn's been ragging on me about how I can't cook?. Fantastic. "That's a splendid idea." The automaton smiled, and I smiled along with it as I retrieved the hand pruner and my gloves from a drawer and headed towards the side door.

"Where are you going?" Quinn asked. "You know the roses are out front."

The outside smile stayed full. "Of course! What was I thinking? Sometimes, I'm such a dummy." The inside smile faded to black.

The front yard had a bed of rose bushes, alstroemeria, and daisies. The rest of it was a bland stretch of perfectly edged lawn.

I didn't recognize the tune I hummed as I cut enough flowers for a bouquet. I did figure out how to manipulate the body just a little. If I could learn to do it a little, I could learn to do it a lot. Then I could walk out that side door.

I put the flowers in a vase and added water, then went to put them on the kitchen table, out of the way. As I neared the side door, I had an idea. The linoleum was still wet from being mopped. If I put my foot wrong...

It worked.

I slipped and fell hard against the side door, breaking the glass window and crashing through it. I was suddenly back on the oil platform.

The first thing I noticed was that blood was running into my eyes from a cut on my head. The second thing I noticed was that Malik had lied. The tiles had been falling the whole time I was in that existentialist time warp hell, and now there were only four left.

Plop.

Make that three. The door I had just come through had vanished. I opened the next door over. I still had broken pieces of vase in my hand, and I wedged them against the jamb so the door couldn't close all the way.

On the other side of the door, it was pitch-black and smelled musky. Yellow eyes suddenly glowed in the darkness. Very large yellow eyes. I didn't want to see what they were attached to, but it made me think of Where the Wild Things Are. The thing behind the eyes snarled and charged at me. I ran for the door. I was only a couple of steps away, and I could see a faint shaft of light where I'd propped it open. I've never been so grateful for broken glass in my entire life. I hurled myself at the light, scrambling for the doorknob. My leg burned as the creature's claws raked me from knee to ankle.

My momentum nearly carried me over the edge of the tile. I stopped myself by flopping back against the wall, where the door had been, and huddling against it. I tried to catch my breath. There was one door left, and it had to be the exit. Maybe I'd survive Malik's revenge, after all, and have a chance at my own.

As I started to step over to the next tile and open the exit door, the piece I was standing on dropped. I lunged forward, and found myself draped over the last tile. I hadn't fallen into the ocean, but I couldn't open the door, either. And I had less than one minute to fix the problem and save myself.

I eased over on my side and dragged my hips onto the tile. The blood streaming from my leg made the tile and my hands slippery. I reached up and grabbed the door handle.

The tile dropped out from under me.

I caught the threshold of the door with my nails as I fell. I grabbed on tightly, and clung to the metal strip. Even without a dislocated shoulder and exhaustion, I would have had trouble pulling myself up into the hallway. My fingers were cramping, my arms were burning, and my shoulder was screaming.

"Easy there, girlfriend!"

Delilah stood in the doorway.

"How——?"

"Later. Let go!"

"What?"

"There's a cat walk about ten feet below you. Don't miss, girl."

With all the blood I'd been dripping into the ocean, every shark within a twenty mile radius was bound to either be here or on the way. If I missed, the end would probably be quick.

I took a deep breath and let go.

Chapter 23
The Female of the Species

IT TAKES APPROXIMATELY ONE second to complete a ten foot drop. Either Delilah was wrong about the distance, or this was the longest second in the history of the universe.

I wished it had been longer.

I moaned when I hit the railing. I felt my ribs cave. Searing pain shot through my chest when I tried to breathe. I didn't want to think about moving.

"Come on, girl. Get up!" Delilah said, suddenly beside me.

Not sure I can. I gasped as I tried to sit up.

Talking only made the pain worse. I could manage it with short, shallow breaths that didn't move my ribs too much. Then it was merely excruciating, instead of unbearable. On the up side, I wasn't noticing my shoulder so much now.

"You went through all this to get Fellowes, and you're just going to lay there and let him get back on his boat?"

I knew she was right. But that didn't make it any easier. The cut on my head had mostly clotted, so I didn't worry much about it. I whimpered as I took off my shirt and used it to bandage my leg. It was still bleeding, and moving would just make it worse.

I cried, big hot tears scorching down my cheeks, as I struggled to my feet. I held onto the railing as a coughing fit shook my body. I tasted blood. Of course.

I needed a punctured lung to go with the broken ribs. Why break up such a nicely matched set?

"I know it hurts, Marti. But you got a job to do. You got to let those girls out. That's the only way anything gonna happen to Fellowes today. Come. On."

I struggled to keep up with Delilah. I was dizzy and felt I might vomit at any time. But I would have crawled through broken glass to take Tucker Fellowes down. And I did crawl up three flights of no-slip grip metal stairs, which was pretty much the same thing.

"We're here," Delilah said.

I had to lean against the door frame to catch my breath. I heard a gurgle as the air went in and a rattle as it went out. That was so not good. I also heard crying on the other side of the door, so I knew we were in the right place. I turned the dead bolt and opened it.

"Girls," I whispered as loudly as I could. "It's me, Marti. C'mon, let's get out of here."

They were very cautious in coming to the door. I assumed they were expecting a nasty trick. Or perhaps it was because I looked like a refugee from a slasher film. Either way, I understood, but they were wasting precious time by being so timid.

"Hurry up! We don't have a lot of time." I don't have a lot of time.

Rayne shooed them along.

"What happened to you?" Rayne asked.

"Long story. Tell you on the boat. Can you get there?" I had to lean on the door to keep myself upright.

"Sort of. I had to help them unload groceries once."

"Go. Don't wait for me."

Rayne led and I staggered behind. Crystal, the one with the bloody stains on her pants and bruised face, was leaning on Veronica. Then she stumbled and fell to her knees. She was pale and sweaty. Veronica helped her up.

"Sorry. I'm just a little lightheaded," Crystal said.

"It's okay. Do the best you can," I said.

I wondered if she had internal injuries, because she sure looked shocky. And there wasn't a damned thing I could do for her out here. Me either, for that matter. She was going to shut down if she didn't get help soon. That made two of us. But I only had to make it long enough to get Tucker Fellowes. After that, it didn't much matter.

Rayne got us to the upper deck. Progress was slow, but we made it.

Delilah appeared and held up her hands "Stop."

"Wait," I rasped. I leaned against a crate and panted, trying not to cry from the pain.

I really hoped there was nobody on the receiving platform – they would see us, if they took the time to look. There were still traces of the sun on the western horizon, but it was dark. An enormous orange moon was just breaking the eastern horizon. I guessed it was somewhere between 8:30 and 9:00. Artificial daylight blazed on the deck, bleaching colors and darkening shadows.

Voices came from the opposite side of the deck, and we stayed put. Tucker Fellowes opened a door and Salinger dragged something heavy through it. It was Ian Chambers. He was at the very least unconscious, but I was too far away to see anything more.

"Yeah, well Billy and Trey couldn't find their asses with both hands. You go look for that bitch," Fellowes barked. "She's getting to be more trouble than she's worth."

Salinger disappeared into the innards of the rig.

I had hoped that Fellowes would follow him, but he didn't. I don't know what I thought I was going to do. I could barely stand up. Even if I could sneak up on him, and if I had a weapon (two pretty big ifs), I didn't have the strength to use it. My original plan had been to knock him out, tape him up and turn him over to Nick. And tell him that he was the one who killed Ryan and blackmailed Chambers. Unfortunately, I didn't have a Plan B, the one that outlined how to capture Fellowes when I was somewhere between half and three-quarters dead.

My legs were shaking so hard that I had to sit down. I unstuck my raw palms from the crate, leaving bright bloody handprints, and slid to the deck against the crate that had been holding me up. My eyes didn't want to stay open. If I could just have a nap, everything would be clearer. Maybe just rest my eyes for a minute.

A scrabbling sound interrupted my snooze.

"Where is she?" A woman emerged from the dark behind a stack of boxes. I couldn't be sure, but she looked like the stripper Quinn had given $100 to at Specials.

"Waynette. What a nice surprise." Fellowes answered, unperturbed. "Just out of curiosity, how'd you get out here? Happened to be in the neighborhood?"

"Cut the crap. My aunt said you took her. Where is Veronica?"

"I don't know. I don't have her," Fellowes said, taking a step backward.

"Mom!" Veronica shouted as she ran out onto the deck.

"You bastard! You told me if I worked for you, you'd leave her alone," Waynette shrieked at Fellows, her voice rough with fury and loathing.

"And you believed me?" Fellowes was easing his way towards the woman, and she was backing away at the same pace.

She raised both her arms, chest level, hands clasped together. The barrel of a handgun gleamed in the harsh floodlights. Veronica stood frozen on the deck. Both she and her mother were crying.

"I'm warning you! I will shoot," Waynette shouted.

"No, you won't. You're just strung out. You're going to give me the gun, then we'll go up to the lab and Charles will fix you up. Then you'll be back at work tomorrow." Fellowes voice was calm and soothing.

"Not another step!"

Fellowes took another step.

A small black hole suddenly appeared between his eyes, followed immediately by an earsplitting bang. I've never seen anyone look more surprised as he sank to his knees and toppled over, face down. He bet wrong on that one.

I was torn between the intense satisfaction of Fellowes getting what he deserved and the disappointment of it being someone other than me who gave it to him. The acrid smell of spent gunpowder drifted past me, and it made me think of Ryan, on days when he came home from the firing range, that smell clinging to his clothes.

Veronica ran onto the platform. "Mom! Mom!" she yelled as she threw herself at her mother.

Still holding the pistol, Waynette wrapped her arms around her daughter. They held each other and sobbed.

There was no sign of any bad guys, and they had surely heard the gunshot. The rest of the girls ventured out to where Veronica and Waynette were standing, and milled around the two of them.

Then there was a loud clunk, as if a heavy switch had been pulled, and all the lights went out.

I was grateful for the light from the almost-full moon, but it still took some time for my eyes to adjust.

Something snarled and snuffled in the shadows. Two points of red light hovered about three and a half feet off the ground. I recognized those eyes. They belonged to a werewolf, maybe even the same one that had hurled itself against my patio door a few nights ago.

It burst into the open, destroying the distance between it and the girls with frightening speed, fangs glinting in the silvery moonlight.

I saw a muzzle flash and heard another bang. The creature was knocked back a little. A dark stain spread through the pale fur on its chest, but it didn't slow down much. Waynette squeezed the trigger again. Nothing happened. The monster was closing in for the kill. Waynette frantically shook the pistol and pulled the trigger again. There was an explosion from the back of the gun, and Waynette collapsed.

I knew I wasn't going to make it.

I couldn't keep my eyes open any longer. But at least had the satisfaction of knowing Fellowes wasn't going to hurt anyone else. Ever.

I thought of Ryan and Cassie, and let myself relax into the dark.

Chapter 24
Flight

"MARTI, GIRL! GET UP and come with me. Somebody need to talk to you."

Delilah? What's going on? I – where am I?

"Just come with me, girlfriend."

I couldn't tell if my eyes were open or closed, and I stretched out my arms in front of myself to feel my way. Pudgy fingers closed around my hand.

"Come on, Marti."

Delilah and I shuffled through the dark. I'm glad one of us knew where we were going. I gradually became aware of light. Then Delilah was gone and I was in a strange room where the floor, walls and ceiling were all bright white. It was hard to tell where one left off and the other started.

"Hey, Bright Eyes."

I turned to see Ryan standing behind me. I ran towards him, but I seemed to be on a treadmill. I ran and ran, but he never got any closer. Finally, I stopped.

"Ryan? Why can't I reach you?"

"Because you don't belong here. You have to go back."

"Aren't I dead?"

He smiled and shook his head. "Temporarily. But you can't stay here."

Why was he smiling? "I saw you, and I assumed that you were here to take me to the other side, and you, me and...wait a minute. Where's Cassie? You do know about Cassie, don't you?"

Ryan laughed. "Of course I know about Cassie."

I felt a little disappointed. "She didn't come with you?"

"She's not dead."

"I saw Tucker Fellowes drop her over the side of the boat."

"Maybe, but she's waiting for you back there. But first, you have a visitor."

"Hey, chica."

"Spam."

"You know that unfinished business? It's finished now. Couldn't have done it without you." Spam grew a little more transparent.

On the one hand, I didn't like Spam. He was a self-centered jerk who was responsible for a lot of human misery. On the other hand, he helped stop someone who was responsible for a whole lot more human misery, and who had arranged to have Ryan killed. If he hadn't shown up at the party, Tucker Fellowes would still be trafficking young women, selling drugs, and living well off other people's suffering. Grudgingly, I said, "Thank you, Spam. If it wasn't for you, I would never have known what really happened to Ryan."

Spam grinned. "Yeah, well you know Waynette bought that gun at a pawn shop with the c-note Quinn slipped her at Specials."

"So you want credit for stopping Fellowes as well?"

"Un poquito," he said, measuring a small space between two fingers.

An elderly couple with a small baby in a frilly dress popped up next to Spam.

"Mamá! Papi!" He hugged them both and took the baby from the old woman. "Maria, me buena." They all got brighter and brighter until I couldn't look at them anymore. And then they were gone.

"You have to go now." Ryan said. He still looked highly amused.

"You don't have to look so happy about it," I complained.

"Seems weird, doesn't it? But every time you look into Cassie's eyes, you'll see me there. I'm always with you. Always."

"Not sure if that makes it better or worse. But at least I get the chance to say goodbye this time."

"Not goodbye. Until next time, Bright Eyes. You've got a lot more living left to do. And it shouldn't involve living in a convent." He cocked his head and lifted one eyebrow.

I smiled back at him. "Hint, hint, nudge, nudge?"

"Be happy. I love you."

"I love you, too."

I felt like I was falling, and reached out to try and stop my fall. I was shocked that my hands made contact with something firm and warm.

I opened my eyes. The sun had just cleared the eastern horizon, and Quinn was sitting next to me. My fingers were digging into his thigh.

"Sorry!" I said, quickly releasing him.

"Welcome back."

His eyes were dark, almost black, the way they were supposed to be. I smiled at him, glad to see him looking werewolf free.

"Not that I mind, but you might want this." Quinn handed me a tee-shirt.

It took me a second to remember that I was only wearing shorts and a nursing bra. "Thanks," I said, pulling the shirt over my head.

"Somebody's been looking for you."

A woman I didn't recognize came over, carrying something.

She was holding Cassie.

I leaped to my feet and snatched my baby from her arms. I hugged that child so tightly that she squirmed and fussed. I knew my eyes were streaming, and I must have looked like I'd been through a blender, but I was too happy to care. I held her at arms' length to look at her. She was wearing the same dress, although there was something that might have been banana smeared all over the front of it. And instead of a diaper, she had some shop towels duct taped to her bottom. She grinned at me. "Mama! Mama!"

I looked at Quinn. He shrugged. "The Coast Guard didn't have any diapers. This was the best we could do."

"The Coast Guard? There's a whole lot of this story that you need to fill me in on."

And that is when I realized that my shoulder and ribs didn't hurt and I could breathe without gurgling. I tore the bloody shirt off of my leg. If I looked carefully, I could see four thin white scars.

"Did you do this?"

"Not me. I just know the right people."

I thought of the woman with dark hair, and wondered if he meant her.

Quinn chuckled a little as he stood up. "Now. Where were we? I'll start where we parted company. First of all, do you know how much Styrofoam those baby carriers have in them? They're extremely buoyant. I don't know if you saw Cassie floating around after Fellowes dropped her in the water. Some of my friends looked after her and kept her under the platform so she didn't get sunburned and dehydrated. They gave her something to eat, too. Don't ask me what, because I don't know, but she seems happy enough."

He reached out and tickled the side of Cassie's neck. She squealed with delight and hid her face against my shoulder. Then she looked around, eager for him to do it again. He didn't, but he motioned for us to follow him down the stairs. The woman stayed on the upper deck. We ended up on the level where Fellowes had kept the five girls imprisoned. I felt cold and oppressed just being down here. Residual energy, perhaps.

"Before they snatched me yesterday afternoon, I could feel Salinger coming for me. Maybe because he's the one who infected me, I was hyper-sensitive to him."

"Wait, Salinger was the werewolf?"

"I thought you knew that."

"I only knew that you'd tracked the werewolf to Specials."

Quinn rummaged through some large cabinets and storage lockers as he spoke. "Sorry. Anyway, I knew Salinger was coming, and that he'd kill anyone in the house with me, so I asked them to take me outside, into the sun, and leave me alone. They did, and when Salinger and Chambers came for me, I pretended to be sicker than I really was. They dropped me trying to get me into the back of the SUV – that's how my lip got busted."

"I thought they'd beaten you up."

"No. They thought I was coming over to their side. And they were right. The werewolf parasites were winning. I couldn't fight them much longer. I knew that the best thing I could do was drown," Quinn continued.

"Drown? You don't look dead to me."

"Well, of course not. Water can't kill me. I am water. But what lying on the bottom of the ocean for an hour did do to my human form was to make it inhospitable enough to the parasite to kill it. And as powerful as dragons are, they are not as powerful as an entire ocean. Because I was in the sea, I was able to override the amulet."

"I thought you weren't a sea monster."

Quinn shrugged. "Water is water. A little salt doesn't make all that much difference, although I couldn't live in the ocean full time. It dries out my skin and makes me itchy." He winked at me. "By the way, did you want to keep it?" He pulled the anti-shifting amulet from his pocket.

"No. I want to unmake it."

"That's what I thought."

He found a metal tank and rubbed some dust off the label, then checked the pressure gauge. He attached a hose to it, and rummaged around until he found a welder's helmet in one of the cabinets.

"You might want to step around the corner. This is going to be bright."

I took Cassie a little way down the hall and sang her a song. She looked so much like her daddy that it hurt, sometimes. I though she also might be hungry. I was right. I ran my finger along her jaw as she nursed.

I could see Ryan clearly in my mind, standing in that white, white room, smiling at me and joking around like he always did. I supposed what I had now was closure. I'd gotten to say goodbye, at long last. And got his not-so-subtle hint that I should move on. After all this time, I finally felt at peace, that whatever happened would be okay. I leaned against the wall, and closed my eyes.

Behind us, I could hear the hiss of an acetylene torch, and smelled hot metal.

Cassie was finished and burped before Quinn joined us in the corridor. He held a chain with half of a melted pewter circle suspended from it, all that remained of the anti-shifting amulet.

"That should do it," he said.

We went back up the stairs and came out onto the deck, washed in fresh new sunlight. Seagulls were already diving and squawking around the platform. Quinn led me to the edge of the deck. I heard a splash and then saw an enormous creature rising from the water. It made Fellowes' yacht look like a bath toy bobbing next to the platform leg. Above the metallic aquamarine body, bat-like wings unfolded and stretched. It raised its snaky neck up until it was almost level with us. Its emerald green eye was bigger than my head. Then it opened its armored jaws and roared.

It was so loud it shook the platform, and it made Cassie cry. I patted her back and jiggled her gently up and down with my hip.

"That's dragon for 'thank you,'" Quinn said.

Water fell on us like rain as the creature flapped its wings and rose into the air. Cassie stopped crying and stared at the dragon as she flew higher in the sky, her silhouette soaring above the orange morning sun.

"There she goes!" said Quinn, waving.

"Won't people see her?" I asked.

"Not unless she wants them to."

We watched the dragon until she faded into the horizon. After discovering kelpies, dryads and werewolves, a dragon seemed perfectly normal to me, no more unusual than a mocking bird in the backyard. I was glad she was free.

"So…just out of curiosity, why was a dragon living underneath the oil platform? I didn't think they lived in water."

"They don't. Dragons fly, of course, but they also travel through the earth. Being bound to the amulet, she was forced to follow it around. It wasn't her fault there was 1,200' feet of water over the little bit of the Earth's crust she was hiding in. Remember, they're the ultimate shapeshifters. They can take any form you can imagine, and quite a few you can't."

"So, while I had the amulet, there was a dragon hanging out under my house?"

Quinn nodded.

What the HOA didn't know wouldn't hurt them. "Where do you think she's going?" I asked.

"I don't know. Watch the news for earthquakes in the next day or two. That'll probably be it. They move around a lot, trying to get settled in."

"Earthquakes. Right." I nodded. "Now, tell me about the Coast Guard."

Quinn led us over towards the personnel basket that had lifted us from Fellowes' boat yesterday afternoon.

"That was all Delilah. She's a wizard with electricity and radio. She called in an SOS from this location. Coast Guard Search and Rescue arrived just after the shots were fired."

"She could have called someone earlier, like when Salinger ran my car off the road."

"She could have. But then no one would have known to rescue the girls he had locked up out here, and Fellowes and Salinger wouldn't have gotten what was coming to them. And I'd be a werewolf by now."

"Funny how things work out, huh?" I looked at Quinn, very glad that he wasn't a werewolf.

Quinn picked up Cassie's waterlogged car seat and put it in the metal basket, then helped us in. An engine rattled to life, and the basket shuddered and lifted off the deck.

I held tightly to Cassie as the arm swung out over the water and the personnel basket started to descend.

"The Coast Guard found the three bodies - Fellowes, Salinger and Chambers - on the deck. Turns out that Waynette used silver slugs. No idea where she found those. The bullet she put in Salinger got him, eventually, but using those rounds also caused her gun to blow up. The slide hit her in the face and fractured her skull. I don't know if she'll survive. It's hard to tell with these things. They took her, her daughter and one other girl by chopper. The remaining girls, the chemist, and the dead ones, went by boat. I hid you and Cassie while he was working on putting you back together. Didn't think you'd mind."

"He? Anybody I know?"

Quinn looked down to the deck. "Kind of. It was Malik."

Anger surged up from my belly. "That's awfully decent of him, since he's the one who nearly killed me."

"Technically, you were dead. And I can't blame you for being upset with him—"

I threw my free hand in the air. "Upset?" I snapped. "It goes way beyond upset."

"I hear you. I was quite angry with him, too, when he told me what had happened. But keep in mind that he'd just been attacked by a sahir who was trying to make him a slave. His mind was poisoned. He wasn't himself. He hoped healing your body would go some way in making it up to you."

It made sense. But it wasn't so easy to forget what he'd put me through. "I'll keep that in mind."

"He also tweaked the girls' memories. As far as they remember, Waynette rescued them. It's like you were never here."

That would save me a very uncomfortable conversation with Nick.

"Speaking of Waynette," I asked as I shifted Cassie to the other hip. "How did she get here and how did you know to give her the money for the gun?"

"The first part's easy. She packed herself into one of the supply crates Salinger took out to the yacht. The second part is a little more complicated. Let's just call it intuition and leave it at that."

I didn't want to leave it at that, but I suspected Quinn wasn't going to tell me any more about it. He had turned away from me, watching the boat below us. Sweat stuck his loose cotton shirt to his back. The image of him in my bed flickered across my memory and I felt myself smile. Then I looked at Cassie and blushed. Still, I wondered if I'd have a different reaction than hopping out of bed and wrapping up in a sheet, if I ever found myself in a similar situation with him.

Cassie squawked when the basket bumped down on the deck of Fellowes' yacht. We stepped out of it, and it rose off the deck. When the basket was back on the platform, the diesel engine stopped. A dark blur sliced into the water near the boat, as if someone had dived off the deck.

"Don't worry about her. She lives here," Quinn said, then frowned at the locked door.

I took the key out of my pocket and unlocked the cockpit. I suddenly realized that not everyone was accounted for.

"And what about the other two? Fellowes had a couple of guys here on the platform other than the cook."

"They won't be causing you any more trouble. You think they've got any fizzy drinks on this boat? I've got terrible indigestion."

The Hanged Man's Wife

Bonus Material

Last Night at the Roquefort

_____✆_____

PAUL SAMSON PULLED THE plug from the bathtub, and listened to all the sweat and grime from his longshoreman's job gurgle down the drain with the bathwater as he dried off. He'd have to hurry if he was going to make it to Club Roquefort on time. He quickly dusted his body with lilac scented powder, then tucked the hot pink box underneath a towel in the linen closet. He had brought his elderly mother to live with him after his sister moved to the west coast, and he would just as soon not have a discussion with her about why a lifelong bachelor would have fancy ladies' powder in his bathroom.

Paul had brought his clothes into the bathroom with him. He pulled a stretch knit panty girdle most of the way up. Then he folded a small towel and tucked it inside, carefully arranging his parts and using the towel to smooth out any bulges. He shaved again, slicked his damp hair back, then dressed in khakis and a pale denim shirt.

In the living room, his mother had fallen asleep on the couch, bible in her lap. He kissed her softly on the top of the head, then pulled an aluminum travel case out of the hall closet and left.

Club Roquefort was far from being the Moulin Rouge, Paul's dream venue. Even in its heyday in the mid-1920s, the Roquefort had been neither grand nor new. Ten years later, was tired and dingy, but it was a fixture. It was the sort of place his mother had told him never, *ever* to go near when his banker father had uprooted the family of five from New Orleans, Louisiana and replanted them in New York City. That had been 1916, and Paul was nearly a grown man then.

The bouncer looked up when Paul came in through the grimy stage entrance, then went back to his newspaper. The dressing room door stuck, as usual, and Paul had to put his shoulder against it to shove it open. He'd been performing here on Friday and Saturday nights for a dozen years, and in all that time, the door had never been fixed. Bursting into the room like Eliot Ness had become a ritual for Paul, almost like a mini rebirth.

He set his burden down on the dressing table and fumbled in his pocket for the key. The Halliburton locking aluminum case – the hot new thing - had been a splurge, but it made Paul feel safer. The Great Depression had caused a social backlash against the mores of the freewheeling 20s that had been slow to dissipate. He feared what might happen if strangers knew what was inside.

He hung up the sequined red gown and set the corset, stockings and makeup box on the table. He'd made the dress himself, spending many a wee hour hand-sewing the sequins while his mother was sleeping. He'd often toyed with the idea of opening a dress shop and designing fabulous custom gowns. After all, if Main Bocher could design Wallis Simpson's wedding dress, and gowns for Mary Pickford, there was no reason Paul couldn't do the same thing. But somehow, there was never enough time, or money, or this, or that, and Paul kept working at the docks.

He sprayed the perfume atomizer around the room, hoping to cover up the eau de mildew of the place while he got ready. It took the better part of an hour to apply the makeup and get the wig just so. Paul slipped on white cotton gloves so that his labor-roughened hands wouldn't damage his stockings. No amount of buffing or lotion ever made the thick callouses truly go away, the price he paid for nine years working at the docks. Before that, he had worked for his father, until that fateful day in 1929 when the bank failed and his proud, but financially ruined, father opted to take a header out of a twenty story window. He'd been thinking of his father a lot, lately. Especially, since he'd been having a recurring dream where his father came home from work, tottering crazily on smashed and broken legs, blood covering one side of his face, and asked to have fried eggs for supper.

Paul sucked in his stomach. The corset had been getting tighter over the last few months. He'd been promoted and was doing less manual labor. It was just as well, because he wasn't as young as he used to be, and as he neared middle age, a certain softness was settling in around his body. It made for nice cleavage, though.

The stage hand knocked on the dressing room door. "You're on in five."

"Zip me up, Irv?"

"Sure thing." Irv stepped in and tugged the long zipper up Paul's back. "You look great," he said.

"Thanks.

Paul strapped on his heels and made his way to the stage wings.

"Please give it up for Nehi, the Indian Princess!" the MC boomed into a bulky silver microphone.

The crowd was not large and the applause was not loud. Nehi, whose wife knew him as Jim, minced off the stage, swinging long black hair.

"And now, what you've all been waiting for! The one and only! The spectacular! The faaaabulous Miiiiss Deeeeeliiiiilaaaah!"

Paul took a deep breath and let *her* out. She strutted out to the MC and took the mic. Miss Delilah owned the stage. She was everything Paul was not – stylish, powerful, and happy. She surveyed the audience. The Roquefort was half full, three-quarters if she counted the patrons who were no longer living. The dead ones came, attracted to drunk people like flies to carrion. They crowded in, hoping to steal energy, memories, life from those who spent their time trying to drown their misery in alcohol. Unfortunately, misery floats.

"How y'all doing tonight?" In spite of living so many years in New York City, Delilah had not only kept her unique New Orleans accent, but embellished it with faux southern-ness. The regulars hooted and cat-called.

The spotlight came on and the footlights went out. Delilah closed her eyes. Tiny rhinestones glittered on her eyelids. The pianist stroked the keys.

Delilah's smoky voice eased into her set, a selection of popular torch songs and a Gershwin medley.

When Delilah finished her act, she got a standing ovation. Delilah always got standing ovations.

She went backstage, then came into the bar from the front. Rudy, the bartender, handed her a glass of tepid water. She perched on a barstool and waited. After the main show was over, and the paying customers had either left or were too drunk to care, the manager let some aspiring performers take the stage – comics, singers, strippers and occasionally, sideshow working acts.

"Great show tonight, Delilah! Good on ya," a young man said as he approached her. He was handsome, blonde, and had been dead for almost a hundred years. She hardly even noticed the gash on his head or the bloodstain on his shirt anymore. He'd fled the Potato Famine, only to die here three months later.

Thanks, Bram, she thought, knowing he could hear her. She'd talked to dead people all of her life, and had been twelve years old before she realized that most people didn't see them.

The majority of the ghosts in the place were ugly, leering, nasty. But Bram had been killed in a textile mill accident nearby. The owner had covered it up. The mill was long gone, but Bram's bones were still buried in the now cement-filled basement.

"Now would you look at that?" he said.

Delilah followed his pointing finger. A strange, misty blob hovered over the head of one of the patrons. A half-empty bottle of whiskey and an empty shot glass sat in front of him. Delilah guessed that he had no clue that a cloud, flickering with what looked like red and orange heat lightning, was slowly lowering itself towards his head. *What* is *that?*

"Have you never seen them before? Not sure what the educated fellas ud call 'em, but I rekon they're a sort of parasite. It's like a possession – they take over yer mind and make you do all and such as you'd ne'er do on yer own."

Come with me. Delilah got up and went to the man's table. "Mind if I sit down?" she asked, pulling out the chair across from him. Bram floated behind her.

The man looked up slowly, his eyes half closed. "It's a free country."

His breath stank of whiskey and despair.

"I ain't seen you around. First time here?" Delilah asked the man. *What are you? What do you want?* She thought at the cloud. It was almost touching the whiskey drinker now.

"Leave us alone!" the cloud screeched at her, its voice like shattering glass.

Delilah imagined a large bubble, formed from pure white light, enclosing the table, surrounding herself, Bram, and the drunk.

The cloud flashed dark red and screamed, a shrill keening that made Delilah's temples throb. But it left, moving off to hover against the high ceiling in the corner.

"Well, mister, I hope you enjoyed the show." Delilah stood up. The drunk grunted and poured more whiskey.

"Lady D! You bring your gorgeous self over here!" Princess Nehi called from the end of the bar, surrounded by the other performers and a handful of patrons.

"Girl, ain't nobody tell me what to do," Delilah answered with mock indignation. She took her glass of water and joined the group.

It was close to 3:30 AM when Delilah went to the restroom. She would have to revert back to being drab, lonely Paul soon, and she was putting it off as long as possible.

"Psst!" a voice from the shadows called.

"*Who* is that up in there? Are you *really* hissing at me?" Delilah's fists planted themselves on her hips.

The drunk from earlier stepped from the shadowy hallway. "Miss Delilah? Is that your name?" He appeared to have sobered up considerably.

"What do you want?"

The man lunged at her, pushing her against the wall and pinning her there with his forearm across her throat. "Just wanted to show you some appreciation, that's all." He grabbed hard at her crotch.

"What the hell?" he shouted as he stumbled backwards.

He doesn't know. Oh. My. God. He doesn't know. "Sweetheart, this is Club Roquefort. What did you *expect* to find down there?" Delilah smoothed her dress and fixed her wig. Her heart raced and she just wanted to get back to the safety of her friends. But she would be damned if she would let this piece of human garbage intimidate her. She may even have let Paul out to pop him upside the head a few times.

When he looked up at her, Delilah saw red lightning flashing behind his eyes. Somehow, he'd found the baseball bat that the bouncer kept in the umbrella stand near the stage door. She turned to run.

Her skull suddenly filled with white light and she couldn't see.

"Don't look down," a disembodied voice said. "You don't want to see that. Just follow me." She found herself floating near the ceiling, at the end of the hallway that led to the restrooms.

A pinpoint of light appeared before her, then spread out into a tunnel.

"Is this…?"

"It is where you need to go."

"Wait! Please. Please bring my friend Bram along."

"Call to him. See if he'll join you. There are a lot of friends waiting for him."

"Bram? Bram! Come here! Please, come with me!"

In an instant, he was by her side. She clasped his hand, and they walked into the light together.

Delilah found herself in a garden. Sweet olive bushes, sprinkled with tiny white flowers, grew in large terra cotta pots in each corner. A fancy wrought iron fence scrolled around the grassy square. Gravel paths quartered the place, meeting in the middle and turning into a rectangle that bordered a parterre garden with a gushing fountain in the middle. White birds fluttered by.

"Hello," said a woman in a long blue dress, whom Delilah was certain hadn't been there a moment before. "Are you ready for your review?"

"My what?"

"Your life review. Everyone gets one when they return here, remember?"

And Delilah did remember. She remembered every second, every feeling, every thought of Paul Samson's life, yet it only seemed to take an instant. And she cried. There were so many grand plans that she'd never gotten around to. So many problems she had planned to solve, but she'd spent too much time clinging to the bank, and not enough time swimming in the river.

"I failed, didn't I?"

"Failed? Of course you didn't. When folks leave here, they are often…overly enthusiastic about what they can accomplish. No matter how many times they've been down there, they always forget that living on the material plane is like wading through chest-deep water – it's much harder work than they think. Evolution of any sort takes time to unfold."

Delilah nodded and looked down, still feeling ashamed. Then she noticed something that had not been there only moments before. Her hands flew to her chest. "These boobs are *real*!"

"Of course they are. That's how you see yourself, isn't it?"

"But I have a male body."

"This is the astral plane. You manifest instantaneously here. If you want boobs, you have boobs." She snapped her fingers. "When you took a body, you chose to be Paul because one of your challenges was to find your authentic self. Don't worry. You'll remember everything before long. It's just reintegration shock."

A piece of astral paper appeared in the woman's hand. She looked at it and nodded her head. "Have you considered Spirit Guide School?"

"What?"

"Spirit guides. People on this side who help people on the other side. More and more people are choosing to incarnate with the ability to see ghosts. You were pretty good at handling that. The counselors are always looking for those with the right qualifications. There's a little training, a few rules to learn – mostly common sense, really."

"I don't even know what to say," Delilah responded.

"Well, we've got a batch who've decided to be highly intuitive getting ready to go down soon. Many of them have never incarnated before. They could really use your help. Why don't you get to know some of them, then decide?"

Time was different on the astral plane, perhaps even irrelevant. And yet there must be some connection to the material plane. Souls came and left. Some succeeded and some failed, but all had assignments. Delilah was reunited with old friends and made new ones. She attended Spirit Guide School – she was happy to stay discarnate, at least for the foreseeable future. She got to know the souls she was assigned to guide, even sat with them in the Antechamber – the room where incarnating spirits wait until it's their time to descend into the material world. They had to forget what it was like to live without a body, or else they'd never take to the clumsy things. They had to forget the easy bliss of the astral, or else they'd never survive. But they would remember little fragments of peace and love, so they'd always try to recreate those feelings. As their memories started to go, they often got frightened, not sure of what would be awaiting them on the other side. It didn't help that the tunnel went from dim to dark as it telescoped down. Delilah was there to hold their hands and guide them into the passage that would take them on their material adventure. She watched over them and helped them while they were down there, and she welcomed them back when they were done. It kept her very busy.

"These are the last two of this intuitive batch," said the lady in the blue dress.

Delilah had been taking a break, relaxing on the incredibly comfortable couch with a book when the woman appeared. She handed Delilah two sheets of astral paper.

"Their identities and life plans for downstairs. Give these a good looking over. This one could get tricky. Let me know if you need any help," the woman said.

Delilah nodded, but the woman was already gone.

She would read the plans, just as soon as she got to the end of the chapter, then go and meet the two souls. But she did glance at the names as she set the pages down on the coffee table. One would be called Marti Renee Schmidt Keller. The other would be named Tucker Wayne Fellowes.

* * * * * * *

BONUS PREVIEW

Of

The Magician's Children

Book 2 in the

Marti Keller Mysteries series

* * * * * * *

*Fate is like a strange, unpopular restaurant, filled
with odd waiters who bring you things you never
asked for and don't always like.*

Lemony Snicket

The Hanged Man's Wife

Chapter 1
Five Rubles

Sveklá wiped the blood off his face with the back of his hand. Bertram Kounis wasn't dead. Yet. But it wouldn't take much longer. Sveklá frowned at the gasping man on the ground, blood spurting from his throat with each heartbeat. He'd gotten sloppy and only severed the jugular and carotid on one side of Kounis' neck. He blamed it on the arthritis settling into his shoulder. This was a physical job, and he wasn't as young as he used to be. Sveklá took no joy in killing. But sometimes it was part his job, and he did it as he would any other.

"*Do svidaniya*, Kounis," Sveklá said, taking a five ruble coin from his pocket. "You should have paid." He dropped the silver coin at the other man's feet. "Now, you must be example to others."

A sharp pain pricked him, and Sveklá dropped the edger and shook out his hand, thinking an insect had stung him – he'd always been terrified of wasps. A large splinter was jammed into his palm, and droplets of blood were oozing out of it. He pulled the sliver out and cursed the wooden handle of the garden tool he'd just used to dispatch his victim.

Men like Kounis disgusted him. Greedy, grasping men who thought the world owed them whatever they desired. Kounis had made an agreement with Sveklá's boss to pay $5,000 every other week, a pittance for such a man, really. And in return, the boss would refrain from providing proof to the Securities Exchange Commission that Kounis' investment firm, Kounis Securities LLC, had devolved into nothing more than a Ponzi scheme.

Kounis had gone from investor to the well-connected captains of Houston's thriving industry to shell-game con artist when he'd compounded a spectacularly bad real estate investment with an expensive mistress.

The first time Kounis couldn't pay, the boss had gone easy on him, letting him off with the addition of a 100% interest payment. When Sveklá had come to collect the $15,000, Kounis had gotten angry and refused to pay.

If Kounis didn't pay one way, he'd pay another. Making an example of someone from time to time kept the others in line.

A noise from the street caught the enforcer's attention. Someone was coming. *Damn.* A glance at Kounis confirmed that he was beyond help. Sveklá fled.

"No. As far as I know, my husband has never been to Russia," Lilian Kounis said.

Her face was pale and her eyes were glassy and red. Head lowered and body slouched, she sat like a beaten dog in the interrogation room. Her voice was barely above a whisper when she answered questions.

FBI Special Agent Hadrian Galanti watched her from behind the one-way glass. He felt sorry for her. Not only had her husband just been murdered, but his death had caused the implosion of the carefully constructed upper middle class façade he had created. His struggle was over, but she was still being wounded by the shrapnel from her shattered life.

Lilian was the second wife, the trophy wife, barely older than Kounis' son, a senior at Princeton. Her job was to look good. And look good she did, her designer sportswear perfectly matched to her pale complexion. Her handbag alone probably cost more than the monthly rent on Hadrian's apartment. As far as personal image went, she was a master. On the other hand, business acumen, or cognitive skills in general, were not required of her. Whether her ignorance was willful or honest was difficult for Hadrian to determine. But she appeared to be just as shocked and surprised as anyone else when Bertram's house of cards came crashing down.

He didn't believe for a moment that she knew anything about her husband's business. What troubled him was the Russian coin found near the dead man's feet. In fact, it was the only reason he'd gotten involved in the case. He felt it was unlikely that it was there by accident. The same type of coin had been found at six other homicides in the past year and a half. The forensics team had recovered a partial print, and was waiting for results from the AFIS database search. If it came up empty, he'd check with Interpol. He doubted he'd get much help from Russia's FSB if the Interpol query failed.

Lilian had reported that she heard a noise, and when she came out of the garage, there was some poor schmuck named Benjamin Fayllor holding the murder weapon and standing over her husband's body. The two men had some heated words earlier in the day, and they were bitter rivals in the upcoming homeowner's association election. It was true that Fayllor had motive, means and opportunity, but Hadrian doubted that he killed Kounis. For one thing, all of the blood was on the bottoms of his shoes. There was none on the tops. There was also no evidence of any blood on his clothes. Several of his coworkers confirmed that he was wearing the same clothes he'd worn to work earlier. For another thing, there were traces of blood on the handle of the edger.

The DNA results hadn't come back yet, but both Kounis and Fayllor were blood type O+. The blood on the handle was AB-. Unless Hadrian was very wrong, Fayllor hadn't killed anybody.

That's why it pained him to keep Fayllor in jail. If the five ruble coin meant what he thought it meant, it would be better for the real killer to think that he had gotten away with it. He'd relax, and be off guard. Hadrian would not.

When he'd joined the Multi Agency Gang Task Force three years ago, he'd expected to see mostly narcos from south of the border, and some Asian triads. That was still true, but European gangs, like the Chechens and the Russians, were on the rise. Being a transportation hub made Houston irresistible to them. A breakaway faction of New York City's Odessa Group had set up shop in the warehouse district, and they were just like any other invasive exotic – unappealing to the local predators, but out-competing the native organisms for resources. The Russians didn't have the strength to challenge the more robust, well-established organizations head-on yet, but Hadrian knew the day was coming. There would no bloodless coup, and a lot of innocent civilians would get slaughtered in the crossfire. If he had to hold Fayllor in order to catch some really bad guys, he would do it. Even if he hated it.

Chapter 2

Edging out the Competition

My husband, Ryan, was still dead.

But at least I had finally gotten to say goodbye.

I talk to ghosts. I didn't use to. Not until one of them insisted I help solve his own murder. And that journey led me to discover whole other aspects of good and evil, in ways I'd never imagined. But I digress.

I babysat while my sister, Emily, and her husband, Nick, went to Ian Chambers' funeral. Nick had recently tried fixing me up with Chambers, and that was an epic disaster. But that's a whole other story. As it stood, I wasn't glad he was dead, but I wasn't exactly sorry about it, either.

My daughter, Cassie, and her brand new cousin, McKenzi, were having their morning naps. The late June heat was already fierce, so McKenzi's brothers, Kyle and Aiden, wrestled on the floor with my Labrador retriever, Bruce. Or at least that's what they thought he was. As far as my family knew, he was a stray dog I found and adopted.

They were wrong, but it was just easier to let them keep believing that.

I was very grateful to Bruce for keeping the boys occupied. I had just started working Tuesday and Thursday afternoons at the Tenth Sphere metaphysical shop, and this was one of my days off. It was harder to get back into the routine than I thought it would be.

I felt a little guilty about wishing Nick and Em would hurry up and get back. I adore my family, and I'd do anything for them – but I really needed some space. After narrowly surviving what was quite possibly both the most horrible and most wonderful weekend of my entire life, I've had one or more them in my house nearly 24/7 this week.

Quinn, Cassie and I, had only just gotten home on Monday afternoon. Mom had a scrapbook club meeting, so Dad came for an early dinner and spent the night. Most of the time he's fine, but he sometimes has seizures, so Mom doesn't like to leave him alone for too long. Also, his artificial leg occasionally gives him trouble. On Tuesday and Wednesday nights, McKenzi was colicky, so Nick and the boys camped out in my living room. Last night, Emily slept over because she was on the verge of sleep deprivation psychosis. Mom and Dad stayed at my house with Cassie while I was working. Poor Bruce. He hadn't been able to shift out of dog form the whole time. I hoped it wasn't uncomfortable for him. Actually, Bruce is only his name when he's a dog. That's what I called him before I knew what he was. Otherwise, he's known as Quinn. But he's really a kelpie, sort of like the Loch Ness Monster. He's also a little like an undercover agent, and his job is primarily hunting demons and undoing the damage they cause to this world.

And I desperately needed to talk to him. It was torture having him curled up next to me on the couch (or bed), knowing who he is, what we'd just been through together, and unable to talk about it.

The head, and only the head, of Delilah, my Creole spirit guide, popped up inches away from my face. "Heads up, girlfriend!" she said. Before I could say anything, she was gone. She did that a lot, and it was the most annoying habit that ghosts had.

This did cause me to glance out the window, where I could see my brother-in-law coming up the sidewalk. They only lived six doors down, so it was easier to park the car at their house and walk the kids home. Delilah stopped in to let me know Nick was outside? Must be a slow guide day.

"Guys? Your dad's coming. Go get your stuff together, okay?" I said to the boys.

"Awww. But Aunt Marti..." Aiden complained.

"Bruce will still be here later. I'm sure your dad needs a hug. He's probably feeling very sad."

No, at that moment, I was not above using guilt to manipulate the six year-old twins. I went and unlocked the side door for Nick.

My cell rang. *Uh-oh.* Caller ID said it was The Tenth Sphere. Had I forgotten to do something at work?

"Lulu?" I asked.

"Oh, gods! Marti I don't know what to do." It wasn't Lulu. It was her partner. And she was crying.

"Belinda, what's wrong?" I was concerned. She was not the sort of person to fall apart easily. It had to be something bad.

"Lulu." It was all she can say before her voice dissolved into sobs.

"What's happened to Lulu?"

"In jail."

"What? That's crazy. Why?"

The screen door slapped against the frame as Nick came in. "How were –"

I held up my hand to silence him.

"Accessory to murder," Belinda whispered.

"Murder!" I echoed, too loudly. McKenzi woke up and started crying. Nick went to get her, giving me a quizzical look on the way.

Belinda answered, but all I could hear was "nephew" and "homeowner's," because Cassie also started crying. "Hold on a sec, Belinda. I'm going to have to put the phone down. Do *not* hang up."

I put the phone on the kitchen table and rushed to sweep Cassie out of her crib. I gave her diaper a squeeze. Excellent. She was dry. I plopped her in the high chair and poured some Cheerios on the tray. She knocked them to the floor.

"Come on, Cassie. Please cooperate. I really need to talk to Auntie Belinda."

"Ning!" she shouted.

I took her out of the chair and set her on the floor next to some toys.

"I'll just let you get back to your call," Nick said. I could tell he was curious about why I was having a phone conversation about murder. He had already gotten the kids packed up and the dog slobber washed off boys' hands and lower arms.

"Thanks. Talk to you later," I said.

Cassie found a large plastic ring from a stacking toy and started using it to whack the other toys in the basket. Bruce lay on the floor nearby.

I hurried back to the phone. Belinda, of course had hung up. I called her back.

"Okay, now tell me what's going on," I said as soon as she picked up.

Belinda sucked in a few deep, shuddering breaths. "Last night, we were coming back from dinner. Our elderly neighbor, Mrs. Thompson, was standing on the sidewalk, crying. We stopped and asked her what was wrong. She said that she was taking Cranberry – that's her Standard Poodle – for a walk. He started to chase a cat and got away from her, running across the street. He got hit by a car, and she couldn't lift him. So Lulu walked across the street and picked that dog up. He wasn't dead, like Mrs. Thompson thought, so Lulu wrapped him up in a jacket she found in her trunk, and we all went to the emergency clinic. I took Mrs. Thompson and Cranberry inside, while Lulu stayed in the car and called Mrs. Thompson's son to come get her. He said he was on the way, so we left her at the clinic while Cranberry was in surgery. When we got home, Lulu realized she had blood all over her clothes and the jacket, so she changed and went to the Laundromat, where she could get the stuff washed before the stains set. Probably ten minutes after she left, a couple of police detectives came to the door. Said they needed to ask Lulu some questions about her nephew. I didn't think much of it –" Belinda fell apart again. It took a few moments for her to stop crying. "And I told them where she was." More sobbing. "When they got to the washateria, they found her with a pile of bloody clothes, waiting for a washer, and arrested her."

"For what? Being a Good Samaritan?"

"No. Her nephew was seen fleeing from a crime scene...it was a murder...and they thought that she was destroying the evidence."

"I can't believe that. Surely the people at the emergency clinic can verify she was there. When they do the DNA testing on the blood, they'll see it isn't human."

"She never actually came inside the clinic, and DNA tests could take weeks. They haven't actually charged her yet, but I don't have money for a lawyer. Everything's tied up in the shop. I don't even know if I'm going to have enough to bail her out." Belinda began to sob again.

"Belinda, it's going to be okay. My sister's a public defender. She'll know exactly what to do." I paused for a moment. I hadn't realized that Lulu had a nephew. "Who did Lulu's nephew kill?"

"Benjamin didn't kill anybody! He'd never hurt a soul. He was running for president of the homeowner's association. The man that got killed was the current president. His wife said that she went outside and found Benjamin standing over her dead husband, holding a bloody Japanese edger. I don't care what she thinks she saw, Ben would never kill anybody."

"Okay, then. Let me talk to my sister, and I'll get back to you."

I dialed Emily's cell, and was worried that it would roll to voice mail. When she finally answered, her voice was soft and a little gravelly. She said she was very tired and sore from going to the funeral – she'd only had a c-section two weeks ago, after all. Still, she humored me and listened to my problem. That was Emily, always taking care of me.

"Ok. There's nothing I can do about it. I can't even drive yet," she said.

"But—"

"Let me finish. Have your friend call Crammwell, Stanford & Malloy."

"They sound expensive."

"Stop interrupting. Call Crammwell, ask for Leonard Peltier. They'll take care of it. Now, I really need to go lie down. Good luck."

Cassie had changed her mind about eating lunch. She'd pulled herself up on the coffee table and staggered into the kitchen. "Mama! Ma ma ma!"

Yesterday was her eleven month-iversary. I still had some cupcakes left, so I put one on the high chair tray with the few remaining Cheerios. Once I strapped her in, she tried to smash the whole cake into her mouth. I took it away from her, although most of the frosting stayed on her cheeks, and broke it into little bits. I got her a sippy cup of water, and paced around the kitchen, looking for my cell phone. Bruce came in and sat down near Cassie's high chair. She stopped stuffing herself with cake long enough to throw him some cereal.

I called Belinda back, but she didn't answer. I left a message on her voice mail, telling her what Emily had said.

Then I got up, closed the blinds and double-checked that I'd re-locked the door after Nick left. Bruce was no longer in the room. A few minutes later, Quinn came in, dressed in a pair of shorts and tee-shirt I'd managed to pick up for him during the week. That's the slight drawback of being a shapeshifter – clothes don't shift with you.

I wanted to run to him and throw my arms around his neck, partly because I had missed him – missed his human form – and partly because I wanted him to convince me that everything would be fine, and Lulu would be home in time for dinner.

Instead, I stood by the high chair. "Lulu's in trouble."

"I heard."

Someone banged the knocker on the front door.

Even though I knew it couldn't possibly be Belinda, I still hoped it was, as Quinn and I hurried into the entryway.

I thought I must be on some TV hidden camera show.

A woman stood on my front porch wearing painted-on jeans tucked into fur-lined boots and a low-cut, too-tight white shirt. A beaded leather pouch was slung around her hips. Two long blonde braids fell to her waist, and her eyes were ice blue. A glossy black raven perched on her shoulder.

"Halle?" Quinn asked. "It's been...a very long time."

The Hanged Man's Wife

If you enjoyed this book
Please consider leaving a review on
Your favorite book-sharing site.
Thank you!

About the Author

Artemis Greenleaf has devoured fairy tales, folk tales and ghost stories since before she could read. Artemis did, in fact, marry an alien and she lives in the suburban wilds of Houston, Texas with her husband, two children and assorted pets. She writes both fiction and non-fiction and her work has appeared in magazines and as novels. For more information, please visit artemisgreenleaf.com.